Hillcountry
Warriors

Hillcountry
Warriors

Johnny Neil Smith

Johnny Neil Smith

SUNSTONE
PRESS

SANTA FE

Sunstone books may be purchased for edcational, business, or sales promotional use. For information please write: Special Markets Department, Sunstone Press, P.O. Box 2321, Santa Fe, New Mexico 87504-2321.

FIRST EDITION

Printed in the United States of America

10 9 8 7 6 5 4 3 2 1

_____

Library of Congress Cataloging in Publication Data:

Smith, Johnny Neil, 1939-
     Hillcountry warriors: the Civil War South seldom seen / Johnny Neil Smith.—1st ed.
          p. cm.
        ISBN: 0-86534-247-4
        1. Southern States—History—Civil War, 1861-1865—Fiction.
2. Mississippi—History—Civil War, 1861-1865—Fiction.
3. State rights—History—19th century—Fiction.   I. Title.
813' .54—dc20   96-6893
                                                     CIP

_____

Published by   SUNSTONE PRESS
               Post Office Box 2321
               Santa Fe, NM 87504-2321 / USA
               (505) 988-4418 / orders only (800) 243-5644
               FAX (505) 988-1025

Dedicated to Susan
without whose encouragement and assistance
this book could not have been written

PREFACE

Many people, when thinking about the antebellum American South, view it as a land of plantations, columned mansions, slave holders, harsh overseers and a society that supported slavery as an institution that was both moral and necessary to maintain the economy. But this is not a totally correct summation. True, slavery helped promote and strengthen the financial system of the South, but many Southerners did not own slaves nor did they have any desire to support this so-called "peculiar institution." So it was with many of the pioneers who settled the hillcountry of east central Mississippi.

These early settlers were living on land that did not lend itself to plantation farming. Most only raised enough food for themselves plus a little extra during the better farming years. In addition, many pioneers were first and second generations of Scotch-Irish folk possessing the ideas and values of their parents and grandparents who had struggled to get to America in order to seek a better life and, in some cases, just to survive.

These immigrants were from economic conditions not much better than those who were in slavery in the United States. In Scotland and Ireland, they had been poor tenants who were paying rent for land that barely provided a living. If the land did not produce, they still would owe the landlord his required sum. Many were then pushed off their land and in some cases were imprisoned for debts to their landlords. They knew about poverty and oppression and upon coming to America, many were sympathetic toward the plight of the Southern slave.

Even though these immigrants had been free to go as they pleased in the old country, in America they were not much better off than the Southern Negroes. Hillcountry people, who held little regard for the plantation system and what it represented, nevertheless found themselves entangled in the conflict that divided this nation, destroyed thousands of promising young lives, and turned family against family.

When the Civil War finally came to an end, the economy of the South had been destroyed along with its armies. Even though the hillcountry itself did not show the destruction that many areas of the war-torn South displayed, the destruction could be found in every family and in individual lives. In some cases physical injuries handicapped the Southern soldiers when they returned home, and all faced crushed dreams and a lack of hope that would plague them for the remainder of their lives.

Although many of these hillcountry warriors only fought to preserve their states' rights, and not for the institution of slavery, when the bloody conflict ended, they bore the same yoke of oppression as the slaveholders who fought to keep slavery legal in the South.

As a young boy growing up in Mississippi, I enjoyed listening to stories told by the older generation, many who were children when General Sherman came through Newton County, Mississippi, on his raid on Meridian. Many of these accounts pertained to slavery and the Choctaw Indians. I was assured that there was a strong belief that slavery was morally wrong and that many people were disturbed by the unjust treatment of the Choctaw Indians. I did exhaustive research to confirm the plight of the Choctaws and the actuality of the Civil War and slavery.

In regard to the native Choctaws in Mississippi, to my knowledge, no book has ever included the facts about their love of their land and how the land was stolen from them along with their style of life and their pride. Readers will also note how the southern Negroes were once again placed in bondage following the Civil War, and only by the work of the FBI in the 1960s was the government able to free the African Americans from the bondage that some of the Mississippi Delta planation owners had placed on them.

The main character in my book, John Wilson, was named after my grandfather and many of the accounts of battle and prison life relate to my great grandfather, Joseph Williams, who lost an arm in the battle for Atlanta and was sent to a Federal prison in Illinois. I have tried to recapture the emotion that existed during this time in history as was told to me by the people who lived during that era.

In a real sense, this is their story.

— Johnny Neil Smith
Monticello, Georgia
1996

PROLOGUE

Mississippi seceded from the union on January 9, 1861. Young men all over the state began to gather in specified areas to form military units and prepare for a war that not all were sure would ever occur. It was with this feeling that Lott Wilson allowed his two oldest sons, James Earl and Thomas, to enlist in the first military company that Newton County organized. It was assembled in Decatur, a small town in east central Mississippi about eight and one half miles southwest of Little Rock where the Wilson farm lay. They called themselves the Newton Rifles.

Lott knew its commanding officer, Montgomery Carleton, very well and felt his boys would be in good hands if any fighting did occur. Lott also sensed that when the United States Government saw that the South was willing to fight for its states' rights, the politicians in the North would then probably sit down and peacefully resolve their differences. War was about as likely as a snowstorm on the Fourth of July, Lott thought.

But that didn't change the fact that while James Earl and Thomas were away playing war, their father was hardpressed to get everything done on the farm, especially since it was planting season. The boys had only enlisted for six months so Lott had determined to get by as well as he could until they returned. The demanding work now fell in the hands of John, his youngest son, and himself. Lott knew the work done by four would now have to be done by a boy and a worn-out old man. He prayed this excitement about a possible war would soon be over.

But hope fell on April 12, 1861, when Pierre G. T. Beauregard and his troops fired on Fort Sumter, out in the Charleston harbor, one of the four Federal forts flying the Union flag in Confederate territory. After that, the war escalated with each passing month and James Earl and Thomas were caught in the conflict. Their six month enlistment became an indefinite commitment.

1

SPRING PLANTING 1862

THE SPRING OF 1862 WAS LATE IN COMING. THE OLDER FOLK who had seen many come and go, said this delay meant a season of unusual beauty. Across the woodlands, at first glance it seemed that a young snow lightly covered the ground. But closer examination revealed that what appeared to be snow was nothing but multitudes of dogwood trees in full bloom. Many of the hardwood trees were still dormant, so these white blossoms dominated the forestlands.

Among the dogwood trees were purple blossoms of native redbud trees dotting the landscape. In the open meadows where deer had once fed in abundance and where no plow had yet disturbed the earth, thousands of wildflowers displayed their colors.

Back in the quiet farmhouse, the predawn breeze gently pushed John's bedroom curtain back and forth while outside the rays of daylight were just illuminating the sky. Down through the hollow came a chorus of music from the whippoorwill. Occasionally the plaintive call of these lonely sounding birds would be interrupted by a screech owl somewhere near the creek bottom. Everything was peaceful, but Old Preacher Jack, the king rooster of the barnyard, began to let everyone within a good country mile know of his presence with one of the loudest voices God had ever given a creature. Jack could give ole Satan himself a headache.

But worst still was a sound John Wilson hated to hear. "John . . . John Wilson . . . Son . . . it's time to get up. Yore paw's already gone to the barn. You got work to do and ole man sun'll be up 'fore long."

John couldn't believe it was time to start another day's work. It seemed only a minute ago he had put his head on his pillow to sleep.

"Mom, you sure this ain't Sunday and I'm just havin' a bad dream?" said John jokingly. Being a religious family, the Wilsons never worked on Sunday. John settled deeper under the cover and before long was sound asleep.

This time, a more aggressive and mocking sound woke him. "John . . . John Willy . . . it's time to get yore lazy butt out of bed. Yore good friends who you loves and resembles is a waitin' for ya. I'm talkin' 'bout Zek and Abner, the mules, you know . . . jackasses as Professor Hendon calls them."

"Sister, how dare you talk to yore brother like that. He's worked hard since the boys been gone," scolded Sarah.

Lucretia, called Sister, was the only daughter and the youngest child in the family and her parents had overprotected her. The boys felt she was spoiled rotten.

Before the feud with the North began, Lucretia seemed to always be getting her way around the house. Now that the South needed men, some of the young girls, like Sister, became less important. The Wilson boys were enjoying their moment of triumph.

John slowly dressed and made his way across the open hall to the kitchen at the back of the house. There he found a breakfast of bacon and eggs with the best biscuits in Little Rock.

He finally finished and as he rose to leave the table, Mrs. Wilson also rose as if by habit, "John, let me look at ya boy. I want to see what kind of young man you is growin' up to be."

"Maw, why do I go through this inspection might near every day? You can see I'm still a growin' and I wash my face and comb my hair every morning. This is embarrassin'," stated John in frustration.

"Stand tall young man," Sarah commanded.

"Yes Ma'am, I'm a-standin' tall."

And so he was. John would not turn seventeen until October, but he was already over six feet with a slim, but muscular build. The hard work on the farm had shaped him well.

His hair was black and mostly straight, except for small curls in the back and his eyes were a deep sparkling blue. He wore his hair long; but when working he would wet it, comb it straight back, and tie it up with a piece of cloth to keep it off his shoulders. As the summer sun tanned his upper body, he could almost pass for one of the neighboring Choctaws.

Mrs. Wilson, acting like a military officer, slowly looked him over. "Okay, Mister John, I guess you look good 'nough for me this morning. You can go help yore Paw now."

She gave her son a kiss on the cheek and tenderly pushed him toward the door. "I love ya boy."

"I love you too, Maw," John responded as he bounded down the front steps and trudged through the dark toward the barnyard located across the road from the house. As he walked, he could hear his mother and sister clanging pans and discussing his new status in the family. They seemed to always be arguing, especially since James Earl and Thomas had left.

"Mamma, why does John get all the special treatment 'round here? All I hear is 'John works so hard everyday,' and 'Oh, John is such a good student,' and 'John was first in his class,' and 'John has been savin' his money so's he can attend college at Oxford,' and 'John is going to study law and come back to Newton County' and 'John this,' and 'John that,'" mimicked his sister.

"That's enough, Mary Lucretia," her mother sternly interrupted. "I'm proud of that boy and I'm proud he's got the ambition to make sump'n of himself.

Since his brothers has gone away, yore paw and I has got to depend on him. He's got to help us hold this here farm together. He's not a boy no more. Manhood has kind of been pushed on him."

Sarah put her arm around Lucretia, tenderly pushed her silky blonde hair away from her face, and quietly in almost a whisper said, "Daughter, you're important to us too. I don't know what I'd do without you to help me keep up this household."

She paused for a moment and looked at her rough and callused hands. "I ain't as young as I used to be. I would have a hard time doin' everything without yore help. You know I love ya."

As Lucretia moved silently toward the sink, her eyes wet with tears, she reached back and grasped her mother's hand and with a weak voice murmured, "I know you loves me, and I know you're worried about what could happen to James Earl and Thomas up in Virginie, but just tell me, just sometimes, that I'm special too."

John glanced back and instead of seeing a mother and daughter confrontation, he saw his mother wrap her arms around Sis and give her a hug that seemed to say everything is going to be just right.

John then picked up his pace and made his way across the front yard and on toward the barn. Once across the road, he could see a faint glow from an oil lantern hanging on one of the beams in the barn. Lott already had the mules harnessd, fed, watered, and ready to go.

"John, that you comin'? These mules told me they is going to make a man out of ya today," he joked.

"Yes, it's me, Paw," reassured John.

It wasn't long until they reached the fields, and there they stood, silhouettes in the soft morning light. Way up the hollow behind John and his dad, they could hear Joe and Spot, Lott's prize hounds giving some critter a run for his life.

"Paw, you think they's after a coon?" John asked as he turned to catch a clearer sound.

"Naw, Son, they sound like they might be after that cat who's been a-catchin' our chickens. I hope they is."

The two stood silent and seemed to forget about the day's work before them. But all of a sudden one of the mules snorted as if to get their attention.

"John, I believe I can see to plow a straight row now. How 'bout you? You ready boy?"

"I'm ready as I'll ever be, Paw."

Every day, Monday through Saturday was the same schedule . . . up before dawn and in the fields until it was too dark to see. It had to be like that. It was the only way they could keep the farm going. Lott placed the harness lines around his neck and John and he stood together facing over a hundred acres of young corn to plow plus seventy-five acres of cotton land to be broken and prepared for planting.

"John Willy, this here land ain't going to get worked with our eyeballs. Let's hit it one row at a time."

Occasionally, when things were going well and Lott felt that he had the fields in control, he would give John Saturday afternoon off. But Saturday afternoon off was a rare event at this time of the year.

Finally, John heard what he longed for, "Okay, Mister John Willy, we ain't workin' this afternoon. I don't want to see hair nor hide of ya till dark. No hard liquor, no wild women, and ya better bring me a fresh mess of fish from the creek. Ya hear? Oh, by the way, I don't mind if'n you do go see that cute little Walker gal."

"Yes sir, Paw." John gave his father a brisk military salute and ran toward the house hollering loudly.

For this moment, John Wilson didn't have his mind on the beauty of the spring nor on the war raging in the East and along the Mississippi River. His thoughts were on simpler things—the afternoon off and his fishing trip to the rock hole.

As John strode down the road toward the creek, he could still hear his father's morning prayer. "Dear Lord, thank Thee for this another day to see Thy beauty. Help me to be able to feed and clothe my family; and Lord, take care of my two boys away fightin' with Mister Bobby Lee. And, Dear God, thank Thee for my faithful wife and hardworkin' son; and, Dear Lord, please forgive me for all the things I'll be a-callin' that stubborn animal of burden today. Amen."

As John recalled all the long hours of work done to help the family, he was proud of himself; but his mind quickly returned to his fishing trip. He began to run, leap, and skip in joy as he savored this little time he could relax by himself.

Soon he reached the creek and worked his way through the underbrush that grew along the road. Once through the entanglement of vines laced with prickly blackberry bushes, he stepped into a large stand of virgin oak and hickory trees that grew in abundance along the creekbanks. John was glad his father had not cut down any of the trees in this lower section and had left them exactly as the Choctaw Indians found these timbers hundreds of years before the first white settlers came. The trees were so large it would take several men holding hands to reach around their trunks. When the trees were covered with leaves, very little direct sunlight could reach the ground so little vegetation grew underneath. This lack of growth left a clear path of vision for almost a quarter of a mile.

As John worked his way through the woods and along the creekbank, he passed ferns and several different kinds of canes that grew in abundance. It took only minutes to reach the bend of the creek, and finally he approached the high bank overlooking his favorite fishing hole. Glancing down, John found the water clear enough to see the large stone boulders settled into the sand. Other stones reached up and out into the deeper part of the creek and gave John a perfect place to sit and dangle his feet in the cold, crystal waters. He quickly slid down the steep creek bank and settled himself on one of the larger stones.

John couldn't believe the week's work was over and not only did he have the afternoon off, but Sunday as well. As his father always said, "Sunday is the good Lord's day. The animals rest, we give the fields a day off, and we thank

God for givin' us this land of plenty, and besides I need a day away from them damned ole mules."

John took his shoes off, and before one could swat a mosquito off an ear, he had his hook baited and had cast it out into the deeper water near the bend of the creek.

"Okay, Mister Catfish, it's time for you to head for our supper table. You hear me?" whispered John.

It wasn't long before his fish line bulged with catfish and red-bellied bream. Confident that he could more than place a meal on the table, John's mind began to wander. He stuck his pole down into the soft creek mud and lay back on the bolder that had now become pleasantly warm and comfortable, especially welcomed on this cool spring afternoon. As he looked up through the massive tree limbs, he studied a clear blue sky with puffs of white clouds moving slowly as if to say, "Can you make out my face?" or "Who or what do you think I might be?" John picked out funny faces and weird looking animals. Then one cloud caught his attention. It looked like a beautiful young woman. It suddenly began to look like his own Rebecca Ann. Her hair was bouncing just like when they were running the horses at full gallop.

He had known Rebecca since they were children. Her father had come to Little Rock to open a general store when she was three years old, and he and Rebecca were always taking up for one another . . . kind of puppy love, he often thought. It seemed Rebecca, or Becca, as they called her, was just one of the boys. She loved to go fishing and hunting with John and his older brothers, and it was many a late afternoon that she helped the boys clean a mess of squirrels out behind the woodshed. She also could outrun and outride most of the boys in Little Rock.

As the years passed, she grew into the most beautiful girl in the community. Not only was she pretty with her silky reddish hair, emerald green eyes, long but muscular legs, and full bosom, but she was a lady in every way, at least every way John could imagine. Becca always loved competing with John and the other boys. Whether it was in the classroom or in a political debate after church, when the ladies and girls were supposed to be cleaning up the tables after lunch, Becca always found a way to get the best of her adversary. She felt women didn't have to be just housewives. Becca would often say, "Us girls, one of these days is going to change this country. I might even be the Gov'nor of this great and glorious State of Mis'sippi." But what John liked the most was the way she could say, "Mister John Wilson, you know one day I'm going to be Mrs. Rebecca Wilson, whether you like it or not." John would always answer, "We'll see young lady, we'll see."

Meanwhile, as the clouds were finally swept from the sky, John sleepily recalled the stories of how his grandparents came to the United States and how his father and Uncle Jake settled in this wilderness.

2

LAND OF HOPE

CREWMEN WORKED RAPIDLY TO STRIKE THE SAILS AND PRE-
pare for docking at the port of Savannah. The area was swarming with people.
Supplies were being moved from other ships to wagons ready to deliver their
long awaited cargo. Breezes rushing across the Savannah River caused sails to
flap vigorously and scare seagulls that had encircled the ships seeking a hand-
out. The sky was filled with screams of distress as they flew in a frenzied search
for food. The latest arrival edged slowly to the dock where it was then secured
and made safe for unloading. A gust of unanticipated wind caused passengers
to grab their caps and bonnets or lose them forever to the muddy, swirling
currents of the river. Near the side of the ship a young couple stood quietly,
feeling a special joy at the realization that they had at last reached Savannah
after long weeks at sea. But this joy was tinted with the uncertainty of what this
new country would hold for them.

"Mary Ruth, I'm not sure what our future is going to be here in America, but
at least it's a new beginning. They say there is a fresh kind of freedom of expression here which may even keep my spontaneous and unrestricted pen out of
trouble," said Jonathan Wilson as he placed his arms around his wife and pulled
her close to his side.

Mary stared out toward the wharf almost ignoring his attempt to make her
feel secure and breathed the reply, "Look at all those people! They are moving
like ants and Jonathan we don't know anyone. Not anyone."

Jonathan turned her around and, looking straight into her face, reassured
her that they did have a contact waiting for them.

"Remember," he said, "we are to get in touch with a Mister Albert Haskins
who will help us."

Suddenly, Mary's thoughts were interrupted.

"Alright, all you Scotch-Irish, get your belongings and get off this ship unless you want to sail with us to the African coast," bellowed the Captain. "I
guess you've probably had enough of this old crate."

The crowd of passengers gathered their boxes and suitcases and briskly
moved down the walkway leading to the pier.

The Wilsons soon found themselves on the cobble-stone street below the
ship, surrounded by people disappearing in all directions.

"What do we do now, Jonathan? Where do we go?" asked Mary as she held tightly to her husband's hand.

With the clamor of talking, laughing, and carts and goods being moved from one area to another, Mary could hardly hear her husband shout, "Mary, let's just wait until some of these people leave, and then we will begin our search for Mister Haskins."

All of a sudden, above the ruckus came the most beautiful sound the Wilsons had ever heard, "Jonathan! Jonathan Wilson! If you're here, raise your hat above your head!"

Jonathan immediately raised his hat and bellowed in reply, "Jonathan Wilson is here. We are here."

Through the crowd came a large burly man with a most pleasant smile. "You Jonathan Wilson?"

"Yes indeed, and who might you be?"

"I'm Albert Haskins, and I've been waiting for you two. Let me help with your baggage. My wife is expecting you for dinner."

"Mister Haskins, we are certainly glad to see you, and let me introduce my wife. This is Mrs. Mary Ruth Wilson," said Jonathan proudly.

Haskins tipped his hat and in a polite manner stated, "Welcome to Savannah and to America. I hope this country is as good to you as it has been to me. Let's get out of this crowd. I hate crowds. Shall we go?"

They soon reached his wagon and were on their way to the Haskins' home on Liberty Street, just two blocks from the docks.

Mrs. Haskins was waiting at the door. "Welcome to our humble home. I know you must be completely famished from your long trip. Please come in."

After dinner while the Haskins and Wilsons were relaxing and getting to know each other, Mister Haskins tipped his glass to Jonathan and almost like a toast said, "Jonathan, tell me about your problems in Ireland; and by the way, I've heard some good things about you. Talk straight, you're in America now."

Jonathan leaned back in his chair and recounted what had happened during the winter. As a promising young printer and writer, he had become too bold and aggressive. Several of his editorials displeased the local politicians and the Crown, and soon he was without a job or a future. His salvation came when one of his wealthy friends offered to lend him enough money to make the trip to America. The debt would be repaid as soon as Jonathan was financially able. In addition, a contact in America would be made for the Wilsons.

"Mister Haskins, you are going to help us, aren't you? You can help us?" inquired Jonathan as he once again reached for Mary's hand.

"Yes, Jonathan, I think I can be of help if you think you can put up with my cantankerous ways. I run a little printing and newspaper shop here in the city, and I need someone who is somewhat spirited. You know, that's exactly what sells papers here in this country. How about it?" Mister Haskins questioned with a tilt of his head and a twinkle in his eyes.

Jonathan moved quickly out of his chair and rushed in excitement to embrace Mary. He picked her up as effortlessly as if she were a feather, then spun her around and around.

"Mary, can you believe I've . . . I mean we have employment. Can you believe it?"

"Jonathan let me down this minute so you can shake this gentleman's hand," exclaimed Mary.

Shaking hands in Ireland was the way men always sealed an agreement. Jonathan reached eagerly for Mister Haskin's hand as Mary thanked him and Jonathan accepted Mister Haskin as his employer.

I

The year was 1807. Jonathan enjoyed working for Mister Haskins, and he slowly began to prosper. It seemed this new country was everything a hard-working young couple could ever want. They soon repaid their debt, made a downpayment on a house, and Jonathan was prepared to offer Haskins a bid to buy into the business.

One afternoon when Jonathan came in from work, he found an arrangement of flowers attached to the front doorlatch. Entering the house cautiously, he found Mary waiting for him in the hall with a most unusual, but pleasant expression on her face.

"Mary, what is the occasion for the flowers? I've never received this kind of welcome.?"

"Sit down my love. We have plans to make," said Mary as she led him to his favorite chair.

"Alright Mary, what is it?"

She placed her hands in his and softly whispered, "There is another Wilson on the way."

Jonathan was flushed with excitement as they began to prepare for the welcomed addition. The first son, Lott, was born in the fall of 1808, and two years later, a second son whom they named Jeremiah.

Life, in general, had been good to the Wilsons, but in the winter of 1812, a massive epidemic of influenza struck the city claiming over three hundred lives. One was Jonathan Wilson. The death of Jonathan was devastating to Mary and her two young boys.

Mister Haskins did all he could to help the Wilsons, but the war with England had made it impossible for him to remain in Savannah. During the past revolution, he had sided with the colonists in their struggle to separate from the Mother Country and once the British had seized Savannah, his newspaper articles had endangered his life. He had been beaten twice by a group of Loyalists, his shop had been almost destroyed, and the safety of his family had been threatened on several occasions. He felt he was too old to go through this kind of ordeal again.

Haskins knew he must warn Mrs. Wilson about the danger that existed for him and his wife if they remained in Savannah. Mary had been working in his business since Jonathan had died and always helped him clean up the shop each afternoon before closing. Telling her he was leaving Savannah was no easy task, and day after day, he procrastinated until he knew he could wait no longer.

One afternoon as they were about to close for the day, he knew he could put it off no longer. "Mary, I've got something to tell you, and I don't know exactly how to begin."

Mary quietly stopped her cleaning and sat down. "Mister Haskins, just tell me what's on your mind," replied Mary. "I'm a good listener."

"Mary, I must leave Savannah. If the British take the city, my life could be in danger."

Then he told her his dilemma and that since his business would be closed, she would be without a job.

"Mister Haskins, what am I going to do?" she breathed as she slowly stood with fingertips on her temples and the palms of her hands over her eyes. Then she ran her fingers backwards through her unbounded hair and said, "How will I support my boys?"

Mister Haskins reached for Mary's hand and gently held her. "Mary, you can go with Mrs. Haskins and me to the Carolinas where my oldest son lives. We'll take care of you."

"Thank you, Mister Haskins, but I can't do that. You have your own family to support. We would be just an extra burden to you. I'll trust the Almighty God to take care of us."

Mary was eventually forced to give up their comfortable home and move to an apartment near the Savannah River docks, a section far from respectable. To support her family, she worked during the day at a textile mill; and during the evenings, she was employed to cook and help maintain a kitchen in one of the local taverns located on River Street. Even though the food was the best in the neighborhood, the establishment often became a roughhouse late at night.

Meanwhile, the years passed quickly, and the family managed. Mary kept her job in the tavern and even found satisfaction in cooking there.

One day, a rare surge of cold weather dropped the temperature below freezing, but the kitchen of the High Step Tavern was warm and comfortable. The tavern was called the High Step Tavern because of the steep steps that led up to the front door off the main street. These steps were an immense hazard to the intoxicated.

This day, Mary stood over the woodstove stirring some of her savory stew listening to the murmurings of people enjoying their meals, but with each passing minute the restaurant's patrons became more lively and boisterous.

"Mrs. Wilson, we need four more servings right away!" shouted Ed Jenkins, the tavern's owner. "People are waitin' and are hungry!"

"It's about ready, Ed. Be patient," she exclaimed.

Lott, Mary's oldest son and now a young man, was sitting near the woodbox laboring over his schoolwork. Hearing Mister Jenkin's tone of voice, he slammed his book to the floor in anger and hurled his pen at the door barely missing Mister Jenkins.

"Mother, how can you stand to put up with these people and their rude behavior? I hate this place. Why don't you quit this filthy work? We don't need the money that much."

His mother stopped what she was doing, carefully placed her stirring spoon down, and angrily addressed Lott, "Young man, we do need this job if we are going to survive. Without the money I take in, you laddies couldn't stay in school. I don't want to hear any more about it. You just keep studying."

She turned quickly from Lott and looked around the kitchen. "Where is your younger brother? He is supposed to be doing his work, too."

"Mother, you know Jeremiah doesn't like to do schoolwork. He hates school. He's probably in the big room entertaining the men. They like to tease him and make him do silly things. He likes all that rough house and racket in there. His language is getting as profane as theirs. Some of them men think it's funny to hear him cuss."

"Son, you go get him out of there right now and make him do his work. I don't want him in there with that crowd. You keep him out!" ordered Mary as she returned her attention to getting the food ready.

"Yes ma'am. I can get him back in here, but I can't make him learn," said Lott as he stomped toward the door in defiance and, in a few moments, returned dragging Jeremiah by the collar.

Once again, Mary stopped what she was doing to address her boys, "Jeremiah, I don't like for you to be around those men when they are drinking, and I don't want you in there. You hear me, young man? And that cursing has got to stop."

Jeremiah looked up at his mother and with a smile that could charm the Queen, reassured her he would never do it again.

"You boys settle down and get to work. We'll be going home soon. Your schoolwork is important. One of your late beloved father's dreams was that you boys would be educated, no matter what the cost."

"Mother," interrupted Lott, "Professor Johnson wants to talk to you."

"What about, Lott? It's hard for me to get to the school and work at the same time."

Once again Mary stopped what she was doing. "It's Jeremiah, isn't it? What trouble is he in now?"

Suddenly their mother's face turned red in anger, "Jeremiah, who have you been fighting with now? Has it been those McCarley boys again?"

Jeremiah hung his head and in a whisper said, "No Ma'am, I haven't fought in a long time, Mamma. I don't know what Mister Johnson wants."

Mary took great pride in the fact that her boys were able to attend school. Very few boys in the backwoods area could read and write and most of the boys in Savannah were unschooled. With the help of her Presbyterian minister, she arranged for Lott and Jeremiah to attend their church school for boys.

"I'll tell you one thing, Mister Jeremiah Wilson. We will get to the bottom of this by tomorrow afternoon, and you had better not be in serious trouble.

The following afternoon as soon as Mary finished her work at the factory, she hurriedly made her way to Saint Andrews School for Boys and Mister Johnson's office. A secretary opened the door and directed her to a seat next to a large desk positioned in front of the most massive windows Mary had ever seen.

"Mister Johnson will see you soon. He is up the hall taking care of a problem. Please, make yourself comfortable."

It wasn't long until Mister Johnson, a tall thin man in his early thirties, came storming down the hall and entered the room unaware of Mary's presence.

"These rowdy youngsters are going to get the best of me," he mumbled as he walked past the desk and peered through the window that overlooked the campus below. "Why do I stay in this profession?" he sighed.

Mary cleared her throat.

Mister Johnson quickly turned in surprise to see who had witnessed his moment of aggravation. "Oh, please excuse me. This has been a most difficult day. You must be Mrs. Wilson."

"Yes sir, I'm Lott and Jeremiah's mother, and I'm here to talk to you about Jeremiah."

"Lott and Jeremiah," He seemed unable to remember the exact intent of his appointment. "Oh yes, I know now. It's Jeremiah, not Lott, that I'm having some trouble with. Actually, I"m having a lot of trouble with that young man."

"What kind of trouble, Mister Johnson?" questioned Mary as she quietly pulled her chair closer to his desk.

"Mrs. Wilson, you have two very different sons. Lott loves to study and is always reading and completing everything assigned to him and he is especially sharp in mathematics. But Jeremiah is quite a different story."

"What do you mean, Jeremiah is a different story?"

"Mrs. Wilson, I'm going to be honest with you. Jeremiah doesn't seem to like school, and he doesn't seem able to sit still long enough to perform his school tasks. His mind wanders off to fantasy lands or somewhere, and he simply is not passing his work. In fact, he's not passing anything."

Tears began to ease down Mary's cheeks. "Mister Johnson, I can help Jeremiah do better. He's just a restless lad."

"Mrs. Wilson, I told you I was going to be honest with you and I must. The truth has got to be told. Jeremiah is basically a good, friendly child, but he has a quick and violent temper that at times is uncontrollable."

"Mister Johnson, I know he has a temper, but . . . . "

"Mrs. Wilson, please let me finish. Jeremiah is quite a bit larger than the other boys his age, and the older boys are endlessly encouraging him to fight with someone. If he's not in a fisticuffs with the older boys, then he's defending some other younger boy who's being aggravated."

"Is it wrong for my son to defend himself?" questioned Mary in an attempt to justify Jeremiah's actions.

"It is when he fights almost daily, Mrs. Wilson. He must learn self control. He should have come to me when he had problems with the other boys. Then I could have helped him."

"Mister Johnson, Jeremiah is large for his age and with unruly red hair that stands straight up, those boys call him names and make fun of him."

With tears now streaming down her cheeks and in a tone of anger Mary once again defended Jeremiah, "Mister Johnson, I've told him to take up for himself.

I've told him to fight and to be proud of his appearance. I'm the one who told him to fight."

Mister Johnson, feeling the anguish and pain Mary was experiencing, gave her his handkerchief and spoke softly. "Mrs. Wilson, this isn't pleasant for me either, but there is more."

"How can there be more, Mister Johnson? What more?" sobbed Mary.

"Mrs. Wilson, this is the part of my job I detest, and there is no easy way to tell you," he said.

"Go ahead and tell me. What more can there be?"

"The Board of Directors has met and Jeremiah has been expelled—I mean asked to leave the school. They feel that since he is not passing his work and is constantly causing problems, it is to the school's best interest that he not remain a student here."

"Do you mean he can never come back? Mister Johnson, he is only in the sixth grade. What is he to do?"

Mary slowly rose, not knowing what else to do. She placed her hands on the edge of the desk as if to hold herself upright and pleaded, "He's only a boy, Mister Johnson. Why didn't you call me in earlier? I could have done something. I could have tried."

"Mrs. Wilson, I am truly sorry our board has taken this action, but they feel they must make room for other students who genuinely want to learn. You probably know I've only been serving as headmaster for four months, and I wish I could have helped your son more. I wish I could have known him better."

Down deep Mary knew that Mister Johnson was right. She could recall how she had tried desperately to get Jeremiah to study over the years, but nothing worked. He loved to run, tussle, and play with the boys on the streets. He cared nothing for books. His education was her dream, not his.

But, Lott was different. Learning seemed to be stimulating and challenging for him. There was always a new book to read and knowledge to be gained.

In Lott's spare time, he worked for Albert Haskins, who had now returned to Savannah. It was there that he met Cyrus McCorkle, a state surveyor, who was looking for a young man to help him survey property in the surrounding area. McCorkle needed someone good with keeping figures and healthy enough to carry his gear through rough country, when necessary.

McCorkle was a short slim man who walked with a slight limp caused by his being thrown from a horse when a boy. He was intelligent but at the same time fatherly. Lott had grown to respect and admire McCorkle and called him Mister Mac.

Although Lott was somewhat younger than Mister McCorkle's expectations, Lott impressed him with his ability in mathematics and his pleasant personality. During the following months, McCorkle depended on Lott to travel outside Savannah to survey land for the state.

Lott was immature physically for his age, but was becoming a strong, handsome young man. He stood at almost six feet tall and was slim. He had thick

22

black hair and blue eyes that seemed to always sparkle. People who knew his father felt Lott was very much his image. In the meantime, life continued to present Mary Wilson with more hardships than she felt she could bear. Supplying the basic needs for two growing boys while sending one of them to school and worrying constantly about the future of the other, was beginning to bring moments of depression. She prayed nightly that God would send her relief.

Mary's prayers eventually seemed answered and life did improve for the Wilsons. Lott graduated at the top of his class and, at the same time, gained valuable experience as a surveyor's assistant. The extra money helped to support the family.

As for Jeremiah, he continued in his rough and tumble ways and eventually found work on the docks loading and unloading cargo. In the evenings, when Mary was working at the High Step Tavern, Jeremiah worked clearing and cleaning tables. Due to his strength and size, he also often served as the establishment's bouncer.

At fifteen, Jeremiah was already over six feet tall and weighed approximately two hundred and twenty pounds. He rapidly gained the respect of patrons because of his ability to survive a tough scrap and he seldom lost a fight. When he was only fourteen, Jeremiah had a dispute with a well-known ruffian and with one punch to the chest, had sent the unfortunate character sailing across the floor, shattering the solid oak entrance door.

Because of Jeremiah's questionable reputation and hard drinking binges, Preacher Amos, a local Methodist minister, who was a frequent visitor to the High Step and a friend of Jeremiah's gave a special nickname. When testing the spirits one night, he directed his mug of ale to Jeremiah and in a tone of religious nature toasted, "Jeremiah, you are too wicked for an Old Testament name. You drink, cuss, and fight, the same. So from henceforth, Jake will be your name, and I don't give a damn who you blame." The High Step erupted with laughter and cheers, and from that night on Jake was his name.

New Year's Eve of 1826 found Mary still working in the High Step kitchen, and this evening Lott was sitting in the kitchen keeping his mother company.

"Mother, let me know when you need help. This is going to be one long and lively evenin'. They are gettin' loud mighty early."

Suddenly, a thunderous crashing caused Mary to drop a plate of food and rush to the door to see what was happening.

But, before she could reach the door, Jeremiah poked his head in and with a big smile reassured her that everything was all right. "Mamma, it's just Mister Amos. He's drinkin' again and knocked over a table. Everything is going to be fine. I ain't in no scrap."

"No scrap. No fight. I hear it every night it seems. Lott, you have got to get your brother out of here . . . out of Savannah. One day he's going to get hurt," pleaded Mary as she began to clean up the pieces of broken dish and food that was strewn on the floor.

Lott knelt down and began to help. "Mamma, how can I change what he's like. I do good just to take care of myself."

Lott paused for a moment, wondering whether or not to say what he was thinking. "It seems to me I am always taking care of him now. What more can I do?"

"I don't know, Son, but you and I have got to come up with something. We have got to help that boy."

The evening grew louder and louder. Around one o'clock, when things seemed to be slowing down, a loud shot rang out and a few seconds later, another burst of gunfire. Mary ran toward the door as she had so many times before, only to be stopped by Lott.

He pushed her back toward the stove and said, "Don't go in there. I'll go. It could be dangerous."

In what seemed to be an hour, but in actuality was only a few minutes, Lott burst back into the kitchen exclaiming, "You had better come in here. Jake's been hurt."

Mary began to cry as she ran into the tavern searching for Jeremiah. She pushed people aside and struck others who got in her path as she worked her way through the crowd. She screamed, "Where's my laddie? Where's my Jeremiah? Get out of my way. You are all nothing but drunks, thieves, and murderers."

Suddenly, the crowd cleared and she stood staring at what she feared to be the dead body of her beloved son, but instead was a still-alive Jake sitting on the floor holding a pistol in one hand and pressing his other hand to his forehead near his hairline. Blood was streaming through his fingers and down his face, and a gaping hole in his shirt revealed where a bullet had ripped into his side.

Mary knelt down, not knowing whether to touch him or not. "Son, what have you gotten into now? Lott, go get a doctor. Get him quick!" shouted Mary.

"Mother, the doctor has already been sent for. He's on the way," reassured Lott. "Just calm yourself. You ain't helpin' Jeremiah at all actin' the way you are. Please, just calm down."

Jeremiah was now sitting in a chair with a handkerchief over his scalp wound and sipping ale as though nothing had happened.

"Mamma, how about settling down and quit makin' such a fuss about this. I ain't going to die, and if I do, it will be the Lord's will. Somebody's going to have to shoot me with something bigger than that pistol," mumbled Jeremiah.

The Wilsons were Presbyterians and avid believers in predestination. They believed that the Almighty God had a plan for every believer and what happened to one was God's divine will.

"Son, how did this happen?" questioned Mary as she cleaned the blood from his face.

"It's all right," reassured Lott. "Mister Liddle saw the whole thing. Jeremiah is not at fault. He says Albert Brewer had been drinkin' too much and pulled his pistol on Joe Langley. He claimed Joe had been makin' advances toward his wife. Mamma, Jeremiah grabbed the pistol out of Mister Brewer's hand to stop a shootin'. From what they say, the first shot hit Jeremiah in the side and when he pulled the pistol up in the air, the second shot hit his head. Mamma, this ain't Jeremiah's fault," reassured Lott.

Doc Haley soon arrived and examined Jeremiah and dressed his wounds. As he finished, he sternly addressed Jeremiah. "Jake, the Lord was with you tonight, young man. You are indeed lucky. That first shot appears to have cracked a couple of ribs but did not penetrate your ribcase. I found what was left of the bullet down in your shirt. Must have bounced right off of you. And for the other, it only grazed your scalp. It's a damned good thing you got such a hard noggin. If you take care of yourself, you'll be fine. But, you might have a permanent part in your hair from here out," joked Doc Haley. The whole crowd broke into relieved laughter and cheers.

Peace was soon restored and Jeremiah was moved to a bedroom upstairs above the kitchen. Mary and Lott sat by Jeremiah's bedside and together thanked the Lord for saving his life. Doc Haley had given Jeremiah a strong sedative and soon he was sound asleep.

For a long time the two stared at Jeremiah and at each other without a word. Finally Mary broke the silence, "This is all my fault. It shouldn't have gone this far."

"Mama, what do you mean?" replied Lott, confused.

"I should have disciplined him better. I quess I kinda gave up on him. I could have stopped his fighting and cursing and I knew he was doing some drinking. What did I do? I just scolded him a little and thought that would do it. I'm part of the blame for him lying there on that bed."

"Mama, you ain't the blame for Jake's problems. You were strict on us. It's many a day you wore us out with them ole switchings. Jake is just different from most boys. Sure he gets into trouble, but he has a lot of good in him too. He ain't never turned down anybody in trouble and you can't say that about most folks. No, you ain't never given up on neither one of us. Mama, you've had it hard since Papa died. We've all had it hard."

"Lott, don't you ever give up on him, you hear me. Don't ever."

"Mama, I promise you I'll never stop caring for him. I'll look after him. You can count on that."

"Lott, we have got to get Jeremiah out of this city."

Lott reached for his Mother's hand. "I think I have a way, but it's going to take us a long way from here. The bad thing about it is we won't be near you in case you need us."

"I don't mind son," interrupted Mary. "Tell me what it is."

"Mister McCorkle has asked me to go with him into the Creek land in west Georgia to help him survey the area for the government. It's a long way from Savannah. They just moved the Indians out, and we have a big job ahead of us."

"But Lott, what has this got to do with your brother?"

"Mother, Mister McCorkle wants me to find someone else to go with us, and that someone else can be Jeremiah."

"But Lott, what if Jeremiah doesn't want to go?"

"He'll go. I'll think of something. He's got to leave. If he stays in Savannah, somebody is going to kill him."

3

HOME IN THE WILDERNESS

THE YEAR WAS 1832 AND THE WILSON BOYS HAD NOW BEEN surveying land for the state of Georgia for four years and recently had accompanied Cyrus McCorkle westward to Mississippi to survey the land acquired by the state of Mississippi from the Choctaw Indians.

While in Georgia, the group had surveyed land in the western part of the state that had once belonged to the Creek nation. After that McCorkle had been contacted by an associate in Mississippi and was employed to survey the large area of land ceeded to the state by the Choctaw nation at the Treaty of Dancing Rabbit Creek. The surveying group sailed from Savannah around the tip of Florida by the way of the Gulf of Mexico, and finally reached Mobile, Alabama. Leaving Mobile, they took a flatboat up the Tombigbee River to a small settlement, and by traveling overland they soon reached the eastern section of the Choctaw lands located in east central Mississippi.

At this meeting place, several groups of surveyors gathered to design a plan in which the area could be charted thoroughly and quickly. The state wanted the Indian lands ready for settlement and sale as soon as possible.

Land speculators and traders had already begun to move into Choctaw lands to locate the choicest property and to trade with the Indians. In some cases, speculators were devising plans to cheat the Choctaws out of the more desirable sections. By the recent treaty, an individual Choctaw male could remain on the land but with restricted rights if he would give up his tribal allegiance and agree to become an American citizen. In return, he would be given 640 acres which was defined as one section. If he did not accept these terms, he and his family would be forced to move to the Oklahoma Territory, where most southeastern tribes were being relocated. The vast majority of the Choctaws chose to relocate in the Oklahoma Territory. Some decided to remain in the only homeland they had ever known, the hill country of east central Mississippi.

In addition to Lott and Jake, McCorkle was assigned an extra surveyor to assist with mapping a large area located to the northwest of their organizational point. The assistant, a young man named Franklin Olliver or Frank as he wished to be called, was the son of a Louisanna land speculator and a French Creole woman. He seemed to be likable enough, but acted strange at times. More was on this man's mind than surveying.

I

The early March winds sent the leaves swirling softly around the campfire causing the horses to shuffle back and forth nervously. Every once in a while, the breezes would gust through the leafless treetops creating a ghostly whistling sound that caused goosebumps on those not accustomed to life in the wild.

The group traveled all day to finally arrive at the work site where they would lay out the land sections. Before reaching their campsite, they had ridden in the dark for over an hour, unaware of the landscape's appearance. When Mister Mac finally decided to stop, it didn't take the men long to set up camp and bed down. Later, he was worried over the restlessness of the animals.

"Jake, get up and check the horses. Be sure they's tied up well for the night. If we loose them, we walk, and I ain't wantin' to do no walkin'," stated McCorkle as he pulled the blanket closer around his head to keep his ears warm.

Jake slowly moved from his warm place near the fire and with his blanket wrapped around his massive shoulders walked toward the horses grumbling, "Why is it always Jake that has to do all the lousy jobs. Hell! I was better off in Savannah."

Jake soon returned to the campfire complaining under his breath. He finally blurted out, "Mister Mac," as he settled once more in his place by the fire, "I want to ask you sump'n, and you bein' more intelligent than my brother Lott, I think you can give me a more sensible answer."

"What is it now, Jake? I'm about ready to settle down for the night. I ain't talkin' long."

"My brother, that smart ass over there rolled up like a cocoon, hoodwinked me out of Savannah by takin' advantage of me when I got drunk one night. He said I got in a fight and killed a man," explained Jake.

"Well, was it true?" asked Mister Mac as he raised up on an elbow to hear Jake's reply.

"Hell, no. You know it weren't no truth to it. You knowed it was a joke. The worse thing about it was that officer Crandell was also in on the trick. He bein' a friend of the fam'ly, made it more real by goin' along with their scheme. They had me scairt to death that I was going to be arrested and sent off to jail or maybe even hanged. They had me scairt crazy."

"Jake, the way I heard it was that yore mamma wanted you out of Savannah. She felt like you was going to get yoreself killed if you stayed there, and I agreed with her and so did Lott," answered Mister Mac. "I knew about their plan."

"Okay, you answer me this. I got hoodwinked out of Savannah to save my life, but here I am in this damned wilderness where I'm goin' to either freeze to death, be eaten by one of them wild bears, or one of them Choctaws is going to stick me full of holes!" explained Jake, now moving closer to Lott to get his brother's attention.

"Jake, just shut up yore complainin'. We've been over this time and time again. You ain't going to freeze. We ain't seen a bear in several days and them Choctaws ain't warlike," said Lott firmly, trying to ignore Jake's agitation.

"We went through that village a couple of miles south of here this afternoon and there was hund'rds of Indians there. There was some mean-lookin' ones too. I don't think they liked us and they kept lookin' at me, kind of strangely," Jake exclaimed.

"They probably don't like the idea of losin' their land, Jake, and we ain't helpin' them too much either," added Frank who had been wakened by the loud talking.

"Jake, settle down. Them Indians ain't going to hurt us, and if they do, this is as good a place to die as any. And by the way, if they did stare at ya, they was probably thinkin' this is the biggest and ugliest white man they've ever seen," joked Lott, as Mister Mac and Frank broke out in laughter.

"See, Mister Mac, what did I tell ya? My brother is nothin' but a smart ass and an educated fool," resounded Jake.

"Jake, why do you resent my education? You had the same chance I did," answered Lott. "You have as much sense as I do, when you want to use it," continued Lott.

"I know that, but common sense is better'n book sense any day. Besides, I just couldn't keep my mind on the subject. There was always more important things to think about, like what I wanted to do when school was out. Weren't no way I could sit still and listen," said Jake, pulling his blanket around his shoulders and settling himself next to a giant oak tree located twenty feet from the fire.

Everyone became quiet, even if they were not asleep, and Lott wondered if they might be able to stave off any more complaints from his brother.

"You asleep?" hissed Jake, trying to revive the argument. "Lott, you remember Mrs. Barton, our fifth grade teacher? She gave me problems, too. She had the biggest set of tits I ever seen. Frank! Frank! You awake? Each one of them was this big." Jake's voice rose and he held his hands in such a way as to create an image of something large and round.

"Jake, just shut that damned mouth up and leave us be. Mrs. Barton's titties weren't that big either," corrected Lott. "Every woman's tits are watermelon size in yore mind."

Laughter once again shattered the quietness of the woodlands.

"Well it's good one of us was distracted by women; you're going to miss out on the best of life. Books ain't better than women!" answered Jake.

"All of ya just be quiet and let me get some sleep," insisted Mister Mac. "You won't see no watermelons or women out here in these woods. And Jake, them Choctaws ain't going to bother us."

"Well, I ain't sleepin' tonight. If them Choctaws get me, they is going to get me wide awake," Jake answered as he rose from the ground.

"Lott, Jake's got a right to be afraid in these woods. It pays to be cautious out here. Things could happen to ya," said Frank as he got up and walked toward the horses to relieve himself.

"Them Indians ain't nothin' but filthy savages. I'll be glad when they is all gone west or better still, I think we ought to just round 'em up and shoot 'em," continued Frank as he returned to the campsite. "It would save the trouble of movin' 'em. I ought to know not to drink so much coffee. I'll be gettin' up all through the night."

"Frank, I'm not sure I agree with you about them Indians," countered Mister Mac. "Them Choctaws ain't done a thing to anyone I've talked with, and this here is their land that's bein' taken."

"Just my opinion, Mister Mac, my opinion," answered Frank.

Later in the night, the winds subsided and cloudy skies gave way to a dark heaven filled with thousands of twinkling stars. Everything was finally quiet around the campfire.

Jake was the first one up and stirring the following morning and wrapped snugly in his blanket, he stood and admired the unusual rays of pink, blue, and purple bands of clouds gathering on the eastern horizon. After gazing at the sky for several minutes, he turned his attention to the forest and suddenly realized this was the most magnificent country they had traveled.

Behind him was a deep forest of long leaf pines stretching as far as he could see. Their massive trunks seemed to reach to heaven. Through the years, fires and bolts of lightning had scarred the sides of these ancient trees, but even these markings made them that much more majestic. As he looked southward, the pine forest gave way to stands of oak, hickory, poplar, beech, and other hardwood trees. Looking closer, Jake noticed a small area of open meadow freckled with deer gracefully gathering around the hardwood trees where an abundance of tasty acorns had fallen.

Jake had the impulse to walk into the forest to see this miracle of beauty, but the fear of the wilderness seized him.

He mumbled to himself, "Why am I afraid of them woods? It ain't as rough as some of the places I've found myself in. I've faced guns and knives and some of the roughest men in Savannah. Hell, I ain't going to let them trees make a coward out of me. I'm goin' in."

Grasping his rifle in one hand and his hunting knife in the other, he quietly and cautiously crept over the dampened, newly fallen leaves and noted dozens of squirrels scurrying around the bases of the trees trying to unearth their morning meal.

Creeping closer and closer to the meadow, he saw a large herd of deer. Suddenly, a large flock of turkeys wandered out into the opening and began feeding on the plants and insects in the field. Occasionally, sun rays would strike the backs of these enormous birds and Jake could see shades of gold, bronze, and orange glittering from their long feathers as they fed from plant to plant.

Jake laid his rifle and knife down so he could crawl a little closer to observe these creatures. Turning his attention once more to the deer herd that had now moved within one hundred feet of him, he began counting.

"Fifty-two, fifty-three, and fifty-four," whispered Jake. "Lott and them just won't believe this," Jake murmured to himself. "Well, I'd better get back to camp before they think something has got me."

Jake started to get up, but suddenly a forceful hand pushed him down. A muscular Indian was standing behind him with an arrow notched in the bow-string and fully drawn.

The Indian looked down at him with dark, piercing eyes, and it was obvious to Jake, that he must be a fierce warrior. A long scar ran across his nose and down his cheek. Jake was terrified when he quickly realized his rifle and knife were lying on the ground thirty feet behind him. Feeling he could not get up in time to stop the arrow, he decided to try to jump the Indian anyway, hoping he would not be hit in the process.

Looking at the arrow once again, Jake reconsidered his plan. To his surprise, the Indian raised his bow toward the nearest deer and sent an arrow racing through the air striking the deer in the lower section of the neck. The animal ran but came crashing to the ground underneath one of the large oak trees across the meadow.

As it struggled to stand again, the hunter sprinted toward the downed animal, screaming and chanting. His long, black hair, shining in the early morning sunlight, bounced across his shoulders as he ran toward the kill.

Jake thought to himself, "Which is the more magnificent of these creatures? The deer or this Choctaw who came up behind me without my knowledge and could've taken my life had he wanted to?"

Jake retrieved his weapons and ran back toward the camp without a backward glance to see whether the Indian was at the kill or after him. Upon reaching the site, he found everyone just as he had left them, sleeping and snoring. Nothing had changed, at least not for them.

Jake contemplated whether or not to share his experience with his friends, but decided to keep it to himself.

"They won't believe me if I tell them what I seen, and if they do, they'll probably just make fun of me," murmured Jake. "But I survived my first venture into them woods, and that Indian didn't even try to kill me. Hell, he was probably more scairt of me than I was of him. Get up, get up, you lazy bastards! It's a fine day to be alive and nary a bear, panther, or Indian has got ahold of this lovely carcus of mine. We is going to tame this here wilderness," hollered Jake as he shook the men vigorously.

"You sound mighty brave this morning, Mister Jake. I guess the daylight makes all them fears go away," said Frank, pulling himself up to the coals to make a pot of fresh coffee. "You is a daytime warrior and a night-time chicken."

"Don't get him started again, Frank. We got to work today," ordered Mister Mac.

The group straightened up camp and loaded the pack-horses with their equipment, but Mister Mac decided to make a change in plans.

"Boys, since this here is a pretty good place for us to camp, I think we'll just use this spot as our base. From this point we can lay out a township in each direction. This can be what you call, the crossroads. That sound all right with you men?"

The group agreed and only loaded surveying equipment on the horses.

A township consisted of an area of land six miles square divided into 36 sections of 640 acres each. To survey four townships of land was a large undertaking.

But by late May, the surveying had been completed in the immediate area and the men were ready to move farther westward. During the past two months, they had covered every inch of the land and made it a point to stay out of the way of the Indians. With each passing day, more Choctaws were seen wandering through the woodlands and closer to the crossroads camp, but at the same time, they kept their distance. The Choctaws minded their own business and continued to live in peace, unaware of the evil future the white men would bring.

With the work finally finished, it was time for the crew to move farther west.

Mister Mac and his men paused at the creek below their now deserted camp and let the horses water before moving out.

"Mister Mac, you know I've kind of got attached to this here place. There's sump'n special about it," said Jake as his horse wandered upstream while watering.

"I have the same feelin' as Jake," replied Lott. "What more could you ask for? Someone is going to be mighty lucky to get a piece of this here property. One could make a fine livin' here."

"Well, young folks like you could probably make sump'n out of it, but for me, I'm too old to start a life out here," answered Mister Mac. "I've got other plans 'fore I go back to Georgia."

The group led the horses up the steep bank above the creek and were soon headed west through an immense swamp bottom covered with heavy hardwoods. The horses struggled to make their way through the entanglement of ferns and canes. Never in their lives had these men seen such an abundance of wildlife. It seemed like every time the horses broke through the thick foliage, some kind of wild creature would bolt out seeking safety from the horses' hooves. They soon crossed an Indian trail that led them out of the swamp and into open woodlands.

"Mister Mac?" questioned Frank. "What do ya plan to do when you finish this job? You said you had sump'n more to do. You mind tellin' us?"

"Not at all. I plan to help the state sell all this land that we've mapped out," he replied. "It was part of the deal I made with the authorities. All the head surveyors got the same arrangement. Who knows the land better than us? Nobody, except the Choctaws."

Later that evening, the men once again settled around a fire tired from too many hours on horseback and the hard work involved in setting up a new camp.

"Mister Mac," questioned Jake nervously, "would you sell me a piece of land?"

"Sure, I would, but I don't own no land in Savannah, Jake," answered Mister Mac.

"I don't mean in Savannah. I mean here."

"Here!" exclaimed Lott. "You must be crazy. You don't like these woods. You're scairt of them, Jake. You wouldn't last a year out here," snapped Lott.

"Lott, had you rather me live here or go back to Savannah when this job is over?" answered Jake. "I've kind of learned to like this rough country. It's a challenge to me, and I believe I can lick it."

Surprised that his wayward brother would consider living in this practically uninhabited land, Lott looked Jake in the face to see if he was really serious.

"Jake, I love this land, too. I just haven't said much about it. I'll stay if you will, providin' Mister Mac will sell us the property. How about it, Mister Mac?"

"You boys' money is as good as any. I'll sell you any piece you want, if'n it ain't already taken by the Indians who plan to stay on here,"

"That's a deal, Mister Mac. When we finish this job, you take the money we've made and place our names in the section of land where we first made camp, if'n the Indians don't want it," insisted Lott.

"And we want that meadow southwest of the camp," added Jake. "It's kind of special to me."

"You boys have worked hard for me the past four years, and I owe you more than the price of this land," stated Mister Mac. "Not only will I register your property, but you should have a nice sum of money left over. And by the way, if'n they has a drawin' for the sections, I think I can work a deal where you two can still get yores. You boys got a deal."

"What about me?" questioned Frank.

"What ya got in mind, Frank?" answered Mister Mac.

"You remember when we traveled south of that Choctaw village on the way up here. There was a large patch of open bottom land next to the Chunky River that would make some kind of fine farmin'. I want that land, Mister Mac. It could make me a rich man one of these days."

"I'll see what I can do, but that's in another surveyor's area," said Mister Mac, "and somewhere I think I heard some talk that a few Choctaws may want to settle there. I'm not sure though."

The campfire was almost out now with only a few glowing coals remaining visible. It wouldn't be long until each would go in different directions. They had become close in many ways but in the years to come, events would shatter the friendships developed during the long summer of 1832 and would bring pain and suffering to the Wilsons.

4

BACK TO THE WILDERNESS

Lott AND JAKE DECIDED TO TRAVEL WITH MISTER McCORKLE to Jackson, the state capital of Mississippi, to purchase the supplies needed for life in the Choctaw lands. With winter coming, they felt it would be better to remain in Jackson until spring which would give them several months to prepare for their return to the wilderness. They would have the long summer to build a house and begin limited cultivation before the cold weather arrived.

One obstacle blocked their return. The state government did not want settlers in the area until the Choctaws were removed. This had been planned for the coming summer. Already there was a rendezvous point in the southern part of Newton County where the Indians were beginning to gather. Some Choctaws were still undecided about remaining on their tribal lands. If they did, they would have to adopt the ways of the white man. Worst still, they would have to adjust to living on a small area of land instead of being able to freely roam over thousands of acres of woodland.

When it seemed the Wilsons would have to spend an extended amount of time in Jackson before they could finally return, McCorkle brought them some unexpected news.

Trudging down the muddy street, he spotted Lott and Jake sitting out on the front porch of the hotel casually observing a group of children playing on the steps.

"Boys, I've got some good news for ya. I got a legal way for you two to get the land you want and to make a little extra. You want to hear about it?" said McCorkle as he settled in a chair and filled his pipe with tobacco.

"We sure do want to hear about it, Mister Mac. I'll be damned if I want to spend another winter here in Jackson. All we do is sit around this flea-bitten shack of a hotel, and Lott won't give me no money to spend. There is women and plenty of liquor here for the takin', but what do I do? Sit and look, and when I get tired of that, Lott tells me to keep on sittin' and lookin'. I just can't take it much longer," answered Jake.

"Jake, just shut up yore complainin'. Go on, Mister Mac."

Their former boss leaned back in his chair and put his arm on Lott's shoulder. "All right boys, here it is. I've got ya the land you wanted and here's your job. When spring comes, you two go back into the Choctaw lands. There ain't supposed to be settlers in there for a while. If you find them, run them off. If that fails, report them to the county authorities."

"Where will they be?" questioned Lott.

"They'll be located in a camp about seven miles west of your place. Also, when people start comin' in there, they's to see you two first. We don't want no fussin' and killin' over land lines. The place is going to be rough enough like it is. There ain't going to be much law out there for a while," continued Mister Mac.

"When can we leave? Jake and I can handle it and we know the area better'n anyone," said Lott slapping Jake on the back.

"That's left up to you boys, but you need to get on in there before we have some squatters sittin' on someone else's land. Spring will be soon enough."

"What about Frank? Did he get the piece he wanted?" questioned Jake.

"Well, from what I understand, he wanted some bottom land below your place. The problem is some Choctaws have already taken claim to the place. Can't say if'n Frank got any land at all. Lott, you boys watch Frank, that is, if'n you ever see him again. I just don't trust him," warned McCorkle.

"I don't see how them Choctaws is going to make it. We going to tell them that they has to live on a piece of land only one mile square and provide for themselves when they is used to roamin' and huntin' and doin' a little bit of gardenin'. I don't think so. It just ain't going to work," said Lott.

I

Lott and Jake reached their hillcountry on the 26th of March, 1833. For the past two days, they had driven their wagon through torrential rainstorms, some of the worst they had ever seen. They had lost two weeks by having to wait for streams to subside before safe crossings could be made. But finally, they reached the old surveying camp which would now be their new home. They wasted no time constructing a house, because soon the cold winter winds would be upon them.

"Lott, why do I always have to get in the hole to saw, and why can't we just make us a simple log hut to live in?" complained Jake.

"Well, little brother, we're going to build us a house that's going to be here a long time. Maybe our grandchildren will be livin' here some day, and you're in the sawin' pit cause you are the strongest," replied Lott.

"Damn you. I'll bet you want a real floor instead of dirt," answered Jake as he pulled the saw blade down through the massive log above his head, almost jerking Lott from his position on the top side of the big timber.

"Most folks is satisfied with just a one-room hut, and that would suit me fine too," continued Jake.

Being frustrated with Jake, Lott sat down and decided to address Jake's habitual use of profanity. "Jake, why do you always use them words? It's 'damn this' and 'hell that' and everybody you don't like is a 'son-of-a-bitch'. Mamma never let us talk that way 'round her, and the church don't go for it either."

Jake bounded out of the pit and sat down on the ground below Lott and wiped the sweat from his forehead. "Well, Mister Brother, I don't call 'damns' and 'hells' and 'sons of bitches' as cussing. Has you ever heard me call the Lord's name in vain? No, you never has. I been to church lots of times in my life, and I do believe in God. And, by the way, saying them words makes me feel better. I can release my tensions, and that keeps my temper down, and when I keep my temper down, I don't get in fights," concluded Jake.

Lott had no reply. It was obvious Jake had got the best of him.

Jake began to laugh as he realized his brother was at last speechless and jumped back down into the saw pit, "Hell, Lott, let's get back to work and build this mansion of yores, and about this house for our grandchildren, I ain't seen no women around here to start foolin' 'round with. What about you, preacher Wilson, you seen any women lately?"

"Jake, just shut up and work. I don't want to talk to ya for a few days. You make me so mad I could cuss and I don't ever cuss," replied Lott as he shoved the saw blade down through the log toward Jake as hard as he could.

Between working on the house, cutting firewood for the winter, and starting a good size garden, the Wilson boys had little time to venture out into the adjoining property. Only on Sunday afternoons did they take time to saddle their horses and explore the countryside. They tried to stay out of the way of the Choctaws. There was a large village about a mile south of the southern boundary of their property called Bissa Aisha [Blackberry Place]. Jake still remembered how the Choctaws looked at him when their crew had traveled through before. Lott could not entice him to visit and maybe do some trading. Jake still remembered how that Indian had almost scared him to death.

One good thing about the summer of 1833 was that it gave Lott and Jake time with one another, and they became more than brothers, they became friends. They learned to accept the parts of each other's personality and character that had previously caused conflict between them.

"Lott, when we going to stop this housebuildin' and try to find sump'n fun to do. I'm tired of sawin' and workin'," said Jake as he finished nailing the last of the white oak shingles on the roof.

"You right Jake, and I'm tired too. We've worked like dogs for the past five months and I'm about burned out. We fixin' to slow it down, little brother."

"Praise the Lord and get out the Good Book. I can't believe you's becomin' a human," shouted Jake as he slid off the roof and landed on the ground with a thud.

"I'm going to go get the brew, Lott. We going to celebrate and I does mean have a party," exclaimed Jake as he ran down the trail leading to the spring.

"When did you have time to make brew, Jake? What did ya make it out of?" shouted Lott, trying to get Jake's attention before he was out of hearing range.

Down in the woods, Lott could barely hear Jake's reply, "Corn! Brother, corn! Ain't you missed some from our patch? I'm puttin' it to good use."

Tired, but now relaxed, Lott and Jake sat down under one of the large oaks growing in front of the new house, sipping brew and admiring their work. It was an unusual sight to see such a fine cabin in the middle of a wilderness with not a single white settler except for them in the area. The house had three rooms down the left side. The first two were bedrooms and the last was a kitchen with an adjoining well where water could be easily drawn. Across an open hall were two more rooms Lott planned to rent out to travelers.

"Jake, it ain't bad lookin' is it? I wish Mamma could see it. She'd be proud of us, wouldn't she?"

"Yeah, she sure would," replied Jake as he guzzled the moonshine. "Lott, I'm as hot as a tater in hell. I'm goin' to the creek to take a swim and cool off a little. You want to go?"

"Naw, I'm going to stay here and start some plans on a barn. You go on," replied Lott.

"Barn! Damn a barn! I thought we was through workin'. You just lied to me, Lott," stormed Jake. "To hell with you and that barn. You build it yoreself. I ain't workin' no more and that's it," shouted Jake, stomping and fuming as he headed toward the creek.

"I don't mean now, Jake. We'll work on it durin' the winter. Okay?" shouted Lott, trying to get his brother's attention.

Jake, ignoring his brother's attempt to reconcile their differences, made his way through the woods toward the creek stopping often to tip the jug. The further he walked, the dizzier he became. When he had almost reached the creek, weary and a lot drunk, he sat down to catch his breath.

Suddenly, out of nowhere, floated sounds of women talking, laughing, and squealing.

Jake being drunk and confused, thought that his "spirits" were working on his mind.

"Hell, this stuff must be killin' me," he mumbled.

But the sounds continued and they were coming from the direction of the creek.

"I'm going to go down there and see what's going on, and if'n I am crazy, I'm just crazy," said Jake, trying to convince himself that he wasn't hallucinating.

He dropped to his knees and crawled across the soft, leaf-covered ground as quietly as a bobcat stalking its prey, still dragging his precious jug of spirits behind him. Finally reaching the high creek bank above his favorite swimming hole, he peered down on a scene he thought must have been heaven sent.

There were four beautiful Choctaw women swimming and playing in the stream and enjoying every moment as they splashed the cold creek water on each other. They wore no clothing, at least from their waists up.

Jake lay still, admiring the group, especially one of them. She resembled the others, but her complexion was lighter and she appeared to be taller.

"Damn! This is sump'n," thought Jake. "I can't believe what my pore eyes are seein'. I wish they would get out of the water so I can get a better look. Damn, this is sump'n."

As the afternoon passed, the women seemed to be in no hurry and Jake became impatient.

36

"Well, if they ain't gettin' out, then I'll just route them out," reasoned Jake. "I'm going to strip down, take a few more swigs of brew to get my conf'dence up, and I'm going to leap off this high bank and splash them out of there. All I'm going to see is women's butts runnin' up that creekbank on the other side."

Jake quietly stripped off his clothes, took several big gulps and lay his jug on the ground. He then backed off to get a running start. With one giant leap he was on his way through the air and headed directly toward the middle of the Indian women. When Jake hit the water, it sounded like a huge boulder striking, a sound so loud it could be heard all through the creek bottom.

No sooner had Jake submerged, than his head popped up as he expected to see nude Choctaw bodies scrambling up the creekbank terrified at the unexpected guest who, one could say, dropped in on them.

But to Jake's surprise, the Indians had simply lowered themselves into the water with only their heads exposed, and were just calmly staring at him. After a few moments, they began to talk to one another. No one moved.

Suddenly, the women looked up toward the top of the creekbank, and Jake sensed company had arrived and he knew it wasn't Lott. He slowly turned around and was horrified at the sight. Standing on both sides of the creekbank were at least fifteen Choctaw men, weapons in hand, staring down at him. Some had spears, others had bows and arrows, and two had some kind of strange club.

Jake prayed to himself, "Dear Lord, this is it. I sure didn't mean no harm to them women, and I never called yore name in vain. Have mercy on my soul. Amen and amen."

Feeling his time was over, he then began to talk and pray out loud, "Lord Jesus, forgive me of my sins, and Lord don't hold it against these here savages for killin' me. I probably deserves it."

Suddenly, one of the men interrupted Jake's prayer. "Oka akocha! Tunshpa!" [Get out of the water! Quickly!]

The women hurriedly emerged and gathered their clothing from a big boulder near the edge. In a matter of seconds, they had vanished into the woods. To Jake's disappointment, all had been clothed from the waist down.

Looking closer, Jake recognized the Choctaw who was giving the orders as the same one he had encountered before. He remembered the scar.

The tall Choctaw pointed to Jake and spoke to the others. "Katima hon nahullo kmat minti. [Where did this white man come from.] Im anukfilit iksho. [I think he is crazy.] Homa Chitto kat nata katimi. [Something is wrong with Big Red.] Imakfili ikono, kano hon hotupa la he keyo. [He acts crazy, but does not seem to want to hurt anyone.] Chihowa im alla isht anumpali. [He also talks of Jesus.] Okla hasha takmalini. [We will leave him alone.] Chukaia Homa Chitto! [Go home, Big Red!]"

Jake did not understand, but one thing was clear: they pointed at him and then in the direction of his house.

Jake gathered his courage, "I think what you fellows are tellin' me is, to get the hell out of here. Ain't that right?" said Jake, not expecting a reply.

"Yes," said the Choctaw, to Jake's surprise. "Get hell out. Stay away from women."

They turned and walked away leaving Jake alone and naked in the cool creek water.

He wasted no time getting up the creekbank to retrieve his clothes and check on the jug. But to his surprise, all he found were his boots and socks.

"Damn! Damn you savages! You stole my clothes and took my jug. You sons of bitches! You might as well have killed me!"

Jake headed toward home after pulling on his socks and boots. "How am I going to explain this to Lott?" he thought. "He'll laugh at me for the rest of my life."

Back at the house, Lott had finished designing a plan for the barn and sat on the front porch steps enjoying the end of the hot summer day. Cool evening breezes ruffled the leaves at the tops of the trees in front of the house, and afternoon shadows were creeping across the front yard.

"Jake should've been home long 'fore now," thought Lott. "I think I'll saddle up and go check on him."

He realized that, for the first time, he was worried about the safety of his brother and also that he had become selfishly dependent on Jake. If anything happened, how could he continue to build their dream? Worst still, he would lose his best friend.

Lott headed for the horses, but something moving in the woods caught his attention, darting from tree to tree and working its way toward the house.

"Somebody or sump'n is up to no good," thought Lott. "It could be an Indian or a trader trying to jump me. I wish Jake was here."

Lott returned to the house, eased down the hall and gently picked up his rifle, powder, and shot and quietly crept down the back steps. He would work his way through the woods and come up behind whoever or whatever was approaching the house.

He quickly moved through the forest and was soon in a position to challenge whatever was in front of him. Something moved again, and even though it was almost dark, he could tell that it was human. Lott took several bold steps and leveled his rifle.

"Stop just where you are. If you move an inch, you'll have a hole in ya big enough to see through."

Crouched in front of him, naked as could be, except for his boots, was his one and only brother trying to cover his private parts with his hands. His face was as red as his hair.

"Jake! This is one heck-ov-uh sight. What in blazes are ya doin' without yore clothes? Where are they? I've been worried about ya."

Jake's embarrassment quickly turned to anger.

"Lott, this ain't none of yore bus'ness, and I'll be damned if'n I ever tell you what happened to me," said Jake as he stalked toward the house.

"You don't have to tell me anything Jake, and why are you mad at me? I've been worried about ya, but you do look kind of funny. I didn't know you did have such a white backend," said Lott as he followed Jake to the house, trying to conceal his laughter.

"See what I mean. All you doin' is makin' fun of me. Hell, you don't understand at all," said Jake. "You can laugh all ya want, but tomorrow, I'm leavin'. I've had enough. And by the way, see this big ole white ass." Jake slapped his backsides. "You can kiss it goodbye."

"Jake, how can I understand? You won't tell me what happened. I ain't laughin' at ya either," replied Lott. "Not too much, anyway."

That evening, the brothers were silent. Each stayed in his own room, not knowing how to handle the awkward situation.

Hours later, right before daybreak, Lott heard a commotion near the barn site. Something was disturbing the livestock.

"Jake! get your rifle. Sump'ns out there botherin' the horses and cows. We can't lose them animals," whispered Lott.

"I'll be right with ya," answered Jake.

They eased the door open and sneaked down the hall quietly as possible. When they reached the front porch, they noticed a small bundle on the top step.

"What do you think it is, Jake?" said Lott as he picked it up to examine more closely.

"Jake, these look like yore clothes! What in heck is they doin' here?"

Before Jake could answer, five Choctaw men moved slowly from the woods near where the horses were secured and approached the house.

Lott and Jake raised their rifles hoping a show of force would discourage the Indians if they intended to start trouble.

"Alright, that's close enough. You can stop right there," said Lott, praying they would understand.

The Indians stopped and raised their hands to show they were not armed and motioned to talk to Jake. Once again, it was the Choctaw with the scar that seemed to be in charge.

"Homa Chitto pist okla laya," [We have come to see Big Red,] said the Choctaw pointing toward Jake.

He stepped forward and presented Jake with a large bundle of furs and then handed Jake his empty jug.

"Trade furs for spirits, Homa Chitto. Want more," said the Choctaw.

"How do you know English?" questioned Lott surprised with his ability to communicate.

"Jesus, Mary School teach us English," he answered, still pushing the jug toward Jake.

"Jake, I've heard that Catholic missionaries have been workin' here with them Choctaws. I believe it now," said Lott. "Come up on the porch. We'll talk."

Conversation was difficult since the Choctaws could speak only a few English phrases. At one point, Jake went under the house to get a jug, but not before he received a lecture from Lott about how the government would not approve of his trading liquor to the Indians.

Lott and Jake soon realized the Choctaws had been observing them without their knowledge since the first day they had arrived. They knew much about them, even their names. They preferred to call Jake, Homa Chitto, which means Big Red in Choctaw language.

The Indians were fascinated with Jake. They had never seen a red-headed white man, especially one with such size and strength. At the same time, they did not understand why he acted as he did. They had observed how Jake appeared afraid of the forest, but yet, had wandered off into the woods by himself and like a crazy man, leaped into the creek amidst the women. They weren't sure Jake was sane.

As the days and weeks of autumn crept by, the Choctaws visited the Wilsons almost every day. Often in the early morning when Lott opened the front door, they would be sitting quietly on the front porch steps waiting.

It was always Jake the Indians wanted to see and, in turn, Jake was outwardly pleased at the attention he was receiving. He looked forward to their visits and after several weeks, gained enough confidence to go with them into the forest.

Winter finally arrived and Lott was relieved that the house and barn had been completed, but Lott was concerned about the relationship Jake had developed with the Choctaws.

"Jake, you going to help me get some firewood up today or you going to go off with them Choctaws again?" questioned Lott feeling jealous that his brother preferred their company to his. Lott was spending more and more time by himself, and loneliness was beginning to take its toll.

"Sure, I'll help ya. I always do, don't I?" answered Jake as he pulled up his suspenders and put his heavy coat on. "But I'm s'posed to go with Hatak Minsa [Birth Scar] huntin' rabbits this afternoon. You know Lott, they hunt them damn things with sticks."

"How in the devil do they kill them with a stick?" questioned Lott. "And tell me more about Hatak Minsa and you."

"Well, I just call him Minsa, and he's the man I first met in the woods. I thought he had a scar down the side of his face, but it turned out to be a birthmark. That's how he got his name. I never told ya that story about the woods, did I?"

"No ya didn't, Jake, and I think you haven't told me a lot of things you been doin' lately. I just hope you is not gettin' into some kind of trouble out there. And what about that huntin'?"

"Lott, a bunch of us get together and surround a thicket or briarpatch and then start closin' in makin' all kind of racket, really raisin' some kind of hell, and when them rabbits start runnin', we start throwin' our clubs at them. Damn! if'n it ain't fun. We kill them by the dozens," bragged Jake. "You want to go with us?"

"Might as well, little brother. I'm gettin' tired of stayin' here by myself, and I want to see some of that stick huntin'," answered Lott, chuckling as if he thought Jake was making a joke with him. "You get the saw, Jake. I'm going to get the splittin' ax. I'll meet ya at the barn. We got wood to get up 'fore we go."

After an afternoon with the Choctaws, Lott understood why Jake spent time with them. They were a lot like Jake: free-spirited, humorous, and excellent hunters. Well, Jake was not really that good of a hunter, not yet anyway.

The sun was going down when the hunting party finally decided to give up. Minsa handed Lott two big cane cutter rabbits which Lott eagerly accepted since he and Jake had not been able to make a kill with their borrowed sticks.

"Onakma owata kiliachin, Homa Chitto? [We hunt tomorrow, Big Red?]" asked Minsa. "You too, Lott."

"We probably will," answered Lott. "We'll see ya later."

It was dusk as the Wilsons found their way home through the forest trails barely able to identify landmarks in the darkness.

"Jake, what about that Choctaw woman you were talkin' about the other day? You ever see her?"

"Yep, I sure do and she's some kind of a looker. You know what, Lott? She's Minsa's sister."

"Then ya better behave yoreself around her or you might get some of them holes shot in ya like you always talkin' about," laughed Lott.

The two men finally got the rabbits cleaned and settled themselves in front of their fireplace to reflect on the day's activities.

"You know, Jake, we better enjoy this quiet livin'. It's going to change you know, and it won't be long," remarked Lott.

"What ya mean by that?" answered Jake as he got up to put another log on the fire.

"Come the first of the year, settlers will be in here by the droves to take this land," explained Lott. "And Jake, most of them Choctaws will be leavin' for land across the Mis'sippi. You going to like that?"

"Hell no! I ain't going to like it," replied Jake angrily. "These is good people. They don't harm nobody, and they mind their own bus'ness. When the white people come in here, all they going to do is cause trouble and rape mother nature of these woods and animals. I might just go with the Indians."

"Jake, when you talk about white folks, you know ya talkin' about yore own kind, don't ya?"

"I guess so, Lott, but I don't feel like white folk. Them Choctaws taught me a new feelin'."

"I feel the same way, Jake. I don't look forward to what the new year's going to bring," said Lott. "I'm ready to turn in. How about you?"

"See ya in the morning," answered Jake.

Several days later, Jake saddled up his big buckskin and left at daybreak, not telling Lott where he was going nor when to expect him back. Since Lott didn't worry about him as much as he used to, he went about splitting white oak shingles for the barn knowing Jake would probably be back before sundown.

About mid-morning, Lott stopped his work and looked up when the sound of a galloping horse caught his attention. In a few seconds, the horse bounded from a clearing in the woods two hundred yards south of his work site, and Lott could clearly distinguish Jake's red hair and massive body astride his big buckskin. Looking closer, he detected a rider sitting behind him holding on for dear life. In a matter of seconds, Jake brought his horse to such an abrupt stop that it threw dirt and grass all over Lott.

"Dadburn it, Jake, I thought you was going to let that horse run over me. You gone crazy?" exclaimed Lott as he brushed the debris from his clothing and shook the dirt out of his hair.

"Damn it, brother. Can't ya be a little more sociable?" laughed Jake. "I've got somebody I want ya to meet."

Lott, looking up, saw the most beautiful woman he had ever seen. She had black shiny hair that flowed below her waist and dark brown eyes that returned his stare and curiosity. She wore a buckskin dress that had worked itself up to where all her legs plus a hint of buttocks were exposed. Her legs were long and muscular, almost as long as Jake's. She wore buckskin moccasins characteristic of the Choctaws. Lott could also see she had an ample upper body. Lott stood speechless.

"Lott, you can shut yore mouth now. I told ya she was a looker, didn't I?" bragged Jake sitting tall in the saddle and reaching back to pull the young woman closer to him.

"This here is Ohoyo Hatta, which means Pale Woman. You can call her Hatta. She's the one I've been talkin' about."

"Chi pinsa li ka achukma [Good to meet you], Lott. Homa Chitta speak good of you," said Hatta offering her hand.

Lott reached to return the greeting and muttered, "Nice to meet you too."

"Well, help her down, big brother. We plan to visit a spell."

Lott grasped Hatta around the waist and slowly helped her off the big stallion. Lott momentarily held her close, feeling the warmth of her body and admiring the beauty of her face which was only inches from his. His heart began to beat rapidly and he felt that the blood veins in his neck and face were going to burst. Lott realized this woman had excited him in a way he had never felt. He was inwardly embarrassed at what he was feeling and the thoughts entering his mind.

"Jake! This is some kind of woman you're runnin' around with. Where did ya meet her?" questioned Lott, letting go of Hatta and easing her toward Jake.

"She was one of them women that was bathin' in the rock hole when I jumped in."

"I don't know nothin' about that, Jake. That's one you've kept to yourself."

The three spent the rest of the morning and most of the early afternoon talking. Lott learned that Hatta was the daughter of a Choctaw woman and a white missionary. Her father had come into the Choctaw lands to convert the Indians to Catholicism and teach them something about the French and English languages. Even though Hatta spoke mostly Choctaw, she still was fairly fluent in English. Lott quickly realized that not only was she beautiful, but intelligent as well.

Hatta told Lott about how her father had died, and later her mother took another man for her husband. This time, it was a Choctaw and the father of Minsa. She was his older sister.

During the weeks to follow, Jake spent more and more time with Hatta. He would often stay overnight with the Choctaws who were still camped south of the Wilson property.

In early January of 1834, Jake had been gone for almost a week, and Lott began to worry once again that something had happened to him. He decided to ride down to the village called Bissa Aisha [Blackberry Place], but found it almost deserted, and the Choctaws who were left could not speak enough English for him to find out about Jake. A feeling of despair crept over Lott as he realized that Jake might have gone with the Choctaws to Oklahoma.

The short ride home seemed like an eternity as he recalled all he and Jake had been through and how he truly missed and loved his brother.

"I'll just have to learn to live without him, because I can't live his life for him," thought Lott, riding his horse up the creek and finally mounting the bank on the opposite side that led to the trail that would carry him home.

Lott was still in bed the next morning when he heard shouting and singing. "What in the world is goin' on?" thought Lott as he quickly rose and ran onto the front porch.

Coming down the path was Jake and some of his Choctaw friends. As they approached, Lott saw that Jake was covered with skins and beads and looked as if he had been in some kind of fight. He had bruises and cuts all over his face, and even his legs had large purple marks where someone or something had hit him. Lott had never seen Jake so beat up and bruised, yet at the same time hilariously happy.

"Istaboli, Lott, istaboli, you ought to been there!" exclaimed Jake. "It was legal warfare. We made all these bets before it started, and when it did start, it was sump'n to behold!"

"What ya talkin' about, Jake? And what's a istaboli?" questioned Lott racing across the yard wearing only his long-john underwear.

After a warm embrace, Jake revealed what had happened. "An istaboli is sort of a ballgame, Lott. There was probably a hund'rd on each side, and we had to use a stick with a pouch on the end of it to throw a small leather ball through these two trees and the field was about a quarter of a mile long," exclaimed Jake, still excited.

"And Lott, everything goes. You can hit each other with them sticks. You can bite and slug the hell out of them. I mean the Choctaws on the other side, that is. And I did! I beat the hell out of droves of them. I was knockin' them out faster than they could tote them off. I knowed I broke two of thems leg. I was the hero, Lott! Our clan won and we got our bets. Look at all this stuff we won. Damn! It was some kind of fun. If'n the good Lord wants me in heaven, he better have some of these kinds of games up there."

That afternoon Jake had finally calmed down and was sitting on the front porch letting Lott clean and dress some of his wounds when Lott began to reveal something that he knew would anger and disturb his brother.

"Jake, we had a visitor today, a Mister Williams."

"So what," answered Jake. "What'd he want?"

"He came here to claim his land and wanted me to show him to the place," continued Lott.

"I hope you kicked him out of here, Big Brother. We don't need that kind 'round here. Hell! We'll run them all out. Everyone that comes in here."

"Jake, we can't do that. They have their legal rights, and they bought their land," said Lott. "And the Williams seem to be good folk. They said lots of settlers would be comin' in here in a few days. You understand what I'm saying?"

Jake picked up the chair where he had been sitting and slung it across the porch. "Damn them folks! They ain't nothin' but a bunch of sons of bitches. I hate 'em all! I wish you hadn't told me," shouted Jake, going into his bedroom and slamming the door.

Lott knew it would be useless to try to reason with his brother right now. He would stay away from him until the next morning.

Lott sadly contemplated the change that would bring their time as the sole white inhabitants in this virgin timberland, living in harmony with nature and these remarkable Native Americans, to an end. Soon he would hear the sound of axes as the forest would be cleared for farming and the smell of smoke as these magnificent timbers would be stacked and burned. He also knew he would hear the sounds of gunshots causing the large herds of deer and flocks of turkeys to vanish from the hills and hollows that had for centuries protected and nourished them.

Lott prayed, "What will become of these wonderful, peaceful people who have been such diligent keepers of this land. I can't imagine a future for them here. We going to need yore help Lord."

5

SETTLEMENT BEGINS

As McCORKLE PREDICTED, OWNERS BEGAN TO ARRIVE DAILY to claim their property. By mid-May, 1834, the Wilsons could not find enough time to tend their own farm because so many families needed directions. Often Lott would go with one family while Jake would direct another. With each passing day, Jake became more irritated because he knew the serene life with his Choctaw friends would soon end, never to return.

And again, as Mister Mac had also predicted, conflict and violence over land lines occurred with such regularity that Lott and Jake had to re-survey and settle many disputes. In some cases, they had to refer these problems to Judge Henry who was in charge of keeping law and order in the newly-formed Newton County. Judge Henry's office was in a crude log cabin in the small but growing settlement of Union. The town lay approximately six and one half miles west of the Wilsons, and it took time to travel back and forth to settle the arguments. When Newton County was created from the southern part of Neshoba County, the county seat was then moved to Decatur, a small village nine miles south of Union.

An unexpected problem between the Choctaws and settlers developed because some Choctaws chose to stay on their native land. Still unaccustomed to being restricted, the Choctaws felt they could roam at will in pursuit of wild game. They also resented the way settlers were slaughtering the deer and turkey. Two settlers boasted that from the latter part of January to the first of July, they had killed almost a hundred deer and planned to continue their hunting. The black bear, that Choctaws hunted with great pride, were now only tales to tell when settled around the campfires at night. They were gone forever.

Some settlers felt the Indians did not deserve the same rights as themselves. They felt they could take wild game at will from the Choctaws' land and often ran the Indians off their own property.

Lott and Jake could see a serious conflict developing, and knowing how the federal government in Washington felt about Indian rights, they realized the Indians could not expect the justice they deserved. President Jackson had already made it clear that this country was meant for the white man and when the Indians got in the way of progress, the Indians were to be removed, one way or another.

Minsa and several other Choctaws had decided to remain on the land where their village was established. It was relatively flat and extremely fertile since it lay next to the Little Rock Creek. An area that had been cleared years before by Minsa's clan to host the famous stickball games would be perfect for cultivation, if the Indians chose to work the land; but Minsa could not think of breaking the ground where so many fierce games had been played. This land was part of the property Frank Olliver had asked McCorkle to purchase for him earlier.

Minsa's sister, Hatta, chose to stay with him and with the man she had grown to love.

On one particular day, the summer sun seemed hotter than usual so Lott and Jake settled themselves under the shade of one of the large oaks on the edge of their freshly plowed field to rest a while and regain their strength.

"Lott, this heat is about to get the best of me, and we still have a long way to go 'fore dark," remarked Jake as he lay back on the ground.

"I know how you feel, Jake, but sundown'll come and we'll be proud of this field."

Lott stood up when movement at the edge of the woods on the other end of the field caught his attention. It was Minsa and Hatta.

"Jake, get up. We got company comin'. Wonder what they want this time of day?" questioned Lott, nudging Jake.

Jake quickly rose and walked through the loosely plowed soil to meet them.

"Lott, sump'n ain't right. They never visit this time of day."

"Jake, bring them up here under the shade. You hear me," hollered Lott.

"I hear ya," replied Jake over his shoulder as he walked even faster to reach their friends.

Lott could tell something was wrong by the way Minsa and Hatta were talking with Jake.

"What's goin' on Minsa?" questioned Lott as they approached.

"Got trouble with white man and black man too," answered Minsa. "They cut my trees and break my ground."

"Wait a minute, Minsa. You tellin' me someone is on yore land," interrupted Jake, getting angrier by the minute. "We'll just run those sons of bitches off right now."

"Jake, let him finish," said Lott. "Minsa, are you sure they is on yore land?" questioned Lott, hoping it was just a mistake.

"On my land. Minsa know where Lott and Jake marked trees," answered Minsa. "White man say us get, or he shoot hell out of us."

"I'll tell ya who is going to get the hell shot out of him. That's that bastard down there on yore land," exclaimed Jake.

"Why didn't you go get the rifle I give you and run him off. You had the right," continued Jake.

"Afraid to do. Minsa cousin try to run whiteman off land, and they had big fight. White man was on top of cousin chokin' him. Cousin pull knife and stick him dead," murmured Minsa.

"Judge arrest him and said he murder. Judge hang cousin. Minsa no want to hang. We come to get help from Wilsons."

Lott saw the fear in their eyes and sadly remembered that Minsa had once governed this land and ruled the woodlands and disciplined anyone who did not follow the tribal law. Now Minsa's independence was gone and he had become an outsider in the land he once possessed.

"That's smart to come get us to help ya," replied Lott. "Jake and I'll go get the horses, and we'll put a stop to this. And I did hear about that killin'. I thought the judge made a mistake," said Lott.

"Minsa, you and Hatta come up to the house with us. Lott and me is goin' down there and create a livin' hell for someone," blurted out Jake as he reached for Hatta's hand.

"Minsa, you unharness my mules, leave the plow and gear here, and bring them animals to the barn," said Jake.

"Jake, we going to go down there and see if a mistake has been made, and there ain't going to be no bloodshed. You hear me," shouted Lott still trying to get his mule out of the field and headed in the right direction.

Back at the house, it didn't take Lott and Jake long to put the mules in the barn and get the horses saddled. In a matter of minutes, they galloped out of the barnyard and headed for Minsa's land four miles south.

The brothers couldn't say a word as they raced through the forest weaving their way through the open woodlands. As Jake's big golden buckskin stallion approached a thicket near a stand of virgin pines, he flushed a covy of quail which caused the stallion to stop suddenly sending Jake sailing and headlong into a thicket. To Lott's surprise, Jake didn't say a single curse word. He just remounted his horse and pushed the animal harder than ever to catch up.

As they approached Minsa's land, they could hear a crosscut saw and smell smoke. They knew from the markings that this was Minsa's land.

They slowed their horses as they approached two men who were dropping a huge beech tree. One was a big black man, almost as large as Jake.

"You men workin' hard," questioned Lott, as he and Jake brought their horses to a stop.

"You might say that, and what is you doin' down here?" replied the white man pushing his hair out of his eyes.

It was Frank Olliver.

Lott quickly dismounted and went over to shake Frank's hand. Recognizing Lott, Frank laid his saw down and hurried to meet his old companion.

"What the hell you boys doin' down here? I heard you was down here somewhere in these woods, and it's about time we had a get together" laughed Frank as he shook Lott's hand and patted him on the back.

"What the hell you doin' here?" said Jake angrily as he remained saddled and made no effort to greet his old friend.

"Get off that ole horse, and let's talk a spell," replied Frank trying to avoid the question.

"You boys has changed some since I last seen ya. Just look at them beards, and Jake you seem to have lost some weight too. Lott, you's gettin' a lot of gray hair mighty early, ain't ya?" chuckled Frank.

Jake reluctantly dismounted and walked slowly over to greet him. Jake and Lott had mixed emotions about Frank. They still considered Frank a friend, but he was up to no good and they had to stop him. Their anger gradually changed to suspicion.

After about an hour of sharing the past year's experience, Lott finally asked Frank the question both parties had been avoiding. "Frank, do you know that this land you's workin' ain't yores?" stated Lott. "You's workin' another man's land."

Frank squirmed nervously. "Lott, I want you to meet the first niggar in these parts. This here is Toby. My paw-in-law in Louisanna let me borrow him to help me get this place started."

Toby raised his hand to acknowledge his introduction but remained seated at the base of a large beech tree studying this unusual pair that had ridden in on them so suddenly.

"Is he a slave, Frank?" questioned Jake.

"Well, he ain't my slave, Jake. He's my paw-in-law's slave. When I get through with him, I'll send him on back to the bayou country."

"Frank, we don't like slavery, and I hope there ain't no slaves kept in this county. It ain't right," stated Lott.

"Lott, let me tell ya sump'n. Slavery's legal, and these niggars are property just like yore mules, plus we treat them a helluvah lot better than you treat them animals of yores," said Frank, becoming angry at the way Lott and Jake were questioning him.

"And yes, I know this here is a Choctaw's land I'm workin', but they ain't any better than that niggar sittin' over there under that tree. Them Choctaws don't know how to work this land."

Jake had all he could stand and before Frank could make another statement, Jake jumped up and grabbed him by the shirt and lifted him off the ground until his feet were barely touching ground.

"Let me tell you sump'n, Frank Olliver! This Choctaw you's talkin' about is a friend of mine, and he is a helluvah lot better person than you is ever going to be," shouted Jake, shaking him with each word.

Frank fearing for his life called out, "Toby! get this fool off me. Get the ax, Niggar! He's going to kill me."

Toby reached for the ax but Lott intervened.

"Wait a minute men! This here's gone too far. Jake, let him down and just cool off some," said Lott, getting hold of Jake and pulling Frank away from him. "And Toby, you don't want none of Jake. He'll hurt ya."

"Yessuh, I didn't want none of him, but I has to mind Mas' Olliver," replied Toby, laying the ax down.

"Frank, the only problem we has, is you is farmin' a friend of ours land. It ain't right; Judge Henry won't go for it, and we need to stay friends, if'n we can," stated Lott trying to restore order.

48

Frank straightened his clothes and stammered some apologies.

"Maybe I did make a mistake to take this land, Lott, but I didn't think the Choctaw would mind me using a few acres, and hell, Jake, I didn't know he was a friend of yores," replied Frank. "We got to live together."

Lott and Jake nodded, straightened their clothes and mounted their horses for home. They doubted Frank's sincerity and knew that their problems with Frank Olliver were just beginning. Mister Mac always said Frank couldn't be trusted.

As they rode, little passed between them, but as they approached the house, Lott cautioned Jake about what had been forming in his mind.

"Jake, I got sump'n bothering me, and it's got to come out," said Lott reining his horse to a stop.

"What's up brother?" replied Jake, pulling his horse up next to Lott's.

"Jake, you embarrased Frank in front of that big black. What's his name? Toby, that's it, and Jake, Frank ain't going to forget it. He's going to get you someday, somehow. You better watch yore back."

"I ain't worried about that bastard. It'll take more than him to bring me down," replied Jake.

Minsa and Hatta were sitting on the front step, waiting.

"Good to see you, Wilsons. You kill white man?" questioned Minsa, stepping forward to stop the horses.

"Naw, we didn't kill nobody, but I sure felt like it," said Jake, dismounting.

"That man ain't going to pester you no more. If'n he do, you just tell me and I'll get him," said Jake as he walked over to embrace Hatta.

"Minsa, you is going to be fine. Let's go to the kitchen and see if'n we can round up some vittles," said Lott pointing toward the back of the house.

Later that night, Minsa and Hatta left and Lott and Jake were alone on the front porch. Lott packed his pipe full and lit it. Tobacco was a new habit for him.

"Jake, can I ask you sump'n personal, and will you not get mad at me?" said Lott, feeling uncomfortable about what was bothering him.

"You sure can, brother. That's what brothers do," replied Jake, not paying a lot of attention.

"Jake, ain't Hatta gained a little weight? You know, in the middle?"

"What you gettin' at?" answered Jake, trying to avoid looking at his inquisitive brother.

"Jake, now don't get mad at me. Is Hatta going to have a baby? And if'n she is, it's all right with me."

"Lott, I love that woman, and she is going to have my baby," replied Jake as he stared hard toward the barnyard.

"I been 'fraid to tell ya 'bout it. I didn't know how you'd take it. I thought you might get mad," continued Jake, pleased that Lott was not scolding him for once.

"Jake, this is how I feel. Hatta is carryin' my future niece or nephew, and I think the child should carry the Wilson name. My brotherly advice to you is to go down there tomorrow, ask Minsa if'n you can take her for yore wife, and bring her to our place. You two can have the other side of the house. And, the first time a preacher comes to this here country, he can marry you two and make it legal," said Lott, with finality.

"Lott, what's people going to say 'bout us havin' a Choctaw in our house?" asked Jake.

"Jake, I don't give a hooter's damn what they say 'bout that. We were the first to settle this country, and we'll set the rules," answered Lott, leaning back in his chair and blowing a large circle of smoke into the air.

Jake eased up out of his seat and motioned Lott to stand up.

Lott was apprehensive about Jake's intentions since he had been meddling, but he stood anyway. Lott hadn't had a fight with Jake since they were teenagers, and he sure didn't want to test his strength against a brother that could tear a man apart and not break a sweat doing it.

"Lott, you mind givin' this ole brother of yores a hug. You know to be such an ass sometimes, you really is sump'n," said Jake.

"I love ya and I'm going to go get her tomorrow," concluded Jake.

"I love you, too, you big ox. That is, most of the time," laughed Lott, relieved that Jake had not taken offense.

The following morning, Jake was gone by good daylight and before noon had returned with Hatta and her few belongings.

In the weeks that followed, Hatta brought many changes to the Wilson's household. She kept the house spotless, cooked better than either brother and with her pleasant demeanor, kept Lott and Jake from their habitual arguing.

Four months later, in November of 1834, Hatta gave birth to a healthy and beautiful boy. Since the Choctaws had named Jake, Homa Chitto. Hatta and Jake decided to use the name Homa, but to change it to Homer, the English name. Homer had brown skin and dark eyes like his mother, but his hair was a light shade of red, almost golden like his father's.

Never had a man been more proud of his son. Jake continually spoke of future plans for Homer and Hatta and how he wanted to set good examples for the boy. Jake even tried to control his temper and tongue.

I

Lott always got up early and read a few chapters in the Bible before starting the day's work. One morning he had an unexpected guest.

"Lott, you mind if Homer and Hatta listen to you? When I was small, my father read stories to me in God Jesus Book," said Hatta. "I want to know more."

"Come on out here. I can use the company," replied Lott. "You ever hear 'bout King David and the giant?"

"Tell me," urged Hatta.

After Lott finished the story, she looked puzzled.

"Lott, why missionaries no come here with settlers? White men all know God? God not important?"

"Hatta, God is important but not all white men believe as this book teaches.

And they'll come, the preachers that is, and when they do, this country is going to get back on the right track. You and Jake is going to get married up right when the first one comes by."

From then on, Lott, Hatta and Homer began their day reading and talking about the stories in the Bible. When the weather permitted, they met on the front porch, but when it was cold, they would sit around the fireplace in the kitchen.

Jake, always a slow riser, finally decided to join the group. Before long, he was taking an active part in the devotions and enjoyed impressing Hatta with his ability to read and discuss the scripture.

As Mister Mac had predicted, the first few years of settlement had brought a lot of violence and turmoil to the hillcountry. Meanwhile, there was not enough law enforcement to settle the continuing disputes. Judge Henry had moved from Union to the new county seat located near the center of Newton County, and he had only one sheriff and one deputy for the entire county.

There were violent fights among neighbors, heavy drinking and gambling. Men would meet every Sunday for horse racing, dog fighting and anything else they could dream up for entertainment. Often these meetings would end in brawls when losers were forced to pay their gambling debts.

Judge Henry always advised his sheriff, "Go out and see who started the trouble and if it was a fair fight. If one of them got killed and you think it's fair, to hell with them. Don't bring no one to me to judge on."

Lott and Jake stayed clear of trouble. They worked hard and minded their own business. Jake still didn't much care for farming, but he had two special interests. First, to Lott's objection, he earned the reputation of making some of the best homebrew and corn whiskey in the county. People would come from miles around and most homes kept it as a normal household commodity. And second, as much pride as he took in his whisky making, his real first love was horses.

He had never even been on a horse until he began surveying with Mister Mac, but since then he was obsessed with how fast a horse could run carrying a man on its back. He searched and traded for the best horses in the state, and once a purchase was made, Jake bred for speed only. Eventually Jake made large sums of money buying and selling horses and he seldom lost a bet at the tracks.

One day Jake heard about a new breed called a quarterhorse, a mix between a thoroughbred and the type of horses the Spaniards had brought into Mexico centuries earlier. A man in Natchez was raising them, and the more Jake heard about how quick the horse was, the more he wanted such an animal. It took all the money he had put away from his liquor and racing, but he traveled to Natchez and returned with the first quarterhorse the Newton countians had ever seen. His goal was not only to raise a fast horse, but also one that could carry his own massive weight.

▌

A sudden downpour of rain was followed by a refreshing cool northern breeze, which swirled the leaves in the tops of the trees sending them fluttering toward the ground. This signalled an end to the extremely hot and dry summer of 1836. Fall was in the air.

On one of these cool days, Hatta was hanging out some clothes she had just finished washing when the sounds of a wagon rattling and creaking up the rough path leading to the house caught her attention. The noise startled Red and Sourdough, Lott's prize hounds, who were curled up under the front porch. They bolted out and raced toward the approaching wagon barking and yelping loud enough to warn the entire community.

Hatta quickly walked to the front of the house to get a closer look. As the wagon reached the house, Hatta nervously called out, "This is the Wilson place. What you want here?"

"I assume you might be Mrs. Wilson," responded the man who was driving as he politely tipped his hat. "I'm Samuel Thompson and this here is my wife, Sarah, and that young lady on the end is my daughter, Sarah Alice. We've come to talk to Mister Lott Wilson."

"My name is Hatta, not Mrs. Wilson. Lott and Jake has gone to check on horses near the creek. They be back soon. Get down and come to porch."

Shortly Lott and Jake rode up with their splendid horses in tow. They were surprised to see guests but assumed they were settlers wishing to locate their property.

Walking up to the steps, Lott introduced himself and Jake and then sent Jake into the house to get some chairs. Lott was introduced to Sarah Alice last and he noticed that she was only a few years younger than he was.

"Mister Wilson, this here is Sarah Alice, our one and only daughter. She's a petite thing, but she's some kind of musician. She can play anything she gets her hands on," said Mister Thompson.

Lott took his hat off and bowed slightly as he reached to shake her hand. She was pretty and only stood about five feet tall with long curly blond hair and deep blue eyes, much the same color as his.

They stood awkwardly holding each other's hand not knowing how to continue the introduction.

Sarah thought, "This is the most handsome man I have ever met in my life and with such good manners. I hope he isn't with that Indian lady. I'll just die if he is."

Lott was embarrased and finally found words to get himself out of his predicament.

"I'm Lott Wilson, and Jake and me was the first white settlers in this country. You all please have a seat," said Lott directing Sarah to a chair.

"I heard about you 'fore we came over today, and I'm also proud to meet ya," answered Sarah, taking her seat next to Lott.

"Mister Wilson, I'm going to get right to the point of our callin'. I'm a Methodist preacher who is workin' for the Lord in this county, and I want to hold a preachin' on yore place and invite all the folks 'round here to come," stated Thompson.

52

"A preacherman!" exclaimed Jake. "Hell, we's been waitin' for you for two years."

Realizing his tongue had gotten away from him, he apologized, "Pardon me, preacher, the devil gets a hold of me sometimes."

"The Lord will forgive ya, Jake," laughed Mister Thompson. "I get excited myself sometimes."

"Amen," replied Mrs. Thompson.

"Mister Thompson. Do you marry people?" asked Hatta reaching for Jake's hand and nudging him.

"I sure do and I bury them too," he chuckled. "Who wants to get married?"

Sarah Alice prayed, "Dear Lord, please let it be Jake, not Lott, please not Lott."

Jake placed his arm around Hatta and pulled her close to his side.

"It's us, Preacher. We been together for over two years, and ain't been nobody come by to marry us. I want to marry this woman," Jake shyly replied.

"Mister Thompson, we have son too. We want preacher to bless family," said Hatta.

Sarah was elated as she pulled on her father's coat to encourage a positive respose, "Sure he'll marry you two. He does it every day."

"Sarah Alice, that decision will be mine. I don't need yore help young lady," replied Mister Thompson, somewhat peaved at her brashness.

"But yes, I'll marry you two when you get ready, but you'll have to go to the county seat in Decatur and register it. I'll take care of God's part, and you two take care of the gov'ment regulations."

A week later, the community's first revival was held, and sermons were delivered from the front porch of the Wilsons' home. An unexpected crowd turned out each evening and went away filled with the spirit, and a few of them went away filled with some of Jake's special spirit corn whiskey.

Reverend Thompson brought a pump organ to the meeting, and everyone was impressed at how Sarah Alice could play any song that was requested. On the first night when Sarah began the introduction to a hymn, Red and Sourdough began to howl so loudly the whole congregation broke out in laughter. The highlight of the final night of the revival that ran for seven evenings, was the plantive voice of Hatta as she sang "Amazing Grace"in her native Choctaw language. This time, even the dogs felt a special reverance and stayed quiet.

Even though some of the settlers frowned on Jake for living with Hatta, they had learned to respect the Wilsons and also accepted Hatta because there wasn't a kinder or harder working woman in the community.

During the revival, the Thompsons stayed in the Wilsons' home. This gave Lott and Sarah a chance to spend time together. Each day they would walk the fields and meadows together, take horseback rides into the open woods and at night sit for hours on the front porch until Reverend Thompson called Sarah to bed.

Lott had always been fascinated with Hatta's beauty and personalty, but in Sarah, he discovered in himself a deep love and affection. In Sarah's eyes and touch, he knew she cared for him. On Christmas eve of 1836, four months after their meeting, Lott and Sarah were married.

They lived on one side of the house and Jake and his family lived across the hall. Homer enjoyed the best of both families. He would often cross the hall and spend the night with Lott and Sarah and at times wander from bedroom to bedroom making this a night time game.

"Jake, can you hear me?" questioned Lott one night from deep up under the covers.

"Sure can brother. What ya want?" muttered Jake from across the open hall.

"You want some nephews or nieces someday?"

"I could stand a few, I guess," replied Jake.

"Then you need to keep H-O-M-E-R in yore bed and out of ours."

Jake and Hatta snickered, because they could hear Sarah scolding Lott for discussing their sex life so openly.

I

The cold dreary days soon began to lessen as the spring of 1837 came to the hillcountry bringing a luster of wildflowers, blossoms and a sense of renewed life.

On one of these days the two families rode to Decatur to visit Sarah's parents and to pick up needed farm items before spring plowing. Upon returning home, they were shocked to see Mister McCorkle, their old surveying boss, sitting on their front porch whittling on a stick and whistling some unrecognizable tune.

"Thought you never would get home," said Mister Mac, as the Wilsons pulled up to the porch. "And who all you got with ya? Where'd you find them good lookin' things out here in these sticks?"

Jake leaped out of the wagon even before it had come to a complete stop and sprinted out in front of the horses to greet his old friend.

"Question is, where the hell you come from, you old codger?" replied Jake as he picked up Mister Mac like he was weightless and whirled him around. "Them hounds ought to have eat ya up 'fore you got on the porch."

"Put me down, you overgrown ox! I'm gettin' old and my bones might break. And them so called bad hounds of yores aint nothin' but house cats. I hollered one time and they took off under the house, tails tucked."

After introducing their families, Lott asked, "Mister Mac, did you get to see Mamma? How's she doing?" As they settled in front of a fresh crackling fire, Mister Mac replied, "Boys, I got good and bad news. What ya want first?" He took a big breath and filled his pipe.

"Mister Mac, don't fool with us when we talkin' about Mamma. This here is serious bus'ness," scolded Jake.

"I'm sorry, boys. I forgot it's been so long since you two has seen her."

"Well first, she's doin' fine and is as healthy as ever. That's the good news and the bad news is she's going to marry 'Fessor Johnson."

"Johnson! That son-of-a-bitch had me kicked out of school," shouted Jake, enraged at the thought. "She must have gone crazy or sump'n. Damn, that makes my stomach turn."

Lott, usually calm in such situations, suddenly became angry and grabbed a piece of firewood and hurled it at Jake barely missing him.

"Jake, I'll tell you sump'n. You is the son-of-a-bitch, and Mister Johnson didn't get ya kicked out of school. Yore sorriness done it for ya. He's a fine man, and if he loves Mamma and wants to take care of her, we ought to be proud for both of them. You ought to be ashamed of yoreself."

Jake was shocked at his brother's reaction. This hadn't happened since they were children in Savannah. Jake quickly realized he had over-reacted.

"Lott, you didn't have to throw that stick at me. You could've hurt me," said Jake as he straightened himself and tried to think of what to say to make amends.

In seconds, Sarah, Hatta, and Homer appeared to see what was happening.

"What in tarnation is goin' on in here!" exclaimed Sarah looking the room over to see what caused the racket.

Mister Mac was leaning as far back in his chair as possible to avoid any melee and held his pipe behind his back to protect his treasured smoke.

Lott and Jake were glaring at each other, waiting for the other to make a move.

"That man over there throwed a piece of wood at me," said Jake. "And it almost hit me."

"Lott, you have never done sump'n like that to Jake before. What has come over you?" questioned Sarah.

"I throwed it and I wish it had got him, too," muttered Lott, still angry.

"Jake, what you do to make Lott this mad?" questioned Hatta. "You talk ugly to him?"

"Naw, Mister Mac says Mamma's gettin' married to 'Fessor Johnson, and Lott was takin' up for him," answered Jake who was now feeling embarrased about the fuss he and Lott had made in front of Mister Mac and the family.

"Jake, is he bad man, this Johnson?" continued Hatta. "Does he steal or kill someone?"

"Naw, he don't do none of them things."

"I don't see why you boys ain't happy about yore mamma's marriage. Ever since I known you, you been worried about yore mamma and concerned about what's going to happen to her. If this man is good, you ought to be rejoicin', not this fussin' and poutin'," concluded Sarah who had become angry herself. "And Lott Wilson, you ought to be ashamed for almost hittin' yore brother. You could've hurt him bad."

"And Mister Jake, yore bad words are comin' out again and in front of little Homer. Devil is after you again," scolded Hatta.

"And until you two get things straightened out, there ain't going to be no supper tonight," stated Sarah as she and Hatta took Homer by the hand and led him across the hall to Hatta's bedroom.

Mister Mac, who had remained silent, finally spoke. "I can see you two ain't changed a bit. Always fussin' and makin' fools out of yoreself. You ought to be gettin' tired of that by now. Either you two make peace and get them women back in the kitchen, or I'm takin' this scrawny butt of mine somewhere else for supper, you hear me?" said Mister Mac as he tried to relight his smoke. By the tone of his voice, the boys could tell he was serious.

"Yes Sir," replied Jake quickly.

"We are kind of good at being a pair of jackasses, ain't we, Jake," added Lott.

"Yeah, we is. And you got some kind of kick when you get that temper up," replied Jake, reaching out his hand.

When supper was finished, Lott turned to their guest.

"Mister Mac, I know we has always been the best of friends, but I feel you've come a long way to tell us sump'n besides a social call."

"You always could read my mind. As soon as we finish our table talk, I want to talk to you and Jake in private, if'n that's fine," replied Mister Mac.

"Good as done, Mister Mac," said Jake. "I'm ready to go up front now. Ladies that was some kind of fine meal."

"Sure was. It was some of the best squirrel dumplings I ever put in my mouth," said Mister Mac as he rose from the table and gave the ladies a bow.

"We're glad you liked it, but remember, no fightin' up there when you start that talkin'," said Hatta.

It didn't take the men long to get relaxed around the fireplace, and in the meantime, Jake went out back to bring in some of his corn whiskey.

"Well, I'm going to get right to the problem, and I want you both to listen and don't interrupt me till I'm finished," said Mister Mac. "As you already know, the gov'ment's gave the Choctaws a chance to stay here and live on their own piece of land. Our politicians didn't think many would do it. But, the problem is, the gov'ment wants them all out. They think they ain't going to make a living on the land and they're going to get in the way of civilization. The bottom line is, the Choctaws gotta go. And 'fore you say anything, listen to what the Gov'nor told me. If'n an Indian and a white man has a problem and even if'n the white man is wrong, the Indian is the loser. The gov'ment's going to move them all to the Oklahoma Territory just as sure as the sun's going to rise in the morning."

The brothers sat quietly looking at one another, too shocked to respond.

"Mister Mac, there can't be over fifty or sixty Choctaws left in Newton and Neshoba County, is there?" responded Lott.

"There is about six or seven thousand registered at the state office now," replied Mister Mac.

"Six or seven thousand!" exclaimed Jake. "I ain't seen them around here. Sounds like a bunch of lies to me."

"They is here, Jake. I has never lied to you boys. They's here."

"What's the President's feelin' about this?" asked Lott. "And Jake, you better pass yore jug to me. I don't usually fool with whiskey, but I think, I need a little help right now."

"Lott, you boys been keepin' up with Gen'ral Jackson through the years? I know you has, and you also know what he's done to the Cherokees. They took their case to the highest court in the land, up in Washington and won," stated Mister Mac, blowing a large circle of smoke toward the ceiling.

"Did the Cherokees get to stay on their land? Hell no. President Jackson moved them anyway. That tell you boys anything?" he concluded.

"Sure does, Mister Mac. Them Indians who fought with Ole Hick'ry against the Creeks and Seminoles were fightin' on the wrong side. They should have killed that son-of-a-bitch long time ago. You know, I heard one of them Indians actually saved his life. Can you believe it? They saved that bastard's life," added Jake.

"What can we do to help them Choctaws, Mister Mac?" asked Lott.

"Jake, I don't know what you can do. From what I has experienced, I don't see nothin' you can do. You two better get on yore knees and do a heap of prayin. It's going to take the power of the good Lord to save that bunch."

"Well, Mister Mac, Jake and I is going to try to help them, and that damned Jackson ain't always going to be pres'dent. Them fancy politicians up North ain't seen the fury of the Wilsons when we get our dander up," said Lott nodding at Jake to get his approval.

"You right brother. Preach on. I like the way you is talkin'," added Jake.

No sooner had McCorkle left the following morning, than another visitor rode up to the house. He introduced himself as Thomas Walker, a merchant from the nearby settlement of Meridian, and he had a proposition for Lott and Jake. He wanted to purchase ten acres of land about a mile south of the Wilsons' home so he could build a general merchandise store and construct a water mill on the nearby creek to grind corn and wheat for the growing community.

When Lott and Jake selected their site, they thought a transportation route would be running right in front of their house some day. But they were wrong. The settlers chose an Indian path that had been used for centuries. It ran through the southern section of the Wilsons' property, and it was there Mister Walker proposed to build his store.

Walker explained what his purchase could do for the community. "This store and mill could be the beginning of a town. And with growth, you can expect, someday a church, a school for yore children, and a group of people who can help one another in this here new country. Without yore help, it can't and won't happen, at least not here."

Lott and Jake agreed to sell.

Soon a village grew rapidly from the forest. At first it was called Coon Tail for all the raccoon tails Mister Walker nailed to the side of his store commemorating his many successful hunting trips. Later it was renamed Little Rock.

The Wilson brothers were dedicated in their support of this village but were powerless in saving their Choctaw friends who were seeing a destruction of an environment that had sustained and protected them since the time of their forefathers.

6

COON TAIL

By 1850, DRASTIC CHANGES TRANSFORMED THE FORESTLANDS of Newton county into many thriving communities. Large stands of virgin pine and hardwoods still sheltered most of this land, but where ancient, majestic trees had once stood like sentries guarding their fellow comrades, now open fields of grain, log cabins, and split rail fences were emerging. Where paths made by the Choctaws once weaved themselves through the entanglement of swampbottom reeds and canes and twisted endlessly into the open forest, roads wide enough to allow wagons to pass now crisscrossed the county like a huge spiderweb and where vast herds of deer had once roamed at will, cattle, sheep, hogs and horses now grazed in the same open fields and meadows. The wilderness was gone.

By 1850, Little Rock was growing and prosperous. Thomas Walker's general store and mill were thriving and he also sold lots to others who built a blacksmith shop, a livery stable and a tannery. One structure the entire community deeply valued and appreciated was its United Church. People of several protestant faiths came together to build this first edifice in the eastern section of Newton County. Each group only met once a month on its designated Sunday for its own worship. It was also in this church that people came together to discuss problems and have fellowship with one other. They also took great pride in organizing a school which was held in the building. All children in the community were invited to attend and most took advantage of the offer whenever they could be excused from their farm chores.

Lott and Sarah now had six children, but of the six, two died as infants; one during delivery and another of typhoid fever when only a few months old. Of the remaining four, the first three were boys and their last a girl.

Their eldest son, James Earl born in 1839, was a sickly child who suffered from asthma and could not stand the long and tiring days in the field. But, he could take care of livestock and gained a reputation as the most knowledgeable person in the community. People from all parts of the county would come to talk with him about problems they were having with their cattle and horses.

The second son, Thomas Stanley, was born in 1841. He was strong and energetic and much like his Uncle Jake; he grew into a large boisterous man who never met a stranger but had difficulty controlling his temper. Thomas loved working in the fields with his father and often would keep at it after his father called it quits. At times when they were behind and the moon was full, he would remain in the field with the company of only the night creatures.

The third child, born in 1845, was called John Lewis. He became a versatile young man loved and respected by all in the community. Like Thomas, he was strong enough to stay in the fields and could work along with his father and Thomas on an equal basis. He also liked helping James Earl with the livestock and horses and became fascinated with horse racing. What made him different from his brothers was his intense desire for education. His ambition to become a lawyer and judge drove him to hours of reading late into the night.

Finally in 1847, Sarah bore the girl she had wanted and needed for so long. Mary Lucretia was the prize of the family. Sarah, Lott and the boys all loved and overprotected her. In fact, she was so spoiled she considered herself the most important member of the family and felt her every wish should be fulfilled. But she was quick to learn and, like John, valued her education at the First United Academy.

Jake and Hatta were not so fortunate. Once while Jake was shoeing one of his racehorses, a spirited mare kicked him in the groin, seriously injuring him. It took months to recover, and the injury put an end to their additional family expectations.

Jake had wanted a house full of children, so he gave Homer his full attention and love often to the point of neglecting his wife.

I

It was now 1850, and fall was in the air. The Wilsons were almost done with their harvesting of cotton, corn and wheat. Work was beginning to slow down so the families could spend more leisure time together and the men had time to venture into the woods to hunt squirrels, rabbits and raccoons.

One of the family treats was a Saturday afternoon ride visiting neighbors. This gave the children a chance to play with each other, a chance they seldom saw during the summer and early fall months due to their farm work. The excursion always ended at Walker's store where the family would purchase supplies for the next week, see if any mail had arrived and watch the arrival of the four o'clock stage from Meridian.

It was just such an afternoon as this, when the family pulled up to the front of Walker's store. Before the wagon had come to a complete stop, the children bounded out of the back and scrambled up the steps to see who could be first to ask about the mail.

"Lott, Hatta and me is going to step up the road a piece to visit Mrs. Walker and Rebecca. You come get us when you want to go home. Okay?" said Sarah as she began walking toward the Walker house.

"That's fine. Me and Jake got a few things to do and we're going to sit the stage out," answered Lott. "Jake, you need any help with them jugs?"

"Naw, there ain't but about twenty of 'em," replied Jake who was already making his way up the steps with two jugs in each hand and one under each arm.

"Walker, you in there? Get yore back door open, and let me store some of this precious water 'fore I decide to drink it," laughed Jake.

"Yeah, come on in. I been waitin' for ya," said Mister Walker holding the door open and giving him a low bow as Jake struggled to work his way through the narrow opening. "Jake, you know folks ain't hittin' the jug as heavy as they used to. I think religion's gettin' to them. Preacher Jones laid a sermon on us last Sunday 'bout the evils of liquor, and he even made me feel guilty," stated Walker.

"Hell, Walker, you can't believe everything a preacher says. We had one in Savannah that could drink you and me under the table," replied Jake as he headed out toward the wagon to get another load.

He stopped at the door, paused as if in deep thought, and turned to share his revelation. "You let a preacher show me in the Bible where it says you can't drink liquor. He can't. It says you just don't overdo it, don't drink in excess. That's in Matthew 20:14. Walker, them preachers going to ruin this community."

"Jake! Get out here. I want to show you sump'n," said Lott who had been sitting on a bench on the front porch of the store, but was now standing and staring down the street toward the blacksmith's shop.

"What's got you in a stir, Big Brother? I ain't seen you this heated since you chunked that piece of wood at me."

"Jake, you see that wagon down there. It had a bunch of Negroes in it, and one looked like that Toby from back then."

"So what. I don't see nothin' and so what if'n it is?" answered Jake disappointed that Lott's excitment was only about a wagon load of Negroes.

"Jake, there ain't s'pose to be no slaves 'round here and Toby ought to be in Louisiana. I'm goin' down there and see what's goin' on."

"Damn Lott, you know you just a busybody. You know there's some slaves here'bouts, and I heard ole Frank was bringin' them in to work his fields. You ain't going to stop slavery here," said Jake trying to catch up with his brother.

Reaching the wagon, Lott could see five Negroes inside preparing to load a box of plow heads and Toby was among them.

"Toby, that you ain't it?" questioned Lott, pushing the door open so he could get a better look. "What ya still doin' here in Coon Tail?"

"Yessuh, it's me and I lives here now. Master Ollivah done brought me back. It's been a long time since I see'd you Wilsons. You need sump'n?"

"Naw, we don't need nothin'. We just meddlin', that's all," replied Jake, bored with Lott's questioning.

"Toby, how many slaves Frank got down here?" continued Lott.

"I don't rightly know, Mist' Wilson. Maybe, twenty or so. I don't knows 'bout no countin'," said Toby, uneasy about answering Lott's questions.

"Twenty!" exclaimed Lott. "I knowed he was a no good scoundrel. I had a feelin' he was going to do sump'n like this."

Suddenly a large, heavyset man appeared from the back of the shop carrying a whip in one hand and a keg of powder under his arm. Jake recoiled, recognizing the type of person approaching them. He had seen them in Savannah. This man was a slave overseer.

"You niggers get that wagon loaded 'fore I takes the hide off yore back," stated the man, ignoring the Wilsons. "We gotta get this gear back 'fore dark."

The man stepped up on the wagon wheel, settled himself on the seat and then stared directly at Lott. "I heard what you said 'bout Mister Olliver, and I think it best you keep out of his affairs. These here niggers is slaves and it ain't a damned thing you can do about it. I also know who you is and know yore reputation. I guess you is Lott and the big ugly one over there is Jake. Just remember the name Jason Talbert and if'n you is smart, you'll stay out of my path and leave my niggers alone.

"Man, I've had all yore mouth I can take. You need to be taught some manners," said Jake as he rushed over to the wagon.

Quickly, Talbert pulled a revolver from his coat and pointed it directly at Jake's forehead.

"Lott Wilson, you get this idiot out of my way or I'll blow his brains out in the streets," warned Talbert.

Lott hurried over to Jake and pulled him back toward the livery stable.

"Jake, let's just drop it. It ain't worth you gettin' shot over. I'm the one who started the whole thing."

The wagon pulled away from the stables and headed south for the Olliver farm.

"Talbert!" shouted Jake, "this ain't over. One day I'm going to show you how I dealt with yore sorts in Savannah."

"I hear ya," answered Talbert, the wagon now approaching Walker's Store. "You just keep fightin' with the boys, you ain't ready for a man yet."

The children came running from the store to see what was causing the commotion. Homer was the first to reach the street and almost ran in front of Talbert's wagon.

He jerked the reigns quickly to the right to pull out of Homer's path. He was surprised at what he saw. At sixteen, Homer was tall and handsome but did not resemble the other children of Scotch-Irish descent. His hair was golden but he had large brown eyes and reddish-brown skin. A most unusual boy.

"Boy! Or ever what you is. Keep the hell out of my horses' way. Next time, I'll just run over ya," shouted Talbert as he brought the horses under control and quickly made his way out of town.

"What'd that man say to ya, Son?" questioned Jake as he put his arms around him.

For several moments, Homer could say nothing but finally mumbled, "I'm alright, Papa. He just scairt me a little. I'll be fine. I don't like that man. He's got too much hate in his eyes."

"Lott, let's get the chill'un and women and go on home. I don't feel like waitin' for the stage," said Jake.

"This has ruined my afternoon, too," answered Lott who had slumped on the store steps to calm himself.

John ran up to the Walker's house to get Sarah and Hatta and told Rebecca and the others what had happened.

The women hurried down to the wagon where they found Lott, Jake, and the children quietly waiting.

About half way home, the children asked if they could get off and take the shortcut through the woods. Away they ran, jumping and screaming like youngsters who have been kept in the house too long.

The wagon slowly moved up the road with neither man saying a word. Finally, Sarah broke the silence.

"Boys, what did you two get into down there?" asked Sarah, nudging up to Lott the way she would when something was wrong.

Lott pulled the wagon to a sudden stop and turned to Jake. "I acted a fool down there, didn't I? I was meddlin' in someone else's bus'ness, and I could have got you killed. I pray you'll forgive me, and I ain't going to meddle no more."

"Lott, you hate slavery, and you got yore own feelings about it. I don't care much for it neither, but for that Talbert, he's got a lesson in manners comin' some day, and I'll be delivering the sermon to him. And for the apology, I owe you a thousand that I ain't yet extended."

As the wagon crept slowly toward the house, Lott told what had happened in town.

"Jake, I want you to stay out of Talbert's way. That man sounds like he's nothing but trouble. I don't like for you to fight and hurt people, and I don't want nothin' to hurt you either," said Hatta.

The women got off at the front steps and the brothers continued to the barn to unhitch the wagon.

"Jake, I heard that Bible verse that you was tellin' Mister Walker 'bout. You know, about drinkin'. You sure it's in that verse in Matthew?" questioned Lott, impressed that Jake knew the scripture.

"Hell naw, I just made it up. I thought it sounded kind of good. Didn't you?" laughed Jake.

"Jake, the Lord's still got a lot of work to do on you 'fore he can take you home. I just hope he gives ya the time it's going to take," replied Lott, grabbing his brother playfully around the neck in an attempt to wrestle him to the ground.

"Well, it may take a while, but he sure got a helluvah job to do on that Talbert, and I might not give the Master enough time to reform that bastard, 'specially if'n he messes with my Homer again."

The next morning was Sunday, so the Wilsons were in no hurry to get up. The adults usually had coffee on the porch before the men and boys fed the livestock.

Lott, the last to arise, noticed Jake and Minsa down at the corral lazily looking over their prize horses.

Through the years, Minsa had adopted some of the white man's ways. He still wore his hair long and often braided it back to keep it out of his face. But, with the shortage of deer and other wild animals, he now wore shirts and trou-

62

sers made from a blend of cotton and wool. He especially liked red calico shirts. Most of the time he was barefooted; otherwise he preferred the leather moccasins worn by his people.

Minsa still lived with his wife and mother-in-law on the section of land he had chosen years before, but he had not tried to cultivate it. Instead, he worked for the Wilsons, taking care of their hogs and cattle which roamed the woodlands, and he took a special interest in Jake's horses. Jake's size still made it difficult for a horse to support his weight while racing, so Minsa who was much lighter and also an outstanding athlete became his substitute. Minsa had been taught the skills that could make him a champion. It was a wise move, because Minsa was excellent with horses and seldom lost a race.

Jake also encouraged Homer and let him race along with Minsa. Having two horsemen in a race doubled their chance of a victory.

Meanwhile, Lott had taken his coffee down to the corral to see what Jake and Minsa were discussing.

"Men, you up mighty early on this Sunday morning. You must be plannin' some kind of campaign or sump'n," stated Lott, making small talk and not expecting much in return.

"Well, Big Brother, we just lookin' at these horses, and we think they's just too short to keep up the winnin'. Sooner or later someone's going to bring in some of them longlegged thoroughbred horses from up north and when they do, our winnin' days is over."

"They look good to me, and you boys has been bringin' in the money on them races. What more do you want?" replied Lott.

"Look at them close. The best we got stands at fifteen hands tall, and Josh Clearman brought in one from up north a while back that stood over sixteen hands. He almost beat us," said Jake leaning over the top rail of the fence to study the horses more carefully. "He could've beat us if'n he knowed how to ride."

"So, what are you tellin' me, Jake?"

"We tellin' you we got to get bigger horse if'n we is to keep on winning," interrupted Minsa.

"Jake, me and Minsa has been thinkin'. If'n we had one of them thoroughbred horses to breed with the strong, quick horses we got now, we can keep on a winnin' races. So what we got in mind is as soon as we get the cotton and corn out of the fields and get the fall hog killin' done where we got the meat in the smokehouse, we goin' north," said Jake. "Me and Minsa got enough money saved to buy one of them animals and if'n we don't, we'll sell the horses me, Minsa, and Homer will ride up there on to take care of the rest," explained Jake.

"Jake, how do you know where to go and who to see?" asked Lott, knowing his brother was serious.

"We met a Mister Sam Jacobson from Tennessee a while back when we was over in Union at a dogfight. He had heard of our horses and we kind of got to talkin' horse bus'ness. He said if'n we ever got up that way, he'd show us some of the finest horse flesh we has ever seen, and he even had some contacts up in Kentucky," continued Jake.

"Well, you two is grown men and if'n that's what you want to do, it's fine with me. Just be sure to be home by spring plowin' or we could have problems," replied Lott. "And you sure better take care of Homer. He ain't never been that far from home."

"Forgot something," interrupted Minsa. "I pick up letter several days ago at Walker's store for you."

He took a folded and crumpled letter from his pocket and handed it to Lott.

"Jake, this here's Mamma's writin. Wonder how she's a doin. Wonder if'n sump'ns wrong."

He quickly opened the letter. The more he read, the more excited he became. What's in there, Lott? What's goin' on?" exclaimed Jake.

"Mamma's comin'! Mamma's comin' to visit us next summer. She'll be here the first of July. She's comin' to Coon Tail, Mis'sippi," shouted Lott grabbing Jake by the hand. In a burst of excitement the two began dancing a Scottish jig their mother taught them in Savannah.

The women up at the house thought the men must be hitting the jug again or had gotten into one of the large wasp nests under the barn roof. They were relieved and excited as the rest when they heard the reason for their unusual behavior.

I

Jake, Minsa, and Homer left the first day of November and headed north. They followed the Natchez trace as far as the middle of Tennessee where they met Mister Jacobson and from there rode into the eastern section of Kentucky. In what has been called "the blue grass country" they found exactly the horse they wanted, but it was priced higher than expected. It took all the money they had plus two of their own horses to acquire the animal of their dreams.

With only one saddle horse left and the magnificient thoroughbred they had no intention of riding, they set out south for Coon Tail. On the long trip back, two would ride and one would walk, leading their prized possession.

Without money, the group had to hunt for food and sleep under the stars. Minsa, used to the outdoors, proved valuable to Jake and Homer in placing food before them each day.

Never had there been a happier group than the one that arrived on the 25th day of February 1851, at the front steps of the Wilsons' home.

The family rushed out to greet the dirty, ragged group that had been gone for almost four months.

Standing before them was the tallest, finest looking animal the family had ever seen. He stood over sixteen hands tall, completely black except for a small white star between his eyes and another patch of white on the back of his right lower leg. Not only was he beautiful, but spirited and strong as well. He was something to behold.

Jake led the stallion up to Hatta. "I want you to meet the newest addition to the family. You name him, if'n you please."

Hatta walked close and gently stroked his nose and patted his neck softly and whispered into his ear, "Your name, my hoofed brother, will be Lightning. You will strike and run quickly as the bolt that streaks across the heavens with power of gods behind you. You and your offspring will bring glory and victory to our family. You will never be defeated."

7

HOMECOMING

JANUARY THROUGH MARCH WERE DREARY MONTHS IN THE east central Mississippi hillcountry but as spring approached, excitement over the arrival of Mama Wilson kept them going. The men worked late into the night with the plowing and planting. They planned to give the matriarch their complete attention so Lott arranged for Minsa to employ several of his clansmen to take care of the animals and fieldwork during Mrs. Wilson's three week visit.

They had also begun to breed the new stallion to the strongest and fastest mares in their herd. Jake was looking forward to seeing his mother, but down deep, he was just as excited about the foals that would be born next winter. He knew he already had some of the fastest horses of the traditional stock in his section of the state and by breeding his choice mares he was anticipating colts that would become the premier attraction in country racing.

Minsa and Lott had built a race track on Minsa's property where the Choctaws had in years past come together for their fierce and competitive stickball games. It lay next to the Little Chunky River where sparkling, pure water was available for watering the horses and the spectators as well.

The settlers had devised three different types of racing. One was the dash where horses would race on a straight away for a distance of a quarter of a mile. This race was usually scheduled for the first event of the afternoon. The second race was a two mile run on the track that encircled the old ballfield. This was a popular event and like the dash, observers could see the entire race from where they sat underneath huge oak trees that bordered the river. But, the most popular and dangerous race was the hillrun. A committee met before each race and mapped out a route that would cover no less than five miles and would involve racing the horses through the rugged hills and hollows, swamp bottoms, and through several creeks and streams that flowed across the woodlands. Each time, the committee tried to pick a different and more challenging route.

Since the hillrun was the longest and most dangerous race, more money was bet on it. Many times a horse and rider were tumbled to the ground when the horse either stepped in a stumphole or simply lost its footing when descending one of the steep hills. Quite a few riders had been seriously injured during past runs, and several horses had to be shot after breaking a leg.

Jake made his top earnings on this race. Not only did he have one of the fastest horses, but with Minsa as his rider, he had the advantage of Minsa's knowledge of every inch of the forest. When given a good horse, it was hard for Minsa to lose. But Jake seldom raced his finest animal because of the danger.

Jake had won large sums of money at the races, but it was a mystery to the family as to where the winnings were being spent. Eventually, Lott began to put the puzzle together but wished his brother would confide in him.

On one afternoon, a severe April thunderstorm forced Lott and Jake to seek shelter in the barn until the rain slacked.

"Jake, I want to talk to you about sump'n that's been botherin' me for quite a spell," said Lott as he sat in the hallway attempting to roll a smoke.

"I know what you gettin' at. It's been botherin' me too. Mamma's comin' and I don't know what she's going to think about me marryin' up with a Choctaw. And you know Homer don't quite look like them other boys 'round here either. What's she going to think, Lott?"

"Jake, don't worry none about that. Hatta is some kind of a fine woman, and Homer, well, you won't find a more handsome and pleasant young'un to be around. Give Mamma a few minutes with him and she'll love him to death," assured Lott. "Mamma looks at a person's heart, not what they look like. You keep forgettin' too, Hatta's father was a white man. It ain't like she's full Choctaw, and it won't make no difference if'n she was."

"Lott, I hope you's right. I want things to be just right when Mamma gets here. I want her to be proud of me and my family. I've caused Mamma a heap of heartache, disappointment and worry through the years, and I want to show her I got my life straightened out. As Mamma used to say, 'Walkin' the straight and narrow.'"

Jake paused a moment then chuckled, "Well, I try to walk it most of the time, I guess."

"Jake, what I want to talk to ya about ain't concerning Hatta or Mamma. I been wonderin' about what you doin' with all that money you been winnin' at them races. You know, we's more than partners, we's also brothers. Our earnings on the farm, we share, and yore racin' money is yores, and it ain't none of my bus'ness what ya do with it."

Jake, seated on the ground across the hall from Lott, picked up a piece of straw and began to gently chew on its stem as he spoke.

"Lott, what I'm going to tell ya, you ain't going to understand, but I want you to hear me out. I've learned to love and respect these here Choctaw people and through Hatta and Homer, I feel a part of them. The gov'ment and our own folks ain't treated them fair. They pushed them off their land and those who did decide to stay, well, they is still cheating the hell out of 'em," explained Jake. "You know they got a outfit called the Choctaw Land Company right here in this county, and they is doin' everything they can to buy Indian land. They offer an Indian ten cents to the acre, and then sell it for anywhere from fifty cents to a dollar an acre. Also, them bastards will get one of 'em drunk and 'fore he can sober up, his land's gone. There's also been times when a Choctaw's run up a debt with somebody, and they tell him that if'n he will sell his land, he won't owe nobody and will stay out of jail. A Choctaw can't stand bein' in jail. Lott, I could go on and on, but the fact is that if'n sump'n ain't done soon, there ain't going to be a single Choctaw livin' on Choctaw land. Hell, it's about like that now. They doin' everything possible right now to try to get Minsa to sell his to the company. Lott, if'n somebody don't help them, they ain't going to be much better off than them pore slaves that you always takin' up for," concluded Jake spitting the straw out of his mouth in disgust.

"What's this gotta do with yore winnings?" prodded Lott.

"Well, I guess it's got a lot to do with it. Me and Minsa got a plan worked out. First, we try to tell the Choctaws how to deal with the white men who's tryin' to get their land, and if'n they get in debt, we loan them money where's they won't have to sell. That's where my money's goin', Lott. I hope you understand what we's doin'. I'm tryin' to save them people's land."

By now the rain had almost stopped and the sun peeked between the rainclouds giving the land a fresh and radiant appearance as its rays streaked across the freshly plowed red soil in the field behind the barn

"Jake, what ya doin' is a noble thing, and if'n that's what ya want to do with yore racin' money, that's yore bus'ness. I just hope you ain't throwin' money down a empty stumphole. Lot of folks think the Choctaws just ain't going to adjust to settlin' on a piece of land. They don't know how to work it, and eventually they going to lose it and when they lose it, the only choice they got is the Indian Territory in Oklahoma. But I'm proud of what you doin', Jake, and I know the good Lord lookin' down from heaven has got to think highly of ya, too. You ready to hit the fields?"

"Ready brother, let's get them pretty for Mamma."

Later, Jake told Lott more about the Choctaw Land Company. From what Jake could find out, Frank Olliver and several wealthy men from Decatur and Hickory had formed the company and acquired thousands of acres of Choctaw land and were making tremendous profits.

What disturbed Lott the most, was when Jake told him that he felt Mister Walker, a personal friend, was one of the members of the Choctaw Land Company.

Meanwhile, time seemed to move slowly as the family anticipated the arrival of Mrs. Wilson. From a letter received on the 15th of June, the family knew she would arrive on the four o'clock stage from Meridian between July the first through the fifth, depending on the weather and when her ship would arrive in Mobile. Professor Johnson could not make the trip, but sent his regards.

The family decided that beginning July the first, they would stop work each afternoon at two o'clock, clean up and put on their Sunday best, load up in the wagon and go to the stage stop at Walker's Store. To be certain they were there when she stepped off the coach, they would follow this schedule each day until she arrived.

The last day of June was the hottest of the young summer. The women and children were busy cleaning the house and washing down the inner walls and floors, while Homer and James Earl were sweeping the front yard. There was no grass grown in the front yards of the cabins in this section of the country nor did the settlers want any. Lott and Jake were down in the swampbottom trying to get one of their cows out of a bog when they heard a rider approaching.

"Lott, that looks like Thomas Walker comin' down here. He sure is in some kind of hurry. Wonder what's the rush," commented Jake, drenched with sweat and glad that the cow was finally freed.

Walker pulled his horse to a stop and with a grin that could have charmed the Governor stated, "You boys expectin' company?"

"Sure we is, Thomas. You know Mamma's going to be here soon. What you talkin' about?" asked Lott.

"Well, a little ole gray haired lady came into my store a few minutes ago when the stage stopped and asked the whereabouts of two Wilson boys."

Before Mister Walker could say another word, Lott and Jake started screaming and shouting so loudly it caused Thomas' horse to rear up and send him tumbling backwards to the ground.

"Mamma's here! Jake, let's get home! We got to get the folks ready and hurry on down there. I'll race ya!" shouted Lott.

In seconds, the brothers were on their horses and on the way to the house. Lott told Minsa to harness the horses to the wagon and shouted to the family.

"Ya'll get washed up and dressed right now! Mamma got here early and is waitin' for us. Me and Jake's going to go down there and get her right now," exclaimed Lott. "You be ready when we get back."

In their haste, Lott and Jake had no time to clean up and they pushed the horse and wagon to its limit. In a short time they turned the corner leading to the front of Walker's store, almost turning the wagon over in the process. As they came to a stop near the front porch of the store, there she was sitting on the bench with her trunk.

For a few seconds, they just looked at each other. Mrs. Wilson, astonished by the way the wagon had almost turned over, thought these men punishing that poor animal must be some of the local Mississippi frontier ruffians Lott and Jake had written about.

As for the brothers, they stared at the little lady sitting erect and neatly dressed and thought, "This woman don't look like Mamma. Her hair's so gray, and she's smaller than I remembered. But those eyes, it's got to be her."

Studying the men thoroughly, Mrs. Johnson soon recognized familiar features and thought, " These men have got to be my boys."

"Well, I had to look at ye for a spell before I knew who you were, but I guess you can pass for my laddies," she said, getting up from the bench. "I thought you might be here on time, young men. Get up here and let me see you."

The boys quickly climbed down from the wagon now realizing they had not even washed their faces and hands. Dried mud was caked all over their clothes, in their hair and even in their beards, but that didn't matter. Their mother was waiting.

They walked slowly up the steps and looked straight into her deep blue eyes. She turned to Lott and gently ran her fingers through his thick greying hair and kissed him on the cheek.

"Lott, it's been nineteen years since I last saw you. You've grown into quite a handsome and distinguished looking man with all those silver locks. And who is this fine specimen of a gent with ye?" pausing to study his brother more closely. "This can't be my Jeremiah."

She stroked the red coarse beard and reached up to place her hands on his broad shoulders.

"I can't believe this is my baby. Jeremiah, you have grown into one giant of a man. I understand you have a beautiful wife and son. I can't wait to meet them all," concluded Mrs. Johnson as she pulled her sons together and tried to embrace them both.

They laughed and cried as they realized that although many years had separated them and changed their appearance, their hearts were still interwoven.

The boys then quickly loaded their mother's chest in the wagon and began the short trip back home trying to tell her all at once of their many years in the wilderness.

"Laddies, you don't have to tell me everything right now. We have three weeks together," she said. "I'm anxious to meet my daughters and my grandchildren. You have told me so much about them in your letters. I can't wait to see them."

On the road, they met Mister Walker and he was as muddy as they were.

"Well, I see ya finally found them fellows you was lookin' for. They got in such a hurry, they forgot to help me out of that bogg," he laughed, pointing at his muddy pants bottom. "It's all right though. They don't ever get a guest as polite and nice as you is. Welcome to Coon Tail, Mrs. Johnson."

As the wagon pulled up to the front of the house, the family was lined up across the long front porch dressed in their best.

Lott and Jake helped their mother down from the wagon and led her up the steps.

"Homer, you get the chest out of the back, and James Earl you help him tote it in," said Jake.

"No, children, you stay right where you are. I want to meet you all first."

She approached Hatta first and gently embraced her. "Young lady, you are every bit as beautiful as Jeremiah described. I can't wait to know you better," stated Mrs. Johnson. "And you, my dear, are Sarah Alice, and you are a pretty thing, too."

Then turning to her sons she said, "You boys have found some mighty fine looking lassies out here. I just hope you treat them as your father treated me, like the Queen herself."

She went from child to child, giving each a hug and saying a few words to each to let them know how much she looked forward to being the grandmother they had heard so much about and had waited so long to meet.

Later after an ample supper, the family sat out on the front porch in the light of a full moon until the early hours of the morning, reminiscing about all that had happened in Savannah and in the boys' new homeland.

Tree frogs, locusts, and crickets continuously serenaded their newly arrived guest. Down at the spring, several bullfrogs croaked, interrupted occasionally by an owl perched out beyond the barn.

The children had tired themselves out in play and were curled up in the hall on quilt pallets that Sarah and Hatta laid out. It was a treat for them to be able to stay up so late.

About three o'clock, the adults felt it was time to retire, especially since Mrs. Johnson was probably exhausted.

"Laddies, there's one thing I am having a problem with. What has happened to the Queen's language? You know, I can hardly understand you sometimes. And boys, do all the women around here really use snuff?" joked Mrs. Johnson.

"Mamma, people don't talk that way out here. We ain't heard grammar like yores spoken in a long time. The children learn it right in school, but it ain't spoken out here and for the snuff, you going to have to try it 'fore you leave, " laughed Lott.

That night Lott and Jake felt their home was complete with their wives beside them in bed, the children tucked in their rooms and their mother finally with them.

The days that followed were some of the happiest the Wilsons had ever experienced. They took long walks through the woodlands, introduced their mother to neighbors who had come to meet her, went swimming and picnicking at the creek and stayed up late talking on the front porch.

The highlight of the visit was the Fourth of July community picnic and races. Lott and Jake invited the entire community to meet at the race track for a day of fun, fellowship, and country racing.

The morning of the fourth dawned clear and warm. Mrs. Wilson was already up at daybreak and after quietly making a cup of coffee, she wandered out into the front yard admiring the natural beauty of the homestead. Somewhere deep in the woods, she could hear Jake's hounds giving chase to some critter, but suddenly noticing movement at the barn, she was startled to see a strange man approaching leading a mean-looking dog.

Noticing that she seemed frightened, he quickly introduced himself.

"My name is Minsa and you, Mamma Wilson. We wait long time for you to come," he said in a quiet and polite manner. "I come to see you and ask Jake if I ride in race today."

"It is nice to meet you Minsa. I've heard many good things about you," replied Mrs. Wilson, leaning down to stroke the dog that was now sitting on the ground beside him. But the dog growled and lunged toward her only to be pulled back by the leash.

"No touch dog! He fightin' dog, no pet. Dog bite you," said Minsa as he scolded the animal.

Trying to be friendly, she asked, "What's the dog's name?"

"His name Son of Bitch," replied Minsa, still trying to get the dog to settle down.

"Minsa, where did you get such a fine name as that?" stammered Mrs.

Wilson, somewhat embarrassed but determined not to show it.

"Jake named dog. He say dog is fightin' son of bitch and he win many fights. Jake give dog fine name," replied Minsa feeling that she was pleased.

Her embarrasement gave way to laughter.

"I should have known Jeremiah had something to do with that name. Jeremiah!" shouted Mrs. Wilson. "You got company out here and there's something I need to talk to you about later."

By mid-morning, the family was on their way to the racetrack. Jake, Minsa, and Homer each rode the horse they planned to enter in competition.

At the grounds, they were secretly pleased at such a large gathering of friends and neighbors. There were men, women and children of all ages scurrying to spread their blankets on the ground before the choice spots were gone. Everyone seemed to have the Fourth of July festive spirit; even Frank Olliver was behaving like a gentleman.

At twelve noon, Lott stepped up on a platform that had been built next to the racetrack and fired his pistol to get everyone's attention.

"I want to welcome you all to this here Fourth of July celebration, and first off I want you to meet me and Jake's mother. Come on up here, Mamma. This here is Mrs. Mary Ruth Walton Wilson Johnson. But to keep it simple, just call her Mrs. Wilson."

The crowd laughed and gave her a loud and vigorous applause as Lott helped her down and then announced the day's activities. "First, we have some games for the chill'un and young folks, and later on, at three, Jake'll start the races," concluded Lott.

The hours passed quickly and after foot and sack races, a pistol was fired to signal the races. Jake, who had been browsing around the crowd to entice people into the betting, lumbered up on the platform.

"Alright, here it is. The first race is the sprint. And before the grownups race, there's going to be one for the young'uns. After that, we run the full track. No more than ten horses to the race and as many races as we got nerve for. Then last, but not least, we run the hills," stated Jake amidst the shouting and sporatic gunfire. "As usual there's going to be bettin' at will, and when we get through this afternoon, there ain't going to be no fightin' and cussin' from the losers. My mamma's our guest and we is going to behave like cultured South'rn gents. Ain't we?" laughed Jake. "And one more thing. If'n you behave, you is invited up to the house this evenin' for barbacue and good ole footstompin' music. But listen up now, you got to bring yore own instrument, if'n you can play it," shouted Jake above the shouts of approval.

"And listen up. Jacob Clearman, you can't bring that ole bagpipe. It scares the hell out of my hounds, and our chickens don't lay an egg for a week after they hear that racket," joked Jake. "Naw, bring it on, Jacob, we kind of gettin' use to it."

Homer won the young people's race without any close competition. When he went to the platform to receive the ribbon, his grandmother waved for him to come over for a victor's kiss. This pleased him more than winning.

Even though James Earl came in third in his race, he was pleased. At fourteen and competing as an adult, he felt he had conquered the art of horseracing.

Then the time finally arrived for the hillrun. The horsemen anxiously made preparation for the race and Jake took the stand once more to give them the route.

"All right men, when the pistol is fired, you run north for two miles up the hollow to the the place where the Little Rock Creek runs into the Little Chunky. Then you head west for about a mile or more through the hills, and you turn south where Sam Graham killed that big ole bear a few years back. For those who make it that far, you then make yore way back to the tracks as best you can. One thing about that last leg of the race, you going to have to get through one helluvah swampbottom 'fore you get to the finish line," concluded Jake, confident his rider knew the swamp better than most. "By the way, there will be a judge at each turn, to be sure that there ain't no cheatin."

Seventeen riders lined up at the starting platform. Minsa on a large dark bay gelding was wearing his favorite solid red shirt and had his long hair tied back.

At the sound of a pistol, horses stampeded from the starting line, almost losing some of their riders. In seconds, they disappeared into the woods on the northern edge of the tracks. All the spectators could then hear was the sound of branches breaking under the flying hooves and the shouts of the riders.

As the first rider approached a turning point, a judge stationed at the marker would fire his pistol, letting the people at the tracks know how the race was going.

Soon the first shot was heard echoing down the hills to the north and in a few minutes, another one alerted the crowd that a rider was on the last and most difficult stretch, the swampbottom.

Suspense grew as the large group wondered which rider would bolt up from the river bank and through the woods located on the edge of the racetrack.

The people could now hear horses galloping through the swamp and could detect the splashing of horses through the shallow river water.

Suddenly, a voice rang out. "Riders comin! On the other side of the river! Comin' fast!"

One man shouted, "I see it, now! Looks like Ted Harmon's golden chestnut!"

Jake and Lott ran up the track to get a better look.

"Lott, that Ted ain't never beat us before and that horse of his ain't s'pose to run with mine," exclaimed Jake, frustrated at the possibility of losing.

Sure enough, Ted Harmon and his steed bounded over the top of the riverbank and were headed straight toward the finish line.

"Lott! Lott! Ted's going to win," shouted Jake, his face a mottled red.

"Wait a minute, Jake! There's another comin' up the bank. He's wearin' a red shirt! It's our horse, Jake! He's commin' hard!" exclaimed Lott, so excited that he could hardly get the words out.

Over the bank bounded Minsa with his horse showing no signs of fatigue, darting through the forest as if the trees were grass. Leaning forward to where it was almost impossible to detect him from his gelding, Minsa was moving like the wind.

The crowd was wild.

"Lott! They's comin' like a bat out of hell. Look at that gelding run and ain't that Choctaw sump'n! We going to catch him! We going to do it!"

The horses had now cleared the woods and were thundering toward the finish line, neck to neck. With one lash of a whip and a shout of victory, Minsa pushed his horse across the line.

Men, women and children cheered wildly and gunshots rang out as if a fierce battle had begun. The race was over. The day belonged to Minsa and the Wilsons.

But Jake and Lott wanted to see what had made the race so close. Reaching Minsa, Jake blurted out. "What happened to ya? Harmon ain't never come that close to beatin' us. What in the hell?" questioned Jake, confused.

Minsa slid off his horse and with a big smile whispered, "Minsa want to make good race for Mamma Wilson. I stop and got water in creek. No worry. Knew we could win."

Minsa, you 'most scared us to death. We had a lot of bets on you," said Lott, relieved.

That evening, a caravan of wagons and buggies showed up at the Wilson's home where a group had been preparing a beef and pork barbecue that would feed two hundred people.

After the meal, Lott summoned the musicians to the open hall that had been hung with lanterns. The blending sounds of the banjo, fiddle, mandolin, guitar, harmonica and Sarah's pump organ filled the night and drifted with the breezes through the woodlands where once only the sounds of Choctaw drums and the voices of a people singing their ancient songs had been heard.

Soon it was time for dancing. Lott got everyone's attention. "I want to welcome you to our home and we want ya to have a good ole footstompin' time. You can pair up on the porch and use the front yard for dancing. The main thing is we want ya to have a good time. Okay men, grab yore partner and let's stomp them feet," instructed Lott, reaching for Sarah's hand to be the first on the yard.

The more popular dances were the waltz and the square dance. The small children kept up with the adults as they danced to almost every tune.

Mrs. Wilson leaned over to Jake who was keeping her company. "Jeremiah, this has been one fine day. I can't remember when I have enjoyed myself so much. Why don't you get out there with your wife and show me some of your fancy foot work?"

"Oh Mamma, I can't do that. Never could," replied Jake, blushing at the thought.

"Well, look down there. Young John and that pretty little Walker girl are dancing like they are at the governor's ball," whispered Mrs. Wilson, pointing to the couple.

As the dance ended, she walked to the middle of the porch, raised her hands to get the crowd's attention and said, "When I look down there and see my smallest and youngest grandson dancing his heart out, and I look over here at this giant of a son of mine, not dancing, I think it's time for his mother to give him a lesson. What do you think?"

There was so much applause that it spooked the horses that were tied up around the outer yard.

"Would you please play a waltz for us?" Mrs. Wilson asked politely. She then coaxed Jake off the front porch, placed one of his hands on her waist and held the other one out in front.

"Jeremiah, it's just one-two-three, one-two-three."

To Jake's surprise, he took right to it and had plenty of rhythm for dancing.

As the dance ended to applauding approval, Mrs. Wilson turned Jeremiah over to his wife like a horse broke for the saddle.

Around midnight Lott once again got everyone's attention, "I know all of you are about given out, and most of the young'uns has already bedded down in the wagons, but we want to thank you for comin' and to close out this day, I'm going to ask Jacob Clearman to come up here to play some special music for us. Come on up here, Jacob."

He stepped up on the porch carrying the bagpipe Jake could not stand.

"Mrs. Wilson, knowin' that you is Scotch, I want to play some special songs just for you, and I hope you like them," said Jacob taking a big breath and puffing it into the large bag clinched under his arm.

Everyone was surprised at how well Jacob could play and the melody sent tears down Mrs. Wilson's cheek as she nodded her head in approval. There was "The Bonnie Banks O," "Loch Lomon," "Comin thro the Rye," "Will Ye No Come Back Again" and his last selection "Auld Lang Syne."

The days quickly passed and Mrs. Wilson's visit was soon coming to an end. With each day, she had become not only a mother-in-law and grandmother, but now a beloved family member.

On the Sunday before her departure, Lott and Jake made plans to carry their mother and the family to the monthly church service.

As usual, Mrs. Wilson was up before daybreak to enjoy the sounds of the whippoorwill, morning doves, locust, and treefrogs, and on occasion, the chilling cry of a bobcat. As daylight approached, she could hear a rooster down the valley in one of the neighboring farms.

Suddenly, hearing the creaking of an opening door, Mrs. Wilson turned to see Hatta.

"Good mornin' Miss Mary," she whispered, not wanting to wake the others.

"Good morning, daughter. I'm glad you are up early. I wanted to take a walk this morning, and I would love for you to join me," said Mrs. Wilson, taking her by the hand.

They strolled by the barnyard, stopping to admire Jake's fine colts. They headed down the wagon road past the cornfield and to the trail through the woods leading to the creek where they rested a spell before returning.

"Hatta, I can understand why my boys decided to stay out here. It's such a beautiful country and the people seem to be so nice and caring for one another," commented Mrs. Wilson reaching down to pick one of the wildflowers growing on the creekbank. "And, I know why Jeremiah fell in love with you. You are such a sweet and supportive woman. I know it has been a long time since I have seen my boys, but I have noticed a big change in them, especially Jeremiah. Back in Savannah, he was always getting into trouble and his language was not the best in the world, but he's different now. He's calmer, more peaceful. He seems to have direction in his life and I think you and Homer are a large reason for that."

"Miss Mary, I loved Jake the first time I met him and he has been good to my people. He still talks bad sometimes when he's angry, but his heart is big, and he does not mean those things. I love Lott and Sarah, too. We have fine family. We wish you could stay."

"I wish I could too, but I have a husband and responsibilities in Savannah now. Hatta, you and Sarah Alice have been so good to me while I've been in your home. My sons couldn't have picked any finer wives, and I want you to know I have learned to love you both so much. You mind if I hug you?"

"My people hold each other too," said Hatta reaching out to embrace her mother-in-law.

The ladies eventually made their way back to the house exchanging stories about Jake and laughing at the humorous tales from his boyhood frolicking.

That Sunday, when the invitation was given at the close of the worship service, Jake, Hatta, Homer, and James Earl walked down the aisle and accepted Christ as their Savior, a special act of religious faith. The congregation was stirred by their commitment and testimonies.

After the members finished the meal that had been spread underneath the trees behind the church, Brother Thompson, Sarah's father and visiting preacher for the day, stood to make an announcement. "You don't know how good I feel, and I know the good Lord's happy today to see these family members given salvation; and Mrs. Wilson, if you had any influence on what happened this morning, may God bless your soul. We are all proud of your family and what they mean to us, and we want you to come back for another visit some day."

"Brother Thompson, I tried to teach my boys the right way to live, and I've spent many an hour reading the Bible to them, but the salvation comes from above. God in heaven claims his own," answered Mrs. Wilson.

The next morning, Jake harnessed the horses and drove the rig up to the porch where it could be easily loaded.

Once at Walker's Store, a quietness enveloped the group as they waited for the arrival of the eastbound stage from Union.

At eleven o'clock, it came rumbling into town and in a matter of minutes was loaded and ready for departure to Meridian. Mrs. Wilson hugged each one, then stepped up into the coach and took the window next to the store.

With a crack of a whip, the horses lunged forward and the stage was on its way.

Mrs. Wilson leaned out the window, threw a kiss to the group huddled together and waved to them one last time.

"I hope I can see you all at least once more before I get too old," she thought, her heart breaking. She wondered if she would ever see her new found family again.

8

RUCKUS AT WALKER'S STORE

THE MEN AND BOYS SOON RETURNED TO THEIR ROUTINE chores. As for Sarah and Hatta, they had labored steadily with the household responsibilities during their mother-in-law's visit so nothing changed. They still had to cook, wash the family clothes, and keep the house clean. It was just more of the same for them.

But it was worth it, and they missed Mrs. Wilson more than expected. Late in the evening was when they missed her most. Three weeks passed before they received the first letter and this one and the correspondence to follow helped ease the loneliness.

Meanwhile, Jake had always defended the Choctaws when their rights were threatened and was still spending his own money to help them retain their land. But his increasing interest in religion and the Bible made him more sensitive to their plight than before. So his support increased during the fall and winter of 1851. Almost daily, an Indian would come seeking advice and asking him to intercede in a court case.

Jake was now not only defending the Choctaws in Newton County, but traveling to the neighboring counties of Neshoba, Winston and Kemper. In case after case, he worked hard to persuade the judge or court to be fair and unbiased when dealing with the Choctaws but he soon realized that no court was going to favor a Choctaw over a white man.

With personal funds exhausted and an increasing sense of failure, he decided on a different strategy. He began to threaten people who had problems with the Choctaws, even before the case was called. On some occasions, confrontations ended in fights and brawls. From the first of August to the middle of December, Jake was involved in seven fights and one shooting that had left a man crippled for life. Even around the house, Jake wasn't his usual self. His cheerful, happy-go-lucky personality changed and he became silent, moody and troubled. He would often get up in the middle of the night, dress and roam the woods until morning.

On one such night, Jake left and told no one where he was going. Two days later, a rider came to the house. "Mister Wilson, I'm Sam Taylor from Decatur, and I got a note from yore brother."

Lott tore open the envelope and slumped down on the front steps. Sarah and Hatta hearing the conversation quickly surrounded him.

"It's from Jake, ain't it," said Sarah.

"Where's my Jake? Is he well?" questioned Hatta.

"All I know is that Jake is in jail in Decatur, and he wants me to come get him out," mumbled Lott who looked blankly into their strained faces.

"We'll get ready to go with you. Won't take long," said Sarah as she and Hatta hurried down the hall.

"No, you ain't s'pose to go. Jake only wants me to come by myself," said Lott, as he rushed toward the barn.

By mid-day, Lott was in Decatur. At the courthouse, he found Sheriff Parker dozing in the back room of his office. Lott's knocking awakened him and he finally came to the door fastening his suspenders.

"You Lott Wilson, ain't ya? I seen you at the races a while back," stated the sheriff. "It's about time you came and got that son-of-a-bitch brother of yores out of here."

Lott hadn't been angry in a long time, but the sheriff's tone of voice was more than Lott could stand.

"Let me tell you sump'n, Parker, I came in here in a polite way to see what I can do for my brother, and what I found is a smart-mouthed sheriff who needs a lesson in manners. Maybe before this day's over, there could be two of them sons of bitch Wilsons in yore jail," threatened Lott taking a step backward and raising his clinched fist.

"Wait a minute, I was up all night tryin' to track a fellow who broke in the Adam's house here in Decatur, and I ain't worth a damned thing today. Let me try it again," apologized the sheriff. "Have a seat over there."

"What did Jake do to get thrown in jail," questioned Lott, remaining standing.

"Well, we had a court case day before yesterday 'bout a Choctaw who stole some hams out of David White's smokehouse and since he was caught with the goods, Judge Henry sentenced him to thirty days hard labor at the Frank Olliver place. After that, Jake told the judge the Choctaw was hungry and that he would pay for the hams. The judge then told Jake he was tired of his buyin' the savages out of trouble and he weren't takin' his money and the Choctaw is workin' for Olliver."

"Ain't nothin' wrong with that. But why'd he chunk him in jail?"

"When the judge mentioned Frank Olliver's name, Jake went crazy. He called the judge a fat bellied, slime sucker, shoved his chair out of the way and stormed up to the bench as if'n he were going to get him. Almost scairt Judge Henry to death. After the judge settled down, he sentenced Jake to thirty days in jail or one hund'rd dollar fine," concluded the sheriff shaking his head.

"Well, Jake ain't going to stay in no jail. Give me a few hours and I'll get him out."

"Mister Wilson, I'm going to give you some sure 'nough good advice. Yore brother has made a fool out of himself 'bout them Choctaws and the judge is gettin' tired of all the fights Jake is gettin' into. If you don't stop him, somebody will and I mean for good."

Lott made the ride back home in record time and returned with the money to pay Jake's fine. The sheriff then gave him a note for the jailkeeper.

Walking into the blockhouse, he spotted Jake sitting on a bench close to the bars playing poker with the deputy sheriff.

"About time you got me out, Lott. I sent for you as soon as the trial ended," said Jake rising to greet his brother.

"I got the note this morning and got here as fast as I could," replied Lott, handing the release note to the deputy.

"I'm Clements, and I'm sure 'nough glad you come when you did. That brother of yores would have cleaned me out if'n you'd come an hour later," laughed the deputy as he unlocked Jake.

On the way home, Jake told his side of the story. When he got to the part about calling Judge Henry names, Lott interrupted.

"Jake, were you really going to hit him?"

"Naw, you know me better'n that. I was going to just scare him a bit. Didn't know that scare would cost a hund'rd dollars."

After a few moments, Jake became serious and turned to Lott.

"Hold up yore horse a minute. I got sump'n I want to talk to ya about."

They dismounted and walked over to a big pine tree where they could sit.

"Lott, I didn't want the women or chill'un to see me locked up," said Jake in a soft voice. "I was embarrassed, and I could just see the faces of the church folks when they heard about it. And if'n Hatta or Homer had come down here, it'd killed me."

"Jake, you was tryin' to help someone, and you just got carried away," said Lott, trying to make his brother feel better.

"I'll tell ya one thing. I ain't going to help those Choctaws no more. I've lost all my money. I've got in fights and been throwed in jail, and what good has I done? Not a bit. Just caused my family hurt. I'm through with 'em," said Jake as he got up and mounted his horse. "I'll tell ya one more thing, Lott. Last night I heard Judge Henry and Parker talkin outside. They probably thought I was sleepin, but by the way they was talkin, they's in cahoots with the Choctaw Land Company. They's gettin' some of the action when Olliver and his partners sells Indian land, and they mentioned a judge in Kemper County too. No wonder we don't ever win them cases."

"Jake, that's hard to believe. You sure?"

"Sure as the Gospel, Lott, sure as the Truth wrote in the Good Book."

In the weeks to come, Jake made no effort to help any of the Choctaws who sought his assistance. Fortunately, few came looking for him. By now, most had lost their land and were yielding to the white man's authority and accepting a new status: servitude.

Jake returned to his old self. Once more he was the fun-loving chap who felt every day should be full of humor and amusement with maybe a little work thrown in.

Christmas was approaching and the family was busy preparing decorations for a big tree in the house, ordering gifts from Meridian and planning a Christmas day spread.

One Saturday Jake took Homer with him to pick up a few items at the village store. Jake increasingly tried to spend every free moment with his son.

Since time was no factor, they decided to walk, racing the last two hundred yards. At Walker's Store, they were greeted by Thomas who was trying to wrap some Christmas presents for his wife and daughter, Rebecca. Homer eased over to look at some new rifles resting in the gun rack, while jake went out on the front porch and stared down the street toward the blacksmith shop.

"Papa, you going to come in and look at these here new rifles, ain't ya?"

"I'll be there in a minute," replied Jake.

Down at the blacksmith's shop, several Negroes were loading some repaired wagon wheels. Recognizing Toby who through the years had developed a fondness for Jake and Lott, Jake tried to get his attention.

Toby raised his hand and nodded. Jake threw up his hand, acknowledging the greeting.

Thinking that Jason Talbert, Frank Olliver's foreman, was probably with the group, Jake went back in the store, determined to stay out of his way. He didn't need any more trouble with the law, especially at Christmas time.

"Well, how is Mister Thomas Walker doin' these days? You ain't been cheatin' nobody lately, have ya?" joked Jake.

"Naw, you know I can't get away with nothin' no more, 'specially with the likes of you pestering me," laughed Walker.

Jake then went into the store room to count the liquor in case he needed to bring another load down before Christmas.

As Homer was sitting on a large wooden barrel checking the sights on one of the rifles and Walker was next to the cash register going over an inventory list, a drunk Jason Talbert stumbled through the front door. He staggered to the counter where he blurted out how tired he was of working with slaves. Homer caught his attention.

"Well sir, what we got over here? Thomas, I ain't seen nothin' like him in my whole life. Hell, he ain't no whiteman and he damned sure ain't no niggar," exclaimed Talbert staggered over to Homer.

"Leave the boy alone, Talbert. He ain't botherin' you."

Reeling around, Talbert took out his long hunting knife and drove it into the top of the counter barely missing one of Walker's hands.

"You keep yore mouth shut if'n you want those teeth of yores and yore fingers as well," scowled Talbert glaring straight at the storekeeper. "I'm just havin' some fun with him."

Turning back to Homer, he addressed the terrified lad, "You ain't no white man and you ain't no niggar. You know, Thomas, I think I know what he is," said Talbert reaching over and grabbing Homer by the hair and pulling him to the front of the counter.

"He's Jake Wilson's squaw's bastard. That's what he is, Thomas," growled

Talbert, letting go of the boy's hair and pushing him into the wood stove in the center of the building.

"Talbert, you drunk and you better just leave him alone and get out of here before Jake comes in. You don't want none of Jake Wilson."

"Jake Wilson! Hell, I ain't scairt of him one bit," said Talbert.

Hearing the commotion, Jake stormed into the room as Homer was struggling to get to his feet. He calmly walked over and helped his son off the floor.

"You all right son? What did that man say to ya?" questioned Jake, first looking at Homer and then turning to Talbert.

"I'm all right, Papa. Let's just go home. He ain't hurt me none. You don't need no more trouble."

"I'll tell ya what I said to yore boy. I says he's Jake Wilson's squaw's bastard," shouted Talbert, reaching to retrieve his knife. "And I think I'll just whittle a bit on yore stinkin' carcus."

"Son, you go on outside. I'll take care of this," said Jake nudging Homer toward the door.

Jake approached Talbert slowly, watching to anticipate the inevitable lunge.

Talbert eased toward Jake making a couple of threatening short jabs with his knife.

As he made a hard thrust at Jake's midsection, Jake grabbed Talbert's right arm above the wrist as the blade tore through the side of Jake's coat, barely missing his body. With all the strength Jake could muster, he overpowered Talbert and pushed him to the floor. Then with one blow from his massive right fist, he drove Talbert's face to the floor, almost knocking the man unconscious.

Hearing Talbert's head strike the floor, Thomas was sure Jake had seriously injured the man and maybe even killed him.

"You mind if'n I get this bag of slime out of yore store, Thomas?" asked Jake, pulling Talbert to his feet.

"Not a bit, Jake. Get him out and thanks for yore service," replied Walker, glad the ordeal was over and Talbert was alive.

Jake held Talbert up by the collar of his coat and placed the sole of his boot in the center of his back. With one kick, Talbert sailed through the doorway, across the front porch and into the muddy street.

By this time, a crowd had assembled outside and from down the street, Toby came running. Jake appeared in the doorway and motioned Toby to the porch.

"Go get yore wagon and put this sorry piece of trash in it and carry it back to Olliver," directed Jake.

"Yessuh, Mistuh Jake. I'll be happy to," replied a smiling Toby, quickly making his way through the crowd.

After Toby and the other slaves helped Talbert up into the wagon, Jake moved within inches of the bruised and broken man. Talbert was able to sit up in the wagon, but couldn't speak. His jaw appeared to be broken and his left eye was swollen shut.

"Talbert, if'n you smart, you'll listen to me. The next time you make fun of my boy or put yore hands on him, I'm going to kill you," threatened Jake.

As the wagon rolled off up the street, Jake called out, "And by the way, you said I just fought boys in Savannah. Hell, I fought women tougher than you is," shouted Jake amidst the laughter of the crowd.

"Tell Frank, he sure got some kind of tough foreman. You hear!"

On the way home, Jake was quiet as he regretted the confrontation. He had been trying to stay out of trouble and had hoped he was making progress. A deep sense of failure swept over him as he recalled his fight and its possible effect on Homer.

As they neared the farm, Jake asked Homer to tell his mother that he would be spending the night in the barn. When something really troubled Jake, he would get a jug of whiskey, go to the hayloft and drink.

"Homer, get me a quilt," Hatta said softly pointing to the bedroom. "I sleep with Jake in barn tonight. Talbert needed beating for what he said to you. Jake don't need to be by self tonight."

That night, a cold north wind whistled around the corners of the barn causing the timbers to creak and rustling the straw in the loft. But Jake had his jug under one arm and Hatta was cuddled by his side as the moon slowly rose in the sky. Maybe it hadn't been such a bad day after all.

9

DOGFIGHT IN UNION

In EARLY JANUARY OF 1852, FRANK OLLIVER CALLED A MEETING
of the Board of Trustees of the Choctaw Land Company to discuss their yearly
earnings and the future of the organzation. Present were the six men who had
invested in the project: Judge Henry, Sheriff Parker, Judge Addison from Kemper
County, Thomas Walker, and two wealthy business men from Meridian. The
group assembled at Olliver's office in Hickory.

"Gentlemen, I want to welcome you all to what may be our last meeting of
the Choctaw Land Company," began Frank with a smile of confidence and satisfaction.

"Through the years, we have done quite well. We have enjoyed tremendous
profits and our purses have bulged, but as they say, all good things must come
to an end. We've got about all the Choctaw land around here that's worth the
gettin'. Well, maybe one piece that's still givin' me a problem," laughed Frank
above the applause and laughter.

"Tomorrow, I'll be takin' our sign down, and I just want to thank ya for
havin' confidence in me and my plan. I know you appreciate all that money I
made for ya, too. Right?"

The men applauded even louder.

"And for our honorable judges, we thank ya. And last, I thank Thomas
Walker for listenin' to all the gossip that floats 'round his store up there in Coon
Tail. We got many a good tip from him that helped us to control a deal from the
start. And Mister Walker's purse has got fatter too. Right, Thomas?"

"Right," replied Walker quietly, embarrassed that his payoff had been mentioned.

Thomas felt guilty about having anything to do with the Company or Frank
Olliver, but his craving for wealth had driven him to agree to help the Company
spot Choctaws, and whites as well, who were having financial problems and
would consider selling their property at a reduced price.

When the meeting finally ended, the Choctaw Land Company existed no
more but there was still one piece of land Frank Olliver wanted—Minsa's spread
that lay to the north of his own. It included the community racetrack which
Frank cared little about, but its fertile bottom land he desperately needed. Cotton was quickly wearing out his soil, and Frank felt pressured to obtain addi-

tional farmland if he were to continue to prosper as he had in the past.

A few days after the final meeting of the land company, Frank called his foreman, Jason Talbert, into his office.

"Talbert, you know you ain't 'specially pleased me lately," began Frank leaning back in his chair and looking out the window, not even giving Talbert the courtesy of addressing him face to face.

"You even embarrassed me by the way you acted at the store a while back; plus you got yore ass whipped in the process. What you think the niggars thought about yore whipping? I'll tell ya. They ain't afraid of ya no more, that's what!" shouted Frank.

To stress his point, Frank suddenly turned and threw the glass in his hand against the wall.

"If you want yore job and the pay it carries, you get me that Choctaw's land and get it before the spring breaks. Otherwise, not only is yore job over here, but I got a few things to tell Judge Henry about some of yore dealings. You hear me well, Boy?"

"Yes Sir, Mister Olliver, I understand what you sayin," replied Talbert stunned by Olliver's threats.

"But, it ain't going to be easy. That Indian's smart. He don't run up nary bills with folks and bein' Jake's brother-in-law, he knows Jake's going to cover his tracks," said Talbert uneasily.

"There ain't no damned smart Choctaws, Talbert! And for Jake Wilson, to hell with him! I don't care what ya do with either one of them!" shouted Frank. "Come spring, my niggars better be plowin' them bottom lands, or you going to be in the ground somewhere yoreself."

I

It was an early Sunday morning in March when Minsa appeared at the Wilson's home looking for Jake and Lott. Jake was still in bed, but Lott had gotten up early to walk around the place to enjoy the beauty of their long hours of work. The distress in Minsa's face sent Lott back to the house to get his brother.

"Got trouble, Jake. Last night I drink too much, and I roll dice," said Minsa looking at the ground, too ashamed to look the brothers in the eye.

"So what, Minsa, you done that before. A bunch of times," replied Lott, placing his hands on his hips.

"Minsa lost lot of money in game."

"How much you lose?" questioned Jake, becoming uneasy.

"They say, four hund'rd dollars," replied Minsa.

Jake grabbed his brother-in-law by the shoulders and shook him furiously.

"Four hund'rd! Damn, Minsa, didn't I teach you nothin'! You don't drank with white men. You don't trust them, and you sure as hell don't gamble with them!" shouted Jake. "I can't believe you done this."

Lott, more rational for the moment, pulled the two apart.

84

"Just wait a minute, Jake. You act like you never did nothin' wrong. You must think you're perfect. Well, you ain't, and we just going to all sit down and work this out together," said Lott.

When Jake had calmed down, Minsa told about the gambling in the shed behind the Walker's store, and that he had signed his signature, an X, on a sheet of paper. He also said the paper was given to Walker so it could be locked in his vault.

After church that afternoon, Lott and Jake rode down to Walker's house and persuaded him to tell them exactly what had happened. Thomas walked down to the store with the brothers and let them examine the note. Sure enough, it was for four hundred dollars, payable in thirty days.

"Well, Lott, we do have a problem. He owes this money to one Jacob Thompson, and if'n it ain't paid in thirty days, the only thing Minsa's got is his land," said Jake, who had been carefully studying the paper.

"You got a problem too, Jake. You ain't got no money to bale him out this time, and with spring plantin' comin', we can't take family money to pay it," reasoned Lott, reaching for the note.

"And who is this Jacob Thompson?" questioned Lott.

"I'll tell ya who he is. He works for the Choctaw Land Company, and he also works for Frank Olliver at times," replied Jake scratching his head, suddenly realizing the connection.

"Lott, we got a rat workin' in this mess, and we ain't going to let him beat us."

"How you going to raise that kind of money, Jake?" questioned Thomas, folding the note and placing it back in the vault.

"Well, we got some horse racin' comin' up next Saturday and I usually make a couple of hund'rd on that, and the folks up at Union is holding a dogfight that night that might help us some more. Minsa's old fighter is gettin' too old for that, but he got a young 'un that might just do the job," concluded Jake, winking at Lott and giving Thomas a big handshake.

"But Jake, I thought you was through helpin' them Choctaws," said Lott.

"This here's my brother-in-law. I ain't going to let him down. And I lie sometimes too, don't I?" chuckled Jake.

That weekend, Jake and Minsa were successful at the tracks, winning two hundred and forty dollars and were in high spirits as they made plans for their evening trip to Union.

Meanwhile at the far end of the tracks, Frank Olliver sent word for Talbert and Jacob Thompson to meet him as soon as the last race had ended.

Thomas Walker had told Frank about Jake's plan and with the results of the day's betting, Jake was well ahead of himself.

"Talbert, it ain't much we can do 'bout the money Jake done won on the horses, but there sure as hell better be sump'n you two can do later on tonight if'n he's lucky up in Union," said Frank.

"The way I got it figured, Mister Olliver, is that the Indian is got a young dog in the fight, and if'n he gets whipped, well Ole Jake done lost the money he put up and won't have no winnings either. Results, land'll be yores," smiled Talbert.

"And if'n he does win. Well, there's three creeks between here and Union. The first'n is right out of Union, and it's too close; and another one is runnin' right by Coon Tail, it's too close too. Well Sir, the one I like runs about two miles out of Union, below the Rock Branch Church. The banks is steep, and the horses is going to have to work to get up. That's where Mister Jake Wilson is going to get robbed."

"I don't care how ya deal with Jake, you make damned sure that he don't come back with no money," said Olliver shaking hands to seal the agreement.

That evening, Jake and Minsa tied their dog in the back of the wagon and rode over to pick up Professor Hendon who had been begging them to take him to the fights.

The Professor had the reputation of being an excellent teacher and possibly the most intelligent man in east central Mississippi. But his love for hard liquor and women often caused him to be called before the chuch elders for discipline. He was always remorseful for what he had done and would promise never to repeat the behavior again. The elders always accepted his apologies, but knew it would only be a matter of time before he would cross the line again. Since everyone liked the professor and he was an excellent instructor, his behavior was overlooked. Most knew it would be impossible to replace him.

Jake pulled the team up in front of the Professor's house and out bounded Hendon, dressed in his best. Six feet tall, well dressed and handsome, this middle-aged man had trouble keeping the ladies away.

"'Fessor, we just goin' dog fightin' tonight. Why you dressed like that?" said Jake, amused at his appearance.

"Young man, you never know who you will meet in life, and I have learned that one must be continuously ready for the future. And I hear there are some fine looking ladies up in Union who might appreciate a gent such as I," replied the Professor climbing up on the seat next to Jake. "And my good fellow, Minsa, I see that you brought the wonderful containers of the spirits of life as I so directed. May God always bless you. But my fellow comrade, why do you always carry that dreaded hatchet with you?"

Minsa, confused over the professor's appearance and speech, handed Hendon one of the jugs and shook Jake's sleeve to get his attention.

"Jake, this man okay? He talk crazy."

Both Jake and the Professor laughed.

"Minsa, who ain't crazy 'round here? I think you's a little crazy today, too. You been actin' like you scairt of goin' to Union like someone's going to get us," replied Jake as the wagon made its way westward.

"Got bad feelin' 'bout fight and clouds show mahli chitto [bad weather] ahead," replied Minsa, slumping down in the wagon bed.

The wagon team had no trouble fording the creeks between Coon Tail and Union, but a hard downpour as they entered the little village made them worry about crossing the creeks on the return trip since no bridges had been built over any of the creeks in this part of the county.

A large crowd had already gathered at the Burkett's Livery Stable in Union for the evening's events and soon Jake, Minsa, and the Professor were absorbed with the excitement of the fights.

Minsa's dog, Hell's Opener, did well in his first fight and was allowed to fight in a second. When the bouts ended at about two in the morning, Jake and Minsa had won over three hundred dollars. Unfortunately, even though Minsa's dog had won its second fight, it had been seriously injured and had to be put down.

Nevertheless, the jubilant trio boarded their wagon and were soon on the way home eager to share their triumph. They now had enough money to save Minsa's property.

As expected, Hendon had too much of the spirits and had passed out, so Jake and Minsa placed him in the back of the wagon. Up front, Jake and Minsa, somewhat inebriated themselves, were singing. Jake was trying to teach Minsa "Camptown Races," but only weird sounds came out. Some in English and some Choctaw, but they didn't care. The property was safe.

The horses had little trouble pulling across the first creek as they left Union, but when they reached the one that flowed below the Rock Branch Church, they decided to wait and let the water subside, unaware that danger faced them from the wooded banks across the stream.

Talbert had sent Sam Jenkins, a recently released prisoner from Jackson, to the fights to report the results. Talbert knew Jake would not connect him with Frank Olliver.

The three now lay in wait for Jake and his companions. Talbert was armed with two revolvers while Jenkins and Thompson each had a shotgun. Talbert gave instructions.

"Men, Frank told me to get the job done, but I'm 'fraid that if'n we stop that wagon to rob him, it'll give him an edge. That Jake ain't one to fool with. When that wagon gets to the top of the bank, it's going to slow down, and when it does, all hell's going to break loose. You empty yore guns at them and you better go for Jake first," whispered Talbert.

"But, ain't that murder, Jason? Olliver ain't said nothin' 'bout that. He just said rob them," replied Jenkins.

"Well, fellow, you can go up there and ask Jake Wilson for his money, but I ain't. And if'n you got good sense, you'll do what I say," growled Talbert.

At four in the morning, the creek finally dropped enough to cross and with the crack of his whip, Jake drove the horses into the swirling water.

"What about the Professor in back?" questioned Minsa, concerned the high water would drown their unconscious passenger.

Minsa, a little water ain't never hurt no drunk! He's going to get a baptism tonight!" shouted Jake.

Talbert had positioned Sam Jenkins in some bushes directly in the path the horses and wagon would take up the creekbank. He was to shoot the horses, immobilizing the wagon. He was then to move to the right of the wagon where another shotgun was located.

Talbert and Jacob Thompson were hidden in the trees to the left of Jenkins, and they would concentrate on Jake.

The horses were now struggling to pull the heavy wagon up the steep bank and with some loud coaxing finally reached the crest.

Suddenly, the night erupted with gunfire and flashes of light as the assailants unloaded their shotguns and pistols into the helpless riders.

The large gelding on the right side dropped where it was standing, shot in the chest. The mare to its left fought to flee the assault, but was not able to pull the wagon and drag the body of the other horse at the same time.

The force of the shot had blown Jake backwards into the bed of the wagon and had knocked Minsa over the sideboards where he landed on the ground next to the front right wagon wheel.

Minsa crawled under the wagon and called out.

"Jake, you okay?"

"I'm hit good. How 'bout you?" replied Jake struggling to get the words out.

"Not bad. Only scratch. What we do?"

"You slip down the creekbank and make yore way as fast as you can back to Union. Get the Doc and some help. We need a lot of men."

"Don't want to leave Jake," whispered Minsa still lying motionless under the wagon.

"Dammit, Choctaw! Do what I tell ya," grunted Jake, experiencing tremendous pain in his chest and side.

Minsa quietly slid down the creekbank, floated down the stream, and was soon on his way up the road leading back to Union.

Shortly, the remaining horse quieted down and the night became still. Only the sounds of rain dripping from the tree branches and bushes and water rushing over the rocks in the creek below could be heard. The sky was dark with storm clouds hovering above.

Talbert felt the gunfire had reached its mark but knew he had to finish the mission and take the money quickly since dawn was approaching.

"Men, don't take no chances! Put one more load through the wagon and then, Sam, I want you to go check it out," commanded Talbert picking up the extra shotgun he had brought with him.

Minsa had reached the top of the hill on his way for help, when a second round of gunfire echoed through the woods.

The sawed off shotgun Jake kept in the compartment under the wagon bench was within his reach. With all the energy he could muster, he pulled the gun to him and eased both hammers back. Hendon was motionless.

"Sam, move on in! There can't be much left to 'em," commanded Talbert, reloading his gun.

Sam cautiously crept to the side of the wagon with the hammers pulled on his double barrel and carefully peered over the side.

Jake pulled both triggers and sent a double load into the face of his attacker. The decapitated Jenkins went spinning to the ground and down the steep creekbank into the raging waters.

Talbert saw Jenkins fall and knew whoever fired the shot did not have long to reload.

"Thompson, get around to the right. I'm going to come up from the rear. Don't shoot less I tell ya. Jake's mine."

Easing up to the back of the wagon, Talbert found Jake lying on his back, helpless.

"Well, Mister Jake. We finally get to settle our dispute and you ain't in any shape to do nothin' 'bout it," he threatened, leveling his shotgun and pulling the hammers back.

"Talbert, I ain't got but one thing to say. I still fought women tougher than you in Savannah."

"To hell with ya, Jake," replied Talbert taking careful aim.

At that momemt, the storm clouds parted overhead and an erie moonlight instantly settled over the scene.

In a few seconds, Jacob Thompson reached his position to the right of the wagon and heard a loud thud. Glancing up, he could make out the outline of a man with a hatchet buried in his forehead. Talbert tried to pull the object out, only to fall to his knees, screaming and kicking and clawing. Thompson dropped his shotgun in terror and ran for his horse.

Jake, weak and nearly unconscious could barely recognize the tall thin figure approaching the wagon.

"Jake, you okay now. I think I need to come back to help you and crazy professor," said Minsa grimly as he climbed into the wagon to assist his friend. "Professor look dead though."

"You're one crazy Choctaw," moaned Jake trying to sit up, but collapsing from loss of blood.

"We go to Union to get Medicine Man," said Minsa as he cut the dead horse loose.

"No, Minsa. If'n you take me to Union, I'll never see Hatta and Lott," whispered Jake.

Minsa pushed the surviving horse hard over the rough and winding road to Coon Tail knowing that every minute was precious time lost.

Finally they reached the creek bordering the town and Minsa forced the horse into the swollen stream, hoping the mare would have enough strength to reach the opposite side. Water rushed in covering Jake and the Professor, and as the wagon made it up the bank, crimson water rushed out the back and over the wheels.

Minsa pushed the horse even harder as they sped by the village. Nearing the farm he began to shout, "Lott! Lott! Jake hurt! Lott! Need help!"

Lott heard the screams in the distance and as they got louder, he quickly got out of bed and rushed to the front porch, dressed only in his long underwear. A cold chill went through him as he recognized Minsa. A moment later, Lott's fear turned to agonizing alarm as the blood-splattered wagon pulled to a stop at the base of the steps.

As Lott looked past Minsa down into the wagonbed, all the strength in his body left him. He held on to one of the timbers that supported the porch roof and slowly dropped to his knees.

"Oh no! What in God's heaven has happened here?" whispered Lott, barely able to speak. "Is they dead?"

"Got jumped, Lott. Don't know why. Professor dead. Jake near dead," said Minsa, slowly climbing down.

"Sarah! Hatta! Homer! Get out here and quick!" shouted Lott, easing down from the porch. A sickening fear once more gripped his heart when he saw his brother and the professor lying bloodied, pale, and motionless.

The family stood huddled together, horrified at the sight.

"Sarah, get the little uns back in the house. Homer, you and James Earl help me get him in," commanded Lott as his strength returned.

"He's still alive!" exclaimed Lott, as he leaned close to Jake. Let's get him out!"

They eased Jake out of the wagon and awkwardly carried him up the steps, putting him down on the porch to get a better grasp. His left shoulder and side had been shredded by the shotgun blast and his left arm was almost severed from his body.

"Is we home, Minsa? I can't use my left arm," whispered Jake.

They all knelt down to hear him.

"You's home, Brother," replied Lott. "And we going to get you in the house and fetch the doctor 'fore you can wink an eye," promised Lott, starting to lift him.

"Lott, don't worry 'bout no doctor, and don't put me in the house. I just want to see the sun come up, one more time."

Jake turned to his brother.

"Hatta's gone to Oklahoma, ain't she, Lott?" questioned Jake, trying to lift his head. "Why no, here she comes with Mamma now." Jake paused.

"What's Mamma doin' here, Lott?" he gasped easing his head to the floor.

"Jake, we all here and Hatta is right here with ya," answered Lott trying to hold the tears back.

Many times Hatta had seen the pale face of death. She leaned down and softly spoke to her fallen warrior, "Homma Chito, Himak nitak pano pinki chibai nusi [Today you sleep with my fathers]. Himak nitak tushka chitto ish itibai nowa [Today you walk with our great warriors]. Hibi kat imponnah [You have fought well...You die in honor]."

"Sun up yet, Hatta? Lott, I bet Papa had hair like mine, didn't he?"

"Yes he did," assured Lott, surprised that Jake knew about their father's wiry hair since Jake had been only a baby when he died. "Why'd ya say that?"

"He's out near the barn, motioning for me. I want to go see him," whispered Jake. "Sun up yet?"

"Sun's up, Jake. It's up. You go on with Papa."

Lott paused. "Go on now."

"I'm comin' Papa." Jake smiled and a tear trickled down his cheek, losing itself in the thick red beard as he quietly released his last breath.

The children were called and they gathered around the broken body as they prayed for strength to survive the first loss in their family. The men then moved Jake's body to the kitchen table where they could clean him up and dress him for burial.

Turning to Minsa, they found a severe cut to the back of his head and a gunshot wound in his left shoulder. Another shot had pierced his left thigh. Fortunately, none of the bullets had cut an artery or fractured a bone.

"Sarah, get the whiskey and let's get Minsa cleaned up. The shot went clean through him," said Lott, still shaken but now fully in charge of the aftermath. Minsa, who did this to you and why?"

"Don't know. We cross creek at church and bullets fly. Man I hit with ax look like Talbert, but it dark, don't know for sure," replied Minsa.

As they labored over Minsa's wounds, he tried to recall the ambush, but was too weak. He was quietly taken to Hatta's bedroom. Minsa called for Homer and sent him for his two cousins. He had a job for them.

"Uncle Lott, we better go get the Professor and lay him out too," pleaded Homer, as he left for Minsa's place.

"You right, Son, we forgot him, didn't we?" answered Lott, placing his arm around Homer, touched that the youngster could think about Hendon with his own father dead.

Walking into the hall, they were shocked to see the professor sitting up, his legs dangling out of the rear of the wagon and holding his head with both hands.

"How did I get here. What happened?" questioned the professor covering his eyes, unable to look up into the sunlight.

"You mean you don't know," answered Lott, stepping down to examine him.

"No, my fine gentleman. The last thing I remember is winning the first fight," mumbled the professor, falling to his knees, sick.

Lott told Hendon the whole story but couldn't believe he came out of the ambush unscathed. One shot had dented the whiskey flask in his coat pocket and another had cut the heel off his right boot. The white oak sideboards of the wagon had shielded him from the second round of shots, saving his life.

Jacob Thompson, meanwhile, had gone directly to Frank Olliver to tell what had happened. Frank was enraged and was afraid he would be held responsible for the ambush. He gave Thompson one hundred dollars and ordered him to leave the state immediately.

It was about eleven o'clock that morning, as Sheriff Parker rode up to the Wilsons where Lott and Sarah were quietly sitting on the porch. He dismounted and made his way to the steps.

"Kind of hot morning, ain't it Lott?" said the sheriff, taking his hat off and wiping his brow with his shirt sleeve.

"You didn't come out here to be sociable, Sheriff. What's on yore mind?"

"I come to talk to Jake," replied Parker, shuffling his feet.

"About the shootin', ain't it, Sheriff? Why you think Jake knows about it?" said Lott.

"Well, Talbert's dead with a hatchet buried in his skull and another pore man was found floatin' down the creek below the church with his head blowed off. Don't know who he was," said the Sheriff. "Yore geldin' was found next to Talbert with its neck shot in two. And Lott, you know yore brother threatened to kill Talbert a while back at Walker's Store. That's why I just need to ask him a few questions."

Lott still seated, pointed to the back of the house.

"He's down there in the kitchen."

"Is he armed?" asked the sheriff.

"Naw, he ain't armed. Why should he be?"

"You ain't lyin' to me, is you?" said the Sheriff, easing cautiously down the hall toward the kitchen door.

"Sheriff, my husband don't lie, and I want you to go see Jake and then get off our place!" said Sarah.

The sheriff eased his pistol out of his scabbard, pulled the hammer back, and slowly pushed the door open. He quietly slipped into the room, but in only a few minutes returned to the porch with his pistol by his side and his head bowed.

"Lott, Mrs. Wilson, I want you to know I'm truly sorry 'bout this. The judge sent me out to see if'n I could put some sense to this here shootin. My deep apology to ya," said the sheriff as he walked down the steps and mounted his horse.

"Apology accepted, Sheriff," replied Sarah.

"Lott, what about that hatchet, it looks like the one Jake's sidekick Choctaw carries."

"It was, Sheriff. Jake told me before he died that he used it on one of them scoundrels," replied Lott. "Jake killed him with Minsa's ax. You tell Judge Henry that."

"Yes Sir," said the sheriff tipping his hat. "I'll sure tell the judge just that."

The family wanted to bury Jake the following morning but Minsa wanted time to get the word to his people. Hundreds of Choctaws began arriving late Monday evening and camped in a meadow below the Wilsons' barn. This was the same meadow where Jake first encountered the Choctaw hunter years before. During the night, people from miles around could hear clinking of sticks and the strange singing that hadn't been voiced for almost twenty years coming from the Choctaw camp.

After the funeral, attended by the villagers as well as the Indians, Jake was buried on a hill about a mile west of the Wilsons' farm. The Choctaws persuaded Lott to bury Jake in their tribal burial ground. Here, warriors who had been killed in a battle around the turn of the century against the fierce Chickasaws were buried.

Early Wednesday morning, Lott, Sarah, and the children were summoned to the front porch by Minsa. Hatta and Homer were standing in the yard with a large group of Choctaws who had broken camp.

"Lott, Sarah, we go now to Oklahoma with our people. We no longer can stay here," said Hatta.

"What do you mean? You going to leave?" questioned Sarah. "This here is yore home, yore land. You is a part of us. You can't leave us now, not now."

"Our way of life died long ago. Our land is not ours, and the pride we once knew is bein' crushed under the white man's feet. If we are to survive, we must go west so that our spirit can renew its strength," said Minsa.

Lott knew what Minsa said was true. The Choctaws' future was dim if they stayed.

"Hatta, Homer, God go with you and bless you. Go to the barn and get you a horse each. They'll get you where you goin'," said Lott reaching out to embrace Minsa. "I'm also going to give you the money Jake had left over from them fights the other night. You take it, and don't let no white man know you got it. From here to Oklahoma you camp in the woods and stay out of the towns. Don't let nobody get yore horses or money. You hear?"

"We hear you, Uncle Lott," Homer replied.

"And Homer, you and Hatta are always part of the Wilson family. The section of land you fought to keep and cost Jake his life, it'll always be yores," promised Sarah as she hugged Minsa and Homer.

Several days after the shooting, Jacob Thompson was found in the woods near the town of Forrest, stripped naked and brutally murdered. He had been tortured and disemboweled. It was said that the warlike Chickasaws to the north would often treat their captive Choctaws this way, if they had no respect for them. The Choctaws also had a custom. If a family member was murdered, a relative of the victim would take revenge.

Later, Professor Hendon seldom took a drink and became one of the most religious men in Coon Tail. Three months after the shooting, he married the widow Cooper, whom he had been seeing secretly throughout the years and eventually fathered seven sons and four daughters, quite an achievement for a man already over forty years old when he took his vows.

Meanwhile, at a local hearing at the Decatur courthouse. Lott stated that Frank Olliver had a motive to have Jake killed because of Minsa's gambling debt and everybody knew Olliver wanted the property. He also reminded the court that Talbert worked for Olliver and did what he was told to do; that Talbert was completely controlled by Olliver and was Olliver's puppet.

When Olliver was questioned, he said that Talbert hated Jake and that Jake, in the presence of a crowd of people in Coon Tail, had sworn to kill Talbert. Talbert just wanted to kill him first.

Judge Henry dismissed the hearing and declared that since there was no witness to the killings, because Minsa had left the state and the professor had been drunk during the entire ordeal, there was no case.

Lott asked the judge if he could make one closing statement. The judge consented.

"Frank Olliver, before the Almighty God and these here good people of Newton County, I want everyone to hear what I say. Frank, I think you had my brother killed, and I think the reason is that you craved that bottom land more than a human being's life. When I saw my brother lyin' in that wagon with his blood dripping through the cracks of them boards and puddlin' on the ground, I wanted to kill ever who done it. But you know, I was wrong. In the Bible it says, 'Vengence is mine saith the Lord.' Frank, yore fight ain't with me, you got to make peace with the Almighty God and may He have mercy on yore soul."

10

YOUNG GATHERING

IT HAD BEEN TEN YEARS SINCE THAT SPRING MORNING WHEN Jake Wilson was brought home from the shooting. It was a scene John would never forget. He would always remember his uncle lying bloodied and dying on the front porch with nothing anyone could do to save him.

John shook his head, as if to clear the memory of those early years. The sun was setting and he had all the fish he cared to clean. He took up his hooks and retrieved his fish string out of the water. Suddenly, the thundering sound of a galloping horse crossing the wooden bridge a quarter of a mile downstream got his attention. The rider was traveling north, headed in the direction of the Wilson home. Then all was quiet again.

In about fifteen minutes, the silence in the creekbottom was once again shattered as the noise of limbs breaking and twigs snapping preceded an animal and its mount rapidly approaching the rock hole. "Here we come, John Willy, here we come!" yelled the rider.

John scrambled up the steep creekbank and ran head on into one of the longest legged horses he had ever seen. The horse was barely able to stop and it was close enough to knock John off balance and send him tumbling down the bank into the cold water below.

Pulling himself up and wiping water out of his eyes, he recognized the face of his best friend, Frankie Olliver, dismounting the horse and scrambling down the bank.

"You alright, John? I didn't mean to knock ya in the water. I didn't know you was comin' up the bank and this here horse ain't easy to handle. You alright, ain't ya?"

"Yeah, I'm fine, but why in tarnation is you ridin' that horse so hard? You going to kill that animal treatin' him like that," replied John shaking water out of his hair and struggling to keep his balance.

"John, look at that horse! Ain't he sump'n. He's a thoroughbred," exclaimed Frankie, so excited he lost concern about his friend's fall.

"I named him Thunder, kind of like yore horse's name, Lightnin'. You get it. Thunder and Lightnin'," laughed Frankie.

"Well, where'd you get him?"

"Paw got him for my birthday and the folks over in Meridian says he can sure 'nough run," replied his friend, staring up in pride at the snorting and pawing thoroughbred.

"Frankie, you best water that animal before you ride it, and by the way, you need a little water too!" shouted John as he grabbed Frankie's arm and slung him into the creek.

Up came Frankie's hat followed by a surprised and drenched young man.

"What'd you do that for, John? I'm four miles from home, and I don't have no dry clothes," scolded Frankie.

"I thought you could use some water just like I did," shouted John, leaping into the creek and swimming toward Frankie.

The boys splashed and ducked each other, ignoring the cold creek water and how quickly the afternoon was slipping away. Finally tiring from their burst of youthful energy they realized it was time to head for home.

"Let's see that champion of yores up close, Frankie. I need a ride home anyhow," joked John, pulling Frankie out of the water and pushing him up the bank.

"Frankie, you got yoreself a pretty good horse here. But, by lookin' at them teeth, I say he's seen his better years. I bet he can still kick up the dust though," said John, patting the animal on the shoulder and giving an approving nod.

"Old! That horse ain't more'n eight, and he can sure run like the wind," replied Frankie, frustrated at John's implication that his father had given him a worn out animal. "I'll tell ya what. I bet he can beat James Earl's horse, if'n yore Paw will let ya race him."

"Frankie, let's just get on home and get some dry duds. I'm gettin' hungry," insisted John, wanting to drop the subject of racing.

After Jake had been killed, James Earl had taken over the horses and continued to breed and raise some of the finest racing animals in east central Mississippi. Jake had kept around twenty horses, but James Earl didn't have the same interest in racing and gambling as his uncle so he sold off half the herd and kept only the finest mares and a couple of stallions. James also didn't promote the races that had earned his uncle large sums of money. His earnings came from the sale of horses.

When James Earl and Thomas joined the army, John was left to tend the farm animals and this included the horses. One of the last things that James Earl told him was, "You treat them animals like you treat a best friend. You care for them and be careful if'n you race them. No hill runs!"

The boys mounted Thunder, and with a mess of fish dangling from the side of the horse, they quickly made their way through the woods to the farm.

John and Frankie had been friends ever since they could remember. They had gone to church and school together and had always enjoyed each other's company. Frankie, a year younger than John, seemed like John's younger brother. John was always taking up for him and giving him advice whether Frankie wanted it or not.

But Frankie was always bragging about how much money and power his Father had and this often caused him to get into fist-a-cuffs with the other boys.

On several occasions, John had stepped into fights that Frankie had initiated when he thought Frankie was going to be hurt. John overlooked Frankie's shortcomings and felt that with time, Frankie would learn that people just didn't take to braggarts.

In turn, Frankie felt John was the older brother he never had. Frankie's father had returned to Louisiana for a brief period in the 1830's and married a beautiful woman from New Orleans. He had stayed in the city for several months and then brought his new bride back to his Newton County farm. In the years that followed, they had a son and a daughter.

Frankie idolized John in every way. Where John was strong, quick and could outrun any boy in the community, Frankie was tall, clumsy and always stumbling over his own feet. In school, John was considered the smartest and most ambitious boy in his class, but Frankie had to struggle to pass and often cheated to make decent grades. Frankie's idolization actually bordered on envy. At times he would fantasize that he was John conquering some unforeseen enemy and that Becca, John's sweetheart, was in love with him, instead of John.

Frankie's father had overprotected and criticized him, which resulted in a lack of self confidence. Actually, Frankie was handsome and almost as tall as John. He had long blond hair that he kept neatly groomed, and his eyes were dark brown. Where John was muscular, Frankie was slim, but his broad shoulders made him look heavier than he was. Frankie also could carry on a conversation with anybody he met, and his few friends always teased that he was so persuasive he could probably convince the preacher that heaven was really hell, if he wanted. Frankie had special qualities that made him unique, but this didn't seem enough for this boy who always stood in John's shadow.

Lott was just taking his shoes off and making his way up the steps when the boys rode up.

"Woah horse!" commanded Frankie, pulling to a stop.

"Brought yore boy home, Mister Wilson and a mess of fish to boot," exclaimed Frankie pointing to the line.

"So I see and by the looks of ya, I think you must a got in there with him to get them," laughed Lott. "You better change into some dry clothes. John, go in there and get some of James Earl's stuff. I believe it will probably fit him. That's a mighty fine horse you got there, boy."

"Yes sir. My papa give it to me for my birthday," answered Frankie, swelling with pride.

Through the years, Lott had never discouraged John's friendship with Frankie even though he still held Frankie's father personally responsible for Jake's death. When it came to the Olliver family and the relationship that existed between the two boys, Lott had remained silent.

John could always sense his father's hostility with each mention of the Olliver family. At times it was difficult, but Lott promised himself that he would not interfere; if Frank Senior was guilty, it would be the arm of God that would bring him to justice and that alone.

John and Frankie headed down the hall toward John's room. The door opened in front of them and to the boys' surprise, John's sister and Rebecca brushed past them into the hall.

"Well, look here now, Miss Becca. I believe the dogs has done brought in a couple of skunks. They look like wet 'uns too," laughed Sister, pointing at the two dampened young men.

"I don't know about that, Sister. They look kind of cute that way to me. 'Specially that dark haired one," said Becca stepping over to John and pushing his hair out of his eyes.

"I still say they both look mighty ugly to me," replied Sister, backing against the wall and edging her way down the hall as if the boys were contaminated.

"I'll tell ya who the skunk is, and it's you, Sister. You's also a halfbreed skunk. Half skunk and half mule. You know what that makes you? Not a jackass, but a blond haired skunkass," stated John as he and Frankie chased Sister down the hall barking like a pack of dogs.

Mrs. Wilson, hearing the commotion came out of the kitchen.

"What in the world is goin' on out here?" she questioned, catching Sister before the boys could grab her. "You boys botherin' her again, ain't ya? And them bad words. We don't use that kind of talk 'round here, John Wilson."

"No Ma'am, Mamma, but as usual, Sister is runnin' that mouth of hers, and we ain't even touched her," replied John. "Sometimes, I'd like to tear that tongue out of her mouth and feed it to the hogs."

"John, Sister, we got guests in our home, and we going to act civilized, you hear. You boys go get dressed and leave Sister be. Sister and Becca, come with me to finish supper. Frankie, you stayin' the night with us?"

"Yes Ma'am, if'n you don't care," replied Frankie politely.

"I don't mind. You just part of the family anyway."

John grabbed Becca's hand and led her to the back of the porch where he could talk without any of Sister's agitating remarks.

"You stayin' over tonight with us, Becca?" questioned John, hoping Sister had invited her.

"No sir, Mister John, but I wish I was. I might even sneak in yore room and pull the cover off ya," giggled Becca, snuggling up. "I'm just going to have supper, and Papa's going to come get me after while."

"Well, I wish you was stayin' and I'd probably just grab you and pull you under them covers before you pulled them covers off me, that is if'n you had the nerve to sneak in my room," said John, feeling confident that one day Becca would be under the covers with him for good. "Well I'd better get dressed. I got them fish to clean. By the way, how do ya stand that sister of mine? She drives me bat hell crazy at times."

"John, she ain't so bad, that is, when she's away from you. I'd better get used to her, specially if'n, if'n," stammered Becca. "Anyway, when you get dressed, I'll help ya with them fish."

Becca was only a year older than Sister and since her family lived only a mile down the road, they had become good friends. The best part was that when she came to see Sister, she could spend time with her John.

That night after supper, Lott remembered a message for the boys. "John, Robert Clearman and Tim Johnson came by here 'bout noon, and they told me to tell ya that they's campin' and settin' out hooks up at red bluff and for you to come on if'n you can," stated Lott, pushing his chair back from the table. "May I be excused, Mrs. Wilson?"

"Maw, can we go settin' hooks tonight? We won't get in no trouble," interrupted John.

"We got guests, son," replied Mrs. Wilson, glancing over at Becca knowing her feelings were hurt when John had chosen the fishing trip over her company.

John, noticing Becca's downcast face, restated his proposition. "Mamma, I ain't going to go nowhere when Becca is here. But she told me she was goin' home after while, and I ain't wantin' to leave 'fore then."

"You fellows going to carry Toby with ya tonight to keep ya out of trouble, ain't ya?" questioned Lott quickly, to break the tension.

"No sir, Mister Wilson. We kind of outgrowed that long time ago," replied Frankie.

"He sure did take care of us on many a huntin' and fishin' trip," interrupted John. "You remember that time when the creek was up and he pulled us out. We'd been gone'rs if'n he hadn't been there."

"That's the Gospel truth, John. I'd done gone under one time when he got hold of my arm," replied Frankie.

"How's Toby doin' these days, Frankie?" asked Lott.

"He's fittin', I guess for an old niggar that got crushed up. He can't work the fields no more. Papa just lets him work 'round the barn and take care of the livestock. Sometimes he does do some drivin' for us. If'n it weren't for his wife and two boys, Papa would probably sell him off."

"Boys, Toby was the first Negro I ever seen in this country, and we go back a long ways. You better appreciate how he has took care of you two through the years. I sure hope you don't sell him," replied Lott, wanting to defend his old friend.

Toby's hip had been crushed when he and another slave were clearing some farmland. He had tried to rescue his dog that was asleep in the path of the falling tree. It took him months to recover, and when he did, he could barely walk.

It wasn't long before Becca's father picked her up, and as soon as she was out of sight, John and Frankie took off like lightning to the creek.

They could see a campfire and hear the chatter of Robert and Tim as they got the hooks on the lines, preparing for a night of fishing, jokes and the telling of tall tales.

"'Bout time you boys got down here. We done give up on ya," said Robert who was cutting some cane poles for the lines.

"I know why you's late," teased Tim. "That good lookin' Walker gal was down at yore house. I see'd her there. John, you ought to brought that woman down with ya."

"Well, Mister Timothy, believe me, I wouldn't of minded it, if'n I could've left that sister of mine at home," stated John, always amused by the things Tim could bring up.

"I'll tell ya sump'n else. I was just thinkin' the other night. If'n the Good Lord would say to me that I could place a sixteenth of an inch somewhere on that Becca's body to do her some good, you know, there ain't nowhere I could put it," remarked Tim.

"Dream on dreamer," replied John grabbing him and wrestling him to the ground, pretending to be angry.

Tim was a year older than John, but because he was small, he looked much younger. Boys would often pick on him, but to their surprise, he was stronger than he looked, and when angered, he would fight anyone. Many times it was the picker of the fight who went home with a black eye and bloody nose, not Tim.

Robert was just the opposite. He and Tim were about the same age, but Robert was already over six feet tall and weighed nearly two hundred pounds. He had a large stomach that bulged out over his belt. Robert was a bully at times, but when someone threatened him, he would usually back down and laugh his way out of a scrap.

Greetings aside, the boys soon had the hooks in the creek and settled themselves around the fire for their usual night of fun and occasional nips from the bottle. Tim would always sneak into his father's supply and bring at least one bottle of prime corn whiskey with him on these fishing trips. This evening, the conversation turned to the war.

"John, you know what I heard. I heard that Ben Thomas, up the road a piece, just joined the army and he done left for somewhere up in north Mis'sippi. He's going to be a horse soldier, and they says he's ridin' with Gen'ral Forrest," said Tim, lying back and watching the smoke curl up through the tree branches. "If Paw lets me join up, I'll kill the hell out of them Yankees."

"Only thing you'd kill is the whiskey bottles. First time one of them Yanks took a shot at ya, you'd place that little butt of yores in a hole and pull the grass over ya," laughed Robert who, as usual, was trying to get something started with Tim.

Tim jumped up and grabbed a limb as if to whack Robert on the head. "I'll tell you sump'n. If'n you ever got in one of them battles, the only place them Yankees would shoot you would be in the back, cause you'd be runnin' from them, scairt to death," teased Tim as he swished the limb past Robert's head and then instead of hitting him, threw it into the fire.

"I don't think any of us need to do no fightin'. It ain't all fun and games; a lot of folks is gettin' killed up there," commented Frankie.

"We got a letter from James Earl a while back, and he says that we is really givin' them boys up north a hard time and he thinks that this here war ain't going to last much longer," stated John. "You know, they got him workin' with the horses. Sump'n like takin' care of the ones that pull them big cannons."

"Well, I'll tell ya one thing, the next time they tries to raise a company here or needs some more fightin' men, I'm going to join up. Paw done said he ain't going to stop me. Ole Mister Tim is going to shoot him some Yanks," bragged Tim, marching around the campfire pretending to be shooting at imaginary forces.

"You ain't going to join no army, Tim; and talkin' 'bout horses, John, you going to race my thoroughbred tomorrow, ain't ya? I bet he can beat ole Lightnin'," prodded Frankie.

"I don't know, Frankie. Paw don't much like me to race him, not till James Earl gets home. It's my brother's horse, and Paw don't want nothin' to happen to it."

"You just afraid you going to get beat, that's what's got yore dander up," replied Frankie.

"I ain't 'fraid of that. Lightnin' ain't never been outrun, and that ole nag of yores ain't got a chance," argued John. "I might just ask Paw in the morning."

The boys checked the line several times during the night, and each time they ended up with a string of catfish. About three in the morning, they called it a night and tried to get some sleep. Tomorrow wouldn't be just a normal Sunday. Tomorrow, there was going to be a horse race.

The next morning the boys headed home, tired and sleepy, but with a sense of independence for the night to themselves. After lunch, John and Frankie began to execute their plan.

Lott had gone to the smokehouse to get some sausage for the next morning's breakfast, when John called out, "Paw, you mind if'n I use the buggy this afternoon? I thought I might get Becca and go for a little ride," asked John, holding the door open so his father could get some extra light, afraid to ask about what he really wanted.

"You know I don't care nary bit, as long as you take care of Miss Becca and maybe the horse, too," smiled Lott. "I used to be a young'un and there ain't no better way to spend an afternoon, than with a good lookin' woman."

John hurried out to the stables where Frankie had his horse saddled, and after chasing Lightning around the stables for a few minutes, finally had him harnessed. It wasn't long before Frankie on his thoroughbred and John sitting high and dignified in his family's buggy were ready for an afternoon of excitement.

In the meantime, Lott had carried the sausage into the kitchen and was now sitting on the front porch watching the boys as they scurried around the barn.

John and Frankie had to come directly in front of the house and by the porch on their way to town. Studying the boys closely as they rode to the porch, Lott motioned for them to pull over.

"John, ain't ya got sump'n to ask me?" said Lott, leaning over to where he could get a better look into the buggy.

"I don't rightly know, Paw. What you got on yore mind?" replied John, looking surprised and feeling uncomfortable.

"Well, I see you got our fastest horse harnessed up. And lookin' a little closer, I see a saddle in the back. Puttin' that all together, I bet you two is going to do some racin'. Don't ya think you ought to ask yore Daddy first."

John looked down. "Paw, I was afraid ya might not let me race him, if'n I asked ya."

"John, we taught you how to care for them animals and I have confidence in yore ability and judgment. All you have to do is ask," replied Lott. "You boys be careful and John, I expect you to take care of James Earl's horse, you hear me?"

"Thank you Paw. I'll be 'specially careful. I'll ask from here on out."

Frankie rode down to the track while John headed into the village to pick up Becca. She was sitting in her front porch swing eagerly waiting, when John pulled the horse to a stop. He couldn't remember when Becca had looked more radiant. She bounded down the front steps and held her skirt up so she would not trip.

Reaching down to help Becca into the buggy, John was suddenly speechless. He had often seen her long legs, but they seemed more beautiful than he had remembered and her blouse, loosely laced up the front, was bulging.

Noticing John's stare, Becca straightened her dress and slid in next to him.

"John, I hope you don't mind the way I look," teased Becca, reaching over and touching his long curly hair that flowed over his shoulders. "How you going to be able to talk to me when we get married if you're so quiet now," continued Becca, giving him a quick kiss on the cheek.

"Becca, when we get married, don't worry none 'bout my talkin' and you know sump'n else, you got more shape in yore legs than I do. You really get to me sometimes. I guess that's what love does to a fellow," replied John, glad he was able to come up with some explanation for his embarrassment.

"So you do notice my legs sometimes, Mister Wilson. I don't show them to just anyone," teased Becca.

"Yeah, I notice a lot of things about ya that stirs me up," replied John placing his arm around her shoulder and pulling her to him.

John snapped the reigns and they started for the tracks. They talked about the fishing trip and all the boys had done the night before, but John stayed off the subject of marriage, not because he didn't love Becca, but because he wanted to finish his schooling first. Becca was only fifteen years old. He felt she needed to get a little older to give them both a chance to grow up some.

The buggy bounced and rattled as it made its way over the rough country roads. At the McLain house, one of the finest in Newton County, Becca asked John to slow down so she could get a better look.

"John, ain't that house sump'n with its two stories and those tall, white columns? I hope you and me has a place like that someday," sighed Becca, reaching to hold his hand.

"Ain't one like our log house good enough for us, Becca?" replied John, feeling belittled. "A big house don't necessarily make a good home."

"John, you know what I mean. When you become a lawyer and we move to some big town, we might just have a city house like that," replied Becca, hoping she had not offended him.

They finally reached the racetracks where Uncle Jake and Minsa had run many good horses to victory years before. The grounds were still owned by the

Wilsons and with the exception of the track, nothing much had changed.

No one had taken the time nor interest to keep the tracks up, but it was still suitable for racing. The public was allowed use of the area and since it was located next to the Chunky River, many in the community would gather under the hugh oaks for Sunday afternoon picnics and swimming.

Frankie was already trying to make bets that he would beat John's champion, Lightning. Frankie hoped he had finally found an avenue of success.

Robert and Tim arrived about midafternoon and teased Frankie about how bad John was going to beat him. They also circulated the grounds placing bets against him. Their betting irritated Frankie more than the teasing.

"Frankie, Tim and me want to place a bet with ya," exclaimed Robert, pretending to be supporting Frankie.

"Sounds good to me. This is the day the Wilsons and Mister John is going to taste some dust," bragged Frankie. "How much you willin' to bet?"

"Me and Tim going to bet five dollars each," replied Robert. "But, we bettin' on John to win the race."

"You just wait and see, Robert. Ole Thunder is at least a hand taller than John's horse and them long legs is going to take that track apart. And by the way, I'm just going to love spendin' yore money," Frankie replied angrily.

John and Becca finally arrived and leisurely strolled around the grounds to see who was there and to talk with friends. Professor Hendon and his family were settled on a blanket under one of the big oak trees next to the river.

John always had a special relationship with the professor because he had encouraged John in his studies and challenged him to set his goals beyond the Coon Tail community. There was also a family connection since he was the only one left who was there the night of the shooting. John also remembered how much his Uncle Jake had enjoyed spending time with the professor.

Just as they were getting into a discussion about how the southern states had a legal right to secede, Frankie came over and interrupted. "John, you 'bout ready for me to show ya how to run a horse?"

"Frankie, do we have to race them horses? I don't much care if'n you do outrun me," replied John, not making any effort to get up.

"You must be afraid I'm going to beat ya," said Frankie.

"If we got to race, let's get it on. Let's race them horses!" shouted John, jumping up and pointing to the track. "I guess that's what I brought that saddle for."

John and Becca walked over and unharnessed the horse, then placed the saddle and bridle on Lightning. John pulled his hair straight back and Becca tied it so it would not get into his eyes. He slipped his shirt off and quickly mounted.

Becca stood below admiring every move he made. She thought, "Has God ever made a man more perfect?"

The stallion pawed the ground and reared up several times before John got him under control. With muscles bulging and already shiny with sweat, John pulled on the reigns.

"Do I get a big kiss if'n I win this race?" he said, reaching down and stroking Becca's cheek. Suddenly the horse bolted forward and she quickly moved away, afraid of being hurt by the excited animal.

"John, you'll get a kiss even if'n you lose."

"Alright Frankie, let's get this thing over with!" shouted John amidst the shouts of the bystanders.

"I hear ya, John! Let's line them up and, Doc Pinson, you fire yore pistol for the start."

The two boys struggled to get their spirited animals in line so neither would have an advantage. Finally, with the horses fairly close together, Doc fired his pistol and sent the animals galloping down the stretch.

John knew that to win this race against a taller horse and one that appeared to be a strong sprinter, he would have to take every advantage. His Uncle Jake had bred his quarterhorses to have an explosive start that could run the distance. He had to get to the inside rail as soon as possible. That would force Frankie to the outside, and his horse would have farther to run. When it came to the final stretch of the two mile run, John prayed Lightning would have the stamina to withstand the pressure of being pushed to his limits.

As John had hoped, Lightning bolted down the track and headed to the inside. By the time they reached the far end of the run, he was four lengths ahead. When they made their turn and were sprinting down the far straight away, the only sound was the thundering hoofbeats of two stallions fighting for the lead. By the time the horses had reached the far turn, Frankie pulled within a length of John, and John feared that unless there was a miracle, Frankie would take him on the last stretch.

Frankie knew he was closing in on a win and wanted an impressive victory. He had worn spurs and when his horse began to clear the far curve and the final straight away was just ahead, he pushed back with his heels hard against his thoroughbred's flanks, sending blood spurting through the dusty air.

Then the miracle John hoped for occurred. Frankie lost control. The thoroughbred, which had never felt the pain of a spur, broke through the fence and began bucking and kicking as he tried to unseat his rider. The third time the horse reared up, Frankie went flying over Thunder's head to the ground.

John flashed past the finish line and looked back to see how close the race had been. He was startled to see Frankie in the distance frantically trying to catch his horse.

When the crowd realized Frankie was not injured, the incident became amusing. Frankie would ease up to his horse to grab hold of its bridle, and every time Thunder would bolt away snorting and bucking. The spectators roared in laughter every time the animal repeated his hilarious routine.

At first, Frankie didn't hear the laughter, but once he realized he had gone from possible victor to the laughing stock of the community in a matter of seconds, his expected pride turned to disgust and hatred.

John pulled Becca up behind him and they cantered down the track toward

Frankie. Robert and Tim were also headed for the loser but, as usual, were full of mischief.

"Frankie, that thing must have gone wild on ya!" shouted Robert. "You ought to put that act in the circus!"

"Frankie, you ought to ride in one of them rodeos. That's one buckin' son-of-a-bitch!" screamed Tim, laughing so hard he could hardly keep up with Robert.

John and Becca quickly rode to the turn where the horse had left the track.

"You just shut it up right now! He just run one helluvah fine race. Sump'n just scairt that horse. If'n you don't, I'm going to come back up here and deal with both of ya," threatened John.

Frankie, angry, frustrated, and ashamed began throwing sticks and rocks at Thunder and eventually drove the horse into the woods that bordered the track.

John, puzzled, dismounted and walked over to console his friend.

"You had me beat, Frankie. You ran some kind of a good race," said John reaching out his hand.

"I don't want to talk about it, John. My paw gave me a dud of a horse and like you said, 'It ain't nothin' but an ole nag,'" replied Frankie as he made his way to the road leading to his house.

"Wait a minute, Frankie!" shouted Becca. "John and I'll help ya catch yore horse. Just hold up a minute!"

Frankie stopped, turned, and pointed to the woods.

"I just ran that sorry bastard off to the woods, and as far as I'm concerned, he can stay in there, saddle and all. I don't want him. He just made me the biggest fool in Newton County," replied Frankie, tears streaming down his face.

"Frankie, you going to walk home? We'll take you in the buggy. It's might near four miles to yore house," said John, as he and Becca walked behind him.

"You two just leave me be. I'm going to walk home, and I don't need no company."

John and Becca watched as he moved off down the road. They then returned to the track, and with the help of Robert and Tim, caught Frankie's horse. The next morning, John returned him to the Ollivers. Frankie pretended to appreciate their effort, but inwardly, he swore that one day he would beat John Wilson in something more important than a horse race.

11

SLAVE AUCTION

THE COOL DAYS OF SPRING SOON GAVE WAY TO A HOT, HUMID summer and long hours in the fields for the Wilsons and the other farmers in Newton County. Occasionally a thundershower would roll through late in the afternoon, giving both man and beast temporary relief from the sultry heat.

Meanwhile, no one had seen much of Frankie since the race. All the boys in the community worked from daylight to dark during this time of year and had little time to socialize, so it was only on Sunday that John missed his friend.

Frankie had not been at the last two church meetings, and John was concerned. In the past, they would visit every week, even if for only a few minutes.

On Saturday, the first day of August, a slow steady rain forced Lott and John out of the fields, giving them a rest on their front porch. During the night, the weather cleared, and when the sun rose the next morning, a cool breeze ruffled through the tall oak trees surrounding the house.

The family dressed for church, packed their picnic lunch, and after the horses were harnessed to the wagon, started down the wet and slippery road to the First United Church in Little Rock which had now become the official name of the village.

John and Sister could hardly wait to see the other young people. It had been at least two weeks since John had seen Becca, and he wanted to ask Tim and Robert about Frankie. The wagon finally reached the church grounds where a large crowd of people had already arrived.

Robert and Tim sat on the front steps of the church teasing several of the young women, and in the center of the group was Becca, more beautiful than ever.

John leaped from the wagon and headed for the steps.

Robert threw up his hand and waved. "Over here, John Willy. How's our number one plowboy these days?" he shouted, rising from the step to be sure John had heard him over the crowd.

"I'm just as fine as any of you mulemen. I thought Sunday weren't ever going to get here. How ya doin' this morning?" asked John, easing up to Becca.

"You better watch it, young man. My mamma might be just watchin' where you puttin' them hands, if'n you ain't careful," teased Becca, pretending that John had let his hands wander.

"Becca, I can't see yore mamma and she knows I ain't going to get fresh," laughed John as he turned his attention to Tim. "Well Gen'ral, I don't see no uniform on you, yet. I figured you'd done joined up by now and would've had that Union army on its heels and a runnin' north."

"Well, you just keep yore jaws flappin, John. One of these days I'm going to be fightin' them rascals. You wait and see," stated Tim in a convincing tone.

"Yeah, I probably will too, Tim," replied John looking around the church grounds. "Becca, has any of you seen Frankie?"

"I ain't seen him, but Mrs. Olliver and Suzanne is here. I seen them goin' in the church a spell ago. Why don't we ask them," said Becca.

It was almost church time anyway, so the group hurried inside to find the Ollivers.

Mrs. Olliver said Frankie had been visiting her people in New Orleans for the past month and had only come home two days ago. Slightly under the weather, Frankie had persuaded his mother to let him stay home for just this one Sunday.

John was relieved and taking Becca by the hand, escorted her to his family's pew which was located directly in front of the Ollivers'. Ever since Becca was a little girl, she had always sat with the Wilsons.

Tim and Robert had slipped in the back pew where they could sneak out. But more often they were called down for misbehaving. A group of older women sat in front of the boys and during the hymns, they would often feel the spirit moving, and the more spirit they felt, the louder they sang. When Robert felt that the ladies were fully wound up, so to speak, he would nudge Tim and they would start howling like a pack of dogs and disrupt the entire church. On more than one occasion, the preacher would have to call them down and make them sit with their parents, a minor disgrace.

After dinner on the grounds, as John was climbing into the wagon to leave, Tim ran toward him. "John, hold up a minute. I got sump'n to tell ya, and you ain't going to believe it," exclaimed Tim. "I was talkin' with Suzanne, and you know what she said. She said her paw had give Ole Toby to Frankie and that he was a going to sell him at the slave auction in Meridian."

"That's a lie, Tim. I know better'n that. His Paw ain't going to give him to Frankie and if'n he did, Frankie sure wouldn't sell him. Toby means too much for that. I just don't believe it."

"Well, believe what you want, but Suzanne said it, and she don't normally lie," reaffirmed Tim.

"Lie or no lie, if Papa'll let me, I'm going to ride over to see Frankie. We got a lot of catchin' up to do. I'll straighten this rumor out for good."

Lott consented but insisted he get home before dark. Monday was a workday.

John found Mrs. Olliver and Suzanne sitting on their front porch when he arrived. John had always admired the Olliver's spacious home, a large two-story wooden frame style with six square columns supporting the porch roof. The house was painted white with red tile shingles instead of the split, whiteoak ones most people used. It wasn't as elegant as the ones John had once seen in Natchez, but for these parts, it was one of the best.

"Well John, I see we meet again today. Come on up here and sit a spell with us," said Mrs. Olliver, motioning him to a chair next to hers. "We going to cut a melon after while, and you sure welcome to have a piece."

John seated himself and replied. "Yes Ma'am, and I truly enjoyed our preachin' today, Mrs. Olliver. And Suzanne, I could hear yore pretty voice over everybody. Yore notes is clearer than them mockingbirds outside my window. I love to hear you sing."

"John, you just tryin' to be nice. You know yore mind was on Becca," teased Suzanne, pleased that John had noticed.

"John, has you heard from James Earl and Thomas lately?" asked Mrs. Olliver.

"Yes Ma'am. My maw gets letters pretty often. James Earl's been a little sick, but they doin' fine. They still after them Yanks."

"I been prayin' for them. I heard that two boys from Hickory and one from Decatur got killed a while back, somewhere up in Tennessee."

"Yes Ma'am, I heard that too," answered John, looking around for Frankie.

Suddenly, Mrs. Olliver pointed down the road. "Here comes Frankie. I suppose you probably came over to check on that boy."

John eased out of his chair, excused himself and made his way to the stables where Frankie was dismounting.

"Hey fellah. Where you been so long? Me and Tim thought the Yanks might've got ya."

Frankie made no effort to greet his old friend and began taking the saddle and bridle off his horse without looking at John.

"I been gone for a spell. I spent about a month in New Orleans and I been busy 'round the place," replied Frankie as he led the horse into the stable.

"Frankie, is sump'n wrong that you ain't come to see us lately?"

"Naw, John. Just like I says, I been gone and I been busy. That's it in a nutshell. Ain't nothin' wrong."

Glancing over at John, Frankie thought, "You made a fool out of me at that horse race and it ain't never going to happen again, and Becca ain't never going to see me cry again either."

"Well, Frankie, I'm glad there's nothin wrong. We all been worried. There's one rumor I think some fools spreadin' around Little Rock you ought to know about."

"What's that, John?" asked Frankie, puzzled.

"Frankie, I heard talk that yore daddy gave Toby to ya, and you plan to sell him. That's a crazy lie, ain't it?"

Frankie abruptly slammed the stable door and turned to face John. "Alright, it ain't none of nobody's bus'ness, but I'm going to put things straight. My paw give me Toby, and I do plan to sell him in Meridian next week."

John grabbed Frankie by the shoulders, not to confront him, but to get his attention. "Frankie, you can't do that to Toby. Think of all them times he has carried us out in them woods huntin' and fishin' and everywhere else we wanted to go and took good care of us. Surely you can't sell him."

Frankie shook loose and stepped back, "Let me tell you sump'n, John. Toby ain't nothin' but a slave and a worn out one at that. If somebody buys him, he's probably going to have it easy since he can't do no more fieldwork."

"Frankie, Toby's got a wife and two boys. You can't take him away from them. That just ain't right."

"I sure can, if'n I want to. He's mine now," stated Frankie, staring John straight in the eyes.

John spent more than an hour trying to reason with Frankie, but making no progress, John realized the sun was setting. He saddled his horse and turned to his friend once more.

"Frankie, I can't believe you going to do this. I thought I knowed you better'n this."

"John, ain't nothin' wrong with me sellin' a slave, and if'n you want him so bad, why don't you just buy him," said Frankie turning and walking toward the porch where his mother and sister were still sitting.

"I might just do that, Frankie. I just might."

Frankie watched as John rode away and thought, "Mister John Wilson, I'm going to sell Toby and that horse Papa give me, and with the money, I'm going to buy me a thoroughbred that will put yore pride to shame. I ain't going to get embarrassed no more."

When John reached the edge of the property he reined his horse and turned in the saddle to see if Frankie would wave as he usually did. John could see Frankie on the front porch, but no hand went up and no, "Take care, John Willy" came echoing through the stillness.

He had just seen a side of Frankie he did not expect nor understand. John couldn't believe his best friend could sell a man, any man.

It was dark as he quickly stabled his horse. Supper had been left on the table for him, but the ordeal with Frankie left him with no appetite.

In the days that followed, John had little to say and even in his fieldwork, he had lost his humorous side. He aggressively attacked his work to the point of exhaustion instead of pacing himself. When they took a break, John sat quietly by himself, showing little interest in his father's conversation. The entire family was concerned.

After supper on the Wednesday following his visit with Frankie, Lott felt it was time to find out what was bothering the boy. "Sister, you know anything that could have upset yore brother? Did him and Becca have a fallin' out?"

"Paw, John and Becca's doin' fine, but you know, Frankie's been actin' strange this summer. Sump'n happened at Frankie's house the other evenin' that upset John, and I think it's that talk about the Ollivers' selling Toby," replied Sister.

Sarah interrupted and reached for Lott's hand, "Papa, that boy's got a problem he's been battlin' all week. I'm sure he's been a prayin' about it, and sooner or later, he's going to share it with us, and when he does, we better be ready to give him our support, no matter what it be."

"You right, Mamma. John has got a good head on him, and with the good Lord's help, he's going to work it out," said Lott leaning over to give Sarah her usual after supper kiss.

That night John tossed and turned. In his fitful dreams all he could see was Toby standing on an auction platform as the auctioneer sold him to the highest bidder. At about four in the morning, John suddenly came upon a plan. He quietly crossed the hall and tapped on his parents' door.

"Paw, you asleep?" whispered John.

"Well, I guess not, if'n I'm talkin', John. What you want?" replied Lott.

"Paw, I want you to come out on the steps for a while, if'n you will. I need to talk with ya."

Lott reached for a blanket to throw around his shoulders. The two made their way through the dark and settled themselves on the steps in the bright moonlight where they could see each other.

"Paw, you know that rumor 'bout Mister Olliver letting Frankie sell Toby. Well, Frankie's going to sell him. Frankie said he was, and yesterday, Tim was over there and he overheard Mister Olliver and Frankie talkin' 'bout it."

"John, I heard Sister talkin' about the same thing, and you know down here in the South, when you owns a slave, you can sell him. I don't like it, but that's the way it is."

"Paw, I can't let that happen. I'm going to do sump'n 'bout it, that is if'n you'll let me."

"Boy, what do you think you can do? I don't know nary thing you can do about it."

"Paw, I've thought and prayed a lot, and I want to buy him."

"Buy him! Boy, where you think you going to get money to buy that slave? And if'n you did, we Wilsons don't hold slaves," exclaimed Lott, alarmed.

"Papa, I know that sounds crazy, but I got almost four hund'rd dollars saved up for college. Since I was a young'un you has given me a few acres to farm on my own, and there has been times you has given me calves and hogs to raise. I've always saved my money."

"Son, I don't doubt you has the money, but that's yore future you talkin' 'bout. Yore Mamma and me can't let ya spend that money and 'specially on buyin' a slave."

"Papa, I weighed it over and over in my mind, and it just might cost me my chance to go to school, I don't know. But what I do know is I can't let this happen to Toby. Will you please talk to Mamma? I can still make more money."

"I'll talk to yore Mamma, but I don't like it and I ain't promisin' nothin."

After Lott finished telling Sarah what John had proposed, she pulled him closer to her and said tenderly, "Lott, I don't like that boy spendin' his hard earned money on tryin' to buy Toby, but I feel that him and the Lord has been doin' a heap of talkin' these past few days and what he's wantin' to do is sure 'nough Godly. I don't think we need to stop him."

Lott lay quietly for a few moments. "Sarah, I ain't looked at it like that. You got a mighty strong point," replied Lott, getting out of bed.

110

"Where you goin'?"

"Me and you is going to go over to John's room and talk some more about this thing."

The auction would be held on Saturday in Meridian, and John could hardly wait until Friday when he could head over. He planned to take the wagon, spend the night, and be rested and prepared. If Frankie and his father did not show up, then that would be fine too, and he would return home knowing Frankie had a good heart and was the person and friend he thought he was.

Friday finally arrived, and Lott let his son off mid-morning to get ready. John cleaned up, put on some of his better clothes, then headed to the stables to harness the horse. Sarah and Sister were on the porch with some food in a basket. As he was saying goodbye, the hall door opened and there was his father, dressed and ready for the trip.

"You didn't think I was going to let ya go by yoreself, boy. You carryin' a lot of money on ya and you know you's a little underage to make a buy, don't ya?

"You men take care of yoreselves, and don't get in no trouble," said Sarah. "You better be home sometime Saturday."

"Yeah, John Willy, don't get in no trouble. I hear there's a lot of ugly girls over in Meridian that will love the likes of you," teased Sister.

"Sister, watch yore mouth," scolded Sarah. "You better pray for them men, and I hope you hurry up and get out of that gigglin' stage. It gets on my nerves."

Lott and John slowly made their way over the rough and bumpy road leading to Meridian. The summer had been hot and dry, so they crossed the numerous creeks and streams without any problems.

Meridian was a treat for John. It was the largest town in eastern Mississippi and had many fascinating stores and attractions.

As the sun set, Lott and John entered the town, finding it still bustling with people and wagons moving in many directions. The railroad had finally reached the city, and with the war raging on the Mississippi, Meridian had become a supply center for the military for that part of the state. Everywhere they looked they saw men in uniform, and even in the woods at the edge of town where Lott was planning to bed down for the night, there was a whole regiment of horse soldiers camped. This made the trip even more exciting. John couldn't wait to tell Tim and Robert about the soldiers and their army outfits.

Lott and John slept on pallets laid out in the wagon bed, and as soon as the sun was up the next morning, they left the horse and wagon at their campsite and walked to the slave market on the south side of town next to the train tracks.

The auction had just begun, and Lott recognized Samuel Claborn, the Ollivers' new overseer.

"How's it goin', Mister Claborn?" Lott questioned, shaking hands. "Well, is you here to buy or sell this fine morning?"

John eased over, eager to hear what Claborn would say.

"Mister Wilson, this here's a most unusual sale. Mister Olliver done give an old slave to Frankie, and the boy wants to sell him so that he can buy himself one of them thoroughbred horses. Hell, the old niggar ain't worth much, bein' he is kind of crippled, and I sure hate to sell him since he's got a fam'ly on the place. You know, the boy wouldn't even come with me."

John became furious. "Did I hear you say he was going to spend the money on a horse! Damn that Frankie! That's the height of sorriness."

"You know the niggar, boy?" asked Claborn.

"We know him well, and we hope to buy him," replied John, never able to keep his thoughts to himself.

"Well, boy, I hope you well. He ain't worth much though. Good luck to both of ya. I hope you get him," said Claborn, moving over to where he could get a better look at the platform.

John and Lott had never been to a slave sale before and as they brought each Negro up, it startled them to see the sellers strip the slave's clothes down where the buyers could get a better look at what they were purchasing. In some cases, a slave would be brought up on the platform in leg irons; others would be in tears, but in all cases, the Negroes had their heads down in shame and degradation.

John nudged his father. "Paw, I don't want to ever see sump'n like this again. This ain't right. I pray we can just get Toby out of here."

John was interrupted by the auctioneer. "Well, Folks, this here next niggar ain't good for farmin' no more, but they say he can still work around the place and is good with the livestock."

Toby struggled up the steep steps and stood in the center of the platform, stripped from his waist up and head bowed. Even with his crippled legs, he still appeared strong and healthy.

"What do I hear? Do I hear two hundred?" barked the auctioneer.

After what seemed like several minutes, a tall man in the back of the crowd raised his hand and made the offer.

"Do I hear two fifty?"

John quickly raised his hand.

"How 'bout three? Do I hear three?"

A woman up front shouted out. "Three!"

"Do I hear three fifty?"

"Four hund'rd!"

Recognizing the voice, Toby raised his head and searched the crowd until he spotted John and Lott standing in the back.

"What you doin' here, John? You ain't buyin, is ya?" said Toby.

"Shut up, Niggar! You don't talk on the block," scolded the auctioneer.

"We got a bid for four hundred. Do I hear four fifty?" After a few seconds, "Goin' once, goin' twice,"

The woman raised her hand again, "Four fifty and that's my final bid."

John looked at his father. "Paw, how can this happen? I came so close. This just ain't right, Paw."

Lott put one arm around his son's shoulder and with his other hand, he pointed at Toby. "Five hund'rd dollars!"

"Five hundred once, twice. What about it lady?"

The woman shook her head.

"Then sold to this gentleman for five hundred dollars. Get him down."

John grabbed his father as tears streamed down his face. "Paw, where'd ya get the money? I thought that you was against this," sobbed John.

"Just give me yore money and you go get Toby while I settle the account. Where'd I get the money? Well, our birthday and Christmas presents is going to be a little on the short side for a few years, but we'll make it just fine."

John pushed his way through the crowd and threw his arms around Toby.

"Mas' John, what you an' Mas' Lott done here?" questioned Toby, knowing how the Wilsons felt about slavery.

"First thing, don't call us no master. You call me John and I guess you can call Paw, Mister Wilson and what we doin' here? We come to buy you and take ya back home with us."

They made their way back to the campsite, and after a quick meal were on their way. Never was there a happier group than the three men who returned home on that late evening of August 1862.

When Lott pulled up in the yard, Sarah and Sister ran out to to welcome Toby to the family.

"John, you let me off at the house, and you and Toby take care of the rig. Toby, you can stay on the porch 'till we fix you a place."

"Yassuh, Mas' Wilson. I means, Mist' Wilson," replied Toby. "I shore wants to thank you for buyin' me. You mind if'n I call myself Toby Wilson instead of Toby Olliver?"

"Toby, you can call yoreself anything you want, and if'n you will help us make up the money we spent on ya, you can be free as the breeze. Shoot, you can be free and leave here now if'n you want to. We didn't buy ya for no slave."

"Mist' Wilson, if'n it's the same to you, I'll just stay right here," smiled Toby.

That night, Lott lay in bed tired, but proud of what he and his son had done.

"Sarah, I can't believe it. I guess it's against everything I has ever preached about. Tomorrow, we going to have to turn that corncrib in the barn into a room of sorts. Jake and me built it just as solid as this here house with them big timbers and we made it tighter 'an ever to keep them rats out of the corn. We'll just put in a chimney and fireplace and add a window or two, and he'll have might near as good a place as this'n, maybe better."

Sarah raised up on one elbow and pushed her husband's hair out of his face. "Lott, you know how my Papa, bein' a preacherman like he is, can't afford to say much. But he don't take to holdin' slaves. What we going to tell him about Toby?"

Lott lay still for a few moments.

"Sarah, we didn't buy no slave today. We freed one."

12

THE THINNING RANKS

AN OCTOBER FROST TURNED THE OAK, HICKORY, AND POPLAR trees to shades of red, yellow, and gold, making the hillcountry as beautiful in the fall as it was in the spring.

Lott, John, and Toby worked diligently to get the crops gathered. When time allowed, they worked on the living quarters for Toby. They added two windows to the outer walls of the corncrib and cut out a section to build a fireplace. The crib only had one door, so Lott cut another opening in the outer wall for a second. A porch was planned for that side of the barn where Toby could sit and relax.

The only problem was the scent from the barnyard. But when this was mentioned, Toby replied, "Mist Wilson, I don't smell nothin'. All I smells is sweet freedom, and I take that any day."

Lott warned Toby that occasionally he might have visitors at night and he shouldn't be alarmed. The Choctaws who had remained in Mississippi and lost their land were now roaming from farm to farm looking for work or were sharecropping. Toby knew there was a quilt up in the loft in case one of the wandering Choctaws came by looking for a place to sleep.

The Indians were welcome at the Wilsons' place and often stopped to spend the night. Most of the time, Lott and his family wouldn't know when they came, but they always left a gift. It might be a bead bracelet, a split cane basket, or some other item the Choctaws thought the Wilsons could use.

As the weeks passed, Lott found that even though Toby was crippled, he was able to do more work than he had expected. He was excellent with the horses and cattle, and with enough time, he could handle the fieldwork as well.

On October 26, John turned seventeen and on his birthday, Sarah gave him a party. She told John to invite as many friends as he liked; there would be a supper, followed by a dance. John invited fourteen and with his parents' encouragement, he asked Frankie and his sister, Suzanne.

With the money Frankie got from selling Toby and Thunder, he had purchased one of the finest and fastest thoroughbreds in eastern Tennessee. He had already won several races but had not gotten up the nerve to ask John for a rematch with Lightning. He wasn't sure he could handle defeat again, just in case Lightning should prove to be the faster horse.

Frankie was secretly relieved that John and his father had purchased Toby. Frankie regretted what he had done but had been afraid to tell his father. Even so, Frankie finally had what he wanted: a horse that could possibly outrun Lightning.

Now he was determined to get back into good grace with John and his old friends, Tim and Robert, who had been ignoring him since the sale. When he got the invitation, he knew this was his chance to make amends, and he didn't plan to lose the opportunity.

The evening finally arrived, and the boisterous group began appearing on horseback and in buggies. John and Sister were on the front porch to welcome each guest.

Robert was the first boy to arrive and, as usual, began teasing. Getting down from his horse, he bowed and lowered his hat, "Mister John Willy, or do I call you, Master Willy since you has become a big time slaveholder?"

"Robert, you just tie that ole horse down near the barn and watch that mouth of yores. You know Toby's free if'n he wants to be, and we damned sure ain't nary slaveholders," replied John, giving Robert a kick in the seat.

"Well, he works here and lives here. I still say he's a slave and you is the holder," laughed Robert.

It wasn't long before a buggy driven by Becca's father came rumbling up the drive. John had been thinking all week about her and the dance. This was one way he could hold her close without his mother or Mrs. Walker scolding them for being too familiar.

"Good evenin' Mister Walker. I'm sure proud to see ya again."

"Good to see you, John. Looks like yore folks are going to have a house full tonight. I know you is going to have a good time, and you sure better take care of my Becca," smiled Mister Walker, extending a hand.

"Well, John, ain't ya going to welcome me too?" snapped Becca. "And Daddy, I'll have you know that John always takes care of me."

"I know, daughter, I was just teasin' John a little bit. I'd trust that boy with my life, if'n I had to. John, is yore pappy here? I'm going to sit a spell with him before I go back to the house," said Walker stepping down from the buggy.

"Yes Sir, he's in the kitchen helpin' mamma. I'll take the horse and buggy for ya. Go on in and make yoreself at home."

"Papa, I don't want ya to stay too long. I don't need no lookin' after," said Becca as she walked with John toward the barn where they took care of her father's horse and returned to the house hand in hand.

"John, you going to take me for a walk in the moonlight tonight, ain't ya?" said Becca, squeezing John's hand and giving him the slight wink and smile that usually brought on a blush. "I've been savin' my kisses for ya all week, young man, and I got bunches of them."

John grabbed her around the waist and whirled her around so fast it slung one of her shoes off.

"Sure, I'm going to take ya for a walk, and if'n you lucky, I might even show ya the loft of the barn," exclaimed John.

"Put me down right now, you Sampson, you!" exclaimed Becca. "My Papa might catch you if'n you force me in that horrible ole loft, and if'n he don't, Toby would hear us rustlin' up that hay," laughed Becca.

With each passing month, Becca was becoming more beautiful. John had always enjoyed being with her, but lately, he was finding it hard to stay away from her, and the thought of a moonlight walk and her kisses were about all that filled his mind as he looked into those deep green eyes.

Just as they reached the house, Tim came riding up and with a loud yell told his friends to gather round. "Alright folks, you soon going to be lookin' at a soldierboy. My paw done give me the go ahead to join up as soon as the next one is mustered in around here. I'm goin' in! We going to get this here war over and quick!" he shouted.

Robert briskly saluted. "Yeah, you goin' in. And them Yanks going to run you back home, too."

The group laughed at the way Robert had stuck out his stomach and saluted Tim while keeping a safe distance from his quick fist.

No sooner had Robert finished his salute, than Frankie and Suzanne pulled up.

"'Bout time you came to see us," said John. "Get out and come on in. It's time for supper."

John shook hands with Frankie and helped Suzanne down from the buggy. Holding her by the hand and carefully catching her around the waist, he eased her to the ground.

"This young lady is really growin' into some kind of a pretty thing," thought John. "That black hair and those dark brown eyes going to capture some fellow's attention one of these days."

"Glad to be here, John Willy. Let's get this party goin'," replied Frankie, slapping John on the back just as he had always done when they greeted one another.

Soon the birthday supper was finished, John had opened his presents, and the young people headed to the porch for the dancing. Mrs. Wilson's organ was brought out in the hall, and several adult musicians were on hand to help with the music.

For the next three hours, the boys and girls shook the very foundation of the house as they danced to every tune. Shrieks of laughter could be heard almost to Little Rock and when they took a break, the girls would gather in one group to catch up on gossip and discuss the boys while the boys talked about the war.

As the evening wore on, they played games that would send couples strolling through the dark shadows where a kiss could be stolen.

Frankie wanted desperately to take one of those walks with Becca, but knowing this was impossible, he asked Sister instead. He always ended up with Sister, but that wasn't so bad.

Frankie seemed as friendly as before, but something was missing. He didn't seem as genuine as he used to be, and he didn't mention his new thoroughbred nor did he ask about Toby.

116

Soon it was time for the guests to head for home. Wanting to talk to John in private, Frankie waited so he and Suzanne would be the last to leave. Frankie then asked John if he could walk with him to the barn and help him with his rig.

"John, I been wantin' to talk with ya for a spell now, but I just didn't know how," said Frankie, leaning on the side of the barn.

"You don't owe me no explanation, Frankie," replied John, reaching down to pick up a piece of straw.

"I think I do. It was wrong for me to sell Toby, and I don't think I'll ever forgive myself. I'm just proud you were able to buy him. I hope you find it in yore heart to forgive me," said Frankie, shuffling nervously.

"Frankie, we been friends all our lives, and ain't neither one of us perfect. As for Toby, we need that man here, especially since my brothers are gone. I always feel things just has a way of workin' out for the best."

The two boys embraced like old times, then made their way to the house where Suzanne was waiting. John helped Suzanne up on the buggy and with the crack of the whip, they were on their way.

"See you Saturday, John Willy!" shouted Frankie.

"See ya, Becca, Sis," added Suzanne.

Frankie wanted to ask John for a race, but not now, maybe in a few months. Their relationship was on the mend, and he didn't want to push it.

John turned to Becca. "You stayin' over tonight, or am I carryin' you home?"

"I'm stayin' over with Sister, tonight. I told yore Mamma I'd help her clean up."

"Well, when you get through, come on out front and we'll swing a little, talk a little, and I might finish gettin' the rest of them kisses you holdin' for me," smiled John.

A little later, as the household quieted down and John and Becca were alone on the porch, the conversation drifted to Toby and the issue of slavery. In contrast to the Wilson family, Becca felt slavery was an accepted way of life in the South and necessary in order to maintain their society and bring wealth to the states.

"John, them slaves is better off over here than they is in Africa and most holders take better care of them than their own folks. They has to if'n they is going to stay healthy for the fields. And look how wealthy them Ollivers has become."

John, angry at Becca's reasoning, got out of the swing and walked toward the steps.

"Becca, I don't care what you say. Just go down to our barn and ask Toby how he'd like to go back to bein' a slave. I'll tell ya right now, he'd say, 'No thank you!' I'm turnin' in. I'll see ya in the morning," replied John walking down the hall to his bedroom. "And for the Ollivers, someday I'm going to do just fine, and I ain't going to need no slaves to help me make a livin'," said John, pointing to his head.

"John, don't be mad at me. I just told ya how I feels," pleaded Becca, following him to his doorway.

"I'll be all right, and I ain't that mad. Let's just don't talk about it no more."

I

As winter approached, temperatures dropped and rains crept over the hillcountry taking the leaves off the trees and leaving the landscape quiet and dreary.

Because of the weather, neither the Union nor Confederate armies were able to mount much of a campaign. They spent this time preparing for the next spring's movements.

Some of the southern soldiers returned home to check on their families, homes and farms. Some had legal furloughs and others simply deserted with the intention of returning as soon as possible. But some never returned.

It was now two weeks before Christmas. The Wilsons were returning from church, huddled close in the wagon to keep warm. A strong north wind was blowing directly into their faces, chilling them as it whistled through the tree-tops and sent sheets of leaves dancing across the road in front of them. As they turned up the drive leading to the house, they noticed a strange horse tied to one of the posts next to the front steps, and by the way the smoke was swirling out of the chimney, they knew a fresh fire had been made.

Usually when someone rode up, Toby would meet them and take care of the animal, but Toby had been sick with the croup and hadn't left his quarters in several days.

As the wagon pulled up to the house, Lott and Sarah's bedroom door opened and out walked a man wearing a ragged gray uniform.

"Thought you'd never get through that preachin' service. I just made myself at home," said the stranger. Faced with a wagon full of blank stares, he bellowed, "You mean you don't even know yore own flesh and blood. I've lost a little weight and my beard's a little scraggly, but you ought to know yore own boy," continued the soldier, walking down the hall toward the wagon.

Suddenly Sarah exclaimed. "Thomas Stanley, what you doin' home? My boy's come home! Lott, our Thomas is home!" screamed Sarah, hustling down from the wagon to greet her son.

The family couldn't believe Thomas was back from Virginia and they crowded around him, almost knocking him down in their enthusiasm.

"Look at them stripes on his sleeve! I bet you's a sergeant, ain't ya?" exclaimed John.

Thomas pushed his chest. "I ain't no sergeant, Little Brother. I'm a corp'ral and that's about as good. But would ya look at how you and Sister has growed. I sure can't believe how you has changed."

"Well, let's get on in the house before we catch our death out in this here cold," said Sarah.

Thomas turned and pointed to the barn.

"Paw, what's Toby doin' here and livin' in our barn? He almost scairt me to death when I rode up to the place."

"That's another story we'll get into after a while and you ain't going to believe what you hear," answered Lott, hurrying the family into the house.

All afternoon the family sat around the warm crackling fire listening to Thomas' many tales of the battles he had fought in and the war in general. They were relieved to hear that James Earl was safe, even though he had been seriously sick at times.

Thomas had always exaggerated his exploits, and since he was an optimist, he painted an unrealistic picture of the war and the Confederate army. True, the southerners were winning battles, but their army desperately needed more men to fill depleting ranks.

"You boys don't mind carryin' yore talk to the kitchen, do ya?" asked Sarah, since it was evening and she wanted to retire. "Me and Sis is about ready to turn in. The fire is still burnin' in the wood stove, and it'll be nice and cozy back there."

"Mom, let me give you and Sis a kiss before you go," replied Thomas. "You don't know how many times I has dreamt about sittin' 'round this here fire, listenin' to that ole clock tick away, and bein' with my folks. This is heaven on earth."

The men then ambled back to the kitchen and made a fresh pot of coffee. Lott and Thomas packed their pipes for an evening smoke, and John sat eagerly ready to devour every word.

"Thomas, you told us a lot about them battles, but how 'bout tellin' me when this things going to get over and you boys can come home," said Lott, blowing on his coffee to cool it enough to take a sip.

"Papa, we's whipping them Yanks might near every time we line up against them, and since Gen'ral Bobby Lee is in charge of this here war, we givin them sure 'nough hell," stated Thomas, pushing another piece of oak into the stove. "I don't think them boys is a going to want to keep on gettin' shot just to keep us in the Union."

"What about Grant and Sherman comin' down the Mis'sippi'sippi? What about them?" questioned Lott.

"Papa, so what if'n they do come down the river. Ain't a damned thing they can do but get them boats sunk when they pass them big guns at Vicksburg. Some of them guns is so big I could crawl up in them barrels," countered Thomas.

Outside, they could hear the wind whip around the corner of the house with such force that it caused the swing on the porch to bang against the wall. Thomas pulled his chair closer to the stove.

"Papa, a while back we brought in a bunch of prisoners and tried to get some information from them and you know, they's boys just like me and James Earl, farmboys from Ohio and Indiana. And you know what? They don't know what they's fightin' for, and they wish Ole Abe would just call off this here shootin' match and let us all go home."

"That sounds good to me, Boy. I been scairt to death that sump'ns going to happen to you two," said Lott.

"Papa, one thing that kind of got us worried is that one of them Yanks, a second lieutenant, told us he heard Lincoln might be plannin' to free the slaves here in the South, if'n he wins this here war," said Thomas. "And you know, that might just give them northern boys sump'n to fight for. Like it is, they feel they's fightin' for nothin'."

Lott walked over to the stove and knocked the ashes out of his pipe.

"I'll tell ya what boy, I consented to let you fight in this here war cause I believe a state should have the power to govern itself to some extent, and our South is just too different from them northern States, anyway. And it ain't no reason for all them tariffs on everything we buy either. But from the start, I didn't think it would go this far. And I'll tell ya one more thing, if'n this here war becomes a fight to stop slaveholdin', then I don't care if'n you and James Earl just bring yoreselves on home."

"Papa, I don't think ole Abe is fool enough to try to free no slaves. Hell, some of them folks up north hold slaves too," reasoned Thomas.

John had been sitting quietly, content to listen to his father and brother's discussion, but now he had a question he had been wanting to ask them all night.

"Thomas, we's glad you got to come home, but just what you doin' here and how long you going to be able to stay?"

"Well, John Willy, Mister Bobby Lee has sent the word down to every outfit to pick some soldiers and send them home durin' the winter months to drum up some new recruits before spring. The Gen'ral feels that if'n we can get our army up some more and take the war to them real hard next spring, them northern folks is going to force ole Abe to quit this fight. And the quicker we can whip them, the more lives we'll save, and then me and James Earl can come on home."

"How many you going to try to get, Thomas?" asked John, excited about the mission.

"Well, me and Sergeant Stallings from over near Union is suppose to raise about a hund'rd soldiers in the north end of the county and have them ready to leave here by the first of the year. That's what we gotta do, John Willy."

Lott patted Thomas on the back as he rose from the table.

"You boys can stay up as late as you want, but for me, I've heard too much about this war, and I'm turnin' in. And John, don't you get no wild idea about joinin' no army. You too young."

"I don't want him, Papa. Two boys up there is enough for this family. Sure is good to be home. Me and John just going to stay up a little while longer. I got to ask this young'un about some of them local girls I been wantin' to hear about."

For the first time in John's life he felt one of his brothers was going to treat him as a grownup, and he couldn't believe Thomas was going to talk about women with him.

"How about that Sally Williams I had my eye on for Mrs. Thomas Stanley Wilson? I bet she's going to sure be glad to see this here soldierboy," smiled Thomas.

"Well, Big Brother, you might have to fight her ole man before you can make time with that woman. She got herself married last summer, and I hear she's got a young'un on the way."

"Hell! Ain't that just my luck," frowned Thomas. "Here I is fightin' for her and the South, and she up and gets married on me. That sure ain't much gratitude, is it?" grumbled Thomas.

"That gal was kind of wild anyway. Well, to hell with her. How about Jessie Clearman? She's better lookin' and can kiss a whole lot better," laughed Thomas.

"Jessie ain't married, and she still looks good," replied John. "Now you tell me about that battle up in Maryland. Did we get whipped?" probed John.

"Whipped! Hell no, we didn't get no whipping up there. We fought them sons of bitches to a standstill, and then marched back to Virginie. The only reason we went up there was to worry ole Lincoln and make him move his boys out of north Virginie to give us some relief. And we did just that. Them folks up in Washington were scairt silly when they heard we was comin' for a visit. Ole Bobby Lee is going to outsmart them devils come hell or highwater."

"I'm proud to hear that, and I sure wish I could be up there doin' some of that fightin'," said John getting up from the table.

"John, you's just where you need to be."

13

BOYS BECOME MEN

THOMAS WAS BIG NEWS IN THE LITTLE ROCK COMMUNITY. Parents and wives of men who had sons and husbands in the Newton County Rifles flocked to the Wilson home for any news. They also loaded him with letters to carry back.

Thomas set up his recruitment center at Walker's Store since most people in the community came in at least once a week to purchase goods and collect mail delivered by the stageline coming out of Meridian.

Over the months, the women at the United Church had been busy turning cotton and wool into cloth that was then made into uniforms. Thomas asked his mother to make him a new outfit since his old one was in rags. In a matter of days, he was sporting a fashionable uniform and a new pair of shoes.

With this new finery, he made a dramatic impression on the men who came by the store to talk about enlistment.

In a few days, as Thomas was sitting next to the woodstove in deep conversatiion, Tim, Robert, John, and Frankie walked briskly through the door. Tim faced Thomas and cleared his voice.

"Corp'ral Wilson, I'm here to enlist in the Confed'rate army, and I'm ready to sign them papers," he stated.

Thomas turned from the men and looked Tim over for a few seconds.

"How old is ya boy? You look like you is a little young, ain't ya?"

"I'm over eighteen. You can ask John here. He knows me."

Thomas laughed, "I remember who you is and I done talked to yore paw about it early this morning. Here, sign right here, and let's get you started on becomin' a sol'ger."

When Tim finished, Robert stepped forward.

"What is this? All you boys want to get in on the action next spring?"

Too bad John and Frankie is too young and by the way, how old is you, Robert?" asked Thomas.

Robert stood tall and straight, "I'm eighteen too, Mister Thomas."

"Well boys, you has now become men, and as of this minute, a member of the Newton County Rifles of the Thirteenth Regiment of Mis'sippi Infantry," stated Thomas.

The boys tossed their hats into the air and yelled as they slapped each other on the back and tumbled on the floor in excitement.

In a few minutes the celebration ended and the boys sat around the stove getting instructions and planning their departure to Virginia. For the rest of the afternoon they listened to Thomas talk about the battles he had fought in and how they, as new recruits, could survive future engagements. Tim had more questions than the other boys.

"Mister Thomas, tell me sump'n. Is it true you just march up close to each other and commence shootin'?"

"It's sump'n like that, Tim. First, each army tries to blow the hell out of each other with them big cannons, and when they think they has done about all the damage they can do, then the foot sol'gers advance," stated Thomas, enjoying every minute with his captivated audience. "We then march up to about as close as from here to that creek down at the edge of town and then them rifles start popping so fast, it seems like a continuous cracklin' commotion."

"Ain't that kind of scaiery?" said Robert, all eyes and squirming nervously in his chair.

"Sure it's a little scaiery, but when everybody starts that yellin' and it's either kill or get killed, you forget about fear. After while them zippin' sounds of shot whistlin' by yore ears and nippin' at yore clothes don't bother you too bad."

Frankie interrupted and looked over at John.

"How about John and me joinin' up too. We both about old enough to do some of that fightin' next spring."

"Frankie, you ain't but sixteen and John here is needed on our farm. You going to have to wait a spell before we need ya," replied Thomas.

John had been quietly listening to his brother's tales all afternoon and thought to himself, "Why can't I join just like the other boys. I'm just as fit as my brothers, maybe better'n James Earl."

He stood up and backed up to the stove to warm up some before he started for home.

"Thomas, I'm going to talk to Papa tonight about joinin' up. I can fight just as good as anybody," stated John, looking his brother sternly in the eyes.

"You can talk all you want, but you ain't joinin'. We need you at the house, and that's final, little brother. And Paw ain't going to waste no time talkin' about it either."

Thomas was eager to talk about his battle experiences and the war, but what he well knew but didn't discuss was the horror, death and destruction. He and James Earl stood a good chance of being shot or killed, and he didn't want to expose another one of the Wilsons to the slaughter that both armies, North and South, were experiencing.

When John reached home he lost no time asking permission. Lott and Toby were out at the woodshed splitting firewood when he made his move.

"Paw, you got time for me to talk to ya about sump'n important?" said John as he started helping his father with the wood.

"Do I have a choice?" grinned Lott, thinking John might be considering proposing marriage to Becca.

"Paw, I'm going to get right to the point. Tim and Robert has just joined the army, and I think I'm old enough to do the same," replied John, easing next to Toby and waiting for his father's reaction.

Lott slammed down the wood and grabbed John by the shoulders.

"Boy, you listen to me and listen well. You ain't joinin' no army, and that's final. I done got two boys up there, and I don't want to have to worry about another," stated Lott as he turned and walked toward the house.

"Just wait till I see that brother of yores. He done put a lot of nonsense in yore head."

Lott was already out of sight, but John heard him exclaim, "You ain't going to go, damn it, and that's final!"

John lowered his head and slumped down on the stack of wood.

"Toby, I can always tell when Papa's upset. He starts that cussin', and that's the only time he does it. But why can't he see I'm no different from any other boy, and about growed up now, anyway."

Toby eased over and placed his arms around him.

"Mist' John, don't get yore pappy wrong. He shore loves ya a bunch. You can tell how he looks at ya and is always talkin' good about ya. Ain't nothin' he can do about yore brothers who is already fightin', but he shore don't want to lose you too."

"I know, but like I say, he's got to realize I'm about growed, and I got to start makin' my own decisions. Toby, I'm going to talk to him again, but it ain't going to be today," concluded John. "You seen yore family lately?"

"Yassuh, I seen my boys the other day down at the mill, and I bet we talked fer an hour. They shore glad you done bought me and give me my freedom. They says my ole lady, Liza, is doin' fine too. I hopes to see her 'fore long."

"Well, I need to go see Frankie, and if'n you want, we might just ride over there about tomorrow," smiled John.

"I'se ready most any time Mist' John, just let me know."

The word spread rapidly that Tim and Robert had enlisted and as soon as Becca heard, she saddled her horse and rode to the Wilsons to see John. Becca knew that the boys had always been together, and she was afraid John might be on the verge of doing something foolish.

When she reached their house, Mrs. Wilson said John had gone to the swamp to check on the hogs that were feeding on the wild acorns and that he was probably on his way back by now. But Becca decided to ride down to meet him so she could talk in private without his sister's interference. She had gotten about a half mile through the woods following an old Indian trail when John suddenly came through the brush.

"Hey, woman! What you doin' down here in these woods?" exclaimed John. "Ain't ya afraid to be down here alone with an ole wolf the likes of me?" he joked.

"Sure I'm afraid, don't I look like it," smiled Becca. "Get up here on this horse, and I'll give ya a ride to the house or anywhere you want to take me."

"Not till I taste them sweet lips of yores," John replied.

Becca leaned down but just as their lips touched, John caught her around the waist and pulled her out of the saddle.

Slipping, they tumbled down a leafy slope and landed in a deep bed of freshly fallen leaves. John playfully wrestled until he had her shoulders pinned lightly to the ground.

"Dadburn it, you is one strong gal. You almost whipped me, didn't ya?" laughed John, rolling over. "Now, about them kisses?"

"No man who pulls me off my horse and rolls me down a hill is ever going to taste my lips. Not until I get good and ready."

She looked over at him and laughed, "And I'm ready. Come here you big ole country boy."

As they embraced, their passion made them forget everything that had been troubling them for the past few weeks.

Realizing they would soon be missed, Becca pushed John away as she spoke. "John, you know I love ya, and I don't want nothin' to happened to ya," said Becca, bending down to give him one more kiss. "And you better not do no foolish thing like joinin' that ole army."

John sat up and pushed his hair back. "Becca, what's wrong about fightin' for sump'n you believe in, and I do believe in the South and our cause. Like Thomas says, 'We going to push them Yanks hard next spring, and it's all going to be over.'"

Becca quickly stood and straightened her dress.

"And what if'n it ain't and what if'n you get yoreself killed? John, I'd die if'n anything happened to you. I plan to be yore wife and bear our chill'un someday."

"Becca, I ain't joined nothin' but the church so far," smiled John. "Let's go. It's gettin' dark."

John mounted the horse, reached for Becca's hand, and pulled her up behind him.

"You better lace up yore blouse before we get home," joked John.

"That's just like a man. Always tryin' to see sump'n he ain't s'pose to see."

"Ain't s'pose to see! They's right in front of my eyes," laughed John.

"Let's just go home and stop this kind of talk right now," replied Becca. "Yore mamma's going to be worryin' about us."

As they raced through the forest at a fast gallop, the horse would leap over a log or ditch and Becca would squeal with excitement while John would scream like Minsa when he was racing.

Arriving at the house, Becca visited a while with Sister, and as it was almost dark, John escorted her home.

A cold rain was falling so heavily the next morning that Lott postponed work until the weather let up. The family took their time at breakfast, and for a change, no one talked about the war.

Suddenly, Joe and Spot, who had been curled up under the house near the chimney, tore out from underneath the porch.

"Them dogs barkin' likes someone's comin' up, Paw," said John, rising from the table. "I'll go see what's goin' on."

He walked down the hall and to the front porch where a rider who was now dismounted hurriedly made his way up the steps with the hounds nipping at his heels.

"Get back up under that house, you devils! Get on now," scolded John as he stomped his feet. "They don't take kindly to strangers."

"That's all right, they didn't hurt me none. I'm Sergeant Stallings from over at Union. Is Corp'ral Wilson here?" he said, shaking the water off his hat and removing his oilcloth.

"Yes Sir, he sure is. Come on in," replied John. "You sure got on a nice uniform and them stripes is mighty impressive."

John led Sergeant Stallings into the kitchen, and after introductions, the Sergeant asked to speak with Thomas alone.

Thomas showed Sergeant Stallings to the front room so they could talk in private around the fire.

Thomas reported on how his recruitment was progressing and how they would have their quota before Christmas if things continued the way they had for the past week. Sergeant Stallings interrupted.

"Thank you, Corp'ral Wilson, but I've got a new order passed down, and we think you're the man for the job."

Thomas looked puzzled as Stallings paused.

"You know, our job is to get soldiers in the field next spring. It was brought to Colonel Carleton's attention that there's one group that we ain't touched yet, and that's them Choctaws roamin' 'round here," stated Stallings.

"Choctaws! That's crazy as hell, Sergeant!" exclaimed Thomas. "Why you think they's going to fight for the South? We cheated them and took their land. They ain't about to do no fightin' for us."

"They've fought in the past, and they'll fight now, if'n the right man asks them," continued Stallings. "And you is that man. Everybody knows how the Wilsons took up for them pore devils in years past."

Thomas took the poker and stirred the logs in the fireplace.

"Paw keeps up with where they's workin' and stayin'. But, what if'n I can't get them to join? What then?"

"Damn, soldier, promise them anything. Tell them we'll give them some land when this here fightin's over. Hell! Tell them anything, just get them in."

"And what if'n I don't do what you say?"

Stallings leaned forward and spit a large wad of tobacco juice into the fire.

"You don't have no choice, corp'ral. This here is a order, and if'n you get us them Choctaws, you is probably going to get an extra stripe on yore sleeve like mine, and if'n you don't, you probably going to lose the ones you got. You hear me clear."

"I got the order, but I sure as hell don't like it."

In a few minutes Sergeant Stallings left, and Thomas told the family what the army was planning to do. Lott agreed that the Choctaws had no reason to fight for the South, but since it was a military matter and Thomas was under order, Lott agreed to help.

For the three weeks preceding Christmas, Thomas rode over a three county area enlisting Choctaws. When they found out who Thomas was, they were eager to listen to him, and to his surprise, many joined.

On the Saturday morning four days before Christmas, Tim and Robert came to get John to go vine hunting in the swamp. On such a hunt and usually on a windy day, the boys would leave the dogs at home and would venture into the woods where squirrels had built nests among the vines that ran up into the large hardwood trees near the creek. One of the boys would shake the vines to scare the creature into the open, while the others would take their shots. On a good day, the boys would have a sack full in a matter of hours.

Tim had also invited Frankie and two of the Graham boys and told them to meet at the rock hole no later than eight o'clock that morning. Before Tim and his group reached the meeting place, they heard shooting near the creek and knew the hunt was already in progress. By mid-morning, the boys had killed over forty squirrels and were headed back toward Little Rock to show their bounty to Walker and the other men who hung around the store.

As they came out of woods, they fired off their rifles to get rid of the shot and powder packed down the barrels. Sergeant Stallings, who was recruiting in Little Rock that day, strolled out on the front porch of the store to see what the shooting was about.

He waved the boys over to the store where several other men who had been sitting inside had joined him.

"What you boys shootin' at? I thought some Yanks might be comin' through here," yelled Stallings. "What ya got there?"

The boys proudly walked up to the porch and dumped the squirrels out at the Sergeant's feet.

"We been vine huntin', and done some sure enough damage to them critters," stammered Tim. "You lookin' at some of the best shots in the county."

"That's right, we try to shoot them squirrels in the head, if'n we can," bragged John, beginning to feel light-headed from the excitement.

The Sergeant studied the young men for a few seconds and shook his head in approval.

"If'n you boys can shoot them squirrels like that, you sure could do some hurt to them damned Blue Bellies. How old is you?"

"I know what you gettin' at, and I'll have you know that me and that fat'n over there is already signed the line," nodded Tim, pointing to Robert.

"Well, that's mighty patriotic of you. How about the rest of ya?" questioned Stallings, looking straight at John. "You look like you fit to be sol'gering. Hell, I bet you is pushin' twenty. Didn't I see ya the other day? Ain't ya a Wilson?

"Yes Sir, I'm John and I turned seventeen in October, but my paw don't want me to do no joinin' up," said John quietly, looking away.

"How about you?" said Stallings, looking at Frankie. "How old is you, boy?"

Frankie walked up on the porch and shook the Sergeant's hand. "I'm Frankie

Olliver and I'll turn seventeen on January the fifth."

"Well, I'm proud to meet ya and let me tell you sump'n. One of the finest sol'gers we got in our regiment was fifteen when he signed up, and he is one sure enough fightin' son of a gun. I bet he done killed himself more than a hund'rd of them bastards. We didn't know he was so young when he joined, and as it turned out, we sure didn't want to send him back home," laughed Stallings.

The boys gathered closer.

"We're signin' up seventeen year olders this time around, and it'll be about the tenth of January before we leave for the front. If'n you want to sign up, the South will be proud to have ya, Mister Olliver, and you can go in with them two friends of yores."

Stallings glanced down at the Graham boys. "I can tell you two squirts ain't old enough yet. We'll get you later."

Frankie straightened himself up and extended his hand. "Give me the pen, Sergeant. The South has just got itself another man in the field," he exclaimed.

Tim and Robert patted Frankie on the back and congratulated him on his commitment while Sergeant Stallings briskly came to attention and gave the young man an impressive salute.

"How about you John? You going to go in with us? You ain't no better'n us. How about it?" said Frankie, looking over the crowd in hopes the group would put pressure on John so he couldn't resist.

John looked into the faces staring at him and tensely shifted his feet back and forth on the wooden planks that covered the porch. He thought to himself, "They'll think I'm disloyal and not much of a man if'n I don't support our cause, and if'n my friends can go, why can't I?"

"Give me the pen, Sergeant, I'll sign," replied John, hardly able to get the words out. "Give it to me!"

But before he could sign, Walker came out of the store and interrupted.

"Wait a minute boys. I'm not sure yore Paws going to like what you about to do. In fact, I know they won't. Sergeant, you better talk to these here boys' folks before they do no signin'," stated Walker, as he reached to take the pen from the Sergeant's hand.

Stallings moved out of his way and pushed him back toward the door.

"Walker, you just get back in yore store and mind yore bus'ness and leave me to take care of the sol'gerin'. If'n we don't kick them Yanks out of Tennessee, they might be comin' down here one of these days, and they might just torch this here store of yores. That'd make ya happy, wouldn't it?"

Walker regained his balance and straightened his coat.

"John, Frankie, I got one thing to say. Lott and Frank ain't going to like this one bit. Just go on and be a fool, if'n that's what ya got to do," he warned as he turned and slammed the door. "And I know a young lady that ain't going to like it none either!"

John looked over at Frankie. They had always been friends, and he wasn't going to let Frankie join the army and go into battle without him. He couldn't let him down now.

"I'll sign, Sergeant."

For a while, John was elated over his decision but soon he must face his father, and he realized he had disobeyed both his father and brother and had placed his family's security in jeopardy.

The mile walk from Little Rock usually didn't take but a few minutes, but this evening, it felt like an eternity. It was almost dark when John reached home, and the cold winter wind that had been gusting all day, pushing the treetops back and forth causing them to screech and groan, finally ceased, leaving the countryside in silence. The chickens that were usually cackling and strutting around the yard had gone to roost in the cedar tree behind the outhouse, and all was quiet.

The darkness and the stillness gave John an uneasy feeling, and the thought of facing his parents caused a sinking sensation to come over him. Even Joe and Spot were nowhere to be seen.

He could see the glow of light shining from his parents' bedroom window and the small curl of smoke coming from each of the chimneys on that side of the house.

John decided to say nothing until after he had finished supper.

When he opened the door, he was surprised at the group sitting there waiting for him: Lott, Sarah, Sister, Mister and Mrs. Walker and Becca. From their expressions, he knew what he was up against.

John eased slowly into the room toward Becca.

"Well, I didn't see yore rig outside. I didn't know we had company."

Lott's face was blushed and his eyes bloodshot. John had seen the same expression on his face years earlier after Jake had been killed.

"Son, sit down over there next to yore mamma. The Walkers were invited to come up here and talk with us about what you did today, and I can tell you, we is all mighty upset. You already know how I feel, and you done went against my judgment," stated Lott.

"How could you do such a thing, John?" his mother asked.

"Mamma, I was going to talk to ya about it after supper," replied John, placing his head in his hands and staring into the fire. "I just felt that if'n all the other boys 'round here were joinin' up, like Tim, Robert and Frankie and even James Earl and Thomas, I ain't any better'n them."

He picked up a piece of loose bark and lightly flipped it into the blazing flames.

"I also heard that all five of them Clearman boys has joined this morning."

Becca got up and knelt in front of him. She gently placed her hands under his chin and lifted his face to where she could look into his deep blue eyes. Tears were streaming down her face.

"John, why didn't ya come talk to me before you enlisted? We've always talked through our problems."

Sister suddenly interrupted. "I'll tell you why. He ain't got no better sense, that's why. He's just plain stupid."

"You just hold yore tongue, Daughter. We got guests here, and you have no cause to talk to John that way," scolded Sarah.

"I'm sorry, Mamma. I'm just mad about what he done, especially since Papa told him not to."

Walker reached over and placed his arm around John's shoulder.

"I didn't mean to meddle in yore family bus'ness, but I figured yore Paw needed to know what was goin' on and the way you and Becca feel about each other, me and Mrs. Walker feel like you is already part of our family. We love ya just like our own."

"I know you do, and I understand how you feel and I appreciate that. I feel the same, but you got to know how I feel, too," said John, facing the group. "You know we's got a war goin' on, and most near all the boys and young men in this here county has left or is going to leave before long. Well, how do you think I feel when I'm still here and the rest is gone? Folks will say I'm disloyal or scairt to fight or that I'm too good to go. What do I say to them?"

"John, you could've said, it ain't none of yore bus'ness. That's what you could've said to them," replied Lott, still angry. "You could've told them yore family needs ya on the farm and right now, we's raisin' extra corn, wheat, and hogs just so we can help feed them boys off sol'gerin'."

John shook his head. "You just ain't understandin', are you? I just can't handle bein' the only one left around here. You can call it pride or stubbornness or whatever you want, but I did what I felt was best for me. And when Frankie signed up, I felt like I had to go with him."

"Frankie! You joined 'cause he done acted a fool! I guess if'n Frankie jumped in a fire, you'd jump in too. Damn boy, what kind of a child has we raised, Mamma!" exclaimed Lott looking toward Sarah.

She reached over and grabbed his arm. "Lott, just settle down. We ain't gettin' nowhere talkin' like this."

John, taking all he could stand started for the door. Lott immediately got out of his chair and blocked his exit.

"John, you just sit down there where you was until I'm through talkin, and then I'll excuse you," said Lott, pointing to the chair.

"Lott, Sarah, perhaps we better go on home," stated Walker, embarrassed over Lott's outburst.

As John reluctantly returned to his seat, Lott realized he was not handling the situation properly.

"Thomas, Mrs. Walker, Becca, please forgive me. Just give me a minute and let me try again," apologized Lott.

They sat in silence for several minutes with only sounds of the ticking grandfather clock on the mantle and the occasional popping of the wood burning slowly down.

Finally, Lott got up and pulled his chair in front of John. Becca stood behind John with her hands on his shoulders.

"John, I hope I can put my feelings out right this time. When Thomas rode up here this afternoon and told me what you boys had done, I got mighty mad, and I went down to the store to give that Stallings a once over. I told him you boys is too young, and if'n you did join, the parents ought to know about it. He told me the Confederacy was takin' boys seventeen years old and some sixteen, if'n they looked old enough. He told me you had signed yore name and that he had always heard that if'n a Wilson gave his word about sump'n, it was as good as carved in stone. I then asked him if'n I could get you out of it. He said that if'n I could find someone to take yore place and pay a three hund'rd dollar fee, then John Wilson could stay home. When I thought about that kind of a deal, it made me mad. I told Stallings he was right about us Wilsons givin' our word and that hell would freeze over before I'd pay for some other man's son to take on what my boy has obligated himself to do.

"John, I know you wonder why I'm so upset about this. Well, I got two boys that's already been up there fightin', and when you go, that'll make all of ya. I now stand a chance to lose all my boys. Now, you put yoreself in my shoes and see how you'd feel."

John reached out and grabbed his father's hands.

"Papa, I feel bad about this too, but when you feel like yore liberty and freedom is bein' threatened like it is by them northern politicians, there is a price to pay and there's a time to stand up and be counted. I'm not completely sold on all that the South stands for, but by stayin' at home, I might lose that pride you is always talkin' about. Like you always say, 'If'n you strip a man of his pride, you might as well take his life with it.' Papa, I can't lose my pride, it's too valuable to me. I understand how you feel, but I just have to go too."

"Son, I ain't the best at speakin' my heart. It don't always make it out just like I feel it. You going to be a soldier just like yore brothers, and I expect you to be a good'n too. I'm going to say a prayer for you and ask the Good Lord to give you a guardian angel to go with ya as well as with James Earl and Thomas and all the other young men like you."

Lott eased down on his knees, held out his hands and motioned for the others to join him. Becca lightly squeezed John's hand. He looked like an unshaven young boy with only a slight trace of a mustache, but in her eyes he was a man facing survival on the battlefield.

14

DEPARTURE FROM NEWTON STATION

Despite the family distress, John was now convinced he could help bring the war to an end. If the Southern troops could muster enough force next spring to bring one or two more defeats to the Northern army, then Lincoln and his politicians would concede to the South and let them go in peace.

The first rays of light streaked across the fields and woodlands revealing a Christmas eve frost softly blanketing the ground. The countryside was so silently beautiful it was inconceivable that a raging war could be shattering thousands of lives.

And now this war reached directly into the Wilson home where meal times usually meant joy and fellowship as they discussed their day's activities. But talk around the table was constrained during the days following John's enlistment.

On this special morning, Lott pushed his chair from the table and walked over to the window to look out on the farmland and think.

"It's a beautiful morning, Sarah," said Lott, still staring out the window.

Sarah walked over to her husband and placed her arms around his waist, "And with that frost it looks might near like a white Christmas. Lott, you ever seen snow at Christmas time?"

"Yes Ma'am, I seen it once. The first Christmas Jake and me come out here, we woke up on Christmas morning and it must have snowed six inches that night. It was one pretty sight. We played in it like we was kids."

Lott spotted Toby stirring around the barnyard.

"Sister, get yoreself wrapped up good and go out there and help Toby with the feedin'," said Lott. "He's movin' kind of slow this morning. His hip must be botherin' him."

John quickly rose from the table. "Paw, I'll go help him. That's my job, not hers."

Lott turned and pointed to Sister, "From here on out, it's going to be her job. You'll soon be leavin' and she's going to have to take on some of yore jobs. I don't mind you helping and showing her what to do, but she's going to take on some outside work."

Sister reached for her coat hanging on the wall and grabbed John by the arm. "Come on sol'gerboy. Let's go see what all you has to do. I bet I'll be back in the house in less than an hour."

John, surprised his sister would even consider doing such chores without complaining, accepted her invitation and determined to keep her busy until noon. "I'll show ya how to work, young lady. But you got one problem. You got to work with yore hands and not yore mouth to get my work done."

The two scampered down the hall like the children they still were and raced across the yard to where Toby was working. Sister threw sticks at John as he darted back and forth playfully laughing at her attempts to thrash him, as she called it.

Lott and Sarah remained at the window watching the two frolic toward the barn. Sarah pulled Lott closer to her side. "Lott, we got some mighty fine chill'un, and I hate to see you and John on the outs. You need to sit down with that boy. He means too much to you to let it keep on goin' like this."

Lott shrugged his shoulders as he continued to stare out the window, "Sarah, I love all my young'uns and to think about my last boy goin' into battle tears my heart out. Why'd he do this to me?"

"What would you have done if'n you'd been his age and all yore friends had joined up, and you was the only one left behind?" said Sarah.

Lott looked down and smiled. "I guess I'd done the same."

About mid-morning Thomas returned from his mission with the Choctaws. Ten days of recruiting showed in his fatigued face and drooping shoulders.

He slowly dismounted, tied his horse to the hitching post and climbed the steps to greet his father.

"Paw, it sure is good to be back at the house," exclaimed Thomas, reaching out to embrace his father. "You ain't going to believe what I done. I don't even believe it."

As Sarah came to the porch, Thomas turned toward John, Sister, and Toby as they hurried across the yard to greet him.

"You might as well come on up and let me tell ya my tale. But I'm going to sit down if'n you don't care. I'm might near worn out," insisted Thomas.

"You have any luck?" blurted out John.

"Luck!" Thomas turned to Lott. "Paw, I rode over every inch of five counties. Looked everwhere you told me, and I'll have you know I has enlisted over sixty Choctaws. Ain't as many as the Sergeant wanted, but I think he'll be proud to get them. When we catch the train at Newton on the tenth of January, they s'pose to be there, and I'm to drill them for a few days before we leave."

"You think they's going to show?" questioned Sister.

"They'll be there, if'n they gave their word," replied Lott. "You can depend on them."

Even though the morning was still cold, the family sat around the steps listening to Thomas' tales till finally Lott said, "Toby, you take John and Sister with you and carry a load of corn down to the mill for grinding."

"Mist' Wilson, we just got some grindin' done a few days back," reminded Toby, confused over Lott's request.

"Toby, I ain't no idiot. Do what I tell ya and don't get in no hurry," replied Lott.

"Yessuh, we'll be on our way. Come on Sis and Mist' John."

Thomas got up and followed his parents into the house while Toby and John began loading corn into the wagon. As they pulled out of the yard about thirty minutes later, Toby said, "Mist' Wilson just wants to get us out of the way fer a spell, Mist' John. When him and Mist' Thomas gets on the outs about sump'n they can get mighty rough talkin'."

Sister shook Toby's sleeve. "What's they fussin' about, Toby?"

John reached across to grab the reigns to stop the wagon. "They's fussin about me joinin' up, and Papa's probably blamin' Thomas for gettin' me stirred up," replied John.

"Toby, let's pull this rig up. I need to go back. It wasn't all Thomas' talkin' that made me do what I done."

But Toby pulled the reins back and kept going. "Mist' John, you don't need to go back to the house. When them two get grumpled up, you just has to let them talks it out and then when they cools down, you can best do yore talkin. The problem with Mist' Thomas is he's got that bad temper like his Uncle Jake."

"I guess you right, Toby. I seen them tie up before. When they get those Wilson tempers up, ain't much you can do with nary one of them."

By noon, Toby had the corn ground, and they were on their way back to the house. Thomas was sitting out on the porch lighting up a smoke. Lott had walked over to visit Donald White, a neighbor who lived up the road a piece.

"Toby, pull up and let me out at the house," said John.

He walked up the steps and pulled a chair next to Thomas.

"Thomas, you and Paw really had a hot'n, didn't ya?"

"Naw, it weren't much to it. We all right now," mumbled Thomas.

"It was about me, weren't it, Thomas? About what I done?"

Thomas looked down. "Well, since you brought it up. It was about you. Paw blames me for you joinin' up, and I guess I did tell some tall stories that probably got you kind of excited. But let me tell ya sump'n," said Thomas, turning to face his brother. "It ain't all purty. Hell, I seen men blown to so many pieces you can't even find all their parts. I seen men hollering and screaming when they gets their arms and legs cut off and given nothin' to kill the pain while the Doc was doin' the sawin'. And as for camp life, we stays hungry most of the time, and in the winter we's so cold the blood in our veins is near 'bout frozen. You get the picture. It ain't all play and games, Boy."

"Let me tell you sump'n, Big Brother. I listened to yore tales but I ain't no fool. You always has a way of stretchin' the truth, and you ain't the reason I joined. I may be yore baby brother, but I made my own decision and you had little to do with it. So you don't worry nary bit about me. As for Papa, I'm going to tell him the same thing I just told you, and I don't want to hear no more about it after that," stated John, speaking his peace for the first time.

"Well, that makes me feel a little better, John, but you talk to Paw as soon as he gets home. You got to get him off my back," insisted Thomas, reaching out to shake John's hand. "You know, this here's Christmas Eve, and we got to get this family in the right spirit before evenin'. As soon as it gets dark, we got to start our serenading."

In this part of the country it was the custom for the young men to saddle their horses after dark and go from house to house visiting friends and neighbors. They made it a point to stop by to see their favorite sweethearts and would often take them along. Families would hang a lighted lantern by their front door to welcome the young people into their home where treats waited.

At mid-afternoon Lott returned and heard Thomas and John making plans.

"You boys gettin' ready to go out for the night I see," said Lott, shuffling down the hall with an armload of firewood from the woodstack at the edge of the porch.

"Yes Sir, Papa. We going to visit all the girls within five miles of this place, that is, Thomas is. I goin' to see Becca tonight," replied John as he quickly stepped into the hall to open the door for his father. "You want to go with us?"

"You know better'n that. We going to have some suitors come visitin' Sister tonight," smiled Lott. "You and Thomas is certainly big enough to go by yoreselves, and Thomas is going to take care of you. Ain't that right, Thomas?"

"Yes Sir, Paw. My job is to take care of John from here on out."

The irony of that reply was not lost on John but he was glad his father and Thomas were on speaking terms again.

As soon as the family finished their evening meal, Thomas and John went to the barn, saddled their horses and picked up some torches Toby had made.

Sarah and Sister waited in the front yard to see them off. "Boys, you behave yoreselves, and be sure to thank folks. Show yore manners, now. Who all's going to go with ya?" asked Sarah.

John stretched down from the saddle and gave his mother a kiss. "Just a bunch of us, me and Thomas, Tim, Robert, Frankie, the Grahams, and I'll probably pick up Becca and carry her over to the Ollivers. Suzanne invited all of us over as soon as we get through makin' our rounds. We'll be home about midnight."

"Sis, I'm going to tell Robert to come by and serenade you a little. You like fat'ns, don't ya," laughed Thomas.

"Thomas, you's a fine thing to be talkin'. You ain't nothin' but a fat hog yoreself, and I bet you going to go visit Betty Hooks and she ain't none too small. John Willy, I bet you put him up to sayin' that. You just wait and see, I'm going to have lots of suitors come see me tonight," shouted Sister, as she ran to the house in tears.

But, it wasn't long until Sister's tears turned to smiles as young men began to knock at the Wilsons' door.

Mrs. Olliver had introduced the idea of serenading when she first invited people to her home on Christmas Eve for refreshments and fellowship. The custom originated in Louisanna, Mrs. Olliver's home state, and it proved to be such fun, that everyone in the Little Rock community looked forward to the festivity.

During their rounds, John gave his full attention to Becca, and about ten o'clock they all headed to the Ollivers. To his surprise, Suzanne Olliver took a special liking to Thomas. John felt the attraction was the fact that Thomas was an older man and a seasoned soldier, for John never considered Thomas particularly good-looking.

Before the party broke up, Mrs. Olliver asked the boys who had just joined the army to meet with her in the parlor. "Boys, we are most proud of you for helpin' us to defend our country, and the ladies at the church wanted me to contact all of you and ask you to come to a special church service on Sunday, the seventh of January. We want you to wear your uniforms and sit together. We know you will be leavin' a few days after that, and we want to show our gratitude."

On the way out Frankie stopped John and Becca at the doorway.

"How'd yore Daddy take to you joinin' up?"

John looked over at Becca. "He hit the ceilin'. I ain't seen him that mad ever in my life. He blamed Thomas for gettin' me in it. How'd yore Papa take it?"

"'Bout the same. He said we is all fools if'n we thinks we is going to whip them Yanks, and he said if'n I wanted to get my head blowed off, then go at it. You noticed he weren't in the house tonight. He said he didn't want to have nothin' to do with no fools."

John and Thomas pushed the horses harder than usual to get Becca home by twelve. Thomas left them at the house, telling John he had a couple of other places to stop before morning. "Ladies of the night," he whispered with a smile.

John helped Becca down from behind his saddle and then stepped down to walk her to the doorway.

"Can you sit a spell, John. Daddy won't care none," Becca said softly, pulling him closer.

John eased down on the top step, "I can't stay too long. Mamma's expecting me. Can't have her worried any more than she is."

"John, I think it's nice for the church folks to honor you all before you leave, but I wish you weren't going at all. I wish that ole war would end tonight."

John leaned over and gave Becca a long and tender kiss. "I've got to be goin'. I'll see ya after dinner tomorrow. You know, I've got you sump'n special for Christmas. And you know what you said about me not leavin' and wishin' the war would end, that'd be the best Christmas present this whole country could get."

The holidays passed quickly and soon it was time for John to put on the new uniform and attend the church service. That Sunday morning, a large crowd gathered at the church. John and eight other men sat together on the first two rows to the right with their families behind them. Other friends and neighbors sat in the benches to the left. Five were in their teens, and the other three were in their forties and fifties. Men in their twenties and thirties were already on the battlefield.

John, Frankie, Tim, and Robert had never felt so special. Their uniforms were tailored to fit; coats and trousers were gray homespun wool, and each boy sported a new black wide-brimmed hat. The boys wanted the snappy looking kepi some of the soldiers wore, but Thomas told them the slouch hat was the best, especially when it rained, because it kept the water from running down the back. Thomas said the most important item was a well-made pair of shoes that should never be taken off so no one could steal them.

Lott had mixed emotions about his son. He knew he would miss him on the farm, and he feared for his safety as he did for Thomas and James Earl, but he couldn't help but be proud of the way John looked and conducted himself, sitting there so straight and manly. Lott closed his eyes and silently prayed these young men would return safely.

Becca and her parents sat with the Wilsons. Becca never took her eyes off John who was sitting in front of her. His curly black hair was rolling over his collar, and several times she caught herself wanting to run her fingers through it the way she so often did when they were alone.

Becca had never seriously thought anything would happen to John, but suddenly she realized that thousands of men were being killed and lamed and that John was no different. This could be the last time she would ever see him. She could lose the boy that had always been the center of her life. Tears began to roll down her cheeks.

Lott reached inside his coat and handed Becca his handkerchief. "It's going to be fine. He'll be comin' back to ya."

The service finally ended with a prayer from Professor Hendon.

Days passed and finally it was time to leave. The train was to depart from the Newton Station at three in the afternoon. Lott realized it would take around four hours to make the eighteen mile trip. They must leave the farm no later than nine o'clock that morning.

Thomas had left several days earlier to meet the Choctaws at the station as they came in from the surrounding counties and to help Sergeant Stallings make arrangements for their training.

The Walkers and Becca were planning to ride along with the Wilsons so Becca would have more time with John.

Lott stepped up into the wagon and motioned for Sarah and Sister. "All right ladies, here comes the Walkers up the road. We can't be late."

Sister hurried down the hall. "Papa, we's comin'. Mamma's right behind me."

Sarah stopped John as he came out of his room.

"Alright young man. Come to attention and stand tall for me one more time. Let me take a good look at ya."

"Maw, do we have to do this again? We go through this seems like every-day," complained John as he took his usual erect position.

"Today it's for real, son. Today you has become a soldier."

She slowly walked around her son, straightening his jacket and brushing lint off his sleeve. She then looked into his deep blue eyes and reached up to stroke his thin dark mustache.

"Son, you's really about growed up, and when you get away from home, you remember yore upbringin'. You make us proud of ya and you make yoreself proud. And you better come home to me when this war's over."

At that, Sarah embraced him as she had so often done through the years, but this time she held him much longer.

"Morning Thomas, Miss Walker, Becca. I hate to make this trip, but I guess we got to get it done," stated Lott as he welcomed his guest. "Thomas, if'n it's alright with you, I'd like Sister to ride down there with you where we can make room for Becca to sit here with John."

"That's fine with us if'n it's okay with Becca," teased Mrs. Walker.

John helped Becca down from the wagon, and Sister jumped into the rear of the Walker's rig and paused. "You know, I think I'll just change my mind and ride with John and Becca. I ain't got but about six more hours to pester him, and I'm sure going to miss it."

"Sister, I'm glad you ain't serious," smiled Becca. "I can't take you and John fightin' all the way to Newton."

A cold winter rain had fallen for the past three days, and even though the night had brought clearer weather, a drop in temperature left a chill in the morning air. John pulled Becca close and placed his arm around her.

"Becca, you is as pretty as an angel this morning."

A gust of wind swirled her hair in her face and she quickly pushed it out of the way.

"I see you's wearin' the locket I give ya for Christmas. I hope you like it. When I get back, I'm going to give ya a ring, but for now, this locket's got to do," said John, smiling down at Becca and tenderly smoothing her hair. "Every time you wear it, I want ya to think about how much I love ya."

Becca reached up and kissed him on the cheek. "John, I ain't takin' this locket off til you and I is husband and wife, and that's a promise from the depths of my heart."

"I believe you Becca, I truly do," whispered John.

The wagons were leaving the yard when Toby hobbled out to see them off. Lott pulled the horses back and stopped the rig.

"Toby, you want to ride down and see the boys off? You can sit there in the back," said Lott, pointing.

"Thank you, Mist' Wilson, but I best stay right here and look after things. I just want to say a few things to Mist' John," replied Toby, edging up to the side of wagon. "Mist' John, you always been nothin' but good and kind to me, ever since I knowed you. I wants you to be careful and don't take no chances. You special, and I wants the Lawd to bring you home to all of us."

John reached for Toby's hand. "I'll be back, Toby. Probably next fall when this war's over. You take care of Papa for me," whispered John.

Toby smiled and winked. "Yessuh, Mist' John, I going to do just that. You can depend on Toby."

138

The creeks were still swollen from the rains and crossing took longer than usual. The party finally reached the northern outskirts of Newton a little after two.

John anxiously leaned forward and placed his hand on Lott's shoulder. "Papa, we going to make it on time, ain't we?"

"Sure, we going to make it. We'll be turnin' down Main Street in just a minute," assured Lott.

During the trip, John had been rethinking his decision. Looking over at Becca and then to his parents, he wished they could just turn around and go back.

"Remember last time we came down here to see Thomas and his outfit leave? There was hund'rds of folks talkin', laughin', and cheerin' and Lott, you remember that little brass band? That was sump'n weren't it?" remarked Sarah.

"Yep, it was," replied Lott as the wagon turned on to Main Street. "And I'd say that we got a pretty good turnout today by the looks of all the people in town."

There was more than a good turnout as the street was literally churning with people on their way to the train depot at the south end of town. Soldiers mingled with the crowd, grasping the little time left with their loved ones.

"Thomas, we better just stop the wagons here. We can't get much closer," yelled Lott over the noise.

"Fine with me. Let's pull in here," replied Thomas.

Suddenly, a familiar uniformed soldier ran up to the wagon. "John, we been waitin' for ya. The sergeant's been a callin' roll, and you and Frankie's going to be in trouble if'n you don't get there and report in!" shouted Tim.

John jumped over the side of the wagon. "I'm here now but I don't know nothin' about Frankie. He's probably like us, havin' a hard time crossin' them creeks. Has you seen Thomas?"

"Yeah, I seen him a while back roundin' up his Choctaws and gettin' them on the train. He's probably down at the tracks. We best be goin'. Yore folks can meet us down there," said Tim, pointing to the train.

The two quickly made their way to where Sergeant Stallings was sitting, and John nervously signed in. "Sergeant, what we s'pose to do now?" yelled John above the confusion. "Has Frankie signed in yet?"

The sergeant stood up and looked down the tracks.

"Wilson, how much more time you need with them Choctaws. You got them all?" shouted Stallings.

John heard a familiar voice shout in return, "Got them! Hell, I got more'n I thought. They is present and accounted for."

Stallings turned to John. "You best say yore good byes and load up on that flat car over there right now, cause we're leavin' this place in five minutes."

Stallings then turned to Thomas. "Tell the engineer up front to get it rollin'. I can't take much more of this racket."

John rushed through the mass of people and found his family and Becca who had worked their way as close as possible to the tracks. The whistle blew for departure and large billows of smoke puffed from the smokestack as the wheels screeched and the train slowly rolled forward.

John quickly hugged his parents, Sister, and the Walkers. Then he grabbed Becca and wrapped his arms around her, his heart seeming to float away as their lips touched. Feeling the warmth of her body and the sweet taste, John vowed he would survive and return to this girl and to the land he loved.

Pistol shots brought John back to reality, and he turned and saw scores of soldiers sprinting for the flatcars now rolling down the tracks. Standing up, arms wildly motioning for him to hurry were Tim and Robert.

John turned and started racing through the crowd toward the moving train. He yelled over his shoulder, "I love you, Becca! I'll be back before you know it!"

With that he reached up to get Robert's hand and the boys were on their way.

15

NORTH TO VIRGINIA

THE TRAIN WENT WESTWARD TO JACKSON. HERE THE CHOCTAWS would be transfered to another train and sent to Camp Moore, near Tangipaho, Louisanna to receive special training.

Meanwhile, John, Tim, and Robert went from flatcar to flatcar searching for Frankie, but no one had seen him. The boys finally figured he must have gotten there earlier and Sergeant Stallings had probably put him on a work detail.

The train made stops at Forest, Morton, Pelahatchie and Brandon. Each time the train pulled into a station, new recruits and supplies were loaded on the boxcars.

The train finally arrived in Jackson a few minutes before midnight, and the soldiers were directed to sleep on the boxcars or find shelter under the porch of the large depot. For the most part, the new recruits were too excited to sleep and spent the night roaming from campfire to campfire, meeting new friends and future comrades.

Morning finally dawned, cold and clear, with a brisk north wind forcing John to wrap his blanket around his shoulders to keep warm. He walked toward the boxcar where the Choctaws were staying, determined to find Frankie before the train turned north to Tupelo, a supply center in the northern part of Mississippi.

He peered into the doorway and spotted his brother arguing with a captain further down the tracks. Before he could reach Thomas, the conversation had ended and Thomas was kicking the gravel along the track and mumbling to himself as John finally caught up with him.

"Thomas, you sure is in a rough mood this morning. What's got yore dander up so early?"

"Hell, they sendin' me down to Louisanna with the Choctaws," grumbled Thomas as he jumped up on the edge of a nearby flatcar. "It weren't enough that I had to round all them Indians up, but they want me to go down there to be sure they get settled in. They say some of them don't talk English too good, and they know I can talk their lingo. So Little Brother, come noon, I'm headed south."

A feeling of despair crept over John and a sinking feeling settled in his stomach. Thomas had given John a sense of security about battle. The thought of his absence made him apprehensive.

"You say you goin' with the Choctaws and ain't comin' with us," muttered John, who had crawled up next to his brother. "You ain't comin' with us?"

"You heard right. The Cap'n said I'd have to stay down there in that hellhole for at least a month."

"Then you's comin' on up," replied John, relieved.

"Yeah, I'll get there 'fore too long."

"Thomas, you seen Frankie? We can't seem to find him nowhere."

"Frankie! How you expect me to keep up with you boys? It's a damned near full-time job keepin' them Chocs in line. They's gettin' kind of restless on this train. I ain't for sure I'm going to get them where we s'pose to be goin'," exclaimed Thomas as he slid off the side of the car. "I'd better go check on them right now 'fore some of them decides to take off for home. If anybody knows the whereabouts of Frankie, it'll be Stallings. Come on and walk with me down the tracks. You'll find the sergeant down there somewhere."

Just as Thomas figured, Stallings was directing a group of soldiers loading several large cannons on the train. Seeing John approaching, Stallings ordered, "Wilson, you just in time to bend yore back a little. Give us a hand here, boy."

"Yes Sir, Sergeant, I'll be glad to. Has you seen Frankie, Frankie Olliver. We been lookin' for him."

"Olliver! I ain't worried 'bout no Olliver, right now. We got work to do. Anyway, that ain't none of yore bus'ness. Get in here and do what I told you to do. Let me worry 'bout Olliver."

Promptly at noon, Thomas departed for Louisanna while John and the other soldiers left Jackson for Tupelo. As the train clanked down the roughly laid tracks carrying the boys farther from home, a feeling of loneliness crept over John. With each passing mile, he wondered if he would ever return to his beloved hillcountry.

When the train finally stopped, the soldiers were issued oilcloths to protect them from rain and were given their first full meal since leaving home two days earlier: soup and hardtack, a rough form of a biscuit. A light rain began to fall, and the soldiers sought dry places to eat. John, Tim, and Robert crawled under one of the boxcars.

"Tim, you going to eat all yore soup? If'n you ain't, I could sure use some more," begged Robert.

Tim pushed Robert away. "Just get back, fat boy. I ain't eaten in two days either, so you can just forget it."

Robert straightened himself angrily. "You didn't have to push me so hard. I'm just hungry."

John turned his cup up to get the last drop. "Why don't we go see if'n we can get a little bit more."

"Extra vittles! You can tell you boys ain't been in this here army for long," laughed a soldier who had been eating next to the boys. "This here army don't eat much and sure does a helluvuh bunch of walkin' on an empty belly. When you get on up there where them seasoned troops is, you won't find no fat uns amongst them. My name is Albert Matthew," said the man as he reached out to shake John's hand. "I'm from Philidelphia, that is Mis'sippi, and I been in this army since the beginning."

Matthews had the look of a veteran; older and he had two stripes on his sleeve. It took time to advance in rank and gain the look and confidence of a soldier who had been under fire.

In the days that followed, Albert took a special liking to the boys and tried to help them adjust to military life. He introduced them to Josh Wilcox, a young recruit the boys' age who came from Hickory, a small community south of Little Rock.

After a three day stop over, the train pulled out of Tupelo and moved eastward into northern Alabama then northward into Tennessee. Here the weather changed dramatically. A cold front swept through the Mississippi Valley dropping the temperature to below freezing, and a light sleet mixed with snow began to fall.

Some soldiers crowded into the covered boxcars and found shelter, but others had to remain in the open cars.

Tim was able to squeeze inside, but John and Robert had to fend for themselves in the outside.

"Boys, wrap yore blanket 'round you and then put yore oil cloth over ya," instructed Albert. "Then we'll bunch up together to stay warm."

"Man, I wish I was home right now. I ain't ever been this cold," chattered Robert, shaking so hard he could hardly talk. "Will it get any colder than this?"

"Cold! You ain't seen nothin' yet. Wait till you get up in Virginie," laughed Albert.

"Pull yore hat down, John, so the water won't run down yore back. We'll be all right," reassured their new friend.

The train slightly swayed from side to side as it wound its way through the east Tennessee hills. As evening approached, the sleet changed to a driving snowstorm covering John and the other soldiers. It was hard to distinguish the soldiers from the other baggage on the open cars as the snow accumulated.

As John lay there cold, hungry, and shivering, he visualized his mother and father around the warmth of a roaring fire, sharing the past day's activities. He could imagine himself curled up on a fluffy feather bed with layers of quilts heaped keeping him warm as toast.

The snow continued to fall, and John wondered if anyone in charge of this operation really cared for him and the other young men who had committed themselves to the Southern cause. What good would they be if they starved or froze to death?

I

The sun had been up for more than an hour but Becca still lay curled up fast asleep. Suddenly she awoke, frightened from a disturbing dream. She had envisioned John racing down the track to catch the train, exactly like before, but the the train raced away from him, leaving him abandoned on the tracks. Seeing him standing alone and in distress, she ran to meet him. But as she drew near, he turned and to her astonishment, it wasn't John at all. It was Frankie. He stood there, smiled, and pointed to a stream of smoke rising above a cluster of trees up the way, the last visible sign of the locomotive. Frankie then said, "He's gone and won't be comin' back."

Becca lay wide eyed, listening to the wind whipping around the corners of the house. She remembered how concerned John had been about Frankie and how they couldn't find him at the station. Becca didn't remember seeing any of the Ollivers at the tracks. Something must have gone wrong.

Becca got out of bed and carried her clothes into her parents' room where she could dress in the warmth of a morning fire. Mrs. Walker was sitting there rocking in her favorite chair and mending a pair of Mister Walker's socks.

"Well, look who finally got up. Yore Papa's been gone for more'n hour, but I don't blame ya for sleepin' in. It's mighty cold and windy out this morning," she remarked.

Becca pulled a chair closer to the fire. "Mamma, I had the strangest dream last night."

"You want to tell me about it?"

Becca stood up and tucked her shirt into her pants, then stood staring at the blazing fire for a few seconds. "No ma'am. It was just a crazy dream. It weren't nothin'."

"Oh, by the way, Sister sent word that Toby was goin' over to see his wife and boys at the Ollivers and wondered if you wanted to ride over with him. She's going to visit Suzanne for the afternoon."

"That sounds like fun, and it sure ain't nothin' goin' on 'round here," replied Becca.

"Well, she'll be here about mid-morning. I told her you'd probably go with them," said Mrs. Walker as she rose and walked to the kitchen to help Becca with her breakfast.

"Young lady, are you ever going to stop wearin' them pants? You's growin' up, and them things is just too tight on ya."

"Mamma, they is just warmer than an ole dress, and John thinks I look good in them."

Mrs. Walker chuckled to herself. "He'd like you in a dirty ole sack. You sure got that young man moonstruck."

A few minutes after ten, Toby and Sister arrived and by noon they were at the Ollivers' place. Toby pulled the wagon up to the front steps and helped the girls off the rig.

"I want you to have a good time, and I'll pick ya up 'bout mid-afternoon. We all need to get on home 'fore dark," said Toby.

The front door opened and Suzanne ran out to meet her friends. The girls giggled as they embraced and then scampered up the steps and into the house.

After lunch the girls gathered in the front parlor to catch up on local gossip. Every time Becca or Sister mentioned John or anything relating to the boys or the army, Suzanne would change the subject. At first, Becca didn't notice, but eventually it became obvious that something was wrong.

Shortly, the girls heard a horse gallop up to the front of the house, and in a few minutes, footsteps on the front porch drew their attention. Becca pushed the curtain aside.

"Frankie! Frankie Olliver! What's he doin' here?" gasped Becca.

Frankie entered boldly and sauntered down the hall past the parlor doorway and on toward the kitchen, not noticing the horrified girls.

Becca quickly rose and went to the doorway.

"Frankie, what are you doin' here? You s'pose to be . . . . "

Frankie turned sharply, surprised to find Becca and Sister standing behind him.

"I happen to live here, you know. Where else would you like me to be?" shrugged Frankie.

"You supposed to be gone with John and the other boys. Why ain't you?" questioned Sister.

"He got sick the night 'fore they was to leave, and he's been ailin' ever since. He's still not feelin' too good. You can look at him and tell that," explained Suzanne uneasily as she eased over to Frankie's side.

"Yeah, I had a touch of sump'n. I was out of my head with fever for two whole days," replied Frankie, placing his arm around Suzanne. "I'm just glad I'm still alive and kickin'. I feel kind of weak right now."

Frankie turned quickly and continued into the kitchen. The girls went slowly back to the parlor. Bewildered over Frankie's presence, they sat quietly, not knowing what to say to Suzanne. Finally, Sister broke the silence. "Suzanne, why didn't you tell us? We would've come over to check on Frankie. You know folks around here are concerned about their friends and neighbors, 'specially when they's ailin'."

Suzanne straightened her skirt and pushed her hair out of her eyes, embarrased.

"Sister, we was afraid someone might get what he had, so we just kept him in and tended to him ourselves. We didn't want nobody else to get his sickness."

"John and the boys was lookin' all over the place down at Newton the other day for him. We didn't know where he was," replied Becca.

"Oh he'll be fine, and the next time they get a new group of soldiers up, Frankie will sure be with them. He just can't wait to get on up there with the other boys. You better come get you some hot tea 'fore you leaves. It's going to be a cold trip back home. Ole Toby's going to be here 'fore long to get ya," said Suzanne.

On the way home, Becca told Toby about what had happened.

"Miss Becca, I shore don't know just whats to think, but I tells ya one thing, them Ollivers is a strange family. You can't tell 'bout them. You knows, Mist' Wilson still thinks that Mist' Olliva had sump'n to do with Mist' Jake's killin'."

I

The snow stopped falling as the train pulled into the station at Murfreesboro, Tennessee and the clouds began to break. The glare of sunlight on the powdery white snow almost blinded the troops as they walked around the grounds. It wasn't long before the soldiers were engaged in their first battle: a snowfight. A snowball hurled at an officer started a flurry of snowballs until the sky was filled with flying blobs. The officers took the assault in stride and counterattacked. After fifteen minutes,the officers, outnumbered and exhausted, conceded to defeat and raised a white handkerchief.

The recruits cheered loudly and with the command to form ranks, fell into formation. Captain Sam Maddox, who was in charge of the train, stood up on a platform next to the depot's front entrance and began to give orders.

"Alright men, listen up!" shouted the Captain. "We going to be here for about two days. We got to unload this train and get everything on another'n. The rails up front is a different size, and this ole crate you's been ridin' on won't run on that un," said Maddox pointing to the tracks leading out of town. "I know it's been three days since you had more'n a bite of bread and you got to be half starved."

"Starved, hell Cap'n. Ain't ya noticed that them ole mules we loaded back in Mis'sippi' ain't on here no more. A bunch of us done butchered them pore devils and had a donkey barbecue. There was enough ass to go 'round for the whole bunch," shouted a soldier from the back rank.

With that, the entire group burst out in laughter and began to bray like donkeys. The Captain, unable to hold his composure, laughed as hard as his undisciplined recruits.

"At ease, men! If'n you can fight Yankees as good as you can carry on foolishness, then this here war ain't going to last for long. Let me finish. When you is dismissed, fall in down at the end of the train and draw yore provisions. We got some rice, some pork, and a little bit of cornmeal. You are going to have to cook yore own meal so you might as well learn. You got three hours 'fore we start unloadin' and reloadin' these supplies, and I better have all my asses accounted for. Dismissed!"

The soldiers quickly broke into a sprint and raced down to the rear of the train.

John, Tim, and Robert running together, were unable to get in front of the long line and by the time they reached the men dispensing the food, very little was left.

"John, look at this stuff they give me," complained Tim. "My pet coon back at the house gets more'n this. They expect us to fight on this."

Robert stirred his cornmeal with a stick. "Tim! look a here! I got bugs in mine."

Albert looked down into his cup. "Well, I do see that you's got company, boy. Just cook them up good and they's like fried chicken, maybe better."

"Mine had them too," Josh said.

He then took Robert's cup and poured its contents on the ground as he reached inside his coat pocket. "You boys has been 'specially nice to me, and I'm going to treat all of you to a decent meal."

"Meal! You better fix me a meal or I'm going to bust yore face. You just throwed mine on the ground," shouted Robert.

Josh smiled and pulled a handful of gold coins from his pocket. "See that sign over there? They serves hot food and I got the means to treat all of ya. Let's go eat!"

Robert and Albert hoisted Josh to their shoulders and paraded toward the restaurant.

They were served baked ham, creamed potatoes covered with thick gravy, blackeyed peas, and a pile of hot biscuits with fresh butter. They savored each mouthful as time quickly slipped away.

After eating, they walked out and sat under the front porch on a long bench. As they relaxed and warmed themselves in the noonday sun, John became curious.

"Josh, it ain't really none of my bus'ness, but I got to know sump'n," he said, turning to Josh.

"Ask on, John. I ain't got no secrets."

"Where did you get all that gold?"

Josh spit his toothpick out and stood at attention. "John, you lookin' at a paid soldier. My pappy got four hund'rd dollars for me joinin' up, and he give me fifty."

"Paid soldier! What the hell is that?"

Albert stood up and pulled his collar up to keep the wind out and then turned to John. "He got paid to take some other soldier's place. Somebody didn't want no part of this army. I call that kind of turncoat a son-of-a-bitch, that's what he is in Mister Lee's army."

"Josh, is that right? Did you take somebody else's place?"

"Yeah, I did. My Pappy owed a farmer up yore way some money, and he told my Daddy that if'n I would take his boy's place he would cancel the debt and give him four hund'rd dollars to boot. He said his boy didn't want no part of no fightin'," explained Josh. "And here I is."

John hadn't heard of anything like that around Little Rock. "Farmer up our way? Who is that farmer, Josh? Do we know him?"

"Well, I ain't too good on names, but I think his last name was Olliver. Yeah, that's right. It were Olliver."

The boys stared at each other in disbelief. For a few second they were unable to speak but finally Robert found his tongue. "You could be wrong, couldn't ya?"

"Naw, I ain't wrong. It was a Mister Frank Olliver. I remember now."

"Damn and double damn!" exclaimed Tim. "That bastard has run out on us, and he was so stirred up 'bout us all joinin' this war together. Just wait till I see him."

"Josh, I apppreciate the meal, but if'n that money of yores come from Frank

Olliver and that turncoat son of his, this stuff is goin' to turn sour in my stomach," protested Robert.

John couldn't believe what he had heard. But as much as he felt deceived by Frankie, he was not going to form an opinion about this until he could talk with him.

Later that morning, a southbound train pulled into the station loaded with soldiers returning home from the field hospital in Richmond. At first, the new recruits cheered and tossed fun, but as the train drew near, the recruits became reverently silent. Many of the soldiers were lying on cots and unable to respond to the boys' teasing. Scores of returning men had loose sleeves or pant legs pinned up above the knees.

Suddenly, a command bellowed out from an officer. "Attention! Stand straight and show yore respect. Them men has paid the price."

The boys stood tall and sadly saluted the soldiers as they passed.

After daybreak on February the 15th, 1863, the train pulled out once more, headed northeast to Virginia. Its tracks skirted the western slopes of the Appalachian Mountains and upon reaching the Virginia border, turned eastward to the state's heartland. John sensed they were entering a major war zone because at each stop more troops and supplies were visible as well as men hurriedly attending to duties.

At two in the afternoon, on February 20th, the train made its final stop at Brandy Station close to Culpepper, Virginia, where most of General Lee's army of northern Virginia was in winter quarters.

It was only a two hour march to the camp, and with each step, John became more excited. The mud was ankle deep and the soldiers struggled to keep their shoes from being left behind in the quagmire as they maintained their line. John remembered what Thomas had said, "A good pair of shoes is worth their weight in gold, don't take them off, and sure as hell don't lose them."

The unit made a left turn and marched up a gentle slope recently cleared of trees. Upon reaching the crest, they were amazed at the scene below. Stretching as far as they could see were rows upon rows of tents and crude huts. The tents were laid out in blocks like a large city. Masses of soldiers were mulling around; some were moving in formations, and others were just stirring around aimlessly. From this distance, the men looked like ants from a massive anthill that had just been disturbed.

Tim turned and motioned to John and Robert who were several rows back. "You believe what you seein'? I ain't ever seen so many folks."

John smiled. "Ain't no way we going to loose this here war with them kind of numbers. There must be a hund'rd thousand soldiers down there."

As soon as the unit reached headquarters, John and his Newton County group were taken to an area where the 13th Mississippi regiment was camped. Here they were assigned to the Newton Rifles, their home county unit. The boys recognized several of their friends from the Little Rock Community and began distributing the mail they had brought.

As evening approached, they were assigned places to stay. When the sun went down, the sky was illuminated by the numerous fires burning around the immense campground.

Tim, John, and Robert sat with some of their friends.

"Tell me sump'n. When is I going to get me a shootin' iron?" Tim asked. "You know they can't expect me to kill them with this here stick," he motioned as he pretended to be drawing down on an enemy. "And what about my trainin'?"

One of the older soldiers laughed. "Well, Mister Gen'ral, first you going to have to wait till we lay another whippin' on them blue bellies, then you can go over the field and pick you a rifle off one of them pore dead Yanks. As for yore trainin, them Yanks will train ya sure enough fast when them balls start zippin' by yore ears."

I

Lott and Sarah had been patiently waiting for news. Finally, one afternoon Becca rode up to the house waving a letter that had just arrived on the stage. She quickly dismounted and ran up the steps.

"Well, it's here. He finally wrote us. He had two letters in the same envelope. One for you and one for me," exclaimed Becca as she excitedly handed the letter to Sarah.

"Come on in this house, young lady, and let's see what that boy's been up to," directed Sarah. "Come on 'round the fire."

Sarah carefully unfolded the letter and turned her chair slightly toward the fireplace so she could see clearly.

Dear Mamma, Papa, and Sis,

I pray that you all are doing fine and that everyone is well. This army life isn't quite what I imagined. Our living quarters aren't much better than living out in the open and we sure don't get much to eat. What I wouldn't give to have some of Mamma's baked ham and sweet potatoes. I wouldn't mind if Sister even cooked it.

I have never seen so many men in my whole life. When I first got in camp, our army looked like a horde of tramps, ragged and undisciplined. We had different kinds of uniforms on and a lot of the men didn't even have shoes. Some are continuously talking back to the officers in charge and stay in trouble most of the time. I've never heard so much foul talk in my life, but when we fall into formation and get down to serious training, I must say, we are impressive. I can see how our army has been getting the best of them boys up North.

We have the feeling that it won't be long before we will be seeing some action. The word is that the Yankees are on the move, and it will be only a matter of days before we will move out to meet them.

Tim and Robert are doing fine, and the lack of food is doing Robert some good. Tell Toby that I send my regards and tell him to remember what I told him before I left. Also,

I've got some information about Frankie that has caused me concern. I'll write more about it next time.

I want you to know that I love you all, even Sis, and I want you to remember all of us in your prayers.

Your loving son,
John

See Papa, I may not speak good grammar, but I can write it.

16

INTO THE JAWS OF HELL

IN THE SPRING OF 1863, THE UNION ARMY OF THE POTOMAC with 120,000 troops faced Lee's army of 60,000 at Fredericksburg, Virginia. General Joseph Hooker, the commanding general of the Union Army, divided his forces to get to Lee's flank, thus catching the Southern army in a pinching maneuver that if properly executed, could destroy their opponents in northern Virginia and hopefully end the war.

Lee, discovering Hooker's plan, ordered part of his army to remain in Fredericksburg to defend the city and with his main body of troops, met Hooker at Chancellorsville. Oddly enough, it was a flanking movement used by Lee's "Stonewall" Jackson that turned the right wing of the Union Army while Lee attacked the Union front. Hooker, unable to accomplish his mission, pulled back into a defensive position and four days later, withdrew his army.

The Thirteenth Mississippi Regiment including the Newton Rifles was left at Fredericksburg with General Early's division to observe the Union army troops that had been left behind. They were to confront the enemy if it moved toward Chancellorsville. The Northern army did move and struck Early's outnumbered troops, breaking their line of battle and sending the Southerners reeling backwards. Seeing a possible disaster in the making, General Early ordered up his artillery to protect the rear and was able to slow the Union advance as he prepared to withdraw. The Thirteenth Mississippi Infantry Regiment was placed on Early's right and did not face the brunt of the attack, but when Early began to withdraw, the Thirteenth and the Seventeenth Regiments were positioned in the rear to support the artillery.

For the first time, John found himself firing upon the enemy, hearing the zip of bullets whistle close to his head, and seeing his fellow comrades fall in large numbers. Death was now a reality, and war no longer a game.

When the news of Hooker's defeat reached General Early, the Southern troops were elated. They had wondered why the formidable force facing them had suddenly moved back toward Fredericksburg during the late afternoon, especially when Early's Confederates were fighting for their lives and were on the run.

That evening, campfires seemed to burn especially brightly as the Southerners prepared their evening meal. All around the campground, excitement proclaimed the victory. The sounds of men laughing and singing, the plinking of a banjo, and the screeching of a fiddle could be heard in almost every cluster of soldiers.

Albert, with a large smile on his face, walked up to where John and Tim had just finished cooking. "Well boys, by the looks of the burnt powder on yore faces, I feel you has sent some lead flyin' today. Care if'n I sit and eat with ya tonight?"

Tim pointed at a stump nearby. "Have yoreself a sit with some sure 'nough Yankee killers."

John looked up at Tim in surprise. "Yankee killers! You don't know if'n you hit any of them. You were just pointin' at that bunch and firin', just like me," shrugged John. "And Tim, you were just as scairt as me."

"Scairt!" protested Tim. "I weren't scairt, and I did aim at them just like shootin' squirrels back home."

"Where's Robert?" asked Albert, looking around the group.

John pointed to a tent nearby. "He's kind of sick on his stomach. That fightin' today and seein' them men out there layin' dead got to him," explained John. "It got to me too."

Suddenly John heard a familiar tune as a soldier whistled his way through the dark toward the fire.

As the man approached, he pulled his hat down to duck under a low tree branch. "Any Wilsons 'round here?" questioned the man, struggling with a limb that had snagged his shirtsleeve.

When the soldier freed himself, the light revealed a familiar face.

"Thomas Stanley, is that you? Is that really you?" exclaimed John, jumping up and running toward his brother. "When did you get here?" John said as he grabbed him around the shoulders.

"Don't squeeze me so hard," laughed Thomas. "I just got here this afternoon. Too late for the action, but I understand you boys done just fine. But I did hear some disturbing news," continued Thomas. "They say that Gen'ral Jackson got shot late this evenin' and by some of our own boys who mistook him for a Yankee. I truly hope he makes it."

The brothers walked arm in arm toward Tim and the other soldiers.

"Thomas, I thought you never would get on up here. What about them Choctaws?"

Thomas eased down by the fire. "John, I worked with them for more'n month, and I finally told the Cap'n that he was going to have to find somebody else to get them trained, cause my orders from Col'nel Barksdale only tied me up for thirty days down in that hellhole. So here I is." Thomas paused a minute. "John, has you seen James Earl?"

John scratched his head. "Me and Tim see'd him one time and that would be about three weeks ago. He didn't look too fittin' and was mighty thin. He was coughing a lot and didn't have too much to say."

"I been worried about that brother of ours. He needs to go home till he gets his health back. He don't need to be soldiering just now," said Thomas, nodding at John. "Man, I has been some kind of places since I left Jackson. We got a lot of talkin' to do Little Brother 'fore this here night's over, a lot of catchin' up to do."

John and Thomas sat around the softly glowing embers until the stars were the only lights on the campground. The sounds of men celebrating quietened, and John and Thomas settled in the solitude of the evening interrupted only by the locusts and frogs in the surrounding trees.

"John, just shut yore eyes and listen to them critters. What's it make you think of?"

John smiled. "Thomas, it sounds like we's back home in Little Rock. We just finished a day's work and is a sittin' on our porch with the family. That's what it sounds like."

"You right, Little Brother, and that's probably where we needs to be," sighed Thomas.

Finally, John dozed off curled up next to Thomas who was still awake and remembering the promise he had made to their father. It made Thomas shudder to think how he would have explained to his father how he missed the last battle. What if John had been wounded or killed. Thomas closed his eyes and thanked God for sparing his brother and prayed that James Earl would be sent home before his health worsened.

General Ewell's soldiers remained at Fredericksburg until June 3rd and then were ordered to move. With the unexpected death of Stonewall Jackson, Lee reorganized his army from two corps into three with about thirty thousand men in each. He appointed General Longstreet, Ewell, and A.P. Hill as commanders and disclosed his plan about the army of Northern Virginia moving northward across the Potomac River. Lee felt by moving into Maryland and on into Pennsylvania, he would force the Union Army out of northern Virginia; and if a decisive victory could be won on Union soil, then perhaps the Confederacy would be recognized by European countries who were interested in the Southern cause. By carrying his army onto enemy soil, Lee's troops would also be able to forage the countryside for much needed food.

During the last days of June, Lee's army had crossed the Potomac River, quickly marched through Maryland, and was making its way into Pennsylvania. The weather was extremely hot, and the dust from thousands of marching feet and hundreds of horsedrawn wagons could be seen for miles.

The Thirteenth Mississippi Regiment was assigned to Longstreet's corp and was moving far behind the other two.

A light rain had fallen the night before, but as soon as the sun came up, it didn't take long for the moisture to evaporate. The heat on the first of July was almost unbearable as the soldiers slowly marched up the dry and dusty road. All along the way men were fainting from fatigue and heat exhaustion, and many were sitting under the shade of trees, too weak or sick to continue the march.

Tim had tied a handkerchief over his nose to keep out the dust. He finally reached the top of a large hill and looking down through the valley, was astounded by the long line of infantry weaving its way among the meadows and woodlands.

Turning back to John, he pointed to the scene below. "John, has you ever seen so many soldiers? It looks like a long snake, except the snake goes on for miles."

John wiped his eyes trying to clear his vision. "Hot-ta-mighty, Tim! I knowed we had a bunch of men, but nothin' like this. Reckon how far we stretch out?"

"It's got to be at least twenty miles or more long," added Robert, stumbling over a root and falling into Josh who was walking directly in front of him.

"Robert, watch where you goin'! If'n I get killed, it sure don't need to be by some fat boy squishing me," complained Josh, who had bumped into the soldier in front of him.

"Fatboy, hell, I ain't that fat no more. I bet I've lost might near thirty pounds. This here army is about to starve me to death," protested Robert, struggling to regain his balance.

Tim, always alert, was suddenly perplexed by a thundering sound in the distance. It was a clear day with hardly a cloud in the sky, but he was certain he heard the rumble of thunder.

"John, you hear anything up front?" questioned Tim, turning his head to get John's attention.

"Naw, I can't hear nothin' but feet stompin', and this dust is about to get me," complained John.

Then once more a low rumble in the distance caused all the soldiers to take notice.

"I heard it, Tim, but what is it? I don't see no rain clouds nowhere," replied John. "What about it Albert, you been round more'n us. What's that racket?"

Albert looked at the boys with a solemn expression. "Them is big guns you's hearin'. We has just run into ole Billy Yank, and you best get ready for some tough goin'."

No sooner had Albert finished his statement, than the order was given to double quick step. The boys knew a fight was on, and by the sounds of the guns growing louder, it would be only a short time until they were engaged.

As the soldiers quickened their pace, an officer came galloping down the long line of troops shouting orders. "Pick it up boys! We got a fight comin'! Longstreet needs us!"

After two hours of steady hard walking, Longstreet ordered his corp to stop briefly to rest before reaching the battleground. In the distance, John could hear not only the roar of heavy guns but also the crackling sounds of muskets, and he could see masses of smoke rising above the trees.

Sitting by the side of the road, John considered the upcoming battle; a cold chill went through his body causing his teeth to chatter and a cold sweat covered his brow. Looking at Tim and Robert, he could see a fear in Tim's eyes he had never seen before. Tim had always seemed brave, but not now.

I

On April 24th, 1863, Newton County got its first taste of war. On a bold and daring raid through central Mississippi, Union officer Colonel Grierson with three regiments of cavalry and a few small pieces of artillery, traveled from the Tennessee line southward into the heart of the state. His unit entered Newton County at Union and rode south through Decatur and on to Newton. Here, Grierson ordered the depot and several supply buildings torched along with some boxcars of military goods. Making his way through the state, Grierson tried to avoid conflict and only took livestock, especially horses, when needed.

A few days after the raid, a group of men were sitting out on the porch of Walker's store in Little Rock discussing the outrage. They could not understand why the Southern Calvary had not put a stop to this mockery.

"Well, any Yanks been through here today?" exclaimed Frank Olliver as he tied his horse to the hitching post outside the store.

"Nary one I knowed of," replied Walker, who had come out of his store to greet his old friend. "But I did hear that one of them bastards got killed over at Union. Got shot off his horse."

"Come on up and sit a spell with these other old codgers, Frank. Tell us what ya know."

Frank shook hands with the men and took a seat next to the front door. "I ain't heard much more'n that, but they made a mess down at Newton. Burnt a lot of property up. Can't figure out where in the hell our soldiers was. Damn! We send our boys up North to fight, and there ain't nobody here when we need them. We sure got some smart Gen'rals, ain't we?"

Lucius White, an elderly man who had fought with Robert E. Lee in Mexico leaned forward and spat a large wad of tobacco juice at a fly that had landed near the edge of the porch. "You see how much damage I done to that fly. Well, that's about how much that Grierson done to us. Not a Tinker's Damn. Ole Bobby Lee is doin' just fine, and ain't no doubt he's going to beat the hell out of them Yanks up yonder."

Walker eased down and took a seat on the edge of the porch. "Beat the hell out of them, I just hope we got enough men to do the job. I understand we losin' a lot of men, and it's gettin' harder to fill the gaps. By the way Frank, how's that Frankie doin'? Is he 'bout well?"

"That boy's doin' pretty good, but still a little weak. That fever like to got him," explained Frank. "But I'll tell you folks one damned thing, he sure has made some changes lately. You might say he suddenly just growed up. He's been helpin' me on the farm more, and for the first time I can remember, I can count on him to do what I tell him. He might just make a man yet," laughed Frank.

Becca, who had been inside clerking for her father, walked out to see what the men were discussing. "I can tell by yore talk, that you gentlemen is havin' a good time. Care to share it with a lady?" teased Becca, giving the men a slight smile. "And I did hear some mighty naughty words out of ya. You know that tomorrow is church day, and the preacher is going to do some strong preachin'."

Frank stood to acknowledge Becca's presence, and gave a nod of his head.

"Miss Becca, I swear you is becomin' the toast of this here community. You has become one very beautiful young lady. Here take my seat," insisted Frank.

Lucius leaned over to where he could get a better look.

"Young lady, you is a looker. I wish I was 'bout fifty years younger, I would have to come a callin'," boasted the old gent. "And yes, we has been talkin' a little on the bad side, Lord forgive us."

"He'll probably do just that," laughed Becca, turning her attention to Frank.

"Mister Olliver, before I forget it, tell Frankie we is havin' a get together this evenin' over at the Graham's house, and we girls want to be sure he's there. He's the only boy left round here taller'n us; most of them boys is just too short for dancin'. They only come to my shoulders," motioned Becca.

"I'm sure he'll be there, 'specially if'n you going to be around," replied Frank.

Frankie, for the first time in his life, was receiving the attention he had craved. Even though he had always been the life of a party, when it came to pairing off with the young ladies, he had always taken a back seat to John or one of the older boys. Now Frankie danced with all the girls, and when it came time for the evening walks, Frankie got his choice, with the exception of Becca. Becca liked to dance with Frankie, but when he hinted about courting or an evening walk, she would remind him that John was the only one in her life. Frankie outwardly accepted her position, but deep inside, he swore that come hell or high water, he was going to court her.

A wagon rolling in from the direction of Meridian caught the group's attention. Lott and Toby were trying to get home before dark.

Lott pulled the wagon to a stop and beat the dust off his hat. He stepped down from the wagon, too tired to be sociable.

"Toby, wait up just a minute while I check for mail," said Lott, making his way through the group. "After'noon, Gentlemen. Becca, excuse me," continued Lott as he walked into the store.

Becca followed.

"Mister Wilson, I get a hug, don't I?" asked Becca nudging up to him.

Lott looked down at her with a big smile.

"Sure you does. What has got into me," apologized Lott. "Come here Miss Becca. For the past two days, we has been over to Meridian on bus'ness, and I'm might near worn to a frazzle. I guess I has lost all my manners."

Becca flipped through the mail.

"I'm sorry, Mister Wilson, ain't none here for ya. I sure would like to hear from John. I truly miss that boy of yores."

Lott took Becca by the hand and led her to a bench next to the counter.

"Becca, while we was in Meridian, the news come in that a big battle was goin' on up North, and if that be the truth, I'm worried 'bout the boys. They say it's a rough un," sighed Lott.

Becca squeezed his hand.

"Mister Lott, we has just got to pray that them boys is going to be just fine. We got to depend on the Lord to take care of him. That's what we got to do."

Lott nodded uneasily and walked toward the door.

Walker stopped him as he descended the steps.

"Lott, has you heard from the boys, lately?"

Lott paused for a moment. "Ain't heard much. I'm scairt to hear. Lot of killin' goin' on up there. A big battle is goin' on right now," replied Lott, turning to Frank.

"When's yore boy going to get goin'? Ain't he 'bout well now?"

Frank's face blushed. "Well, Lott, you know Frankie's been sickly, and he's also been a lot of help to me lately. I'm not sure I can spare that boy right at this point."

Lott crawled up in the wagon seat next to Toby and then turned and stared down at Frank. "Well, I couldn't spare none of my boys either, but they's all up there fightin'. All three of them. I even got my daughter in the field helpin' with the plowin' these days. Don't tell me no more 'bout sparin' a child."

I

On July 3rd, 1863, the soldiers of the Thirteenth Mississippi Regiment and the remainder of Longstreet's Corp took partial shelter behind a long ridge of hills as one of the largest artillery exchanges of the war proceeded. John and the other Newton Rifles lay as close to the ground as possible, afraid to even lift their heads to see the large guns at work.

A shell bursting overhead sent limbs and large pieces of a tree trunk sailing in all directions. Another round exploded nearby, throwing dirt and rocks over the soldiers along the slope. Albert eased up to see what damage was done.

Peering through the smoke and dust, he nudged John, who had found protection behind a large fallen timber to his right. "You ought to see this! Them guns is belchin' out smoke like a bunch of giants blowin' huge rings of tobacco smoke."

John pulled Albert to the ground. "You best get yoreself down 'fore one of them giants gets you," he warned.

Suddenly, another shell burst to their rear, instantly killing several soldiers and deafening John and his comrades.

"Damned, if'n that un weren't too close for comfort!" shouted Tim, who was positioned next to Robert and Josh.

"Robert, you all right?" He nodded and kept clinging to the grass underneath him.

"What 'bout you, Josh? You okay?"

"I got a headache and my nose is bleedin', but outside of that, Ole Josh is still sound and fittin'," he replied.

When the two armies had come up against each other on July 1st, Longstreet's corp, marching far to the rear of the other two corps, reached the battlefield too late and too exhausted to take part in the first day's action. At the close of that day, the Union and Southern armies, who occupied a long ridge of hills, faced one another across a large open valley.

Earlier, on July 2nd, Longstreet was ordered to take the Union's south flank

157

that included some hills strewn with large boulders. From this position, his corp could direct artillery fire down upon the Union lines with devastating results. Fighting was fierce and bloody with the Confederates finally taking these heights, only to be driven back by Union reinforcements.

The Thirteenth Mississippi Regiment did its share of the fighting and often was engaged in hand-to-hand combat with the enemy. In the last encounter, Tim was hit by a spent bullet that left a large bruise on his left thigh and Robert was almost killed when a Union soldier knocked him to the ground. But before the soldier could drive his bayonet home, Albert rushed up and struck the soldiers with the butt of his rifle, saving Robert's life.

John and Thomas had stayed close to each other during this engagement and took no unnecessary chances. Men fell to the left and right of the brothers as they, along with the other Southerners, charged and countercharged the Union lines, but no bullet found its mark on the Wilson boys.

The biggest loss to the Thirteenth was Colonel Barksdale who was killed while leading his men through a peach orchard on the lower slope below the large boulders. It was a bitter tragedy for the soldiers.

On July 3rd, the large field pieces ceased firing and an eerie quiet settled over the battlefield, interrupted only occasionally with a musket crack echoing across the hills. Thomas eased up and motioned for Albert. "What ya think, Thomas?" said Albert, moving up to where his friend was crouched.

Thomas pointed to the center of the Union lines, far across the valley. "That's where we been shootin' for most near two hours. Mister Lee's softenin' up that spot for some good reason, I figure. We probably going to hit them there."

"God forbid if'n we do, Thomas. It's might near a mile of open ground across there. God forbid it," protested Albert, shaking his head.

John and Tim, still shaky from the long barrage of cannon fire, crawled to where Thomas was squatting. John eased up to his brother and pulled on one of his pant legs. "Is it safe for us to stand up now? What's you lookin' at out there?"

Thomas pulled John up by the shoulder and pointed "We just lookin' at them Yanks over there on them hills and feelin' sorry for them pore boys. I bet our big guns done chewed them apart. Won't be long 'fore we put them runnin' again."

Thomas didn't mention that when an army's artillery was directed intensively on a target, the infantry wouldn't be far behind.

Suddenly, Sergeant Stallings ran toward them screaming to the top of his voice. They couldn't tell what he was saying, but as far as they could see across the hillside, soldiers were hurrying to pick up their equipment and were falling into formation.

"Get yore rifles and get in line!" commanded Stallings. "We goin' forward! We going to break that Yankee line over yonder!"

Everything was happening so fast that John didn't have time to think. In seconds, they had fallen into ranks.

"Dress right, men! Check yore rifles! Stand at attention!" screamed Stallings.

John looked down the line of soldiers and as far as he could see, men in gray

158

and various shades of brown were standing in perfect formation. They had formed two lines and, by John's calculation, amounted to at least ten thousand.

An officer rode to the front of the Thirteenth Regiment and barked, "Forward men. Keep them straight!"

The soldiers made their way up the hillside and over the crest where they obeyed a brief order to halt at an open field opposite the Union army. All down the line regimental flags were waving and sunlight reflected off thousands of bayonets.

Far down the line to John's left, a high ranking officer was addressing the troops, but John could not make out what he was saying. When he finished, a rider came galloping down the line toward where John was standing and pulled his horse to an abrupt stop in front of Sergeant Stallings.

"Need a rider to send a message, and I want a good one!" demanded the officer, leaping down from his mount. "Got to send a message to Gen'ral Longstreet!"

Stallings turned and quickly scanned his men. "Wilson, Thomas! Up Front!"

Thinking of the vow he had made to his father, he knew he could not leave his brother on the brink of combat. "Sergeant, if'n it's the same, I prefer you to get someone else to ride. I need to stay with my group," replied Thomas, still standing at attention.

The officer ran up to Thomas with his pistol drawn and pointed directly at Thomas's face. "Soldier, I don't give a damn what you want! This order is for Longstreet, and I suggest you get it to him," he demanded. "You don't have no choice. Here, take these reins and get this horse goin'. If'n you get it done quick enough, you can get yore ass back to the line and get all the fightin' you want."

Thomas took the reigns, mounted, and wheeled the horse around. "Where is the Gen'ral?"

The officer pointed to a clump of trees up the slope to their left. "He's up there 'bout two hund'rd yards past them rows of cannons near them big oaks. Go round to the left and stay away from them big guns. Them Yanks is still tryin' to knock them out."

Thomas, sitting tall in the saddle, looked down at his brother.

"John, I'll be right back. Don't have no fear. It won't take me but a few shakes and I'll be back here with ya."

At that, Thomas kicked the horse in the flank and away he sped up the hillside, dirt flying high as the horse's hooves dug into the ground.

John watched his brother in the distance and once again the fear he had felt when Thomas left him at the depot in Jackson crept over him. Watching his brother bouncing in the saddle as he weaved his way up the hill, John sensed he would never see Thomas alive again. He watched as long as he could, but then he turned as Sergeant Stallings raised his sword and pointed it toward the Union line. "Boys. Warriors of the South. Today we will break that line up yonder and send them Blue Bastards straight to hell! Forward!" yelled Stallings.

As John walked down the gradual sloping hillside toward the Union lines, a feeling of pride swept over him at the way this Southern army looked. Thousands and thousands were advancing in order, flags streaming in the afternoon breezes and weapons at the ready position. John felt there was no way the Union army could withstand such an attack without breaking its ranks.

Almost immediately, Union artillery shot raked through the Southern lines leaving rows of men torn apart. The Confederates closed ranks and continued their attack. When they reached the center of the valley they found a road and a slight depression where they were momentarily sheltered from the fire. Marching up the ravine and into the open, the men were now in musket range for the Union soldiers positioned on the crest of the hill.

A captain near John raised his pistol and motioned. "Forward at double quickstep! Direct yourselves to that clump of trees up near the top! Give them your best boys, and let's give them a yell!"

Tim looked over at John as they sprinted up the long grassy slope. "Stallings said we going to send a few of them to hell today, John! By the looks of this open country, I say, a bunch of us is going to be joining them. Let's go, John Willy. Let's go! Let's break that line!"

The Southern army broke its line of battle and ran toward the Union center, now only a few hundred yards to their front. A loud yell from the southerners went out across the countryside sending cold chills into the Union soldiers awaiting their order to fire.

The yell was instantly obliterated by the thunderous roar that erupted from the Union line as artillery and musket fire swept the valley. Smoke quickly covered the battle front and rose into the sky, almost shutting out the sunlight of the clear July afternoon. Hell could not have been worse than what was happening on this Pennsylvania hillside.

John pulled his hat down on his brow and ran as fast as he could toward a clump of trees up front, occasionally stumbling over his comrades who had fallen before him. No sooner had his hand left his hat than a large explosion in front sent him spinning. Before he could regain his balance, another force picked him up and sent him through the air. With the second blast, there was a blinding light followed by a sharp pain to his head and back as he fell. The sound of men screaming and the terrible roar of gunfire gradually subsided. The fragrance of green clover filled his nostrils and all became silent.

I

Becca lay across her bed taking a mid-afternoon rest. A strong wind suddenly blew through her bedroom window and a clap of thunder brought her screaming in terror from her sleep. She was dreaming that John was running to meet her with arms extended, his long black hair flowing behind him and a loving smile on his face. But, he quickly vanished and all she could hear was more thunder as it shook the walls of her room.

She sat up. "John! Something's happened! Don't leave me."

Her mother, hearing Becca's vioce, rushed to the room. She found Becca curled up crying and pulling the covers around her body as she often did as a child when she was frightened during the night.

"What's wrong baby? You have a bad dream?" said Mrs. Walker, kneeling beside the bed. "You're fine now. Everythings just fine. Mamma's here."

Becca looked up into her mother's face with fear and pain in her eyes. "Mamma, something just happened to John. He's gone, Mamma! He's gone!" screamed Becca.

I

In a matter of minutes, Thomas reached the trees at the top of the hill and scanned the area. Seeing a group of high ranking officers, he galloped over and quickly dismounted.

"Message for the Gen'ral," shouted Thomas, holding the reins in one hand and handing the note to a captain who seemed agitated by his abruptness. "Watch yore manner, soldier, and which Gen'ral are you referrin' to?"

Realizing his lack of protocol, Thomas immediately came to attention.

"Sir, Gen'ral Longstreet, Sir."

A bearded officer sitting on a fence rail pulled down his field glasses and stepped toward Thomas. "I'm Longstreet. Let me see the note," commanded the General. He glanced at the letter, wadded it up, threw it on the ground, and shook his head.

No sooner had the note hit the ground, than the earth they were standing on began to shake as the Southern artillery opened fire once more on the Union line. Thomas noted the constant crackle of musketry out front and knew the final assault was being made.

"Sir, may I be excused," asked Thomas.

The general nodded. "Where do you intend to go, soldier?" replied Longstreet.

Thomas pointed to the smoke rising from the far hillside. "There Sir. That's where I'm s'pose to be with the Thirteenth. My brother's over there."

Longstreet pulled his field glasses to scan the battle raging in the distance.

"You best go and may God go with you," he replied. "And may God be with our army today. We may not exist tomorrow."

Thomas quickly mounted and galloped down the slope. In his haste, he forgot about taking a circular route away from where the Southern cannoneers were firing and raced his horse directly across the hillside in front of the long rows of guns.

Shells exploded all around him as he sped down the hillside. The Southern cannoneers stopped their firing and cheered as they marveled at the courage of the horseman headed for the battle front.

One blast blew Thomas's hat off and almost knocked him from his mount, but away he went. He had almost cleared the area in front of the artillery, when another shot exploded in front of him, sending him and his horse tumbling to the ground. The mount was killed instantly and the fall knocked Thomas unconscious. When he came to, he found that he was pinned under the horse, unable to free himself. Lying there, he sensed that the battle must be almost over. Artillery on both sides of the valley had ceased firing and the sound of musketry was now only sporadic. General Lee must have busted the Union line and sent them Yanks a running once more, he thought.

Suddenly, a group of soldiers, face black with powder, appeared. "You got a problem, Sergeant," smiled one of the men looking down at Thomas. "Come on boys, let's get the critter off this fellow."

"Thank you, men. I'm obliged to ya," he said. "I got to get up there with my outfit. It ain't over, is it?"

The men looked at each other and dropped their heads. "It's over and you best not go up towards that Union line, that is if'n you wants to stay alive."

Alarmed, Thomas pushed one of the soldiers out of the way so he could get a clear view of the hillside. He stood motionless, unable to speak. In front of him strewn across the slopes, were thousands of dead and wounded Southern soldiers, many literally blown to pieces. In some places the dead were stacked in piles and in other areas they lay in neat rows where they had fallen. Across the plain, he could hear the steady moaning of men struggling for life.

"My brother may be out there! He might be one of them pore souls!" shouted Thomas, walking toward the battlefront. "I've got to find him."

After taking a few more steps, he collapsed and fell motionless to the ground.

Late that afternoon, Thomas regained consciousness and found himself lying on the ground surrounded by a group of soldiers from a Virginia regiment. Pulling to a sitting position, he looked around for a familiar face. "How'd I get here?" he muttered, feeling a bandage around his head.

"We pulled you up here after we got that horse off of ya. You was raisin' some kind of hell 'bout yore brother, and you finally just fell out. You going to be all right, though," replied one of the soldiers.

"Is the battle over? Did we win?"

"Naw, we didn't win no battle today, maybe tomorrow. We got ourselves shot to pieces near that hilltop. Half of us is laying dead out there," sighed one of the men.

"Then I got to find my brother, and he better be alive," said Thomas, standing to see if he could keep his balance. "Thank you boys for takin' care of me. I'm beholdin' to ya."

During the late afternoon and evening, Thomas searched from group to group, trying to locate the Thirteenth Mississippi Regiment and his Newton Rifles. In the chaos that followed the battle, surviving officers had tried to reorganize the stragglers as they returned to the safety of their lines. As darkness fell across the Pennsylvania countryside, troops were still searching for their units.

"Thirteenth Mis'sippi. Newton Rifles!" shouted Thomas over and over. "Anybody seen the Thirteenth?"

For more than two hours he searched in vain. Exhausted and so hoarse he could hardly speak, Thomas was about to give up hope of finding the Thirteenth and his brother, but he decided to try once more. "Anybody seen the Thirteenth? Anybody seen John Wilson?"

Down near a small fire, he heard a faint voice reply, "The Thirteenth is down here, and I seen him."

Racing through the bushes, Thomas became entangled in vines and fell down the hillside. He quickly got back on his feet. "Who said they knowed John Wilson?" shouted Thomas.

"I'm over here. It's me, Tim," replied a faint voice.

"Where's my brother? Is he all right?"

Tim looked at the ground. "He's gone, Thomas. He got himself killed up there," whispered Tim.

Thomas grabbed Tim by his collar and shook him vigorously. "You lying to me, boy! You lying like hell!"

Too weak to resist this outburst, Tim looked up at him with tears streaming down his powder-smeared face. "Thomas, I was in line right behind him. I saw him get blowed up. I knelt down and turned him over. He was a mess," cried Tim. "You think I'd lie about that? That brother of yores was my best friend."

Thomas released Tim's jacket and pulled the frail figure to his side. "I'm sorry Tim, I knowed you didn't lie. He just can't be dead. Lord forbid it, that boy has got to be alive."

17

PAINS OF WAR

ON THE AFTERNOON OF JULY 4TH, 1863, GENERAL LEE, KNOWING the remains of his army could be completely destroyed by a Union attack, gave the order to leave the field of battle. The weary army of Northern Virginia headed slowly back toward the safety of Southern soil leaving thousands of its dead and wounded on the hillsides south of Gettysburg, Pennsylvania.

Ten days later, General Lee's tired and battered army was massed on the banks of the swollen Potomac River waiting for the water to recede so a crossing could be made. To his surprise, Meade's Army was not in pursuit. Lee had his soldiers dig large entrenchments that stretched between Hagerstown and the Potomac. The General feared if Meade did strike him here, the army of Northern Virginia could easily be destroyed.

That evening, after the Thirteenth Mississippi Regiment had been dismissed from its formation, the men headed to their sleeping area. Instead of his usual joking and pranks, Thomas now stayed to himself and barely spoke to anyone. He had wanted to search the battlefield for John before they were ordered out on July 4th, but he could not face what he would find.

Albert had been looking for the right time to approach his friend. "Hold up Thomas, let an ole buddy walk with ya."

"Can't stop you. You can walk where ya want."

"Where's yore rifle? I ain't seen you with one since the battle," continued Albert. "Of course, we ain't needed nothin' but shovels here of late," he chuckled.

"I don't need no rifle no more. I wouldn't use it, if'n it were in my hand," replied Thomas.

By then, the two had reached the place where Thomas's gear was lying. Since Thomas was at least speaking to him, Albert was determined to stick close and try to find a way to help his friend deal with John's death.

Thomas lay down on the ground, crossed his arms behind his head and gazed into the evening sky, ignoring Albert.

Albert rolled out his blanket and kept up his questioning.

"You miss yore brother, don't ya? I know how you feels, I lost one when I was little. He died of the fever. I lost a sister, too."

"You didn't get one killed in battle," stammered Thomas. "I should've been there, and I should've gone out there on that field and got him. Like a coward, I just walked off and left him. I should've buried him. In the right way."

Thomas hesistated and then in a low voice muttered, "Not in one of them long trenches."

"Thomas, you was ordered to carry that note to the Gen'ral, and if'n you'd gone out on that field, you'd gotten yoreself shot. You done all you could do," reasoned Albert.

Tears began to run down Thomas's cheeks.

"Albert, I promised Paw that I'd look after John and do my best to take care of him. What is I going to tell Paw?" he whispered. "I give Paw my word that I'd stay with him."

Albert sat up and looked over at his friend to get full attention.

"You ain't God Almighty. Folks get killed in wars, and yore Papa is going to be glad just to see ya come home. Sure he's going to hurt for John, but he's going to be glad you got back."

Thomas nodded his head and wiped his face.

"You right, Albert. As soon as this army gets 'cross that river and on Southern soil, I'm going to go get James Earl and we's headed home. I'm quittin' this here damned army, and I'm going to get my sickly brother out 'fore he's dead too."

Albert was stunned. "Thomas, you can't do that. That's desertion. They'd come lookin' for ya. Hell, a while back a bunch of deserters were caught and shot. You don't want to get killed that way, do ya? Yore Paw would be ashamed of you. You can't desert this army, Thomas. Not just now."

"Albert, Paw told me if'n this war becomes a war to free them slaves, then we's fightin' for the wrong cause. And you knows Mister Lincoln is already said that he's going to free the slaves as soon as his army takes over. Paw'll understand me leavin' this army."

Albert placed his hand on Thomas's shoulder. "In a few days, you going to feel different than you do now. You going to see things better, then. You just hurtin' for yore brother, now."

"Albert, I'm a God-fearin' man and before God Almighty who is lookin' down at us right this minute, I swear when these feet of mine get back on Southern dirt, I'm goin' home, and if'n you's smart, you'll do the same. This war's over for me."

I

The Little Rock community impatiently waited to hear results of the battle. At the same time, they dreaded the moment when the casuality list, always slow to reach the rural areas, would finally arrive.

It had now been over three weeks since Lott and Toby had returned from Meridian bringing news of the battle. There was nothing to do but wait.

The evening stage from Meridian had made its usual quick stop in Little

Rock and now only a small cloud of dust remained as the stage rumbled on toward Union.

Walker, watching the stage as it dropped out of sight up a long range of hills west of the village, headed for the door.

"Becca, I'm goin' down to see Mister Sam. Put up the mail and get the place swept out 'fore I gets back," instructed Walker, making his way down the steps. "I won't be too long."

Becca smiled and began going through the mail that was lying on the counter. "Be glad to Papa. I'll have everything neat and clean when you get back."

Walker stopped at the bottom of the porch steps to see if he could get an annoying splinter out of his finger. As he was reaching into his pocket to get his knife, he heard a crash from inside.

He turned and shouted, "Becca, what's goin' on in there! You need some help?"

He dashed up the steps. Becca lay on the floor by the counter, unconscious with blood streaming from her nose.

Walker knelt down and turned Becca on her back. He couldn't tell whether she had fallen or fainted. As he tenderly placed her head on his lap and cleaned the blood from her face, he noticed a wad of paper clinched in her fist. He eased it from her hand, unwrinkled it, and in a matter of seconds, realized what had caused the fall: a lengthy casuality list had arrived with the evening mail. The report had been folded back to the name John Lewis Wilson.

A sinking feeling surged through his body. "Oh my God! This can't be true, not John, not our John."

Becca moved her arms as she regained consciousness and moaned softly. Her father cradled her in his arms and rushed out of the store and up the street.

"I've got to get her to the house as quick as I can. I've got to get her home," whispered Walker to himself.

As the sun was setting, Walker, face drawn with grief, rode his horse toward the Wilson's home. It was just a short ride, but it seemed like miles. He kept thinking to himself, "How can I tell them what has happened? Dear God, how can I tell them John is dead?"

Joe and Spot growled at the approaching horse and then tore out of the barnyard toward the intruder, barking with every breath. Toby, hearing the commotion, stepped outside to see what was disturbing the animals.

"Get back you dogs! Git on back to the barn where you belongs!" shouted Toby. "Joe, you and Spot, ought to be 'shamed. Get on back! Welcome, Mist' Walker. Sorry 'bout them dogs. Let me take yore horse for ya."

"Thank you, Toby. I'm used to them dogs barkin' at me. They don't bother me none."

Walker eased down from the saddle and handed Toby the reins.

"Sump'n ain't right, Mist' Walker? Sump'ns bad wrong."

Walker nodded and placed his hand on Toby's shoulder.

"You best come on in the house with me. I got some bad news for the family."

Lott, hearing the noise outside, opened the door to his bedroom and walked into the hall.

"Well, look who's visitin'. What brings you out at this time of the night, Mister Thomas Walker? And who is that sidekick with ya?" teased Lott.

Shaking Lott's hand, Walker cleared his throat and tried to speak, but he could hardly get the words out. "Lott, we got to talk," stammered Walker.

In the past, Thomas had never lacked for words; he usually talked too much for Lott's taste.

"You two come on in the house," beckoned Lott. "Sarah, make up some tea. We got a guest."

"Right away, Mister Wilson," replied Sarah. "Sister, heat the water 'fore you finish cleanin' them dishes."

Thomas sat down in the bedroom without saying a word. Lott felt a gnawing fear growing inside him.

"Thomas, this ain't like you to be so quiet. Has we got a problem?"

Toby moved a chair close to Walker and shook his head.

"Lott, you best get Sarah in here and leave Sister in the back room."

Sarah was just entering the room with the tea when she heard her name.

"Sarah, you best sit down. I've got some bad news for ya," sighed Thomas.

Sarah eased down by Lott, clinched his hand tightly and stared into Walker's eyes.

"It be one of my boys. It's James Earl, ain't it, Thomas? He's gone ain't he? That boy was always sickly, weren't he, Lott?" whispered Sarah, placing her head on Lott's shoulder.

"No Ma'am. It weren't James Earl, Miss Sarah," replied Walker.

"Then it were Thomas," interrupted Sarah. He's a reckless boy, and I knowed he'd take chances up there with that army."

Toby could wait no longer. "It's Mist' John you talkin' 'bout," moaned Toby, looking at the floor.

Walker could only nod slowly.

Sarah raised her hands and sobbed, then slumped into her husband's arms.

Alarmed by the sound of her mother's weeping, Sister ran into the room.

"Mamma, what's happened? What's goin' on in here?"

Her parents could say nothing. Toby went over and placed his arms around Sister and spoke as gently as he could. "Miss Cretia, Mist' John ain't comin' home. He's with the Good Lord now."

She instantly pushed Toby away and exclaimed, "You lying, Toby, you just a lyin' niggar!"

The stricken family sat in the bedroom for almost an hour without speaking a word. Finally, Lott straightened up and looked over at Walker.

"Thomas, how's Becca takin' this? This has got to be bad for her."

"Lott, Sarah, she's takin' it just like the rest of us. You has lost a son and my Becca just lost her intended husband. Her whole life has been nothin' but that boy of yores ever since she first saw him."

Later that evening, after Walker had left, Sister turned to Toby. "I didn't mean to call you names. I knowed you wouldn't tell me no story, I guess I was just takin' my pain out on ya," apologized Sister. "We love you just like one of the family, and I didn't mean to hurt ya."

Toby smiled faintly. "I know that. I knowed how you feels towards me. If'n callin' me a niggar would bring that boy back, I'd change my name to Niggar Wilson. Hadn't been for that boy buyin' my freedom, no tellin' where'd I'd be now."

The following day, after the Ollivers were seated for dinner and waiting for the blessing, the elder Olliver spoke solemnly, "Before we offer a blessin', I've got to tell ya sump'n that's happened, and it pains me more than you know. War claims lives and we have lost a friend."

His wife, head bowed for prayer, lifted her eyes and stared at her husband in dread. "Who is it, Frank? Is it someone close?"

The family joined hands in fear.

Frank cleared his throat, "It's John. He was killed durin' the last day of fightin'. I'm sorry, I always held a high opinion of that boy."

Suzanne burst into tears, pushed her chair back and ran toward her bedroom. Her mother quickly followed. Frank and his son sat in silence, staring at each other.

Finally, Frankie broke the tension. "Paw, I don't understand this war and folks gettin' killed. John was my best friend. Sure we had our ups and downs, but I just can't see him gone. It ain't no way this is happenin'. I should've been with him, Papa."

Frank reached over and placed his arm around his son, "Now you know why I wouldn't let you get on that train with them other boys. I knowed what war would bring, and I didn't want this to happen to you. I love ya too much for that."

Frankie looked up, astonished. This was the first time his father had ever told him that he loved him.

"Thank you Papa. I love you too," smiled Frankie.

Later that afternoon, Suzanne and her mother paid their respects to the Wilsons, but even though Frankie wanted to go, he did not have the courage to get in the carriage. He knew the Wilsons had always felt he should have gone with the other boys, and with John gone, how could he face them?

The entire Little Rock community grieved with the Wilsons. Even as a young child, people had a special affection for this intelligent youngster with ambition. They realized this war was costing both the North and the South too many promising young lives. When would this killing stop?

Becca tried to accept John's death, but remembering the dream she had during the rainstorm, she felt that in some mysterious way, she had received a revelation from God. John had run toward her, arms outstretched. In that instant, she felt God had let her be with him for just a fleeting second, before taking him home. She would never forget those blue eyes as he rushed toward her.

Meanwhile, Sarah sat on the porch day after day, praying and sometimes singing a hymn. With each sunset, fewer tears came to her eyes.

Lott tried to work around the farm as hard as he could to keep his mind off what had happened, but watching Sarah on the porch day after day, he had become concerned. Losing a child is a terrible experience, one some parents never overcome. Losing John was one thing, but to lose a wife would make it even worse.

Late one afternoon as Lott headed to the house after he and Toby had finished feeding the livestock, Sarah got up from her chair and slowly walked out to meet him.

"Lott, you best get the rig ready for tomorrow, you know it's church time. We got a lot to be thankful for," said Sarah, grabbing his hand and pulling him down for a kiss on the cheek.

"Yes Ma'am, Miss Sarah. I'll have everything ready in the morning," replied a surprised Lott. "What's got into you, woman? You sure seem to be feelin' more fit."

Sarah smiled. "Me and the Lord has done a lot of talkin' these past few weeks, and he told me my John is comin' home. I just needs to be patient. He'll be a'comin'."

Lott, puzzled, placed an arm around her waist as they walked toward the house.

Sarah now seemed much like her old self, except for one thing. She would get up before daybreak, dress, then go out and sit on the front porch for exactly an hour. When she heard the clock strike, she would get up and go about her normal housework. She would do the same thing each afternoon, an hour before dark.

One morning Sarah got up from her chair as the clock struck and called out. "Cretia, get out of that bed, I've got a job for ya."

Moments later, Sister straggled from her bedroom.

"Mamma, what you got on yore mind this early in the morning," grumbled Sister, half asleep. She leaned down and hugged her mother.

"Sister, this afternoon, I want you to go down to the village and get Becca. I need to talk with her," said Sarah.

"Yes Ma'am, but I don't know why ya need to see her. You seen her a humpteen dozen times these past few weeks."

"Just do what I tell ya. That's for me to know and for you and Becca to find out."

That afternoon, after the usual amenities, Sarah said, "Becca, honey, pull yore chair up close to me. And Sister, I want you to stay too."

The girls pulled their chairs close and waited, breathless.

"Girls, when I heard about what had happened to my boy, I first was angry with the Lord for doin' this to me. I swore that I was never going to go back to no church no more, but I got to thinkin' 'bout how the Lord gave his son to be killed on the cross for our sins. Then I was ashamed about what I'd been thinkin' 'bout my own boy. I then began to pray and sing to God and thank him for all my other chill'un who's still alive. One day, I kinda dozed off and all of a sudden a strong voice woke me up. It said, 'He's comin' home. You patiently wait in the twilight.' After that voice spoke to me, I been waitin' every day. I believe the Lord was truly speakin' to me."

The girls sat quietly, not knowing how to respond.

Finally, Becca reached over and grasped Sarah's hand, "Missus Wilson, mind if'n I come and sit with ya on some of these afternoons?"

"Me too, Mamma. I wants to sit with ya," added Sister.

Sarah pulled both girls close.

"It would please me greatly if'n you would. There's power in numbers, you know."

In the days that followed, the three spent many a late afternoon sitting, praying, and singing.

In Sarah Wilson's face, Becca saw a beam of hope that had lifted her out of despair, but in Becca's mind, she could not forget the dream. Spending time with Sarah, she often found herself gaining hope, but then the dream would resurface and her hope would fade.

As the weeks and months passed, Becca became convinced that her dream was God-sent and Sarah's vision nothing but a delusion. Becca's visits dwindled until she came no more. Even Sister stopped the ritual, but Sarah never faltered. No matter what the weather, she was there rocking . . . praying . . . singing.

18

ANGEL OF MERCY

THE CONTINUOUS CRIES OF THE WOUNDED IN THE DARK NIGHT haunted those soldiers who had survived the past three days of slaughter.

In the morning light of July 4th, 1863, the two armies, battered and bruised, faced one another on the same ridge of hills and wondered if the new day would bring just more fighting and bloodshed.

The first streaks of dawn revealed a battlefield strewn with thousands of dead and dying men. Smoke was still curling into the sky from wagons and caissons struck by artillery fire during the previous afternoon.

But, by mid-morning there was no sign of a renewed attack from the Southern army, so General Meade ordered burial details to begin work immediately. The wounded were to be taken to field hospitals as quickly as possible.

Soon, mule-drawn wagons rolled from the Federal entrenchments. While one group of soldiers collected the dead and wounded, another detachment began digging large burial trenches.

"Throw them on in, Private," instructed the sergeant in charge of one detachment.

"Grab them by the arms and legs and sling them. They're dead, won't hurt them none."

After three days under a hot July sun, the stench of decaying bodies, stiff and bloated beyond recognition, was almost unbearable.

Private James Martin of the 71st Pennsylvania Infantry and several members of his unit were detailed to clear an area where the Confederates had broken through a railed fence and attempted to cross a field covered in thick clover.

Private Martin had been working for almost an hour loading the dead when he and another soldier discovered a fallen Confederate lying alone, face down in tall grass on the edge of a clearing.

"Well, Sam, let's heave another one of these Johnny Rebs in the wagon. I swear it was a lot easier shooting them than loading them," complained Martin.

The men grabbed the body by it's arms and legs, but as they lifted it from the ground, they hesitated.

"Martin, this Reb's not stiff. You think he's alive?" commented Sam. "Let's lay him down and check him over."

"Live! To hell with him, Sam. Just look. He's been shot to pieces. If he's alive, he doesn't have much time left anyway. I say to the top of the heap with him."

Sam looked down at the boy, thought for a moment, then agreed. "You're right, let's give him a sling."

Once the wagons were loaded, they were driven to the burial trenches where the bodies were stacked neatly in the open pits and quickly covered with dirt. Captain Joseph Larken was supervising the soldiers. All morning he had been standing on a huge mound of dirt overlooking the site where the Confederate dead were being placed.

"All right men, throw them down below, and the men down there will lay them out straight," instructed the captain. "We got to get this job done, and we don't need to waste time."

As one body was harshly thrown to the ground, a faint moan was detected by the captain. His first impulse was to ignore the sound and get on with his task, but then he noticed a slight movement.

"Hold up a minute. Don't cover those last few, yet," he ordered.

"You people hear anything down there?" questioned the captain, sliding down the steep side of the trench.

A large soldier wiped the sweat from his face and looked down the trench and said, "They make strange sounds sometimes, Cap'n. When they hit the bottom, I figure it knocks what air they got out of them."

"Maybe so, but I'm going to check the last several we laid down," he replied, walking over the bodies. One caught his attention. He wasn't bloated, but there was a terrible wound to the head. Little chance this soldier is alive, he thought.

The captain knelt, closely examined the body, but could detect no breathing. He lay his head on the soldier's chest to listen for a heartbeat and as he rose from his crouched position, a hand feebly reached up and grabbed his sleeve. The captain, startled, fell backwards.

"My God! That boy's alive. We almost buried that soldier. Get him out of here and on a rig to the field hospital," commanded the captain. "We may have to shoot those boys from down South, but we sure don't bury them alive."

Later in the afternoon, heavy thunderstorms erupted sending sheets of rain across the war-torn countryside. One field hospital was set up in and around the church in the village north of the battlefield. Doctors and surgeons from nearby towns were asked to come and assist in caring for the wounded.

Since the church was small, soldiers were placed in long rows outside, waiting their turn for medical help. Many never survived the wait. The rain drenched the wounded as they lay helplessly on the ground.

A group of women who had volunteered to help moved from soldier to soldier trying to assist in any way possible to save lives. It didn't matter whether the wounded were from the North or South.

"If they are bleeding, try to stop it," instructed a tall middle-aged woman. "If they want water, more than the Lord has sent down, give it to them. Help them any way you can."

Among the women was a young girl only thirteen who insisted on being with her mother to serve. Her father was one of the doctors and she had often assisted him in emergency cases. Carrying a large bucket of water, she moved up and down the long lines.

When they reached a group of soldiers who had been placed near the end of one of the rows, about a quarter of a mile from the church, they noticed a young Confederate lying by himself, intentionally separated from a group of Union soldiers. Obviously in pain, the soldier was digging his heels into the mud, trying in vain to lift his left arm.

The woman and daughter, rain dripping from their big brimmed hats, stopped momentarily, watching.

"Mamma, do we help him? He looks like a Southerner," whispered the young girl.

"Southerner! Shame on you to think like that," she reprimanded. "This is one of God's creations, just like these Union boys. Sure we're going to help him. You see what you can do while I try to find some dressings."

This was the first time since they had arrived at the field hospital that Lora Caulder had allowed her daughter to personally look after one of the wounded.

The hard rain had washed some of the blood from the face of the fallen Southerner. A large depression above his right eye exposed by a section of barely attached skin meant a possible skull fracture.

She wondered if her time would be wasted on this dying man, but before she could consider further, the soldier painfully reached up to her. Looking at the struggling figure below, she could not resist. She lifted his head and slowly trickled water into his mouth, almost choking him. She then carefully wiped the remaining dried blood from the man's face and pulled the loose flesh over his wound. The soldier never opened his eyes, never spoke a word.

She straightened herself and stared down at the helpless man. His shirt had been partially stripped, revealing a tanned and muscular upperbody. He was handsome, probably not over eighteen years old, not much older than herself, she thought.

As she stood admiring the boy lying on the grass, a cool gentle breeze came up, pushing the rainclouds from the sky and allowing rays of sunlight to stretch across the hillside. This piercing light seemed to annoy the soldier. He slowly moved his left arm up to shade his eyes and then tried to speak.

The girl knelt quickly to pull his hand away from the wound on his forehead. The soldier sensed her presence, but the sunlight was so bright he could not stand the glare. All he could see was a blurred face surrounded by a sparkling golden halo.

"Am I in heaven? You're an angel?" he gasped in a trembling voice.

The girl leaned closer. "You are alive and I'm no angel, yet. You've been hurt pretty bad," she explained, giving him more water. "You're going to be just fine, I promise you."

The boy feebly clasped her hand.

"Promise not to leave me," he muttered.

She hesitated, then promised, "I won't leave you, soldier boy."

She could not believe she had made such a commitment, especially to a total stranger, especially a Southerner.

In a few minutes the soldier's vision cleared enough so he could examine the pretty young girl leaning over him with piercing blue eyes and curly blond hair. The halo he had seen was only sunlight reflecting through her golden curls. He reached up to touch the silky hair flowing down across her shoulder.

"You're an angel to me," he said. "What's yore name?"

She smiled. "I'm Lucretia, Lucretia Caulder. My Papa's a doctor. What's your name?"

The soldier thought for a minute. "I don't rightly recall; I don't know what my name be."

"Well, Mister No Name, I'm going to call you Johnny, Johnny Reb."

"I don't care what you call me," answered the boy, "just don't let me die."

When Lucretia's mother returned, she told about her experience with the boy and what she had promised. Her mother reminded her that they had others to attend and she could not afford to give all of her time to one wounded Southern boy.

Lucretia obeyed her mother's instructions, but returned to her Johnny Reb as often as she could during that day. Late that night when she had worked her way back down the line to where the young man lay, she found him unconscious and burning with fever. Knowing the danger he was in, she quickly ran to the church to find her father.

She found him almost at the point of exhaustion, working frantically to stop a soldier's severe bleeding.

"Papa, I need your help," demanded Lucretia. "There's a boy dying down there, and I need you, now."

Doctor Caulder ignored his daughter and continued his efforts to save the soldier's life. Finally, he looked to the orderly assisting him.

"Get him off the table, there's nothing I can do for him now. He's gone."

The doctor turned to his daughter. His haggard face and tired eyes relayed a clear message. "Lucretia, there's a lot of boys dying out here tonight. I'm taking them one at a time. You do your best with him, and when I can, I'll see what I can do."

For the rest of the night, Lucretia stayed with her patient and tried to keep him cool. As soon as it was daylight, she cleaned his wound with whiskey she had sneaked from the hospital and carefully stitched the torn flesh on his forehead.

A day later, with Johnny still unconscious, Lucretia's father appeared, examined the wound and then shook his head in dismay.

"Sugar, you did a fine job stitching this wound, but by the looks, he's got a fracture," announced Doctor Caulder.

"Will he live, Papa?"

The doctor shook his head. "Only God knows, Baby. This boy has got a serious injury, and if he does live, he may not have his right mind."

Lucretia and her father then rolled the boy over on his side and found a gaping wound to his back. Doctor Caulder tore his shirt apart and closely examined the injury.

"Lucretia, this doesn't look too promising. His shoulder blade by the way it is shattered, must have stopped a pretty big piece of metal, and some of it appears to be lodged fairly close to his spine. I wouldn't attempt to try to take it out, it could paralyze him."

"What can we do, Papa?" pleaded Lucretia. "I can't let him die."

Doctor Caulder looked down at the boy and then to his daughter. "Try to clean it up the best you can and keep a bandage on it. It's too big of a mess to try to sew up," instructed her father. "And you best do a lot of praying if you want that poor soul to live."

The doctor walked away, never expecting to see the boy alive again. But, three days later, Johnny regained consciousness and his fever was gone. The boy spoke little, and was able to roll over on the side opposite his injured shoulder, allowing Lucretia to apply clean dressings. While removing an old bandage, she almost fainted at what she found. She eased Johnny back on his side and ran as fast as she could to locate her father.

Finding him sitting out behind the church taking a rest, she frantically told him, "Papa, he's got worms in his wound, he's going to rot to pieces!" exclaimed Lucretia. "What do I do now?"

Her father looked at her solemnly. "Is his fever gone?"

"Almost, Papa," nodded Lucretia.

"Is he conscious?"

"Yes Sir, he is."

A slow smile crossed her father's exhausted face.

"Lucretia, it looks like your soldier may be on the mend, and as for those worms, they probably saved his life. They are taking care of the gangrene I was worried about."

"Is this a miracle, Papa?"

"It may just be, Lucretia. Yes, it has got to be that."

After the battle, the Confederate prisoners and those not seriously injured were herded into boxcars and sent to Federal prisons. The seriously injured who could not be moved, were placed in Union hospitals or assigned to families in the Gettysburg area until they had recovered. As soon as they were well enough to travel, they would join the other prisoners.

Lucretia persuaded her father to talk with the Union officer in charge of placing the injured Confederates into homes, and as she had hoped, Johnny was assigned to their family.

For weeks, Johnny was too weak to stand alone and could only walk short distances with help. His wounds slowly healed. Lucretia had done an excellent job stitching the torn area over his eye. Except for the slight recession near his hairline, it was hard to tell he had been wounded.

The wound to his back was another story, but it eventually healed, leaving a large scar. The young Southerner's memory still eluded him.

Due to intense pain in his back, Johnny could barely lift his right arm. Doctor Caulder instructed Lucretia to work the young man's arm as much as possible to condition the shoulder muscles.

Early one morning after breakfast Johnny sat on the side of his bed while Lucretia pulled a chair in front of him to help with his exercise. She admired the muscles in his arms, aware that Johnny was no stranger to physical labor.

"Alright, Mister Johnny, let me see you pick that arm up," instructed Lucretia giving him a determined look. "You're a big boy. You can do it."

Painfully, he picked his arm up trying to make his shoulder move in a rotating motion. He was determined not to let Lucretia or anyone else see him in agony.

"Ain't nothin' to it," he exclaimed. "Won't be long 'fore I'll be just fine."

Each time he tried, he felt like screaming. After a few minutes with sweat pouring down his face, he eased his arm down and carefully eyed the girl who had so faithfully cared for him.

Lucretia blushed and twisted nervously in her chair. "Why are you looking at me like that? Is something wrong with me?"

Johnny smiled. "Nothin' wrong. I just can't understand why you has taken me in and cared for me like you has. You didn't have to show me this kind of mercy. Why'd you pick me?"

Lucretia thought about how to answer.

"Johnny, when I looked down at you lying there on that grass, helpless, something inside told me to see if I could do something. And when I gave you my word that I wouldn't leave you, that's just what I did."

"I don't remember that," he replied. "But I'm sure glad you did," he continued, reaching down for her hand.

"How old are you anyway, young lady?"

Lucretia blushed again. "I'm almost fourteen. Why?"

John began to laugh. "You reminds me a lot of my sister back home, that is, on her good days. Her name's Lucretia, too, but we calls her Sister. She's not as pretty as you, though."

"You think I'm pretty, Johnny?"

Suddenly, she caught her breath. "Johnny, you just told me something about yourself! You're getting your memory back! Papa told me this might happen."

John slowly released her hand and laid down on the bed. "Lucretia, I been recalling bits and pieces for the last few days, but I didn't want to say nothin' till I knowed that what I was thinkin' was real. Your name for me was pretty close. My name is John, John Wilson, and I come from Little Rock Mis'sippi."

John stared out of the window. "My daddy's name is Lott and my mother is Sarah, Sarah Alice. I've got two older brothers, but I can't recall their names. I've told you 'bout Sister, and there's somebody in my family's named Toby or sump'n like that."

John paused for a moment. " Lucretia, that's 'bout all I know."

"I'm proud of you, John," smiled Lucretia, wanting to know more about the handsome young man lying in front of her.

"Do you have a girlfriend back in Little Rock?" continued Lucretia. "I bet you do."

John closed his eyes and tried as hard as he could to bring back his past, but he remembered no one.

"Don't think so. I'm probably too young for that. Why, what difference does it make?"

"None, I don't think. I just wondered. You are kind of handsome, Johnny, I mean John."

Looking into Lucretia's angelic face, John saw for the first time more than someone who had been caring for him; he saw a beautiful young girl blossoming into womanhood.

Lucretia was afraid she had been too bold questioning John, but she longed to reach out, pull him to her and hold him tightly. Her heart pounded just thinking about the touch of his lips against hers.

"Come on John," demanded Lucretia. "Let's go tell Papa about your memory. I can hardly wait to tell him about your family."

That evening at dinner, Doctor Caulder said, "Son, I'm glad you're beginning to get your memory back. That's a good sign."

"Yes Sir, some things is comin' back to me. I can certainly remember my parents and my two older brothers and my younger sister. I can see them as clear as lookin' at you, Doctor Caulder."

Lora eased her cup down. "John, does your family have land and slaves like I hear about all the time?"

John stopped eating and placed his fork quietly on his plate.

"Missus Caulder, we have a lot of land. Papa owns a section and my Uncle Jake, who's dead now, owned another'n. And then Minsa, a Choctaw, well that's a long story."

Lucretia continued her mother's question, "How about slaves, John. Do you own some?"

John shook his head. "No, we don't have none. My family don't believe in holdin' slaves; we do good to feed our own, much less slaves. Most folks 'round Little Rock don't have no slaves either."

"That's good," commented Doctor Caulder. "I'm a little surprised. I thought most Southerner's had them."

Lucretia interrupted her father. "Then why are you fighting against the Union if it's not for slavery. I don't understand."

John took a swallow of tea, picked up his napkin and carefully wiped his mouth.

"Sometimes I wonder that myself," replied John. Thinking clearer now, he shook his head, "It's not just slavery, it's 'cause we believe in states' rights, and the South is just too different from the North. Our culture is different. We don't need tariffs on everything we buy that's manufactured, and we don't care much for them factories and such like that. And when a state joined the Union, who said we couldn't withdraw if'n things didn't work out?"

"John, did you go to school down there in Little Rock. You sound like you have," admitted the doctor.

"I don't rightly recall any school. Perhaps I did. I don't know."

In the days that followed, as John's health improved, he joined in family outings. Doctor Caulder took John and Lucretia with him as he made house calls, and every Sunday, John dressed in civilian clothes when he attended church services with the Caulders.

Lucretia was too young for boys to call on her, and it delighted her to have such a handsome young soldier escorting her about the countryside.

One afternoon, Doctor Caulder took the family trout fishing in a nearby stream. John remembered his own fishing trips back home and each day, he slowly recalled more and more details of his life before the battle.

Three months had now passed since the terrible battle and with John's improved health, it would be only a matter of time until he would be sent away.

During the long stay with the Caulders, John had become part of the family. He helped around the house and assisted Doctor Caulder with his patients, no matter what time of the night it would be. No longer was he thought of as the enemy, a Rebel.

One afternoon, Doctor Caulder came home early. His family was sitting on the porch awaiting his arrival. He walked over, eased down, and kissed his wife and then pulled a chair to where John was sitting.

"John, I talked with a Lieutenant Barker this morning in town and, well, there's a train leaving for Illinois in the morning and you are to be on it. I did all I could to stall him, but the folks 'round here have noticed how well you are doing, and I think the lieutenant felt I have been sheltering you."

John lowered his head, puzzled.

"Doctor Caulder, why is they sendin' me up there, just to parole me and then send me all the way back to Mis'sippi? That don't make no sense."

Quietly, Doctor Caulder replied, "John, the government has stopped paroling Southern prisoners. They are sending you boys to prisons where you will stay until this war is over."

"Papa, they can't do that to John!" Lucretia cried. "Can't they see he's not able to fight any more. He's no enemy. He needs to go home, or stay here with us."

"That's right, Henry, John doesn't need to go up there. Isn't there anything you, we can do?" demanded his wife.

Doctor Caulder took his handkerchief and wiped Lucretia's tears, "I'm sorry, but this is wartime, and we don't have that kind of power. Don't you think I've already tried?"

That evening Lucretia and John sat in the swing on the front porch and watched the sun as it slowly set. Fall was in the air and a cool breeze was blowing out of the northwest. The leaves had turned brilliant shades of red and gold and were already finding their way to the ground. As Lucretia shivered in the cool air, John placed his arm around her and pulled her to his side.

They sat quietly for a while, swinging and watching the leaves flip and spin as occasional gusts shook them from their branches.

Lucretia looked up at John and fastened a loose button on his shirt.

"John, one time you said you thought I was pretty. Did you mean it?"

John squeezed her gently and smiled. "Sure, I meant it. I ain't never seen anybody prettier than you. And Lucretia, you is pretty inside, too."

"John, if you really think so, then I want you to kiss me," she whispered. "I've never been kissed by a boy, and I want you to be my first."

John reddened, turned his head away and coughed nervously. Regaining his composure, he took her by the hand and eased out of the swing.

"Lucretia, I will indeed be more than glad to kiss you. It will be my pleasure," replied John, giving her a polite bow.

Lucretia wrapped her arms around him as she stretched up on her tiptoes, tilted her head upwards toward the young man that she had grown to idolize and closed her eyes. She had wanted to hold John close and feel the touch of his lips against hers for so long.

John gently raised her chin and pulled her closer. When their lips touched, a friendship was thrust aside and replaced by tender passion, a love that had slowly been nurtured through the long months.

Lucretia trembled as she stood in his arms.

"John, you kissed me that time, now I want to kiss you."

Once more the two embraced, but as John looked into her face, suddenly, unexplainably, he saw another girl in his arms. Her eyes were emerald green and her hair was red. The vision was so frightful, he pushed Lucretia away and stood still, puzzled and confused.

"John, I shouldn't have asked you to kiss me," apologized Lucretia, thinking she had offended him by being too forward. "I didn't know what I was doing. I don't know anything about kissing," she said, running toward the front door.

"Lucretia, wait! Something happened I can't explain," pleaded John. "I saw someone that I, please come back and sit with me. You did nothin' wrong. Come back to the swing."

That night as John lay in his bed drifting in and out of sleep, he was haunted by the image of the mysterious girl staring at him. Sometime before dawn he heard a voice in the darkness, "Becca, Becca, Becca."

John sat up instantly. "Becca, I know you. I know who you are now."

Love for Becca filled his heart as he remembered. How he longed to see her again. But what about the passion he felt for Lucretia?

John rose early and dressed in the uniform that had been washed and mended for him. When he learned that the whole family planned to go to the depot, he requested that only Doctor Caulder accompany him. The doctor did not understand why this was so important.

The doctor harnessed his horse to the family buggy and at ten o'clock John eased down the steps and edged his way toward the waiting rig. He turned and embraced Lora Caulder.

"Before I leave, I want you to know that there ain't no way I can thank you enough for what you did for me. You made me feel a part of yore family. I thank ya," stammered John.

He then turned to Lucretia. "And for you, young lady, I owe you my life. I'll never forget them hours we spent together. You're sump'n special. You're my angel," said John, taking her in his arms.

He thought, "I should tell her how I really care for her, but maybe what I'm feelin' really isn't. I just don't know."

As mother and daughter watched the buggy wind down the path toward the main road, Mrs. Caulder pulled her daughter close.

"Lucretia, I know how you feel. We all are going to miss that young man. But if the Lord sees fit, he'll come back some day. A prayer can't do any harm."

Lucretia smiled up at her mother. "Mamma, you think I'll ever see him again? I've just got to."

"That's the Lord's bus'ness. Let's just put this matter in his hands, Daughter."

When Doctor Caulder and John reached the depot, they found Lieutenant Barker, and John was taken to the area where scores of prisoners were being guided into boxcars.

John turned to face his mentor. "Doctor, I want to thank ya for savin' me, too. Yore family is a lot like mine back home, a lot of love for one another. I hope to see you again sometime, and in some way, I hope I can repay you."

Doctor Caulder's eyes filled with tears. "John, you don't owe us anything. Through these last few months, you have become like a son to me. You have taken the place of the boy I lost eight years ago. No, John, you don't owe us. Come back to see us when this war's over."

John shook Doctor Caulder's hand and then, with tears running down his face, embraced the man who had become like a father. He then turned to join the other soldiers, but paused after a few steps.

"Doctor Caulder, I almost forgot. Please get word to my folks that I'm fine. Tell them where they's sendin' me."

"I'll try, Son! You know I'll try!"

19

LONG ROAD HOME

THE HEAVY DOORS SLAMMED SHUT ENCLOSING THE SOUTHERN soldiers in a leaded gloom. Some seventy prisoners and five armed Federal soldiers were crammed in each boxcar. These ragged souls, headed for a wretched Illinois prison, should have been depressed and despondent as they sat shoulder to shoulder. Instead they had a collective determination to survive.

One called out to the sergeant in charge, "Hey Boss, where's you takin' us to?"

The sergeant looked back. "We're carrying you boys to a sure enough hellhole. That's where you're goin'," scoffed the crusty soldier.

"Can't do that, Boss. We done there. We been in hell ever since we crossed the Potomac," replied the soldier amidst cheers and laughter.

"I just hope you boys like cold weather and pig slop. That's what you're headed for," countered the sergeant, irritated by the Southern humor.

Determined to keep the harassment going, another prisoner who had lost an arm to a surgeon's saw, stood up to get the sergeant's attention.

"Bossman, you feel sorry for boys like me that got their arms hacked off?"

The Union soldiers became apprehensive.

One of the guards replied, "We are human beings just like you. We don't take pride in you losin' no arm."

"Well, it be just fine that I lost that damned ole arm of mine. It was causing me to sin over and over," replied the amputee.

"What do you mean, it caused you to sin so much?" replied one of the guards.

The soldier raised his head upward as if addressing the Good Lord himself. "Well, it says in the Good Book that thou shalt not kill, and that ole finger on that long gone arm of mine just kept on a pullin' that trigger and sendin' them pore Yanks to an early grave," concluded the soldier.

So much Southern laughter shook the car that the sergeant felt compelled to fire his pistol into the ceiling to regain order.

The boxcar became suddenly quiet, as the sergeant picked up a double barreled shotgun and moved toward the center of the car.

"Let me tell you Sons of Bitches something. You aren't going to make fun of this army of mine, and I'm not putting up with none of your foolishment. I lost a brother and a cousin to Rebel bullets, and I hope to God some of you bastards try to escape. I'll kill you quicker than lightning strikes."

A tense silence settled over the boxcar. Only the clankity clack of the heavy wheels striking the joints of the track could be heard as the train sped through the darkness.

John, listening to these sounds, remembered the excitement he and his friends felt as they loaded the train at Newton headed for the glorious service in Mister Lee's army. He could still see his family standing there waving to him and how Becca looked so radiant as she blew a kiss. He also remembered how cold it was on the train as the snow covered him and his companions on that trip to Virginia. John then painfully visualized the hundreds of dead and dying men scattered on the battlefields he prayed he would never see again.

One of the prisoners called out. "When we going to get sump'n to eat? I ain't eaten in two days."

There was no reply.

"I can just taste them sweet 'tators and fried ham, back home right now," mummured another prisoner.

"I'm so hungry I could eat a chitt'lin a mile long," chuckled another.

The men howled in laughter.

"Hey, anybody here from Mis'sippi?"

John spoke up, "I come from Little Rock. Some call it Coon Tail. Not far from Meridian."

The tall lanky soldier made his way through the mass of men huddled on the floor and sat next to John.

"I'm Sam Harris. I come from Magnolia, Mis'sippi. Good to meet ya," said the soldier, extending his hand.

For the next several hours, they talked about life in their home state, war experiences and loved ones at home. The two had a lot in common, and a natural friendship began to bind the boys together. Around four o'clock in the morning when all were asleep, Sam nudged John.

"You see that knapsack hangin' on that peg over the sergeant's head?" whispered Sam. "It's got some crackers in it, and I'm going to steal us a bit."

"You best not, Sam. One of them Yanks is s'pose to be watchin'. You might get caught, and they's lookin' for a reason to shoot us."

"Don't give a damn. I ain't eaten in days, and I think that sergeant was just blowin' off steam. I'm a going to try to get us sump'n."

Sam eased up from his crouched position and stealthily made his way through the sleeping prisoners, constantly eyeing the sleeping guards.

Approaching the knapsack, he hesitated for just a moment to make certain no one was looking, then glanced over toward the sergeant who was curled up in the front corner of the car. He quietly reached up and slipped his hand inside. But, suddenly in haste, he knocked the sack from its peg sending the bag tumbling to the floor. No sooner had it struck the floor, than one of the guards awoke, leaped up and grabbed Sam's hand.

"What you think you doing, Reb? You're supposed to be back there with those other men."

"I'm just stretchin' my legs a little," stammered Sam.

Hearing the commotion, the sergeant in charge got to his feet. Seeing the knapsack on the floor, he sensed the prisoner was up to no good.

"Stretching your legs! Hell, Boy, I know what you're up to. You're stealing, aren't you? Open your hand and let me see what you've got," ordered the sergeant.

Sam smiled weakly and opened his hand, as bits and pieces of cracker crumpled to the floor.

"Just what I thought. You're trying to steal army provisions, aren't you? I hate Rebs and I especially hate thieving Rebs," scowled the sergeant.

"Two of you men keep your guns on the prisoners, and the rest of you get a good hold on him. This boy's got a lesson to learn.

Sam struggled to free himself, but ceased when he realized his effort was useless.

"What you going to do to me? I was just hungry. I ain't eaten in days," pleaded Sam.

"You don't steal from the army. Place his hand against the side of the car," ordered the sergeant.

The sergeant took his shotgun and with one jab, slammed the butt of the gun against Sam's outstretched hand. With a loud moan and wrenching in pain, he sank to his knees.

The prisoners, angry at such blatant cruelty, leaped to their feet and rushed toward the guards. A loud shotgun blast erupted, sending the prisoners to the floor in fear.

"Stop where you are!" commanded the sergeant. "The next one of you that gets up is going to get himself killed. This man was caught in the act of stealing, and he deserved what he got. As one of you bastards said, 'That hand of mine ain't going to do no more sinning for a while.' This one won't be thieving for a long time, not with that hand."

The sergeant pointed to John, "You back there. Come get this piece of trash and keep him out of my sight."

John helped Sam to the rear of the car, and with the help of other prisoners eased him to the floor.

John took Sam's battered hand and held it toward the light of a lantern to see how badly it was hurt.

"Easy, John, he might near beat it flat, didn't he?" gasped Sam.

John shook his head, "They did break it up most bad, but I seen Doc Caulder set one that was might near this busted. I'll do what I can to set it for ya, but I ain't promisin' nothin'. Sam, I can't believe they busted you up for tryin' to keep from starvin'."

"Doctor on me, if'n you can," smiled Sam. "I ain't got much choice, do I?"

Right before daybreak, John lay awake thinking how hunger had driven Sam to risk death for only a cracker. Glancing up front, he saw the sleeping soldiers and noted that the knapsack still lay on the floor where Sam had dropped it. He thought to himself how his father had taught him to slip through the woods while stalking squirrels, and a knapsack only twenty feet away should be an easy take. John finally mustered enough courage to cautiously creep on all fours toward his goal. He would move two or three feet and then wait a moment or two and then move again.

In no time at all, John reached his target. He curled up next to the knapsack and pretended to be sleeping. Slowly he reached into the bag. After he had taken four crackers, he quietly eased back to where Sam was lying.

John nudged Sam, pushed a cracker into his hand and whispered, "Just put it in yore mouth. Don't bite down. Let it get soft first."

"Where'd you get this?" Sam said, in amazement, then realized what John had done.

"You must be some kind of fool. They could've got you too," he muttered, "but I is obliged to ya."

John gave Sam a wink. "You deserve a cracker or two after the bustin' they give ya."

The air began to chill as the train moved northward, and then after more than a week, it reached its destination. The prisoners were herded onto a holding yard glazed over with a thick layer of ice and snow. Some of the prisoners had no jackets to protect them, and many were barefooted.

Not far from the railroad yard was the prison camp that would be their home. It was south of Chicago on property Senator Douglas of Illinois had donated to the United States Government. Looking toward the camp, John could make out rows of tents and shacks that afforded little shelter from extreme weather. The mosquitoes and flies of the summer months had made life unbearable for the Southerners, and now winter brought even more misery. Cold winds off Lake Michigan would often hold temperatures far below freezing for weeks at a time. Hundreds of prisoners never survived the cold nights; they froze to death in their sleep. Those who survived the weather, battled malnutrition, diarrhea and dysentery. As John and the other prisoners entered the gate, they had no concept of the hardship and possible death awaiting them.

John slipped several times on the glassy ice and the blistery cold wind sent chills through his body. The inadequate shelters and the haggard appearance of veteran prisoners glaring out at them brought doubt to John's heart that he would ever live to see his loved ones again.

Sam, his battered hand swollen and roughly bound, pointed toward the rows of shacks, "War's great, ain't it, John. We's going to be a bunch of heros when this mess is over."

"Yeah Sam, it's been most good to us," shrugged John.

I

It was now January, 1864. For weeks, Becca hardly ever left her house, and when she did, she would ride up to the Wilsons to visit with Sister and sit with her mother.

Becca's father had been sickly for several days. One day when he left the house following lunch, he asked Becca to come about mid-afternoon to help with the chores. He planned to close early to return home and rest as soon as the afternoon stage had made its run.

But, due to the rainy weather and poor roads, the stage was over an hour late. When it finally arrived, Walker unloaded his ordered items as quick as he could and told Becca to sort the mail.

In a few minutes Becca came from behind the counter waving an envelope.

"Papa, this here is a strange letter to the Wilsons. I mean, just a envelope," exclaimed Becca. "You best take a look at it."

"Well sir. It appears this here letter has had a rough go of it," exclaimed her father.

"It's been torn into and its contents has been lost or taken. And look at its return address. The outer edge is wet and the only thing I can make out is somebody named Caulder from somewhere in Pennsylvanie has wrote the Wilsons a letter."

Becca looked puzzled as she re-examined the envelope.

"Papa, who do they know up there? I ain't never heard them talk 'bout folks up in Pennsylvanie. This don't make no sense at all."

"Well daughter, if you will, and me bein' on the sick side, how about you carryin' this out to Lott and Sarah. This could be important to them."

Becca shook her head, "Papa, I'd rather not go up there. I get funny feelings, now that John is gone, and Missus Wilson is always askin' why I don't come up and sit with her no more. Please don't insist on me goin'."

"I understand," replied her father. "I'll wait 'til tomorrow and carry it myself. I need to see if'n Lott will let me borrow Toby for a couple of days to help me round the store."

The next morning, Lott and Sarah had no idea who could be writing them from Pennsylvania. They knew no one up in that part of the country and were surprised a letter had come across enemy lines in the first place. No wonder it had been torn apart.

Shortly, Thomas mounted his horse and bade farewell to his old friends. "You come down to see us when you can. It gets mighty quiet at the store, 'specially in the winter months."

"We'll do that 'fore long," replied Lott.

Sister came running from the barn where she had been doing the morning milking.

"Tell Becca to come up to see us. I've been missin' her visits," insisted Sister.

"She ain't been feelin' too fittin' as of late," explained Mister Walker. "I'm sure she'll be up here soon."

As soon as Thomas had gone, Sarah turned to her daughter. "Sister, you heard anything about Becca seein' that Olliver boy as of late. The ladies at church is tellin' that they seen the two of them buggy ridin' the other day."

What her mother was suggesting both surprised and embarrassed Sister. Becca was her best friend and Frankie almost like a member of their family.

"Mamma, you ought to be ashamed. Frankie is like a brother to Becca and me, and he's took the both of us for rides. Becca has been through a lot, just like the rest of us, and if Frankie can lift her spirits a little, then what harm can come of it?"

"Sister go fetch the milk," instructed Mrs. Wilson "And for Frankie Olliver, he ought to be up there fightin' that war like the other boys round here . . . like John."

Sister jumped down the steps and skipped toward the barn. "Mamma, you got some funny notions sometimes."

"They may be funny, but you hear me. Our John is a comin' one of these days. And I'll tell you 'bout Frankie. He's always had a fancy for Becca, and I says he's makin' a play for her."

Sister laughed and raced toward the stables, "If you says so, Mamma, but I say we's all just friends."

I

On April 11, 1865, the sound of cannon fire shook the ground around Camp Douglas, sending prisoners scurrying from their shelters. For months they had known the war was not going well for the South and that it would be only a matter of time until their side would have to give up its struggle.

Suddenly, the guards posted around the perimeter of the stockade began cheering as each fieldpiece was discharged. Something important had happened.

Sam ran down the path to his tent and threw up the flap.

"John, get up! You won't believe what's happened! Lee surrendered, two days ago, and they expects all the other gen'rals is going to call it quits too."

John tried to get up, but was so weak he had to let Sam help him to a sitting position.

"'Bout time, Sam. I'm ready to go home to my folks, and as soon as we get there, I want you to stay long enough to be my best man," replied John. "Help me out of here. We need to do some celebratin'."

John had now been inside the confines of Camp Douglas for over two years and had barely escaped death on three different occasions. When he had entered the camp, he had been in excellent health, but now he was only a skeleton. His cheeks were sunken and his once smooth face was covered with a dark black beard. Like his father, he had grayed prematurely. Streaks of silver ran through his hair on each temple making him look older than he was. John had survived the largest military engagement ever fought on American soil, battled disease and the extreme elements of Camp Douglas, but he now faced the greatest challenge: enduring the trip home.

On May 14, 1865, the prisoners were called into formation. Once assembled, Major Ben Anderson addressed the group.

"Men, as you have surely heard, General Lee has surrendered along with the rest of the Confederate Army. This war is over. You are no longer prisoners of the United States. In the morning at eight o'clock, you will be officially parolled."

A loud burst of cheering and screaming erupted that startled the citizens who lived on the outskirts of Chicago and near the camp.

The next morning, John stood in line as each prisoner placed his signature on a release form. Finally, it was his time and after laying the pen down on the table, he and Sam walked out as free men. Approaching the guard at the gate, he asked, "Yank, now that we's free, how's we going to get back home?"

"Get home! You hear that?" laughed the soldier as he motioned to some other soldiers posted nearby.

"This Reb wonders how he's going to get home. He must expect a train ticket or something. Well boy, Ole Gen'ral Lee didn't send you boys no tickets," continued the officer. "Just use those legs and keep the sun over your left shoulder in the morning and over your right shoulder in the afternoon. Sooner or later, you'll get home or you'll have to swim the Gulf of Mexico."

Sam looked at the ground for a few seconds and then back into the soldier's face.

"You know what's wrong with you? You weren't fit to fight us in the field, that's why they stuck you up here at this prison. I bet you is one of them Yanks that run from the fight. You ain't worth me talkin' to, and we can certainly walk home, if'n we have to."

Several Union soldiers rushed over ready for a scuffle.

"Hold back men. This Southern trash doesn't bother me none. They probably won't make it home anyway. Let it be," stated the soldier coldly.

John and Sam turned and along with a stream of Southerners filed out the gateway and down the road.

"Well, John, the sun's over our left shoulder. We must be headed south," commented Sam, patting John on the back.

"Right, Sam, but I'm mighty weak to walk it all the way home. I don't think I'll be able."

Sam chuckled. "John, I ain't plannin' to do a heap of walkin'. We don't have no ticket, but I do know how to jump trains, and if need be, I can steal a horse or two. We going to get you home to that good lookin' gal of yores. And one more thing, we best separate from all these other boys. We'll do best stayin' to ourselves. Easier to find food and not get caught."

It took only five days to work their way through Illinois, and after hiding on a barge crossing the Ohio River, the boys finally reached Kentucky soil. They skillfully sneaked off the barge and sprinted into thick woods near the riverbank.

Huddled in the cover of the bushes, John whispered, "Sam, we ain't eaten in three days. I can't go much farther like this," he insisted, crouching behind a large oak as he tried to catch his breath. "We got to find sump'n to eat."

Sam nodded. "There's got to be a town or a farm near here. Let's see what we can find."

After waiting a while to be sure they had not been spotted, the two sneaked out of hiding and trudged down the road away from the river landing. To their surprise, they had only walked a few miles when they came upon the village of Wickliffe, Kentucky.

The boys walked into town, cautiously watching the people as they stirred about their morning business. John inquired about doing chores to earn food, but no one seemed interested in helping them. Working their way down the street, John entered a general merchandizing store and introduced himself to the merchant in charge.

"Sir, I'm John Wilson from Mis'sippi, and I'm tryin' to make my way home. You got any chores I can do to earn some food?" explained John, extending his hand.

The elderly man raised his head and adjusted his glasses to examine the young man standing in front of him.

"You one of them Rebs, ain't ya? One of them prisoners from up near the lakes. Look at yoreself, boy. I don't want the likes of you in my place. Bad for business. Now get on out of here 'fore I call the law."

John still held his hand out in greeting. "Mister, I'm just hungry. I need sump'n to eat."

"I said get. You ain't the first to come through here. You boys is about to steal us all blind. Now get," ordered the merchant.

John quietly left the store and met Sam coming down the street.

"You have any luck findin' chores? They all but kicked me out of that store," sighed John.

"It appears some of our soldiers has already been through here and caused some trouble."

"Seems so, John. I ain't done much better, but you just go on down near the end of the street and wait for me there. I got a plan."

A half hour passed and Sam was nowhere to be seen.

Suddenly, John heard loud hollering and there was Sam thundering down the street astride a large gray horse with a loaf of bread under his arm and a ham strung across his saddlehorn.

"Get ready, John! We got to get fast!"

As the horse approached, John could see a group of men in pursuit. Two were armed.

"Catch my hand, John, and swing up," shouted Sam.

As he reached up to grab the outstretched hand, he heard a thundering sound from up the street. Instantly, Sam toppled from the saddle and tumbled to the ground. The horse, startled by the loud gunshots, galloped wildly down the road and out of sight.

Sam lay motionless on the dusty street. John rolled Sam over and knelt down by his side. Blood gushed from his chest. The bullet had gone completely through him.

"Sam, why'd you do a fool thing like that. You done gone and got yoreself killed," muttered John.

Gasping for breath, Sam whispered, "You 'member when I was hungry and you stole them crackers for me. I owed ya."

He tried to speak once more, then eased his head over on John's lap.

"You pore boy. I weren't so hungry that yore life was worth this."

The men now encircled John with pistols drawn and motioned for him to stand.

"Boy, you has stole yore last horse in Kentuck'. You going to be jailed, and you is going to see the judge," growled the town marshall.

"You didn't have to kill him. You just shot him down like a dog. We was just hungry."

John stayed in the county jail for three weeks until his case came in review to Judge Clarence Topper. After listening to witnesses and to John, the judge ruled that John had not actually stolen the horse or food, but because of his action to mount the horse, was clearly in on the theft. He was sentenced to one year in the county jail, providing he behaved himself.

As the heavy iron door slammed shut, John shouted, "I'm innocent! I had nothin' to do with it! I never stole anything. I been taught better than that."

He slumped down on the hard cot next to the wall and mumbled to himself. "The only thing I ever took was a few stale crackers, just crackers. My friend is dead and now a year in jail. God in heaven."

Meanwhile, the South anxiously awaited the return of its heralded heroes. In a few cases, entire companies marched in formation over hundreds of miles of rough roads to be officially dismissed when they reached their home county. But for the most part, the men just trickled back into their homeland any way possible.

During May and July of 1865, thousands of soldiers returned to the outstretched arms of their wives and parents. Many who returned had been listed as either dead or missing in action. Their arrival home startled friends and loved ones, bringing unexpected joy. By August most of the surviving soldiers had returned and were rebuilding their lives and homes.

A dry, late summer wind swept across the front porch of the Wilson home, but as usual, Sarah was out at dusk. With the last rays of light, an owl screeched off in the distance and the night became alive with the sound of singing locusts.

Lott, easing his way toward the house, spotted his wife sitting out front.

"Sarah, when you going to finish yore foolishness? He ain't ever comin' home. You got to face what's happened," said Lott, removing his shoes. "All the boys is home now. That is, all that's comin' back."

Sarah continued rocking. "You think what you might, Husband, but he's a comin'. You'll see."

Lott, frustrated, slung his shoes to the floor. "Dadburn it, Woman! I'll swear, you is becomin' as crazy as a flitter. Folks 'round here is beginnin' to talk. That boy's dead, and you best accept it."

Sarah was unmoved and continued her rocking, ignoring her husband's outburst.

"Faith, Husband. Just a little faith."

During that summer of 1865, Becca had also waited for a miracle. She had heard of soldiers who were thought to be dead, and without notice, had shown up at their homes unannounced. Maybe John would come home and surprise her. But by September, she had lost hope.

One afternoon Suzanne and Frankie Olliver came to visit and Frankie invited Becca to go with his family to visit relatives in Louisana.

"Becca, if'n you will go with us, we'll surely show you the time of yore life," promised Suzanne.

"You ain't never seen such a plantation as my grandpapa has. He's got three of them, and we can go into New Orleans, and that is some kind of beautiful city. You'll love it all," exclaimed Frankie.

Becca shook the hair out of her eyes.

"I don't know, Frankie. I'm not sure Mamma'll let me go, but it does sound like fun. I ain't never been that far from home."

I

John peered through the bars as the guard sat leisurely leaning back in his chair whittling on a stick.

"Can I write a letter to my folks, Mister Goss? I need to let them know where I is and what has happened to me," insisted John.

Goss laid his knife down.

"John, you is a prisoner and prisoners don't get them priv'leges. And how you going to pay for the stamp? You got money?"

"No Sir, I ain't got no money, but I can get my folks to send me enough to pay you back."

"Pay me back! Hell, boy, I ain't no banker. I don't loan out no money to prisoners."

20

MIRACLE AT CHRISTMAS

Hank Goss knocked the mud off his boots at the door, then angrily slung his oilcloth on a peg behind his desk.

"I'm tired of rain, and I'm tired of cold weather, and I'm sure as hell tired of all this gummy mud," complained the jailer as he moved quickly to the woodstove near the back of the jail.

Hank, in his late forties, was short, stocky, and almost bald. What little hair he had was cleanly shaven. The only real hair was on his face, a long black mustache that he kept waxed and curled.

"John, you awake? I'm ready for some checkies."

The covers rustled and a sleepy-eyed young man poked his head from underneath a pile of blankets.

"You sure can be loud when you want to. Yeah Hank, I'm awake now. How can a man sleep with all the racket you makin'? And yore complainin' is enough to give a band of angels a headache. And for playin' you in a game of checkies, it ain't no fun no more."

"Ain't no fun! What ya mean, boy? You and I has had many a good time playin'."

John, wrapping a blanket around his shoulders, got out of bed, opened the barred door, and pulled a chair near the stove.

"Hank, look at it this way. We play one or two games; I always win; and then you get mad and throw the checkie board and checkies all over the place. That ain't exactly what I call fun," complained John.

"Hell! That's what I like about it," laughed Hank. "It's gettin' mad and seein' them checkies fly all over the place that makes this game for me. Let's play. Who knows, this might be the day I win one, and then you can throw the checkies," joked Hank.

"Well, I guess I is still the prisoner. Get the board and let's go at it," agreed John. "Hank, has I got any work to do today?"

"Naw, the weather's too bad. We stayin' in," grunted Hank. "You know, we going to miss you when yore time's up. You has sure turned out the work these last six months. I believe you is better than them slaves you said worked for that Olliver man down near yore homeplace."

"You sayin' I been doin' slave labor, Hank?"

"That's right, boy. You has done it well," snickered Hank.

When John was put in jail, he had resented his confinement at first. But, with the passing of time, he gradually accepted what had happened and decided to do the best he could to prove himself. If he could survive Camp Douglas, he certainly could stand being jailed for a few months. Prisoners in this part of Kentucky were expected to work. Any citizen who needed a laborer could contact the county sheriff and, if the prisoner wasn't considered dangerous, he provided free help.

John had quickly gained the reputation of being not only a hard worker, but one who could handle almost any job. His friendliness and trustworthiness made him one of the most requested prisoners in the county.

After only two months, the local Methodist preacher, Robert Thomas, who had used John on several occasions for church work, began coming down each Sunday and taking John to morning services. People soon realized that John Wilson was no criminal.

"Hank, you ever talk to Judge Topper 'bout me? I've been on my best behavior and has done everything I has been asked to do. You know I ain't no bad sort."

Hank laid the checkerboard out and started placing the checkers on their squares.

"The judge knows 'bout you. He ain't no fool," remarked Hank, trying to avoid the issue. "You move first."

Hank soon jumped a few of John's checkers and, when it looked like Hank was going to make a run, John slowly made his moves toward cleaning the board. Hank's face was red with anxiety. With only two of his checkers left on the board, Hank could already sense the outcome. Just as he was about to admit defeat, the door opened.

"Well, what do we have here? I thought you'd be long gone by now John. You must love this place," commented the Reverend Thomas.

"Shhh!" whispered Hank. "I ain't beat yet. I still got two left."

Instantly, John made his move and snapped up Hank's last two. "That does it. The board is clean. Games over. You can throw the board now, that is if'n you want to show the preacher how yore temper can get the best of ya," chuckled John.

"And Preacher, what do ya mean, I ought to be long gone?"

"Hank, you haven't given this boy the note from the judge yet?"

Hank could not look John and the preacher in the eyes.

"I was 'bout to give it to him. I only got it yesterday," replied Hank, reaching into his coat pocket.

Embarrassed, Hank handed John a note, turned, walked to the front of the office, and stared out the window at the rain pounding down on the boardwalk.

John read the note and then quietly folded it and placed it in his pocket. Trying not to show his emotions, John said, "Thank you, Preacher. I knowed you probably had sump'n to do with this pardon. I'll forever be thankful to you all." John then awkwardly embraced the man who had helped to gain his freedom.

"Just glad we could help, and I'm glad you didn't leave yesterday. We also took up a little donation so you won't have to starve before you get home," replied the Reverend, reaching into his pocket for a small bag. "And Hank gave the judge a few good words for you, too."

"That right, Hank? You spoke up for me?"

Hank turned and moved toward John. "When I first met you, I didn't care much for ya, but with time, you kind of grew on me. You're all right, boy," said Hank, extending his hand. "The only reason that I didn't give you the note yesterday, was I wanted one more chance to beat ya in checkies," smiled Hank.

"You can forget that, Hank. You best find you another game or a sorry checkie player, if you expect to win."

John quickly gathered his few belongings and said his goodbyes to Hank and Reverend Thomas.

As he was leaving the jail, Hank caught him by the sleeve. "What's yore plan, boy? How you going to get home?"

"Hank, I ain't going to walk it, and I sure ain't stealin' no horse. That leaves the train."

"Well, it's December the twentieth. You got five days to make it home by Christmas. The train just might be yore answer, but you stay out of trouble, you hear," advised Hank. "And I'm givin' you a little present early. I'm going to send that telegram to yore folks you been nagging me about and let them know you comin'. Who do I send it to and what do I say?"

John grinned and replied, "Send it to Rebecca Ann Walker in Little Rock, Mis'sippi. That's near Meridian and tell her I is alive and comin' home to her."

Struggling to keep his footing in the deep mud, John was oblivious to the drizzling rain and cold December wind. He was finally going home, and nothing was going to stop him from reaching Little Rock by Christmas Eve.

Trudging down the road, he could visualize himself running across the front yard and bounding up the front steps into the arms of his mother and father. He also fantasized how he would get a good bath and put on his best clothes and rush down to surprise Becca on Christmas Eve. John could see Becca's surprised face when she opened the door and found him standing there waiting with open arms. With dreams of home swimming in his head, John felt a joy and excitement he had never felt before.

I

Walker was tending his store as a rider dismounted and entered the front door.

"You Thomas Walker, ain't ya?" said the rider.

"The last time I checked," responded Walker.

"You got a daughter named Rebecca?"

"I have. Why do you ask?"

The rider took a note from his pocket. "She got a telegram from up in Kentucky."

"Kentucky. She don't know nobody up there," remarked Walker. "Let me take a look at this thing."

"Well, I made the delivery, and I got to make a run over to Union. The top of the day to ya, Sir."

Walker nodded and quickly opened the letter.

"Ump," he grunted. "She don't need no note like this, not now. Damn, this is going to create some kind of problem."

Walker crumpled up the letter, walked over to the stove and threw the note into the fire.

I

As daylight slowly broke on Christmas Eve, John stood under a gray overcast sky on the walkway outside the train depot in Memphis, Tennessee. What little money the congregation of Wickliffe had given him was gone. To his surprise, he found jumping trains was easier than he imagined and he had been able to avoid the railroad inspectors who were constantly looking for drifters.

A commotion down the tracks caught John's attention. A train was waiting on the tracks with steam puffing from its smokestack, and the conductors were peering down toward the engine, wondering why the delay.

Walking closer, John saw a man being lowered to the ground from up near the engineer's compartment. Easing up to the group, he discovered the problem.

"Just my luck. This train's ready to pull out, and I got a drunk fireman. How can the railroad expect me to stay on schedule with a no-good drunk firin' my engine?" complained the engineer.

John immediately pushed through the crowd. "Where's this train headed?" he questioned, stepping up to the man.

"Goin'! We ain't going nowhere till I get somebody sober to fire that damned old boiler."

"Where you goin' then?" pressed John. "You headed south?"

"Yep, we headed for Corinth, Mis'sippi and from there south to Meridian and then west to Jackson. That is, if I get this crate movin'."

John shoved his hand toward the engineer. "How about takin' me on. I can fire it. I'm John Wilson, and I need a ride as far as Newton, Mis'sippi. You let me do the firin', and I want charge you a thing."

The gentleman studied the young man for a few seconds and then extended his hand. "You fought for the Confed'racy, didn't ya?"

"Yes Sir. Mis'sippi infantry, and I'm tryin' to get home. Today if'n I can," replied John, excitedly.

"Well, Mister Wilson, yore pay ain't too bad. You have just been employed. I'm Amos McCleary, and as for reachin' Newton, it's going to shove us to make it by dark. Let's see you get up there and fire that thing, and by the way, I rode with Gen'ral Forrest. You heard about him, ain't you?"

"Yes Sir, who ain't heard 'bout Forrest?'"

John knew home was only hours away. By mid-morning the train had reached Corinth, and after a two hour delay, it was steaming south toward Meridian.

John was sitting on a stack of wood behind the boiler, enjoying the north Mississippi countryside when McCleary turned and shouted, "John, you notice how cold it's gotten durin' the past hour. This don't look too good. Might mean trouble."

John nodded his head in agreement. "I know it must be might near freezin', and by the looks of them low gray clouds, it could mean snow," observed John. "But it don't usually snow down here in December."

"I agree with that, but you can't ever predict what the Good Lord's going to send us," replied McCleary.

At ten minutes after five, the train pulled into Meridian. Rain had been falling for the past hour and as the train came to a stop, sleet was bouncing off the sides of the train and surrounding sidewalk.

"I told you it might snow, Mister McCleary. It's too cold for rain," said John, stepping up to the boiler to warm himself. "This going to cause us any trouble gettin' on to Jackson?"

"No sir, Young Man. It'll take a whole lot of that white stuff to slow this engine down. We'll get you to Newton before seven tonight."

John smiled back at McCleary, thankful he would soon get to Newton, but disappointed that he was not going to get home in time to fulfill his Christmas Eve dream. Even if the train reached Newton by seven, John still faced an eighteen mile walk.

The train soon pulled out of the depot and headed west. The sleet that had fallen for the past hour was now turning to snow. John kept throwing logs into the boiler and praying they would reach Newton without a problem.

At ten minutes after seven, McCleary pulled the whistle cord which sent a shrill blast echoing through the darkness.

"John, we pulling into Newton Station. You think you going to recognize the place?"

"Sure will, Mister McCleary. Been down here many a time with my Papa. Seems like yesterday."

"Well, it's changed some since you last seen it. The Yankees burnt the station and some of the buildings with it. A Yank named Grierson made a raid through here. John, look at them big flakes coming down. I tell ya one thing, I ain't ever seen snow like this in this part of Mis'sippi, not in December. I hope you ain't planning to go it on foot tonight. You might just freeze out there."

The train came to a slow screeching stop and John carefully eased down the ice glazed side of the train. "Mister McCleary, it's been might near three years since I seen my folks, and I ain't going to let no snow stop me when I is as close as I is now."

McCleary followed John to the ground, almost slipping on one of the steps.

"Hold up boy!" he insisted. "I want to thank you for the job you done for me. It sure helped us keep this ole crate moving. I just hope the man I picked up in

Meridian can fill your shoes. But I'm more concerned about you being out in this weather. You best stay here in town till morning."

"Can't do that, Mister McCleary. Got to get on home. Ain't nothin' going to stop me now."

"Well, I guess I'd do the same. But, if you start gettin' cold and sleepy, you stop at somebody's house or barn and get out of the cold. Remember now, don't go sleeping out in the open. You'll freeze. You hear me?"

John shook McCleary's hand. "I hear you. Don't go to sleep out in the cold," repeated John. "And, thank you for takin' me on with ya."

McCleary quickly crawled back up to his compartment and threw a blanket down.

"You ain't got much of a coat. This here might help some. You take care boy and a Merry Christmas to ya."

"Merry Christmas to you, Mister McCleary," replied John, as the train moved out.

The streets were completely deserted with only a few dim lights from several store windows silhouetting the street. The townspeople had already retired to the warmth of their homes.

John suddenly felt a surge of loneliness. With no one in sight and a deep snow covering the ground, John thought, "I've got eighteen miles to go. Just one step at a time. That's all it's going to take."

Home for John meant walking nine miles north to the village of Decatur and then another nine miles northeast to Little Rock. This time of the year, roads would be almost impassible by wagon, and since few bridges had been built, several streams would have to be forded. Travel on foot, especially at night, was dangerous.

The snow was now falling heavier than ever and visibility was difficult. Deep ruts in the road helped him find his way through the darkness and to his surprise, the bridges outside of Newton were still intact. After more than three hours, John reached the outskirts of Decatur. Facing a stream south of the village with no bridge, he had to take off his shoes and wade across. As he reached the opposite bank, he recognized a large bent oak tree up ahead and knew he was only a short distance from the town.

Through the falling snow, a dim light appeared. Probably Taylor's Tavern, John thought, the stage stop located on the edge of town. The light and the thought of getting out of the cold spurred him on, but in his haste, he slid down several times before reaching his destination. With hands almost frozen, he pushed the door open and stumbled in. Toward the back of the tavern was a low fire burning in a large fireplace. John's sudden entry startled two elderly men sitting next to the heat, quietly enjoying an evening smoke.

"Hell boy, where'd you come from?" questioned one as he pushed his chair back so the stranger could get to the fire.

John stood, shivering as steam rolled from his wet clothing. He tried to speak, but was shaking so hard the men could not understand a word he said.

"Jacob, this here boy is 'bout froze. Here lad, take off that wet blanket and let me get you sump'n dry. You must be some kind of fool to be out on a night like this. I'm Jimmy Taylor. I own this place, and that there is my cousin, Jacob."

After more than an hour, John began to come around. "Want to thank you for the dry blanket, and I ain't a fool. I'm from Little Rock, and I'm on my way home, tonight. Been gone for most near three years. I'm John Wilson, son of Lott Wilson."

The old men shook their heads. "We know of Lott Wilson and I has had more than a few run-ins with that Uncle Jake of yores. That is, 'fore he got himself killed," commented Taylor. "You sure don't need to be tryin' to get to Little Rock. You best stay here tonight. You won't make it. They'll find you froze dead out there."

John reached for the blanket he had spread out to dry next to the fire. "I'll make it. I come too far to stop this close to home, but I do thank ya for lettin' me share yore fire."

One of the men pointed to a pot hanging near the hearth. "'Fore you leave, there's a little stew left in the pot. You best get a bite to eat, and I still says you's a fool to get out there in that cold. I guess you get some of that foolishment from yore uncle. He used to do some outlandish things 'round here."

John carefully wrapped his blanket around his shoulders and again thanked the men for their hospitality. The severe cold and the perils that lay ahead caused him to hesitate momentarily before stepping out into the night.

When he reached the edge of town, John found the fork in the road that led to Little Rock and veered to the right. Only eight and a half miles more, a short walk from there to his house, and then he would be home.

For the first hour, John had no trouble finding his way, but, the freezing temperature soon began to take its toll. He would fall in the ruts and with each fall, it became harder to regain his balance. Dizzy and confused, he thought, "I'm spendin' more time on the ground than I am walkin'. I've got to stop and rest a while. I got to find some kind of shelter."

Up ahead, he saw a tree that had foliage on the low branches. He crawled up the bank and slid under its cover. From the scent, he realized he had found protection under a cedar tree. He curled up drowsily and pulled the blanket over his head. For the first time since leaving the tavern, he began to feel a sense of warmth.

"I'm just going to take a short nap and rest a spell, then I'm goin' to get on home," thought John. Before losing consciousness, John remembered what McCleary had told him, "Don't go to sleep out there in that snow. You'll freeze."

"I'll only rest a few minutes," John thought.

Later that night, a light wind shook the branches causing snow to come crumpling to the ground. The sound of the wind and the shock of the fallen snow awakened John and he crept from underneath the branches. He found to his surprise that the storm had passed. A clear sky and a full moon reflecting on the snow made the night as light as early dawn.

Suddenly, he heard a horse approaching in the distance and as the rider drew near, he recognized the markings.

197

"Hey, hold up there!" commanded John, stepping in front of the rapidly moving stead.

The rider jerked the horse to an abrupt stop, straightened himself in the saddle and stared down at John.

"'Bout time you got home. We all been waitin' for ya," replied the rider, removing his hat and dusting the snow from its brim.

"James Earl, what you doin' out here?" exclaimed John, rushing to the horse's side. "Am I glad to see ya!"

The horse bolted forward a few steps, startled by John's quick movement.

"Woah, Lightnin'! Woah!" shouted James Earl. "You sure know how to spook a horse, don't ya. What is I doin' out here, Little Brother? It's Christmas Eve, and I'm out serenadin', that's what I's doin'."

John extended his hand, but his brother seemed more interested in calming his mount.

"James Earl, give me a hand and help me up. We'll be home in no time. Help me up. I'm 'most froze."

He smiled down at John. "I got places to go 'fore I go home, and Little Rock is right over that rise. You get on home. Mamma's been waitin' for ya a long time. Every mornin' and afternoon she waits. So don't you go back to sleep. You get on home."

With that, his brother slapped the side of his mount and away they galloped.

"James Earl, you got to take me home!" screamed John, running after his brother. "Serenadin' ain't as important as yore own flesh and blood! We ain't seen each other in years! You actin' crazy!"

The rapidly disappearing rider shouted over his shoulder, "The folks need you. Get on home, John! I loves ya, boy."

John couldn't believe that a brother that he hadn't seen in ages, wouldn't even help him get home. That just didn't make sense.

"Just wait till I tell Papa 'bout how he left me out here. He's going to be in some kind of trouble," mumbled John, angrily stomping up the hill.

At the crest, John paused and stared down at the scene. In the valley below, he could make out the winding stream that bordered the western edge of the village and beyond he could see stores and houses with swirls of smoke curling upward from their chimneys.

John started running and screaming to the top of his lungs. In a matter of minutes, he had covered the quarter of mile, splashed through the shallow creek, and stood in the center of town. Before him was Walker's store, and up the street, he could see Becca's house. She was only a few hundred feet from him.

"Do I rush over and surprise Becca, or do I go on home to my folks?" thought John. Without answering himself, he headed for the Walkers. But, as he drew closer, he suddenly remembered what James Earl had said, "You get on home, the folks is waitin' for ya."

John stopped and looked down at himself. He saw that he was in rags and filthy. "Can't see her like this. Got to clean up first," reasoned John. "Goin' home and rest a bit. I'll see her first thing in the morning. I'm going to be at my best."

John turned and headed north. The countryside was beautiful in its thick covering of snow and its quietness. With the exception of an occasional howl of a lonesome dog, there was no sound at all.

It was comforting to know the village was still standing. John had heard that the Yankees had come through Little Rock on the way to make a raid on Meridian, and he was afraid Sherman might have burned the town.

"Only a half mile to go," he thought.

Once more the cold tore through his body and the dizziness returned. Pushing on, he realized his feet and hands were completely numb.

"Got to get home. Too close now," John mumbled.

A large stand of timber bordered by an open field came into view. He was on Wilson property.

"What happened to the rail fences that used to hold in the stock?" muttered John. "Sump'n must've happened."

"It won't be long now, 'fore I'll spot that big ole log home of ours," thought John. "Hope it'll still be standin'. Maybe the Yankees burnt it. What about the family? How 'bout Thomas, wonder if'n he made it back like James Earl?"

Only a few more steps and he would know. He could feel fear building in his stomach. But, there it stood like a fortress. as he had always remembered.

"And look at the barn, it's there too. Thank God," thought John.

As he neared the house, one of the hounds caught the familiar smell and came tearing from underneath the house, barking with excitement. Bolting through the snow, Spot leaped up and knocked John to the ground. Lying there on his back, with the hound licking his face and beating his tail vigorously in the snow, John remembered how he had raised this dog, along with his brother, Joe, from pups and had spent many a night following the dogs as they chased coons through the hills and hollows in the woods nearby.

John brushed himself off and trudged across the front yard and up the front steps. Spot could not leave him alone. He whimpered and brushed against John, making the icy steps treacherous.

As John reached the porch, he knew only the open hall and a thick wooden door separated him from his family. "What if no one's home; there's no smoke comin' from the chimney."

Frozen and numb, he could barely limp down the hall. He tried to lift the door latch, but it was bolted from the inside.

Lott had heard Spot barking earlier and thought someone might be approaching. But when the barking stopped, Lott just figured some critter had excited the hound.

"That dog ain't never barked like that before," mumbled Lott. "Sounded like he was barkin' at somebody."

"Barkin' at somebody?" asked Sarah who had been awakened by her husband's voice. "Lott, hand me the lantern," demanded Sarah. "Got to light it, quick."

"Ain't nobody out there, woman. You dreamin' again. If you want to check on that hound, do it yoreself. I ain't gettin' up."

She worked frantically to light the lantern.

"Sarah, you be careful openin' that door," warned Lott. "And don't go wanderin' in that cold."

Finally, the lantern was brought to life and Sarah hurried to the door and lifted the latch. Cautiously opening the door, she peered into the darkness and was startled to see the figure of a man leaning against the doorway with a snow covered blanket wrapped around his shoulders. Snow and ice was crusted in his hair and beard, his face drawn and thin. Sarah slowly lifted the lantern and detected a familiar twinkle in the man's deep blue eyes.

"'Bout time you got home, boy. You runnin' a might late, ain't ya," said Sarah quietly, as she placed the lantern on the floor and held her arms open to her son. "I knowed you was comin'."

John stumbled into his mother's arms as Lott came to the bedroom door.

"What's goin' on! Sarah? Who is this man?" exclaimed Lott, rushing up to the intruder and grabbing him by the arm.

Sarah pushed Lott away. "He's home, Dear Lord All Mighty! John's home," cried Sarah with both arms wrapped around her son.

Lott lifted the lantern as he studied the man's face carefully.

John shook his head and smiled at his father. "It's me, Paw. It's John. I'm home," he muttered.

"Sister, get out here! Yore brother's home!" shouted Lott as he wrapped his arms around his son.

John held his hand out to his astonished sister. "Don't you know me?" he said.

"Mamma! Papa! It's him!" exclaimed Sister, grabbing her brother around the waist

Suddenly, feeling weak and faint, John sank to his knees.

"Lott, feel of this boy!" Sarah said. " He's might near froze. Go start the fire and build a big un. His face is like ice. Sister, get some of James Earl's long underwear and thick socks," she instructed. "And make up some hot tea and bring it to the fireside."

"Yes Ma'am, I'm goin'," replied Sister, as she ran out to the front porch.

"Toby!" she screamed over her shoulder. "John's come home! He's here in the house."

Lott soon had a fire going and had helped John into dry clothing. Sarah and Sister placed a thick pallet of quilts in front of the fireplace and wrapped several blankets over him. John was soon able to get the hot tea down, and began regaining his strength. Even though he was covered with thick quilts, his whole body continued to shake.

Sarah motioned to Lott. "We best get him to a bed. It'll be a lot warmer than this here floor."

John shook his head. "Don't move me, Mamma. I dreamt of sleepin' front of this fire for a long time. Just let me be," whispered John as he closed his eyes.

A light tapping was heard at the door.

"Come on in, Toby. We got one big Christmas present here with us," said Lott as Toby shook the snow off his shoes and placed his hat under his arm.

"What ya got there, Mist' Lott? Could it be . . . ?" questioned Toby.

Toby edged up to the man in front of the fire and stooped down. "Good Lawd, it sho' be Mist' John. Where'd that boy come from, Mist' Lott?" marveled Toby. "He sho' don't look like a boy no more. That boy done gone and made a man. Just wait till I tell Liza 'bout this. She won't believes it nary a bit."

Toby soon returned to his wife's bed. She had been freed by Frank Olliver at the end of the war and was now with her husband on the Wilson farm. Their two sons, Andrew and Caleb, had remained with the Ollivers as hired laborers.

Back at the main house, light filtered through the windows as dawn approached. Sister, wrapped in a thick quilt, had curled up on the floor next to her mother and was still asleep. Lott sat next to the fireplace watching the fire pop and crackle as he enjoyed an early morning smoke.

"Lott, the boy's done growed a beard," whispered Sarah. "And look at that touch of gray hair, just like yores," she continued as she pushed his hair back. "Lott, come look at this," insisted Sarah, motioning to her husband. "This boy has got a bad scar on the side of his head."

Lott squatted down and gently examined his son. "Sarah, sump'n sure hit this boy. No tellin' what John's been through, nor where he's been."

"Don't care where. Just glad he's come home," whispered Sarah.

Several hours later John turned over on his side. "Mamma, why didn't James Earl bring me on home last night? Just wait till I get up. We going to straighten that matter out," grumbled John. "He just left me out in that snow and rode off."

"What do ya mean by that, John?" questioned his mother.

"He was out there serenadin' last night and rode up on me. We talked a spell, and he just rode off into the night on Lightnin'and left me standin' there."

Sarah and Lott were speechless, shaken by John's words.

"John, you is just dreamin'. It's hard to tell you this, but James Earl died over two years ago. He got real sick up in Virginie. Thomas told us 'bout it when he come home. Right after that big battle in Pennsylvanie. He's been gone over two years. You just dreamin', boy. Just a bad dream," explained Sarah.

John shook his head. "Ain't no dream, Mamma. I seen him clearer than light. He told me to get on home, and that you been waitin' for me a long time. It weren't no dream," whispered John as he slowly turned toward the fire.

21

DASHED DREAMS

Christmas Day, 1865, dawned splendidly clear with over eight inches of puffy white snow blanketing the hills of east central Mississippi.

John awoke suddenly as he heard the familiar sound of his mother and sister disagreeing in the kitchen. He was wrapping one of the blankets around his tired shoulders and moving closer to the fire as they entered.

"Sister, I can't see why you just can't do like I tell ya," snapped Sarah. "Well, look who's decided to get up," she said, motioning toward John.

"Maw, do you and Sister ever get along?" smiled John. "This fam'ly sure ain't changed much."

"John, where's you been all these years, and did ya kill any of them bad ole Yankees?" questioned Sister, pulling up a chair in front of her brother. "And how'd you get them scars? Why didn't ya let us know where you was?"

John twisted uncomfortably as he took a chair. "Sister, we'll talk about it later, not just now. Mamma, was I dreamin' 'bout James Earl?"

Sarah knelt next to him as she painfully told the story.

"What about Thomas?" asked John.

"John, when he thought you was killed, it tore him apart. When you joined up, he felt responsible. When he thought you was dead and then found out James Earl had died, he quit the army. He come in here late one August afternoon, about dark, with several other Southern soldiers."

"Well, where is he now, Mamma?" probed John.

"He told me if'n he stayed, he was afraid the army would come and get him, and since he was a deserter, he might just get shot. He and the other boys, they said they's from Texas, headed west. Maybe Californie."

John slowly stood up to check the feeling in his feet.

"Sister, where's Paw? I reckon I need to talk to all of ya."

"Paw and Toby has gone to look after the stock. They'll be back soon."

" Sister, how about you boilin' some water for me. I got to get washed up. I got some serious courtin' to do. I been waitin' for this day for might near three years," said John, rolling his shoulders back in pride.

"John, yore water's already been boilin' for a long time, and the tub is sittin' right next to the stove. There's some strong lye soap in there, too," snickered Sister, holding her nose.

As John left the room, his mother and sister turned to each other.

"Mamma, who's going to tell? It's going to kill him. You know it is."

It had been over a week since John had taken a bath, so he savored every minute in the hot soapy water. He then neatly trimmed his beard and combed the tangles out of his long black hair.

Putting on some dress clothes belonging to James Earl, he stepped up to the mirror and took a long look. "Well, I'm a little thin. But I say I'm still a handsome gent, and I'll do just fine for Miss Becca," he mumbled as he returned to his parents' room.

"Well, who's that gentleman there all dressed up?" smiled Lott, who had joined the family around the fire.

"Don't look bad, do I, Papa? A little soap and water can sure make a change in a man," stated John proudly. "How's the stock?"

Lott pushed his feet closer to the fire. "They's fine. That is, what few we got left. Ole Sherman come through, camped down near Beulah Church, and them soldiers of his, might near stole everything eatable round here. They even used our fence rails for firewood. We saved two of our horses and one mule. Toby hid them out. Them devils stole the rest."

"I wondered what happened to our fences. You lucky they didn't burn ya out like they did some folks," commented John. He paused for a few seconds. "Paw, I know you wants to know 'bout what happened to me, and I guess this is as good as time as any."

John then related his near-death experiences and his stay with the Caulders. He decided not to mention Frank Olliver's deal with another man to take Frankie's place. This was a matter John wanted to take up personally with Frankie.

When he finished, they sat in silence, each with his own thoughts. The fire popped and hissed as steam rushed from a burning piece of freshly cut wood. The only sound in the room was the steady tick of the grandfather clock that had been on the mantle chiming out hours for as long as John could remember.

"Sarah, that explains the torn envelope we got from up in Pennslyvanie," remarked Lott, breaking the silence.

In a few moments John stood up and straightened his jacket.

"Well, folks, I got places to go and people to surprise. You are going to have to excuse me."

"Lott?" frowned Sarah, staring at her husband. "We agreed that you would tell him."

Lott glanced at John and then back to Sarah.

"What ya got to tell me?" questioned John, uneasily.

"John, you best sit down," Lott said quietly, reaching out to his son.

John, slowly eased down in the chair by the window.

"Son, it's clear the Lord has saved yore life and that's a miracle within itself, but things do happen, they happen," stammered Lott, unable to continue.

"Papa, what are you trying to tell me?"

Sarah burst out, "Tell him Lott! Tell the boy."

Lott's bottom lip quivered. "John, you can't go see Becca."

"And why not, Papa? Why can't I go?"

"She got married. Two days ago. Day before Christmas Eve."

John looked out the window for a few seconds and then back at his father.

"You just jokin' me, ain't ya. You just tryin' to play a trick. That girl ain't loved nobody but me ever since we knowed each other," said John, standing.

Sarah got up and placed her arms around him.

"Son, we don't make jokes like this. Not about you. She's a married woman. She thought you was dead. Gone."

John slowly eased back into the chair. "Who'd she marry?" he stammered.

"Frankie. Becca married Frankie Olliver," replied Sarah, softly.

"Frankie!" exclaimed John, jumping up. "She couldn't have. She don't love him. I'll straighten this thing out," he stormed. "That bastard is nothin' but a traitor. He signed up like the rest of us, and what did his paw do, he bought his way out. Hired a boy to take his place, Josh Wilcox. That sure makes Frankie some kind of a man," exclaimed John, heading toward the door.

"Hold up son!" ordered Lott, blocking his way. "You ain't going to do a thing till you think this thing out. They's legally married. You're going to leave them be."

"Leave them be! That's a hellava thing to say," countered John, staring defiantly at his father. "I bet you thought that bunch down at Walker's store talked me into joinin' up. They didn't. I ain't that weak. Ever since we has been younguns, I've always tried to take care of Frankie. Tried to keep him out of trouble. When I seen him signing that line, all kinds of things went through my mind. I didn't see no way in God's heaven he could survive no war. I signed that line to go with him, just like what you told Thomas to do for me.

"You say the only reason you joined was to be Frankie's personal bodyguard?" stammered Lott in disbelief.

"That's a big part of it," continued John.

Lott looked over to Sarah, shook his head and then turned back to John. "Don't ya think that was a little foolish?"

John's face burned red in anger and he pointed to himself. "Yeah Papa, just look at me. You is lookin' at a fool. A fool that loved Frankie like a brother and look what he done to me. God forgive me for how I hate that son of a bitch."

"You have no cause to talk to your father like this, John. No cause at all," his mother begged.

John slowly turned away. "It weren't intended for him, Mama. It were intended for me."

I

"You girls sure know how to make a mess," teased Judith Olliver. "I hope these cakes will be worth eatin', come Sunday."

"They'll be fine," snickered Suzanne, flipping flour toward Becca. "If not, we'll give them to Frankie. He'll eat most near anything."

Becca placed some flour in the palm of her hand and blew it at Suzanne, dusting her face.

"You know, you tease Frankie all the time 'bout his eatin' habits, but you is just as bad as him," laughed Becca, taking a cloth and cleaning the flour from Suzanne's face. "And where is that lovable husband of mine. He needs to be here with us when we is questioning his habits."

Judith Olliver nodded toward the front of the house. "He's probably up there workin' on his rifle. I heard him say sump'n was broke about it and he wanted to fix it so he could go huntin' this afternoon."

Suddenly, a loud slam of the front door echoed through the house.

"Frankie! I want to see ya, now! In my study," shouted Frank Olliver. "Get in here!"

Frankie put his rifle down and quickly stepped across the hall to his father's office.

"What's wrong, Paw? What you so upset about?"

His father was seated behind the desk staring out a large window behind him. He paused, and then, "He ain't dead. He's back from the war. John Wilson is home," snapped Frank Olliver.

Frankie's mouth dropped in surprise. "Paw, that's hard to believe. Then, recovering his composure, he said. "But, that's fine. I'm most glad John has made it home. I'm happy when any of our boys come back."

His father swirled around so quickly he almost lost his balance. "Boy, far as I'm concerned, John should've stayed dead!"

"Stayed dead!" shouted Frankie. "I'm glad he's alive. I look forward to seein' him."

Olliver brought his clinched fist down hard on his desktop sending an inkwell tumbling to the floor.

"Damn, Boy, I thought you was beginnin' to get some sense, but you is as stupid as ever. That young, pretty wife of yores has always loved that Wilson boy. Everybody round here knows that. And you bein' the way you is, she will again, if'n you don't do sump'n."

Frankie placed his hands on the desk, glared directly into his father's eyes and calmly said, "You listen to me. Becca is my wife, and she loves me, John Wilson or no John Wilson. And let me tell you one more thing. You don't have no faith in me, do ya? But you know what, I just don't give a tinker's damn."

Judith Olliver, Suzanne and Becca rushed into the room as Frank Olliver was grabbing at his son's coat collar. "What's goin' on here?" his wife questioned. "You men got a problem I need to straighten out?" She was used to separating them.

"Frankie, you take Becca out back and talk to her. Judith, you and Suzanne stay with me," demanded Olliver.

Frankie took Becca's arm and hastily escorted her to the back porch. The afternoon sun had warmed open areas, and there was only a slight breeze.

"Frankie, what in the world is goin' on? What is yore dad so upset about?" questioned Becca, walking over into the sunlight.

Frankie reached for her hands and placed them under his coat as he looked into his wife's dark green eyes. She was so beautiful. When she had agreed to marry him, he couldn't believe she would be a part of his life forever. What now, he thought.

"Becca, I can't believe what Paw just told me and there ain't no easy way to tell ya this. John's come home. He got in day 'fore yesterday."

Becca stood dazed for a few moments, flinched and a smile broke across her face. She grabbed Frankie and swung him around and around. "He's home! He's home! My John is home!"

With fear in the pit of his stomach, Frankie knew what his father had said was true. He took her arms from around his neck and pushed her away.

"Becca, I'm yore husband. You got to put John in his rightful place, and that ain't in our household."

Blankly staring at Frankie, Becca suddenly realized she had forgotten. She was now married to Frankie. In those few seconds, she could see John's face as he waved goodbye at Newton Station and saw herself in John's arms as he took her breath away with his kisses. The love she had always felt once again burned inside her. She walked to the end of the porch, placed her hands on the railing and looked northward toward Little Rock. "What was he like now, probably more handsome and dashing than ever," she wondered.

Frankie nervously placed his arms around her waist. For several minutes they stood in silence.

"Becca, you remember one thing. I truly love you. I don't expect you to get over this right away, but you must remember you is a married woman."

She could not face her husband. "Frankie, I know we're married and I love ya," whispered Becca. "But I have feelin's for John. Always have."

"You take yore time. John was my best friend."

Many thoughts were crowding through her mind. How had he survived the war and why was he so long getting home. Why hadn't he written? Her heart sank as she thought how he must feel. She had so many questions. "Somehow, some way, I must see him," she thought.

News about John Wilson's unexpected return had spread quickly through the community and neighbors flocked to the farm. At first John tried to be cordial, but all he could think about was Becca. Questions, senseless questions were all they hurled at him.

"They just want to see how I feel about Becca, now that she's married," thought John. "To hell with them all. No more for me. I'm through with them."

In the days that followed, when John heard anyone approaching, he would grab his coat and escape down the hall into the woods. The isolation in the forest gave him time to think and place his life into order. No matter how much he thought about rebuilding a life in Little Rock, the thought of Becca in Frankie's arms shattered any hope for the future. He could not face seeing them together.

Alone in the woods, John wept as he wandered aimlessly. one day, lying face down on a carpet of damp leaves, he knew there was only one thing he could do. He got up and headed for home.

When he reached the house, John found his mother in the bedroom, stitching a button on his father's shirt. His father was working with a piece of leather to repair a harness.

John walked over to the fireplace and turned his palms toward the warmth.

"Mamma, Papa, I been doin' a lot of thinkin' these last few days, and come morning, I'm leavin'. I can't stay here no more."

Sarah put down her work and walked over to her son.

"John, the Lord has brought you home for some reason. You can't leave us now," she pleaded. "I know you has got to be painin', but don't leave us. I waited so long."

John embraced his mother. "For days I has thought and prayed about what to do, but I just can't bear what's happened here. Come daybreak, I'm headed west. Maybe Texas, Calfornie. I going to look for Thomas."

Sarah cried quietly as Lott got up from his chair and placed his arm around John.

"Son, I've been watchin' you close since you got home. If you got to go, then we'll try to understand. You take Lightnin' with ya. You'll need a good horse. Don't have much money. I can give you a ten dollar gold piece."

Before daybreak the following morning, John bundled his few belongings, saddled Lightning and with the first sign of daylight headed southwest toward Newton.

By late evening, John had traveled over fifty miles, westward through Forrest and Morton, and felt sure he could reach Jackson before noon the next day. He sighted a high rise above the road and a large stand of hickory trees for a campsite. After taking care of his mount, he gathered firewood and set up a shelter. Soon he was under his cover and staring at a fire as it slowly turned to embers. Occasionally, Lightning would stomp his feet and shake his bridle. A day in the saddle had drained his energy and sleep came easily.

Later that night, John was awakened by Lightning who was moving nervously. He eased his pistol from underneath the cover as he pretended to be asleep. There was the sound of something shuffling through the leaves below and an occasional crack of a twig.

Somebody probably spotted my horse and is planning to steal him," John thought.

The steps came closer and John slowly pulled the hammer back as he thought, "A few more steps, and I'll draw down on ever who's out there."

A limb broke almost in front of him and John could see the figure of a large man standing in the darkness.

"All right, I know you there," he shouted as he jumped to his feet. "I got a pistol. One more step and I'll blow the hell out of ya!"

"Don't shoot, Mist' John! It's me. Toby. I been after you the whole day."

"Toby," muttered John. "One more step, and you'd been a shot Toby. What you doin' followin' me?"

Toby shuffled up to the campsite. "You is shore one hard man to ketch, and I come near to missin' yore camp."

"Come on in and tell me why in tarnation you is after me," ordered John who began laying limbs on the hot coals.

As the flames blazed up, Toby secured the mule he had been riding and returned to the warmth of the fire.

"Mist' John, I was gone yesterdy. Gone to check on my boys, over at Mist' Ollivers. Didn't know you was a leavin'."

"So you rode that ole mule all this way just to say goodbye?" replied John, baffled at Toby's actions.

"Well, no Sir, Mist' John. I come to talk to ya 'bout yore leavin'. You don't understand what shape yore folks is in. They wouldn't tells ya."

"What do ya mean the shape they's in, Toby. What's you gettin' at?"

Toby edged closer to the fire. "You get a good look at the farm since you got back? It ain't been worked much. Mist' Lott hurt his back over a year ago and he can't do much no more. The pain comes and it goes. Sometimes he stays for days on his bed, can't even get up. And for me, you know what shape I's in. Mist' John, there ain't nobody to work the place. Yore Papa's 'bout broke. He don't even have 'nough money to start farmin', if'n we had the workers," explained Toby. "Miss Wilson and Sister was a'tryin' to work the fields last summer."

"Mamma and Sister in the field," muttered John. "Papa's hurt. They should've told me."

"Mist' John, they knowed how you was a hurtin'. They just couldn't tell ya."

Later that night, John tried to sleep, but the thought of his mother and sister working the fields, kept him awake. He thought about how he could get the farm back into shape, and then the thought of Becca would tear his plans apart. He just couldn't go back.

At sunup the next morning, John and Toby prepared breakfast and as soon as everything was packed, John saddled Lightning and then mounted. Looking down at Toby, he gave his old friend an answer.

"Toby, I appreciate yore comin' to me, but I can't go home, not now. I don't expect you to understand what's goin' on inside my head. Tell my folks I love them," said John, kicking Lightning in the flank.

The horse easily maneuvered down the steep bank leading to the road and then galloped westward toward Jackson.

Toby stood next to his mule and watched John until he was out of sight.

"Dear Lawd, what is we going to do now?" he sighed.

Toby slowly mounted his mule and turned eastward. He had never been this far from Little Rock and never had he felt so alone.

Crossing a creek outside of Forrest, he suddenly heard a horse approaching and a rider call out, "Slow down, Toby! Hold up for me!"

Recognizing the voice, Toby couldn't believe his eyes.

"Mist' John! What ya up to?"

Lightning worked his way down the creekbank and stopped in the middle of the stream to water. John removed his hat and wiped his brow.

"Toby, let's go home. We got work to do."

22

OUT OF DESPAIR

THE STEADY POUNDING OF HAMMERS ECHOED ACROSS THE meadow where Frank Olliver and his daughter-in-law stood admiring the almost completed structure. Once finished, the house, along with a large parcel of land, would be turned over to his son and new bride.

"It's mighty pretty, ain't it, Rebecca?" asked Frank Olliver, placing his arm around her. "There ain't another as fine in this here county, except maybe my own place."

Becca drew closer to her father-in-law and gave him a hug. "It is a beautiful house, Mister Olliver. I've always dreamed of livin' in a place like this. I just didn't think it would happen to me."

"When you is a part of the Olliver family, things is done right. Soon as the house is finished, then we'll build you a barn, and then it's up to my boy as to what you does with it. If'n he's the man I expect him to be, you two might just end up the richest couple in these parts."

"Look down there below us. What do you see? I'll tell ya. You seein' six hund'rd and forty acres of the best farm land in Newton County. You is lookin' at a gold mine, if'n it's worked right."

"Yes Sir, Mister Olliver. This is going to be some kind of fine farm. There can't be none better," agreed Becca. "Frankie and me sure appreciate what you has done for us."

Gazing up at the house, Becca remembered her rides through the countryside years earlier, and how she would make John stop the buggy so she could get a better look at a place that caught her fancy. But, that was a long time ago, a time she was trying to forget.

"Rebecca, yore mother-in-law is expectin' you and Suzanne home for dinner. Frankie and me is going to stay down here for a spell," Olliver said, leading Becca across a grassy clearing toward the house.

Halfway there, Olliver stopped under the bare branches of an old apple tree.

"Rebecca, I been meanin' to talk with ya for the past few days, but just couldn't find the right time," he insisted. "I know how you always had a fancy for that Wilson boy, but that's in the past. You is now a Olliver, and I don't expect John to cause us no trouble."

Feeling uncomfortable about what her father-in-law was saying, Becca slipped her arm from his. "What is you tryin' to tell me, Mister Olliver? I'm a married woman."

He shook his head. "I hope so, Rebecca. Women 'round here don't make fools out of their husbands, and they never leave them. They don't do that," he snapped. "Not here, and not to an Olliver."

Becca's eyes widened and she blushed in anger. "Mister Olliver, I was reared that a woman stood by her husband, and I married Frankie for better or for worse. It sounds like you don't have much faith in me."

"Faith! What's faith? You is a young and, I say, a most beautiful woman, and time can only tell what you'll do. Just remember, as long as you stay in this family and treat my boy right, the wealth of this county can be in yore hands. When I'm gone, everything will be Frankie's and believe me darlin', I have plenty. I weren't like lots of them fools 'round here. I didn't take none of that Confed'rate money. I kept my gold and silver, and I hid it where no Yankee or even God himself could find it."

"I understand what you is sayin', and I'd rather not talk about it again, not ever," exclaimed Becca.

"I'm glad we understand each other, cause if'n you don't, you might end up just like this apple tree. Old, brokendown, and out there by yoreself, with nobody."

Becca turned quickly and walked toward Frankie and the other workers. She realized this was a new side of Frank Olliver. He wasn't the polite, sweet talking man who had always gone out of his way to be nice to her. She remembered what James Earl had said, "Frank Olliver is a man you can't trust. He's only lookin' after his own interest, and anyone who gets in his way is brushed aside, just like Uncle Jake was."

Later, the buggy bounced from rut to rut as Becca and Suzanne made their way toward the Olliver's home. At a low bog in the road, it sank almost to its axles. The two got out of the carriage, placed their hands on the spokes, and helped the horse pull free. Once on hard ground, both women, splattered in mud, stepped back up into the buggy and were on their way.

"We sure look a mess don't we?" gasped Suzanne. "But we showed that horse what two healthy females can do, didn't we?"

Becca, with her hand on the reins, smiled. "It was kind of fun, weren't it? You want to try it again?" she teased.

"Try it again! You must be funnin' me. At least I got you to talk. Since we left, you ain't said a word. Sump'ns wrong, ain't it? My Daddy said sump'n that bothered you, didn't he?"

The buggy hit a large hole in the road almost throwing the women from their seat.

"It weren't nothin'. I'll be fine," insisted Becca, regaining her balance.

"My Daddy can say some hard things sometimes. He's just that way, but down deep, he don't mean half the stuff he says. But I bet I know what he was talkin' to you about. It was about John, weren't it?"

Becca pursed her lips and made no reply.

"I knowed what he was up to," continued Suzanne.

They rode in silence for several minutes.

"Suzanne, ever since I became a part of yore family, you has been like a sister. A sister I never had, and what I tell you is just between you and me. I want to be able to trust ya."

Suzanne placed her arm on Becca's shoulder. "I've always wanted a sister too. Someone I could talk with and depend on. You can trust me," promised Suzanne.

"Well, you was right 'bout what yore daddy was talkin' to me about. He's afraid I might try to see John or do sump'n foolish."

"But, Becca, what are you going to do 'bout John? And what about Frankie?" probed Suzanne.

"First, Frankie is my husband, and for John, well, that's in the past."

They were quiet, each in a separate world.

"Why didn't he write me? Other girls got letters durin' the war, why didn't I? When the other soldiers came home early last summer, why didn't John come? I don't understand," thought Becca.

Her mind continued to race, "If only I could talk with him, just a few minutes. There's so many unanswered questions. But could I look him in the eyes? Could I be close and not want to wrap my arms around him as I once did?"

"Becca, folks say John's changed a lot. He won't see nobody when they go to his house. I don't know a soul that's really talked with him. I heard that he spent time in jail after the war. Don't know why. I wonder if'n he'd see me? I might could get some answers, who knows?"

"'Bout home now, Suzanne," interrupted Becca. "As for John, you do what you feel is best for you. I'll be fine."

Suzanne insisted that Becca go on into the house; she would take care of the horse. Walking back from the barn, her thoughts turned to John. As long as she could remember, she had been attracted to him; but there was always Becca, she was always his. So many times she had dreamed of being with John, teasing and laughing as they made their way hand in hand down some secluded path or riding horseback with him, clinging to his firm muscular body as the horse sped across some flower-strewn meadow.

Many a night she had seen Becca in his arms, kissing him passionately. She had wished it had been her.

"Yes, I'm goin' to see John Wilson. Why not? No more dreams, not for Suzanne Olliver."

I

"Get up, son! Time's wastin'. We got ground to cover," said Lott, pounding on the door.

"Man, I hate to get out of this warm bed. I bet everything's iced up this morning," muttered John. "Paw! Is the fire warm yet?" he shouted.

"Been warm!" came the reply from across the open hall.

The day John returned with Toby, he had carefully walked over the farm. John knew the burden of hard farm labor would now fall entirely on his shoulders. He must be up to the challenge.

After breakfast, Lott, John, and Toby walked every inch of Wilson property together. After lunch, while Lott and Toby were resting, John inspected the barn and the outer sheds where plows and farm equipment were stored.

Late that afternoon John removed his jacket, hung it on a peg in the hall and entered his father's bedroom.

"Going to be a cold one tonight, ain't it, Papa?" he said, backing up to the fire.

Lott beat his pipe against the heel of his boot, knocking the ashes to the hearth.

"Yes it is," he replied, reaching into his pocket for his tobacco pouch. "What ya think about the place today? We got a chance to make it go?"

John eased down in a chair across from his father. "Don't look too bad. But we have some problems," admitted John.

"What problems do ya see?" questioned Lott, reaching for a piece of burning treebark to light his pipe.

"Well, Papa, we got land, a lot of it. It ain't been farmed lately, and that's good. Professor Hendon always said he thought it was good to give the land a rest, don't overwork it. As for our plows, we can get them in top notch shape with a little work. But Papa, what worries me is we has only got one mule and two horses to do the plowin', and I don't want to hurt yore feelin's, but I may be the only man on the place that can put in a full day's work."

"I can still work," stated Lott, straightening himself in his seat. "I ain't in that bad of shape."

"Papa, even if'n you can work, to farm like we used to, we need at least four mules, and I need some hired help to get the job done," continued John. "And what about seeds for plantin'? You got any?"

Lott squirmed in his chair. "Don't have nary bit."

"What about money, Papa?"

"John, we supported the South as well as we could. We got twenty dollars in gold left, that's about it."

"Twenty dollars!" exclaimed John. "Papa, that won't even buy the seeds."

Lott dropped his head. "That's all we got. I gave heavy to the Confed'racy. I guess I was just a fool."

John got out of his chair and moved next to his father.

"Papa, don't ever say you acted a fool. My brothers and me was all a part of the Confed'racy. You supported us when you gave." John paused for a few seconds. "Somehow, someway, we going to make this farm go."

Later that evening, John sat quietly thinking how he could raise enough money. He was soon joined by his father.

"Papa, I been thinkin' and the only thing I know that can bring some money in, is if'n we sell off some land."

"Sell our land!" stammered Lott. "Boy, that's all we got, and land prices is hit rock bottom."

John calmly continued, "Papa, we got three sections of land. Ain't no way we can use all of it."

Lott calmed down and replied, "Son, one of them sections is Minsa's. That's Choctaw land that I give my word I would take care of for him, if'n he comes back. The other section was yore Uncle Jake's and that's Homer's. I ain't never touched a tree on it. That only leaves this place, and we ain't gettin' rid of any of it. You understand?"

John shook his head. "I understand Papa, but we need money."

"John, that's my problem. You're soundin' like you is runnin' this place," remarked Lott. "I'm still the head of this fam'ly and I ain't sellin' an inch."

Frustrated, John rose and headed toward the door. "I come back to farm the place, and I'm the only one that is fit to work these here fields. No money, no seed, no help. I sure come back to one mess," he muttered.

Sarah, who had been quietly knitting, peered over her spectacles. "Son, I hear a tone of disrespect in yore voice I don't appreciate. Yore Papa's worked hard to carve this farm out of a wilderness and gettin' rid of a smidgin' of it is like takin' a limb from his body. I think you owe him an apology."

John, his hand on the door latch, turned to his father. "If'n I sounded disrespectful to you, I'm sorry, but what I told ya is how I feels. If'n I stay around here, the load's on my back. And Papa, I think it's time you start treatin' me like a man. The boy that left here three years ago died on that grassy slope in Pennsylvania."

"And, while we talkin' about death," John continued, his voice rising, "there's a place down there where you said them Yankees camped that looks like a grave."

Lott interrupted. "You might say one of them died, but I ain't in no mood to talk about it."

John rose early the following morning and made his way to the kitchen where he found his parents already at the table.

"Today's Sunday, we figured you'd sleep a spell and then maybe go to church with the family," said Sarah, turning to greet her son.

John slid down on the bench next to his mother. "Got work to do. I thought I'd get started on repairin' some of them plow handles."

"What about church? You ain't been since you got home. Folks been askin' 'bout ya."

John's thoughts went back to the time when he enjoyed going to the services. He couldn't wait to get there to meet Becca. He had felt good sitting among his friends and neighbors, holding Becca's hand and dreaming about the future.

"Son, you want to go with us?" insisted Lott.

"I was just dream . . . . No, I don't want to go," replied John.

"You know we never work on Sunday 'round here. Never have," frowned Lott.

As John started to get up, Lott reached over and placed his hand on John's shoulder, pushing him back to his seat.

"Son, yore mother and me got to talkin' last night, and what you said made a lot of sense. You are going to have to carry the load around here and I've got to realize you is a growed man. But I just can't stand the thought of lettin' any of this land go."

"Papa, what about Toby's two boys? Why don't we get them to work for us? We could give them part of what we make and build them homes on our place. They could be right here near their folks."

Lott rose and walked to the window. He watched as Toby and Liza rounded up firewood down near the barn.

"Can't do, John. Olliver won't let them go."

"Won't let them go!" exclaimed John. "Hell, I thought slavery was over."

Lott returned to his chair at the head of the table, "John, when the war ended, if any Negro didn't have a job, then the gov'ment saw to it that they was assigned a job. They called that the Black Law, or sump'n like that. Well, seein' that them boys didn't have no work, Olliver got them signed up to keep workin' for him."

"Well, Papa, from what I heard. That didn't last long. That's over now."

"You right, but that Frank Olliver worked him up a plan to keep them Negroes out on his place. You see, what he done, and Thomas Walker is in on the deal too, was to talk them into workin' for him, on salary. So far, that's all right, but they has to trade at Walker's store for the things they need. He don't give them no money outright and from what I hear, them Negroes, not knowin' how to handle money, is spendin' more than they make."

John smiled. "Papa, lot of white folks do the same. That ain't unusual."

"Son, Walker and Olliver won't let any of them go as long as they is owing a debt. They says that if'n they let them go, then they might skip out, leavin' them with the loss."

"What does the law say about it, Papa?"

"Well, we has got a military gov'ment now, and I went down to Decatur and talked with a Major Everette. He said that he didn't especially care for the way Walker and Olliver was doin' bus'ness, but the Negroes had to learn to pay their bills and had to learn not to spend more than they make," explained Lott.

John slammed his fist against the table. "Damn, if'n that don't sound like a scoundrel for ya? No tellin' what they's chargin' them Negroes for goods. That's still slavery if'n I ever seen it," muttered John. "And I can't believe Mister Walker is workin' with Frank Olliver."

"John, Thomas Walker's been doin' deals with Olliver as long as I can remember. I even heard he was a part of the Choctaw Land Company. And I still say, that's the ones that had Jake killed."

"That's hard to believe," replied John.

Suddenly, the hall door opened and Sister whirled into the room. "My, you men are loud this morning. I'm glad you is on speakin' terms, and by the looks of them plates, I'll say Mister John has eaten his and my breakfast," complained Sister.

214

"I suppose I has eaten too much," agreed John, smiling. "Give me a minute, and I'll fix you sump'n. Mamma's gone down to talk to Liza."

Sister didn't know how to react to her brother's hospitality. "Papa, is he all right? He s'pose to talk back to me and argue like he used to," she exclaimed.

John, standing at the woodstove, looked over at his father. "She can't take it, can she Paw? Bein' nice to her just may ruin her."

"John, you ain't asked about yore friends. Not one word 'bout Robert or Tim or the other boys," added Sister.

John, afraid of what he might learn, turned toward the door. "Don't want to hear about them, not now. Want to be left alone."

"Papa, ain't that a little strange, actin' like that."

"Sister, the boy's been through a lot. Things we can't even imagine. We has just got to be glad he got back."

Later as Lott, Sarah and Sister were in the buggy leaving for church, John ran out and stopped them.

"Papa, just one question before you go. Who actually owns Lightnin'? I mean, legally owns him."

Puzzled, Lott thought for a moment. "Well, he was James Earl's, and he told me if'n anything ever happened to him, well, I guess he be yores, legally, John. He said the horse would be yores. That's what he said."

"Thank you Papa. That's what I figured."

As the buggy moved out of sight, John headed down to the barn.

"Toby! Toby! Got to see ya," he hollered.

Toby came out of his quarters adjusting his suspenders. "What ya so worked up for, Mist' John. Thought you might has gone with them this morning."

"Got a plan Toby, and you can't let Papa know nothin' about it. In the morning get up and give Lightnin' the best brushin' he has ever had and saddle him up. I'll be leavin' 'bout eight. After I leave here, you wait 'bout an hour and then follow me with the wagon."

"Where to, Mist' John? Where we goin'?" questioned Toby.

"We goin' to Walker's Store and if'n it goes as planned, we going to have what it takes to start our plantin'," replied John.

"Oh, Mist' John, Toby ain't shore he likes the sounds of this here dealin', and I ain't shore yore pappy is going to like bein' left out."

Early the following morning, Toby, with a well-groomed Lightning, waited patiently in the shadow of the barn.

John came down from the house and extended his hand. "Looks good. I ain't never seen him look better. He sure favors his daddy. I can still remember Uncle Jake bringin' that stallion in here from Kentucky. He was so proud of him. They looks just alike, don't they? I guess that's why they named him after his daddy."

Toby ran his hand across the horse's flank and patted him. "There ain't none better in this part of the country, Mist' John. Ain't none better."

John nodded his head and rubbed Lightning gently on the nose. "That's what I'm bettin' on, Toby."

John stepped up into the stirrups and settled himself in the saddle.

"Remember, one hour. Walker's store with the wagon."

Riding into town, John visualized Becca standing behind the counter as in days past or sitting out front waiting for him. "What would he say if'n she were at the store?"

Turning the corner, John was startled to see Walker sweeping off his front porch. Their eyes met at the same time. Neither knew how to react.

Walker put down his broom and stared at the man sitting on the horse, thinking, "He resembles himself, but he's changed a lot. What do I say to him? What do I say about Rebecca?"

John spoke first. "Morning Mister Walker. Good to see ya again."

Walker felt like he was addressing a ghost. "Erhh, Good morning, John. Want ya come in? I see you lookin' fit."

"Thank you, Sir. I want to do a little lookin' 'round the store. Let me tie my horse up, and I'll be right in."

"He's sure spirited, ain't he? That horse ain't ever been beat, has he, John?"

"No, Sir, don't reckon he has. I'm just glad the Yankees didn't find him. They stole most of the herd."

Walker stepped down and slowly walked around the animal. "He's a fine un. You ever thought about sellin' him?"

John ran his hand down Lightning's neck and calmly replied, "I don't know. We might, if'n we could get a good price. We do need money to get our farm goin'."

"John, it's kinda nippy out here. Come on in."

As soon as John had settled himself next to the woodstove, Walker continued. "John, if'n you did sell Lightnin', what would ya be askin' for him?"

John thought for a minute. "Oh, he ought to be worth five hund'rd. He is the finest horse in the county."

"Five hund'rd dollars!" Thomas exclaimed. "That's a lot of money, 'specially durin' these hard times."

"Mister Walker, there ain't none better than that horse standin' out there, and I really don't plan to sell him."

Thomas nervously walked around the store straightening items as he went and then headed to the window and studied the horse.

Suddenly he blurted out, "I'll give ya three hund'rd dollars for him right now. Not a penny more."

John stood up. "I don't know, Mister Walker. A person could make money racin' that horse, and he is a stallion you know."

"Tell ya what. I'll loan ya the three hund'rd dollars on him, and if'n you can pay me back by December, then I'll give the horse back to ya. How 'bout that deal?"

Thomas thought to himself. By December, I can win enough by racin' and breedin' this animal to triple that three hundred.

"That horse is mine and I can live with your arrangement," agreed John. "Put it in writin'."

"My word ain't good enough for ya?" replied Walker.

"It's good, but this is bus'ness," replied John.

Walker quickly drew up the paper and counted out the coins on the table. The men shook hands and John tucked the document into his pocket. "Mister Walker, good doin' bus'ness with ya. I need to buy some seed. Cotton and corn. Maybe a little wheat. Need some mules, but I'll get them over at Union."

"I can fix you right up, but I'll tell ya right now, my store ain't stocked like it was before the war. Times is hard. I can spare you some seed, not as much as ya probably needs. What else can I do for ya?" replied Walker.

John scratched his head. "Mister Walker, don't Toby's boys owe you a little money. I sure hope you gets paid someday."

Walker pulled out his ledger and flipped through the pages. "Let's see, John. One of them niggars owes me forty two dollars and the other 'bout thirty six."

John reached into his pocket and began laying ten dollar gold pieces on the table. "Fifty, sixty, seventy, and eighty dollars. That ought to do it, don't ya think."

"What ya mean? What you doin' with that money?" inquired a puzzled Walker.

"I'm settlin' them boys' debts. I'm payin' them off," replied John.

Walker quickly pushed the coins back. "Can't do that. Can't take yore money," he muttered.

John put his hands on the gold and looked up at Walker. "I understand, if'n you offer to pay a debt and a man won't take it, then the debts settled. "Fessor Hendon said that. He told us it was Mis'sippi law."

"Frank Olliver sure ain't going to like this," he mumbled. "He's going to be some kind of upset."

"What ya say, Mister Walker? I didn't hear ya."

Thomas took his handkerchief and wiped his face. "Ain't nothin'. Just thinkin' to myself."

"And by the way, I'd appreciate it if'n you'd put it in writin' 'bout me clearin' them boys' accounts," insisted John.

"I figured you probably would," replied Walker. "But you might just be gettin' yoreself in trouble with them niggars."

"I'll be just fine, Mister Walker, and give the family my regards."

As John left the store, Thomas realized he had just been hoodwinked, but he couldn't figure out exactly what John was up to.

In a matter of minutes, Toby pulled up to the front of the store with the empty wagon. "Right on time. Ain't been here ten minutes. Give me a hand loadin' this grain," instructed John.

"Yassuh, Mist' John. How'd you get these seeds?"

John grabbed one of the sacks and hurled it into the back of the wagon. "Don't ask so many questions. Just help me load her up and be neat with it. We going to need the space."

John gave Toby a wink and a slight smile. "We goin' to get yore boys and bring them home. They fixin' to work for the Wilsons and for themselves."

"Lawd Mercy, Mist' John. You got to be crazy in the head. You shore we going to do that?"

"Toby, I done told ya not to ask no questions. Just get in that wagon and let's head south."

"What about yore horse, Mist John?"

"Let's get this rig movin', and I don't want to talk about Lightnin' no more."

Bouncing down the rough road, Toby was full of unasked questions, but he knew not to probe. John had been one irritable young man since he returned home and Toby wasn't going to cross him.

"Where can we find yore boys?"

"This time of the year, they ain't in the fields," replied Toby. "How 'bout goin' by my ole place down in the qua'ters. They's might be there, or we can asks somebody."

"Sounds good to me," replied John.

To reach the old slave quarters, they would have to go right by the Olliver house. The last thing John wanted to see was the Ollivers, especially Frankie or Becca. John hoped he could just pick up the boys and quietly move out without a problem.

Fortunately, no one was in the yard, nor could John see anyone at the barn up ahead. "Couldn't be better," he thought.

"Ain't much farther now, Toby. Just down the road," commented John as he whistled at the mule to hurry the animal along.

Toby looked over at John with a worried expression. "What if'n we runs into trouble, Mist' John? How far you plannin' on goin'?"

John didn't take his eyes off the road. "Toby, I got the legal paper showin' yore boys' bills is cleared and, if'n that don't work, I got Papa's revolver inside my coat."

As they entered the quarters, several Negroes stepped outside their shabby dwellings. Recognizing Toby, they waved to the wagon.

"How about it, Toby! 'Bout time you drug yore carcus down here to see us. You must thinks you's a high f'luttin' niggar these days, livin' up there with them Wilsons," joked a tall thin Negro who was an old friend.

"I is a high f'luttin' niggar compared to you. At least I don't works for no Olliver," laughed Toby.

John pulled the wagon to a stop in front of the shack.

"To get to the point, we's here to fetch Toby's boys, Andrew and Caleb. Know where we can find them?" asked John.

The tall Negro scratched his beard for a second and then pointed to a row of houses where Toby used to live. "Andy is down there. He be a little sick lately. And Caleb is a workin' over at where Mist' Frankie's house is. He be back for sump'n to eat 'bout noon. But I tell ya sump'n, Mast' Olliver shore ain't going to like you takin' them boys off the place."

John slapped the reins down on the mule's back and the wagon surged forward.

"Thank you for yore help. As for the Ollivers, I don't give a damn what they like."

218

"I hears ya, Mist' John. Good luck to ya."

Andy was in bed, but as soon as he heard he was at last leaving the Olliver's farm, he quickly got up and gathered his few belongings.

Later, twenty minutes after twelve noon, Caleb walked through the door.

"What you doin' here, Papa?" he questioned, startled to see his father and John.

Toby placed his hands on Caleb's shoulders, "We here to take you outta this place. We goin' to the Wilsons."

"Wilsons!" muttered Caleb. "We can't leave this place. We owe up at the sto'. Mast' Olliver ain't givin' us up either. You can forget that."

"Jest sit down and lets me tell ya what Mist' John done up and done," insisted Toby.

Caleb shook his head in disbelief. "Mist' John, answer me this. If'n I go to yore place, is I going to be goin' from bein' a Olliver niggar to bein' a Wilson niggar? If that be so, I ain't none better off at yore place than this'n," remarked Caleb.

"Boy, you watch yore mouth!" warned Toby, drawing back his hand. "These folks has been good to me, and theys'll be good to you as well. Show some respect."

"Hold it, Toby. Caleb has asked a good question, and I think he deserves an answer," said John.

"I ain't even told yore daddy 'bout this. But, if'n you boys help us get our farm goin', then we'll let ya pay yore store debt to us in a share of the crops we make. And if'n you'll stick with us, I'll see to it that you each get eighty acres of good Wilson farmland so you can have yore own place. That sound fair?"

Caleb looked over at his father and then to Andrew. "Sounds good to me. Let's get packed. We leavin' this place. Needs to be gone 'fore the Ollivers miss ole Caleb."

It didn't take long to load their few belongings but as Caleb was about to shut the door, he paused momentarily. "Wait up, Papa."

Toby beckoned to Caleb. "Ain't nothin' in that shack worth takin'. Get on up here."

"Papa, I got a woman now. I can't leave her here," explained Caleb.

"She owe anything at Walker's?" questioned John.

"No Sir. Not a thing."

"Then get her and hurry. We need to get out of here," insisted John. "What's her name?"

"Jest call her Sadie, Mist' John."

"Does I has any grandchill'un, that I don't knows 'bout?" smiled Toby.

"No suh, Papa. Just a fine little woman is what we got."

John hurried the mule along the road still hoping to avoid any confrontation. But, nearing the Olliver's house, he saw a horse and rider approaching. The rider was a woman. John's heart began to pound. "I don't want to talk to her right now, not just now." he mumbled.

John breathed a breath of relief. It was Suzanne Olliver.

She looked down into the wagon loaded with furniture and at the Negroes who were supposed to be in the quarters. She then stared over at its driver who had his hat pulled down on his head.

"Where you takin' these folks?" questioned Suzanne, not recognizing the man with the reins. "I best go get my father, right now."

John slowly removed his hat and pushed back his long black hair revealing the handsome face Suzanne had so often dreamed about.

"You don't know me, Suzanne?" he smiled. "That surprises me, dawlin'."

That smile and those deep blue eyes. "Oh my, it is John," she thought. "He looks so much older, but oh, he's made one handsome man."

Suzanne nervously backed her horse away from the wagon. "I been waitin' to see ya. I mean we has all been waitin' for a visit."

"Suzanne, I say you has growed up since I left," replied John, admiring how time had changed a lanky skinny girl into a most appealing woman.

She was almost six feet tall and her long dark hair almost touched the saddle. Her dark brown eyes seemed larger than ever as she stared back at him.

"What am I doin' with yore Paw's workers? I has just paid off their debt down at Walker's. They is workin' our place now," replied John, spellbound by Suzanne's beauty.

"Papa, ain't going to like it, John. Them's his workers, and he ain't going to take it lightly, you takin' them off. But, I figure you know what ya doin'," smiled Suzanne, regaining her composure. "Tell Sister, I'm going to come see her before long. You tell her that, don't forget."

John pulled his hat back down on his brow. "I'll tell her. And good to see ya, Suzanne."

John turned in his seat as Suzanne galloped off across the field that bordered her house.

"Shore a fine lookin' woman, Mist' John," commented Toby. "She might even make you forget about Bec . . . . "

"Stop it right there!" exclaimed John in anger. "Don't ever mention that woman to me again, you hear. Never!"

"Yessuh, Mist' John. Didn't mean to get yore dander up," apologized Toby.

Nearing Little Rock, John was relieved that he would get home without a hitch. But before this thought was out of his head, the thunder of horses could be heard rapidly approaching from the road they had just covered.

"Sounds like trouble, Mist' John," announced Caleb. "I knowed things was goin' too good."

"Just stay calm. If'n it's the Ollivers, I'll take care of them. Can't be no worse than facin' them Yankees."

The riders quickly burst into view and raced up, surrounding the wagon. One pulled up beside the mule and grabbed the harness, bringing the animal to an abrupt halt.

In front of the wagon was Frank Olliver, his overseer, Samuel Claborn, and John's boyhood friend, Frankie.

He had changed. Frankie sat tall in the saddle, maybe even taller than John.

His blond hair was neatly combed back, and he wore a thin mustache and sideburns. This was not the Frankie John remembered.

"You, Niggars, get out of that wagon and get on back to the farm," growled Olliver, pointing in the direction of his place with his other hand near the shotgun that rested across the front of his saddle.

Looking back at Toby's boys, John could see the same fear he had seen in his comrades' faces as they marched into combat.

Andrew started to move down out of the wagon.

"Hold up, Andy. You ain't goin' nowhere. Stay in the wagon," instructed John, turning to face Frank.

"They ain't goin' back, Mister Olliver. You and Mister Walker don't own them no more. I paid off their debt."

"Paid off their debt! Hell, boy, everybody 'round here knows the Wilsons is broke. What'd you do, steal some money."

"No Sir, Mister Olliver. I sold my horse to Mister Walker and paid them off."

"You got proof of that?" said Samuel.

John reached into his pocket and handed Olliver the papers. Frank carefully studied the document and then crumpled it up in his fist and threw it to the ground.

"That Walker ain't nothin' but a damned fool and a dumb un at that," scowled Olliver. "I ought to knowed better than throwin' in with that son of a bitch. And as for you, John Wilson, you might hold the high hand today, but there'll be other days. You take yore niggars and see if'n you can get them to work. Yore paw's always had a soft heart for their kind anyway. And you stay the hell away from our place. You set foot on my property and you might just get shot."

John slowly reached under his coat revealing the pistol resting on his lap. "Don't threaten me, Mister Olliver, and I don't 'preciate you talkin' 'bout my father. As for you shootin' me, I don't think you got the stomach. You'd just hire somebody to do it, just like you did with my Uncle Jake."

"You is a fool like yore daddy. They ain't no proof that I had anything to do with yore Uncle's shootin'," growled Olliver, pointing down at John. "Let's get the hell out of here. I ain't wastin' any more time."

Frankie wheeled around in the saddle. "John, you didn't talk well about my father either," he shouted. "He didn't have yore Uncle killed. And you stay away from my wife. I better not catch you near her."

As Frankie disappeared down the narrow road, John crawled down and picked up the paper. He carefully smoothed it out, refolded it and placed it in his pocket.

"Mist' John. Tell me one thing? Would you have used that gun?" John settled himself on the seat and slapped the mule with the reins. "In a hell's second, Toby, I'd shot them all."

23

EASTER MEETING

SUZANNE LEAPED DOWN, NOT TAKING TIME TO SECURE HER horse and bounded up the steps.

"You won't believe it, Becca! It was sump'n!" shrieked Suzanne, tumbling over a sawhorse left on the porch by a carpenter and landing on the floor in the front hallway of her brother's new home.

Becca rushed from the bedroom where she had been measuring the windows for curtains. Reaching the hall, she found Suzanne sitting in the middle of the floor.

"Girl, what in tarnation is wrong with you? I thought you'd killed yoreself. Is you all right?" asked Becca.

Suzanne reached up and pulled Becca down beside her.

"Becca," she gasped. "You ain't going to believe what I just saw and who I just seen! He was takin' a bunch of Paw's niggars off the place with him. I can't believe he was brave enough to do that," she stammered.

Becca grabbed her shoulders. "Suzanne, what is ya talkin' 'bout?"

"Becca, I just seen him."

"Seen who, Suzanne?"

"I seen John Wilson. He was ridin' right by our house," she exclaimed. "And he was takin' 'em over to work on his place. He sure was sump'n to see."

Becca sat quietly for a few moments, wanting to know more. She realized this impulse was wrong but impossible to restrain.

"What was he like, Suzanne?" she softly questioned.

Suzanne dropped her head. "Becca, he looked terrible. He was skinny as a rail, face drawn like a old man, and he had a horrible scar across his face. I like to not knowed him," she sobbed.

Sensing the pain in Becca's eyes, she could not continue the tease any longer. A big smile crept across Suzanne's face.

"Suzanne, you foolin' me about John. Now tell me the truth. You ain't even seen him, has ya?"

Suzanne giggled as a slight blush crossed her face.

"Becca," she whispered. "He was truly sump'n to see. He looked taller than ever and got a full beard with a distinguished touch of gray hair. And when he looked at me with them deep blue eyes, I got so weak I might near fell off my horse. I just knowed he noticed it. He is some kind of good lookin' man and I does mean man."

Becca could vividly imagine what John was like.

For a few moments, Becca again forgot her marriage and for that brief time, she was there with Suzanne next to the wagon gazing down at her lost love.

Regaining her composure, she quickly got up. "Suzanne, I'm glad he's fine, but will ya help me with some measurin'. We plan to move in here early next week, and I could use yore assist, if'n you please."

I

When Lott heard that his longtime friend and neighbor, James Thornton, had died, he, Sarah, and Sister loaded up in the family buggy to pay their respects. John had been down with the croup for the past few days and was staying out of the weather in order to get back to work as soon as possible.

Sitting alone next to the fire with a blanket wrapped around his shoulders, John thought back on the past four years. He remembered leaving Newton Station and the tearful faces of loved ones waving goodbye to the soldiers; the long, cold ride to Virginia, smoke belching forth into their faces as thousands of rifles sent whistling balls of death straight into the Southern ranks; the sickening, thudding sounds of bullets hitting their mark; and the cry of men praying for death, rather than life. Then out of the depths of hell, the heavens opened and John remembered a young girl's face, an angel reaching down to rescue him from that dark pit.

Deep in thought, he barely noticed a knock on the door. Without thinking, he uttered, "Come on in. It ain't latched."

The door screeched open and to his surprise two men made their way inside.

"'Bout time you seen us, you ole burly face bastard," remarked one of them, pulling a chair up to the fire without being invited.

John turned his head and stared out the window. "Didn't want to see ya. Still don't," muttered John. "I didn't invite you here. either. Didn't know you was even alive, Tim. Good afternoon, 'Fessor."

"Good afternoon to you, John. We're both your friends, and you can't just keep shuttin' folks out that care about you," stated Professor Hendon, edging up near the fire. "I came by earlier, but your parents said you weren't seein' anyone. Can't keep your doors shut forever."

"I sure can, if'n I want to," replied John. "It's my life."

Tim, quick tempered as always, grabbed John by the arm, pulled him around and started to throw a punch. But, he suddenly lost his balance and fell. As Tim struggled to get up, John noticed that only a loose britches leg dangled where a leg had been.

"How did I miss seein' that?" thought John as he and the Professor quickly reached down to help their friend.

"Just get back!" he threatened. "I'm going to bust yore face, John Wilson, and good. You been sittin' 'round here feelin' sorry for yoreself, and you come out of that war better than most of us. Least you got yore arms and legs," said Tim, struggling to regain his balance.

"Just wait a minute, Tim. Maybe my manners ain't been the best, but I've had a lot on my mind. Let's start over," suggested John, extending his hand to his boyhood friend.

"Hell, we all got problems," replied Tim, taking John's hand and settling himself in a chair.

"I weren't going to poke ya anyway, just wanted to get yore attention," smiled Tim.

For the rest of the afternoon, the three men swapped stories and rekindling their friendships. John found out that Robert had been killed in a battle in the northwest corner of Georgia and that Tim had lost his leg when a minnie ball shattered it as their unit was breaking away from Petersburg. Out of the five Clearman boys, only one of them returned.

"What about Sergeant Stallings and Albert Matthews from up near Philadelphia, what happened to them, Tim?"

Tim thought for a minute. "Well, Stallings got sent back home to help raise another company, along with Capt'n Carleton, and as far as I knowed, Albert made it back in one piece too."

John got up to stretch his legs. "You want some water or sump'n. How 'bout some coffee or tea?"

Professor Hendon looked over at Tim and eased a hand into his inside coat pocket. "I don't think we care for any water, especially when we got some of this with us," he smiled, pulling out a flask.

"This will do just fine."

"Fine, my eye, 'Fessor Hendon. I thought you quit that drankin' back 'fore you got married," stated John.

"Well, my fine young man, I did, but after five offspring and a nagging wife, I have once again found solace in the spirits . . . that is, occasionally, and among friends, and I do tell you it helps my marriage tremendously."

They burst into laughter, and John realized at that moment there was no way he could ever isolate himself from these old friends again.

With the sun setting and the family soon to be returning, the Professor and Tim decided to call it a day, especially since Lott and Sarah never allowed drinking on the place.

"Tim, 'Fessor, I want to thank ya for comin' to see me. I guess I has been keepin' to myself too long. We'll have to get together again before long."

"John, I want to talk to you sometime about going back to school. You know, you were one of my best students," remarked the Professor.

John shook his head. "That was a long time ago. Lot's happened since them days. I spent my college money, and I've got a farm to run now. Won't be no college for me."

Looking at his friend with a crutch under his arm, John thought how fortunate he really was.

224

"And Tim, I been feelin' sorry for myself since I got home. You kind of opened my eyes today. I want to thank ya."

Tim reached out and embraced John. "Somebody had to get you goin' again. You know where we live. If'n you don't come to see us, then we going to come up here and worry the hell out of ya. And I'm one of the best at doin' that."

Suddenly, John remembered. "What about Josh Wilcox? The one that took Frankie's place. Did he make it Tim?"

"Josh Wilcox, let me think. John, after I got shot, they sent me on home, and to tell ya the truth, I just don't know what happened to him."

❙

A strong March wind raced through the bare branches of the oak trees outside Frankie and Becca's bedroom causing the curtains to flutter noisily.

Frankie lay silent, unable to sleep. He had looked forward to the time when he and his bride could move into their new home and have the privacy he knew they needed.

As his father had said, there was no better house in the county than this one. The large framed two story structure contained four bedrooms, a parlor to entertain guests, an office with an area set aside for a future library and a fully appointed kitchen away from the main building. The front porch supported four large bricked columns like many stately homes on plantations in the Mississippi Delta.

Frankie should have been elated, but it seemed to him his good fortune was falling apart. He had never been so happy as when Becca accepted his hand in marriage. But now things weren't the same.

Frankie could sense a drastic change in his and Becca's relationship. There were times when she was as warm and loving as when they were first married, and then suddenly she would become despondent and completely ignore him. Then, he knew her thoughts were not on him, but on another man, a man who was once his best friend.

Frankie finally got up and walked to the window, gazing down at the freshly plowed fields in the distance.

Becca roused to see what was wrong. "Frankie, you all right? It's cold in here. Come on back to bed 'fore you catch cold."

"Ain't sleepy. Can't sleep," he mumbled. "Got a lot on my mind."

Becca held her arms open. "Honey, come on to bed. We can talk about what's troubling you here next to me, where it's warm."

"It ain't me I'm worried about," said Frankie, remaining at the window. "It's you, Becca."

"Me!" exclaimed Becca. "What have I done that's got ya where you can't sleep?"

"What has you done? I'll tell ya. Since he's got back, you ain't been the same. Sometime when you is in my arms, I feel you is makin' love to somebody else."

For a few moments the room was quiet.

Becca pulled the covers over her shoulders. "I'm sorry, Frankie. I didn't know my feelings showed. When you told me about John a while back, I told ya I needed time to sort things out, and I do. I got a lifetime of feelings 'bout that boy I've gotta place in order."

"What about me, Becca? What do I do while you is sortin' out yore feelin's for another man. What the hell do I do?"

"You has got to be patient with me," pleaded Becca. "Why don't ya come on to bed, Frankie. We can work through this together."

Frankie eased under the quilts.

"Becca, why don't ya go talk with him? I'll even go with you, if'n you want me to. You ain't going to ever find yore answers if'n you don't."

Becca had not moved and now made no effort to draw Frankie to her. "Don't think so. I really don't want to see him."

"Don't want to see him, or afraid of what might happen if'n you do," muttered Frankie.

"That ain't fair, Frankie. How can you love me and say sump'n like that?"

"Okay, Becca, answer me this. Tell me that you don't love John Wilson. Just say it out loud."

Finally Becca murmured, "Frankie, I love you, and you has got to take my word for it, but you don't sweep a lifetime of carin' for another person out into the wind. You don't do that."

"You sayin' you love both of us?" he shouted. "That's crazy as hell, Woman! I'm goin' downstairs to sleep. You just stay up here with all yore many loves and see how warm they keep you."

Becca slid out of bed and followed her husband to the door. "Frankie, there's all kinds of love, and the Lord expects us to love all human bein's in some kind of way."

"Damned, if'n that's so! Ain't no way to love like that! Get on back to yore bedroom and leave me be."

Frankie stomped down to the office where a low fire was still burning and settled himself, staring at the glowing embers.

"How can a man love a woman more than I love Becca?" he thought. "This is like drivin' a knife into me. And what if she finds out my father paid my way out of the war? What kind of person would run from his responsibilities? I'll kill whoever tells her, even if it's my own father."

I

Lott had been furious when he was told about Lightning, but calmed down eventually when he realized the advantages it had brought. They now had seeds for planting and three mules for plowing. The mules weren't in the best shape, but good animals were hard to find. Now with the help of Caleb and Andy, land that had lain waste for several years was being cultivated. Day after day, the men would leave before daybreak, and only darkness would drive them home.

One afternoon, after a heavy thundershower had made plowing impossible, John called it a day and headed for the house. As he approached, he was alarmed to see a detachment of Union calvarymen. From a distance, he could make out what appeared to be an officer on the porch talking with his parents.

The sight of blue uniforms brought a flash of anger. Excitement and hatred engulfed him as he ran.

"Get away from us! Get on, now!" John shouted, sprinting across the yard, waving his arms in an effort to scare the horses. "Get the hell out of here!"

The horses bolted backward a few feet, and one began bucking wildly, sending its rider tumbling to the ground. A sergeant instantly pulled his pistol and leveled it on his attacker.

"Hold it Sergeant." ordered the officer on the porch. "He ain't armed!"

Seeing the open end of a barrel and the look of fear in his father's eyes, John stopped at the steps.

Lott rushed down and stood in front of his son. "Everybody just wait a minute," Lott insisted. My son just didn't know what was goin' on."

The young officer stepped down and extended his hand. "I'm James Robinson. You might say I help to keep the law around here."

John made no attempt to shake the outstretched hand and stood glaring at a man that years earlier in combat, he would have killed.

"Let's go on in the house, men. I think we need to talk," insisted Lott, pointing down the hall.

"You go, if'n you want to, but I ain't socializing with no Yankee, not me," muttered John.

"John, you comin' in and you doin' what I say, Boy. You going to give this man a chance to explain some things to ya," ordered Lott.

Lieutenant Robinson explained that their patrol was investigating a complaint about a group of Negroes who were causing problems south of Little Rock and had even bragged that they planned to murder some farmers who had once held slaves and wanted some of their land.

John sat quietly and listened. They had never held slaves. It didn't concern them.

Finally, the lieutenant rose. "I appreciate you listening to me, and I'm sorry if I upset you, John. I think I know how you feel. Your father said you were with the Thirteenth Mississippi. Fought up at Gettysburg. I was on the other ridge. You broke our line near an ole stone wall. Lost an uncle, cousin, and a brother on that hill. I know how you feel. I got pains too. "

Suddenly John felt a sense of compassion. "I think we both understand each other better now. Please accept my apology, Sir," said John, extending his hand.

"Pleased to meet you, Mister John Wilson."

Walking down the steps, the lieutenant paused and turned. "Tell Mary Lucretia I send my regards, and if you'll allow, I'd like to accompany her to church tomorrow. She did invite me, you know."

As soon as the soldiers had left, John exclaimed, "What did he mean by sayin' he was takin' my sister to church. Ain't no Yankee takin' Sister nowhere. He acted like he knowed her."

Sarah smiled up at John. "They has been doin' a little courtin' for a spell. He's really a nice young man. He's a West Point man, he says."

"West Point man, hell. He's still a damned Yankee as far I'm concerned."

I

An occasional gust of warm air mixed with the cool northwest breeze whipped through the hillcountry. The white blossoms of the dogwood trees and the masses of wild flowers were soon showing in abundance. Spring had finally arrived.

Since Sarah was responsible for music at the special Easter church service and needed to practice, she, Lott, and Sister left early. Sarah always longed for John to go with them, but she had grown tired of insisting.

After breakfast, John went down to the barn to plan the next week's work schedule with Toby and his boys.

"We doin' just fine, Toby, so far. The seeds is in the ground, and we just got to let ole mother nature take it from here," commented John. walking out to the barnyard where he could get a better look at the fields to the south.

"We has worked, Mist' John. Them fields ain't never looked better," agreed Toby.

The men leaned against the tall fence railing surrounding the area and stood admiring their work.

Finally, Toby glanced over. "John, you know Mis' Wilson wanted you to go with her to church today."

"She didn't say nothin' to me about it," replied John, still studying the fields below. "She could've asked."

"You couldn't see it in her face, Mist' John? Yore Mamma has got a way of showin' her feelin's. Ain't nothin' would make her any happier, than you sittin' there next to her.

"You know, when most folks thought you was dead, she just sat out there on that porch and just a kept lookin' down that road sayin' one day her boy would be a comin' home. Some folks even thought she lost her mind."

"Ump," grunted John. "I guess we showed them, didn't we, Toby."

"Naw Suh, Mist' John. The Lawd showed them," stated Toby. "It were his works that brought ya. You owe him."

John stood in the warm morning sun thinking. He then pushed away from the fence and walked toward the house.

"Want me to saddle the mule, Mist' John?" asked Toby.

"I ain't going to be seen ridin' no mule to church. I ain't no mule man," replied John. "I can walk it in no time."

A short time later, sounds of singing could be heard as John neared the church. Horse-drawn wagons and buggies covered every inch of the grounds. The church was filled. It seemed as nothing had changed. Time stood still.

John felt suddenly weak as he walked up the church steps. Becca never missed a service. She could be sitting in her family pew, right behind his parents.

"If she's there, what do I say?" he pondered.

John paused at the doorway. "Can't go," he thought. "Just can't face her and the other folks at the same time."

Then John imagined his mother sitting day after day in all kinds of weather waiting for his return and people thinking her insane. "Can't let her down, not now."

He pushed the door open. The large congregation sat in silence with heads bowed as the minister led them in prayer. John quietly stepped down the aisle to his family's pew. Sarah looked up, smiled at her son, and patted the bench beside her. This place was for him. John was mildly irritated to see Lieutenant Robinson sitting next to his sister.

Hearing the floor creak, Suzanne glanced up and reached for Becca's hand. Frank Olliver and his son seldom attended church and had gone to Meridian on business for the weekend. Sitting there behind John was Becca, Suzanne, and her mother.

Becca had watched the tall handsome man in a light gray dress suit make his way to the pew in front of her. His hair was still damp where he had tried to comb it back and Becca knew it would only be a matter of minutes until it began to curl.

The prayer ended and the pastor began his sermon.

As the preacher droned on, John sensed a fragrance familiar to him from the past. For a moment, he couldn't remember, but a light cough behind him suddenly revealed his worst fear.

Becca had not heard a word the preacher said. In fact, to her, the whole church was empty. How broad his shoulders had become, and almost by habit, she lifted her hand in an attempt to touch the curls above his collar. Suzanne pulled her hand down so no one would notice.

Knowing he would have to turn and face Becca, anxiety crept over John. He began to move about nervously, sweat forming on his brow and in the palms of his hands.

Sensing his distress, Sister reached over and took his hand. He smiled softly as his mind raced.

As the sermon concluded, John had his plan of action. To the surprise of his parents, he quickly worked his way down the pew and walked up to the pastor. He whispered a few words and knelt in prayer.

The preacher smiled and turned to the congregation. "Brothers, Sisters, the Lord has surely blessed us in many, many ways. We're all glad to see John worshippin' here with us again, and this morning his request is to spend some time in prayer to the All-Mighty God for bringin' him home. He wants to pray by himself, nobody remaining. So let's all let the Lord work his wonders with this young man and pray silently for John as you leave."

For a short time, conversation and quiet laughter could be heard outside. But soon, everything was still, and only faint goodbyes drifted in from the outside. His plan had worked. He would have no one to face, John thought with relief.

Rising from the floor, he turned to leave but was startled to find Becca still sitting in the pew. She stood and slowly walked toward him.

His first impulse was to run, but how could he run from this woman who had been on his mind for years. She was even more beautiful than he had remembered.

Without thinking, she reached up and gently stroked his beard and then carefully pushed the hair off his brow like she had always done.

With tears in her eyes, she whispered, "Why didn't you write me, John? I would've waited."

Looking down into the familiar deep green eyes, John finally answered. "Doctor Caulder was s'pose to write you, and I sent a telegram."

"John, all we got was a torn envelope, nothin' in it."

"What about the telegram?" questioned John, his heart settling down. "I checked. They said yore Daddy took the message."

"I know nothing 'bout no telegram, John."

"Mamma told ya I'd be comin' home. Why didn't you have more faith?"

Becca began to sob. "John, they said you had been killed. Tim told me he had seen you on the ground, blown apart. I also had this dream that . . ."

"Dream!" exclaimed John. "You had a dream."

"Let me just explain, John. It was so real."

"Just forget it, Becca. I need to get on home," shouted John, moving up the aisle.

"John, I loved you, and I guess I always will. I ain't as strong as yore Mamma. I'm sorry."

John turned. His inner impulse was to pull her close and wrap his arms around her. He could still remember the taste of those lips and the way her body felt pressed closely against his.

"I love you too, Becca. You're all I could think about up there. You kept me alive when gettin' home seemed impossible. You should've waited," whispered John, tears beginning to form in his eyes. "Just a little longer."

"John, I still need to know what happened to you up there. I've got to know," pleaded Becca.

John forced himself away from her and started toward the rear of the church. "I don't think that would look too good, you bein' married and all. And it really don't make no difference, Becca. Not now."

"John, I've got to know. It changed my whole life. Our lives."

"Leave it be, Becca. What we had is gone."

Outside, Suzanne sat quietly in the Olliver's buggy. To John's relief, Tim had the wagon waiting.

"Need a way home, Soldier!" Tim called out. "Told yore folks I'd take care of ya. They and that Yankee is done gone to the house."

John stepped up and settled himself next to his old friend.

"Don't really care to go home. You got any suggestions?"

"Got an idea, Mister Wilson," smiled Tim, reaching under his seat and pulling out a clay jug.

230

"How 'bout us goin' to the creek for the afternoon. It's nice and warm, and these here spirits might just get you through a rough time."

"Lead the way, Tim. I've got to do some serious thinkin'."

A little way down the road, Tim questioned, "John, how did it feel?"

John leaned back and put both hands behind his head to work a stiffness out of his neck.

"To tell ya the truth, Tim, when she was there close to me, my whole body seemed to burn inside. There's no way tellin' you how much I wanted that woman. But then when I thought about her bein' married to Frankie, I hated her. You understand what I mean?"

"Nah, can't say I do, but I ain't ever been in love neither." Tim laughed.

Later that afternoon, Tim pulled up to the Wilson's porch just as Lieutenant Robinson was preparing to leave.

"Tim, is John been hurt?" exclaimed Lott, spotting his son lying in the back of the wagon. "What's happened?"

Tim, trying to stand, weaved back and forth. "Hurt, hell naw he ain't hurt. My paw's whiskey ain't never hurt nobody. In fact, it'll heal the soul," stated Tim, sinking to the seat, unable to stand."

"Tim, you said you'd take care of him, and what did you do, you got him drunk. Both of ya is drunk," snapped Lott.

Lieutenant Robinson stepped over to the wagonbed. "Does he normally drink a lot, Mister Wilson?" he questioned.

"No, almost never," replied Lott.

"Then, maybe he had a reason."

"You're right young man. A damned good reason."

24

A WOMAN'S DREAMS

WITH THE END OF THE WAR AND RELEASE OF SLAVES, THE Southern plantation system crumbled into despair. Most slave holders not only lost their laborers, but many lost their land as well.

During the summer of 1865, severe weather damaged the cotton crop, the planters' prime source of income. But,in contrast, Frank Olliver seemed to prosper. He had not only devised a plan to keep his Negro laborers indebted so they were not free to leave but was also wise enough to plant crops other than cotton. And, since he had not exchanged his gold and silver for Confederate currency, he was now one of the wealthiest men in Mississippi.

"Look at them rows, Son. Ain't it sump'n? Prettiest I ever seen," he commented, stretching up in the saddle to look down the long rows of corn topped with young tassles.

"Ain't none better in Newton County, Paw. Even the cotton is better than last year," replied Frankie. "Last year was rough. Sixty-five is a year to remember. South got whipped, and crops didn't do worth a hoot. But this year is different."

"Let's ride down to see how things is goin' at the lower section 'fore it gets too hot,"said his father.

Frank Olliver was confident that he would again prosper with the fall harvest, but there was one storm on his horizon. He wondered if Frankie would be able to handle his strained marriage. As they trotted down the dusty road, Frank suddenly reached over and caught his son's horse's reins, pulling the mare to a stop.

Surprised, Frankie instinctively jerked the reins back and angrily drew his whip to strike. "What'd you do that for? I most near got throwed!" snapped Frankie.

"Sorry boy, just have to ask ya 'bout sump'n that's worryin' me," explained his father.

Steadying his mount, Frankie replied, "It better be sump'n big for you to act like that."

Nearing a creek, Frank dismounted and motioned for Frankie to water the horses.

"Son, I'm concerned that you need to get yore household in order," advised Frank, clearing his throat.

"What ya mean by that, Paw?" asked Frankie, reaching down to wet a handkerchief and wipe his face.

"I got my household in just as good a shape as yores."

"Damned if'n that's so! I'm sleepin' with yore mother. That's more than you can say 'bout you and Becca."

"Who told you sump'n like that?"

"Don't make no difference. Frankie, you tellin' me you ain't havin' problems?"

"I didn't say that. We've had some disagreements of late, but it's going to work out," assured Frankie.

"The talk is, that Becca stayed after church last Sunday and met with John. Everybody seen it. That right?" muttered Frank.

"That she did, but I told her to," explained Frankie. "There's questions she needed answers for, and I thought it might be a way to end the relationship."

Frank mounted his horse and stormed up the creekbank. "End a relationship! How stupid can you get! That's just a way to get a love affair goin' again," shouted Frank. "Just when I think you is makin' a man, you turn out to be a damned fool again. My advice is to keep that Wilson boy away from yore wife or you going to find her in his bed, not yores."

Frankie, suddenly filled with anger, quickly mounted and raced up to where his father was waiting.

"Let me tell you sump'n ole man! John Wilson ain't never slept with my wife, nor will he. So don't go makin' sump'n out of nothin'. And as far as you sleepin' with my mother, how 'bout them women you been sleepin' with down in the quarters all these years. Folks talk. Mamma know about that?"

In a rage, Frank drew back his whip and brought it down across Frankie's face, leaving a bloody path down his cheek.

Frankie wanted to strike back, but he just untied his handkerchief and wiped away the blood. Swaying in the saddle from the pain and shock, he abruptly turned his horse and headed toward home.

As he reached the opposite bank, he stopped his horse and turned in the saddle toward his father.

"Now, let me ask you sump'n. You ever tell anybody about you buyin' me out of the war?"

"Not a soul. Not even yore mother," came the reply.

"I should've gone with the others. That way I might not have come back to this hellhole! A Yankee bullet would have been better than livin' with you," hissed Frankie.

Several days later, Frankie was surprised to spot a handsome stallion in the corral.

He called out to his father's overseer, Sam Claborn. "What's that horse doin' in here?"

Sam led the animal over. "You recognize him, don't ya?"

"Who wouldn't?" exclaimed Frankie. "Ain't no horse in the country like this. But he 'spose to belong to Mister Walker."

Sam smiled. "Well, yore paw figured he'd come down on you a little too hard the other day, and I guess this is his way to say he's sorry. As for Thomas Walker, what's his is also yore paw's. So, this here horse is now yores."

As he stood admiring Lightning, Frankie felt he possessed everything he had always wanted—six hundred and forty acres of prime farmland, one of the finest homes in the county, and a beautiful wife. There was no way he was going to let his life unravel.

Becca, wandering out on the porch to enjoy the cool morning breeze, glanced down to where her husband and Sam were standing. She instantly recognized the stallion and thought back to the times when she and John spent hours together. She could remember wrapping her arms around his waist and feeling the warmth of his body as they sped across the hills.

Those faraway memories quickly dissolved into the events of last Sunday. It was so strange. In one way, he was the same boy she had waved goodbye to before the war, but in other ways he was a stranger, quieter, elusive, but still extremely attractive. The love she had tried to forget, was still there.

She quickly left the house and ran toward the corral, calling out, "Frankie, that horse has got to go! He can't stay on this place. He s'pose to be at Papa's house."

"You wrong, Lady!" replied Frankie. "This horse was givin' to me and it's stayin' right here."

"I got his woman. I got his horse, and by damn, I might even get his land one of these days," mumbled Frankie to himself as he headed for the barn.

For the past several weeks, Becca had not been feeling well, and she knew arguing with Frankie would be fruitless. These days, long rides about the countryside gave her the only chance to be alone and place her feelings in perspective. And on one of these rides, she thought about the words John had spoken, especially the telegram. Her father owed her an explanation.

Becca often rode up to Little Rock on Saturday mornings to visit with her family. Her father usually opened at six in the morning and since he had few customers until around seven, there would be plenty of time to talk to him.

The sun was barely up as Thomas Walker strolled down the street toward his business. "Damn, somebody's already there. I wish they'd give me a little time to open," he complained, quickening his pace.

"Mornin' Papa, You runnin' late, ain't ya?" greeted Becca.

"Good gracious, Girl! What ya doin' down here so early?" he replied, embracing his daughter.

"Just come to spend the day with ya. Maybe give ya a little help's all."

Becca waited for the right moment. "Papa, I want to ask ya sump'n that been a botherin' me."

"What's that, Sugar?" answered her father, hastily placing money in the cash register.

"Papa, I heard you got a telegram sent to me a while back. Is that so?"

"Telegram! Who told you that?" he exclaimed, nervously closing the cashbox.

"Don't matter, Papa. Just tell the truth. Did John send me a telegram?"

He dropped his head, unable to look his daughter in the face. "I've been wantin' to talk to you about it, but I . . . . "

"You been hidin' it from me, all this time, ain't ya?" she interrupted. "It came in here 'bout the time I got married, maybe before, didn't it?"

Her father edged around the counter and tried to place his arm around Becca, only to have her shrink from his grasp.

"Just give me a chance. Listen to me. You and Frankie seemed to truly love each other and I didn't want nothin' to spoil it. Them Ollivers is good people and owns a lot of this county. By marryin' into that family, you could have anything yore heart desires. As for John and the Wilsons, they's might near broke. Ain't got nothin' but the land they stand on."

Becca could not look at her father. "I need to be goin'. I'm disappointed with you, Papa. You know how I has always felt about John and his family. By not lettin' me know that John was alive and comin' home, you made the decision for me. That decision should've been mine."

Becca quickly walked out of the store and mounted her horse. Her father followed.

"Becca, yore Mamma's going to want to see ya," he pleaded.

"I'm leavin', and I don't care to see any of you. You ain't treated me right. For the first time in my life, I've been deceived. And by my own family."

I

The July heat boiled down on John, Caleb, and Andy as they toiled in the cotton field below the house. Corn planted in the bottom land near the creek had been laid by, and now their biggest task was to clear weeds around the cotton plants. John was shirtless, barefooted, and with britches rolled up. His face and upper body were deeply tanned.

"Hey, Mist' Bossman, I thinks the Lawd is tryin' to tell us sump'n," called out Caleb, who was working a couple of rows over from John and Andy.

"Whats that, Caleb?"

"I thinks he's a tellin' us to get in the shade for a spell. I worked many a day for Mast' Olliver, but ain't never seen one as bad as this'n. I'm sweatin' like a bore hawg in heat," he exclaimed.

"Didn't knowed a bore hawg got in heat," laughed Andy, tying his handkerchief around his head to protect himself from the sun.

Suddenly, the men heard a horse rapidly approaching, and by the pounding of hoofs, they could tell someone was in a hurry. A horse and rider soon appeared in a cloud of dust at the edge of the field.

Slowly reining in, the rider pulled her steed to a halt and smiled down at the surprised man below.

"Well, Mister Wilson, I did tell ya I was going to pay a visit one of these days, but I didn't know you was going to be half naked."

John leaned on his hoe handle and shook his head. "Suzanne, what you doin' out here? You said you was going to visit Sister, not me." She suddenly reminded him of his Aunt Hatta with her black hair and dark eyes.

"Young Man, I can come visit you if'n I wishes. Yore Mamma told me where ya was."

"I ain't got time to do no visitin' right now. We got work to do," explained John impatiently, wiping the sweat from his face.

"Go on and visit, John," exclaimed Caleb who had found shelter in the shade of a large hickory tree next to the field. "We 'bout burnt out anyhows."

"That's right, John, you need to take some time off," added Suzanne, sliding over the back of her saddle. "Come on up here with me," she insisted, extending her hand.

"I don't know about this. Can I trust ya to behave?" he teased, his face softening.

Suzanne smiled at him. "Can't promise that. You'll just have to take yore chances, Plowboy."

Caleb and Andy snickered. "Mist' John, we callin' it a day, and I thinks you needs to do the same," laughed Andy.

"I'm mighty dirty and sweaty. You sure you want me next to ya?" remarked John, moving over to the horse and placing his foot in the stirrup.

"If'n I didn't want ya near me, I wouldn't have asked."

"Okay, let's take a ride," said John, settling himself in the saddle. "And when did you start wearin' britches?"

"I don't like the way my dress flies up when I ride. Somebody might see sump'n they ain't s'pose to."

"Well, you better hold on 'cause I'm going to see what yore horse is made of," instructed John, pulling her up behind him. She put her arms around his waist and pulled herself as close as possible.

"Heaaah!" screamed John and the horse lunged forward. They sped down the edge of the field and into a vast stand of virgin timber. Racing through the forest, they jumped logs and ditches and splashed through several streams. Holding on for dear life, Suzanne shrieked with excitement as they darted through the undergrowth.

Nearing the old racetrack, John slowed the horse to a trot. The platform at the starting place had almost rotted down, and trees were now growing in the center area where years ago the Choctaws had hosted their fierce stickball games. It saddened John to see what time had done, but the track was still there, only slightly grassed over. The desire to run the race again stirred inside him. He remembered the last time, the time Frankie coaxed him into that competition he had long regretted. He could still see Frankie's horse kicking and bucking with Frankie in pursuit. He flinched at the memory of people laughing at Frankie and how hurt Frankie had been.

"Suzanne, slip down for a bit. I want to make a run," said John. "You can start me, if'n you will."

Suzanne slid to the ground and pretended to be steadying the horses on the starting line. She then lifted her hand to fire the imaginary shot that would start the race. "Ready, John! Line them up and steady them horses. Boom!"

Grass and dust flew in all directions as John pushed the horse down the track. Leaning close to the horse's neck, John pretended he was Minsa and that a horde of horsemen were breathing down upon him.

Suzanne watched intensly as John made the first turn and erupted down the straight on the back side clinging hard to the horse's neck. In seconds, the far turn was made and the two thundered toward the finish line.

Suzanne screamed. "John, you beat them all! The grand prize is yores!"

John slowed the horse and then cantered around the track once. He gave Suzanne a bow and then reached his arms to the sky as Minsa had often done.

As he approached, Suzanne motioned for him to lean down.

"Ummp," stammered John. "I ain't ever got a reward like that. Who taught you to kiss?"

"You like it?" she replied, looking into his eyes.

"Well, I think I do. It's been some time since I've kissed a woman. I forgot how it was."

The afternoon heat was taking its toll. John was drenched with sweat, and after the hard run, the horse needed cooling down. They quickly made their way through the trees on the western edge of the track and down the steep bank of the Chunky River below. In a few moments, the cool clear water rushed around their legs as they eased the horse out into the stream.

"I think we all need a little coolin' off," suggested John, reaching down to catch some water in his hand.

"You could be right," replied Suzanne, suddenly grabbing John around the neck and playfully pulling him downward. The two tumbled headlong into the water, startling the horse.

Suzanne emerged, laughing. "Now, you gotta save me. I can't swim!"

"Swim," replied John. "This water ain't waist deep."

They splashed and ducked like children until they were exhausted. John made the first move and swam over to the sandy bank to lie on his back and look up at the heavens.

Suzanne followed and lay beside him. "You like to look up at the clouds, don't ya? You can see all kinds of things up there."

"I guess so," replied John, remembering how he used to seek images in the sky.

They lay there in silence, the only sounds were the ripple of water rushing by and the birds singing in the branches above.

John felt a warm surge deep inside as he eyed the young woman at his side. Reaching over, he pulled Suzanne to him and once again their lips touched. But this time, it was not a winner's kiss. It was a kiss of passion, one which Suzanne had so often dreamed about and one John unexpectedly savored.

Time went unnoticed as John told Suzanne all that had happened to him during the war and how so many times he thought he would never see Little Rock again. Soon, the sun was down and a slight breeze stirred the leaves above.

Suddenly, Suzanne got up and swam out into the stream and dipped under the surface. Emerging, she flung her head back and smoothed her long hair.

John raised up on his elbows and watched intently as she waded toward the banks.

"You know, them clothes clingin' to ya is almost embarrassin' me. I can see everything you got and you ain't no little girl no more, you know."

"You like the way I look?" beamed Suzanne. "How 'bout this?" Standing waist deep, she slowly slipped her blouse down revealing the upper parts of her well-developed breasts.

"Whooa," warned John. "I'm not ready for this yet, and it's gettin' late. We gotta head for the house."

Suzanne laughed, reached down and splashed water toward John. "Foolish boy, I was just teasin' you. I ain't takin' my clothes off for nobody 'cept my husband," she exclaimed, pulling her shirt back up.

"And if'n I have my way," she thought, "you, John Wilson, will be the man lyin' beside me one day and I'll be watchin' you undress."

As they started home, John wondered why Suzanne had made such a bold afternoon visit. She had never done anything like that as long as he could remember.

"Suzanne, did somebody put you up to this?"

"Put me up to what? Oh, you mean this afternoon. No, I just wanted to spend time with you and ask ya to, maybe, escort me to a party tomorrow night over at the Williams."

John waited a few moments before he replied. "Party. Naw, I don't think I need to carry you to no party. Yore folks don't approve of me and I sure wouldn't pick ya up at yore house."

"You don't have to. I'm spendin' the night with Clara, so all you has to do is meet me there. I promise you, we'll have a good time."

"Who all's going to be there?" probed John.

"John, you don't have to worry. She ain't going." Suzanne paused and then asked. "You had a good time with me today, didn't ya?"

John did not answer.

Nearing the house, John was conscious of the warmth of Suzanne's body on his back and remembered how it had felt to have her next to him in the water. He reached back and with one hand pulled her closer.

"I did have a good time today and I'll just have to wait to see how I feel tomorrow. I might go to that party with ya, but don't wait on me."

As John watched Suzanne ride away, he suddenly realized how very much he had enjoyed the afternoon. When kissing her, he had felt emotion and passion stir inside him. He had not thought of Becca once.

Suzanne had never been happier. Her dreams were beginning to come true, and reality with John was even more exciting than she imagined. He was every-thing that she had hoped for and much more.

John had not noticed Sister sitting in the porch swing. Straining to catch a final glimpse of Suzanne, he tripped on the bottom porch step and stumbled.

"Whoaa," laughed Sister. "You must've had an interestin' afternoon. You can't even stand up, and you sure look like you got yoreself wet somehow."

"Mind yore own bus'ness. I don't need none of yore meddlin'," snapped John.

"Andy told me you left the field 'bout mid-afternoon and he said Suzanne was a holdin' mighty tight to ya."

"If she hadn't have, she would have fallen off that horse. And that ain't none of yore bus'ness either," grumbled John.

Sister eased out of the swing and waved a letter over her head. "Got sump'n for ya, Lovah Boy. Letter come in here today addressed to ya," teased Sister. "From some Lucretia Caulder up in Pennsylvanie. You must have all kind of love affairs goin' on."

John stormed toward Sister, but she quickly stepped behind the swing, still waving the letter.

"Give me that, girl! I ain't playin' games with ya."

"If you'll say please, and tell me what all you and Suzanne were up to, I might just give it to ya," teased Sister.

"Give me that letter, and you can forget 'bout knowin' my personal bus'ness," answered John, grabbing for the envelope.

"Here, take it. It's probably from some fat old lady anyhow," added Sister, throwing the letter toward him.

John sat down on the steps, carefully opened the envelope, and removed the letter. For several minutes, he was completely engrossed. When he finished, he refolded the letter and placed it back in the envelope.

"You going to write her back, John?"

Startled to hear Sister's voice directly behind him, John almost fell off the steps.

"Dammit, Sister! You is some kind of nosy. Just wait till yore beau comes courtin' again. I'm going to fix you good," shouted John, jumping up and chas-ing her down the hall.

Hearing Sister screaming and the pounding of feet in the hall, their mother rushed outside. "You stop it, right now! Both of ya!" she ordered, catching Sister as she ran by. "And John, you is gettin' too old for this kind of nonsense."

With a boyish grin, John stood looking down at the little woman who could be as ferocious as a raging bull when it came to disciplining her children, and explained, "Mamma, Sister is pesterin' me, as usual, and we just playin', that's all."

"Playin' or no playin', you two is makin' too much racket. Yore Papa's back's hurtin' him again and he can't get no rest with you two carryin' on like this."

Later that evening as the family sat on the porch enjoying the cool evening,

Sister said, "I know what Suzanne wanted. She wants you to go with her tomorrow night. That's it, ain't it, John?"

"Might be. What about it?"

"I just know, that's all. And James is going to take me. Mamma done said he could," announced Sister.

"Is that right, Mamma? That Yankee going to take Sister out again?"

"John, I thought you was gettin' to like that young man. And yes, I agreed to let him escort her," responded his mother.

"Then, I ain't goin'. I ain't goin' to no party where my sister is going to be," stated John, flatly. "And I ain't sure I'll ever like a Yankee."

As Lott listened he was concerned with John's bitterness. "John, I think you got Johnson all wrong. You don't know everything about the man."

"I know he's a Yankee, and there were a time, he was the enemy. And I know what him and the rest of them devils did to the South, and I ain't talkin' 'bout doin' away with slavery either. I know they stole most of our stock."

In the darkness, only the glow of Lott's pipe could be seen.

"John, you remember, you told me you saw a place that looked like a grave down yonder. Well, that's just what it is. When Sherman come through here, some of his ruffians sneaked up here one night, hit me over the head and was tryin' to have their way with yore mother and sister. Lieutenant Johnson just happen to be patrolin' the place and heard what was goin' on. Them soldiers knowin' they was caught, fired a shot that took the lieutenant's hat off, and before they could shoot again, he drew and killed one of the bastards. Fired again, and wounded the other."

No one spoke for a few moments. Everything was quiet except for locusts singing in the trees and an occasional croak of a bullfrog near the spring.

"Papa, why didn't ya tell me this before now?"

"We don't like to talk about it, Son," replied Sarah. "Just like there's things you don't want to tell us about the war."

Before long, John excused himself, leaving Sister and his parents with their thoughts.

"You know, Mamma," said Sister. "I think John is gettin' back to his old self."

"How do you see that, Sister?"

"You know this evenin' when John was a chasin' me down the hall and callin' me names. It were just like ole times. I enjoyed every minute of it."

The next evening, John didn't attend the party. His mind was too filled with thoughts of Becca. Suzanne was a beautiful young woman who could certainly arouse desire in any man, but John knew his feelings for her were only physical. No more.

The rain finally let up and a brisk, cold north wind moved in, ushering in the long awaited relief of fall coolness. The smell of cotton ready for picking was in the air. Corn stalks, once green and waving, were now brown and shriveled, and the leaves of the hardwood trees had turned red and gold. Harvest season was at hand.

Gradually, Frankie and Becca's relationship warmed. Frankie had made every effort to be patient. Meeting with John that Sunday had strangely eased her longing to see him. She now knew he was well. He could rebuild his life without her.

Meanwhile, Suzanne had said nothing to Becca about her afternoon with John, but these thoughts haunted her. She had been very disappointed when he had not come to the party, but Sister's explanation made sense. She could understand John's not wanting to be at a party with his sister.

Several days later, Suzanne spent an afternoon with her sister-in-law.

"Look down there, Suzanne. Has you ever seen so much cotton? It looks like a sea of white puffy clouds. No tellin' how much we going to make off that crop."

"It is a good un. I know Frankie is proud of it. I guess soon he'll have more than cotton to be proud of," stated Suzanne.

"What you mean by that, Suzy?" replied Becca, brushing some dust off her sleeve.

"Well, a while back, you was mighty sickly. And I do notice you's gainin' weight. I say that you two has a baby on the way," grinned Suzanne.

"Hush yore mouth, girl," replied Becca. "There ain't a soul that knows about it, not even Frankie.

25

BALANCING THE SCALES

AT THE END OF THE WAR, FREED SLAVES EXPECTED A PARCEL of land and a mule to get them started in a new life of independence. To their dismay, they received nothing. Many went back to the fields of former masters, while others became poor sharecroppers. Some Negroes brave enough to pick up and leave, migrated north, while others moved westward.

Many whites found themselves destitute, as well. Money was hard to come by and farmers were unable to buy supplies and equipment. Without resources, many had no choice but to sell and move. For those who did have some reserves, a bad crop spelled disaster.

As white rule ended in the South some Negroes, now protected by the military, became bold and aggressive in dealings with the whites. They openly challenged and intimidated white citizens on the streets and roads. Still angry that they had not received any help from the government, pockets of hostile Negroes refusing to work for white employers, spent their time plotting to seize what they wanted, relying on military protection from the government. Such was a man named Skinner Jackson.

Skinner had been owned by Frank Olliver and when he was freed, he took the name of Jackson after General Andrew Jackson. Under slavery, Skinner continually caused trouble on the farm. When he wasn't trying to run away, he was always creating problems among the other Negroes on the place. More than once he had been beaten unconscious by the master's whip for problems in the quarters. The only reason Frank Olliver kept him was because he could outwork any three men in the field.

When the slaves were set free, Skinner swore that one day he would personally deal with Olliver, even if it cost him his own life.

Meanwhile, Tim, with only one leg, was no help on the family farm. To earn money, he turned to something he and his father already knew well—corn whiskey. Tim also made money raising and fighting dogs.

One Saturday afternoon, John went with Tim down to Hickory for one of his events. Hours later, slightly inebriated, Tim decided to stay over with the Wilsons. In the early morning hours, the men were awakened by shouting out front.

"Mist' Lott! Mist' John! There's big trouble down there! Somebody's going to get kilt. Good Lawd, somebody better stop it!"

John ran headlong into his father as they rushed out of their bedrooms and into the hall. They hurried out to the porch where Andy and Caleb were waiting, so nervous their whole bodies shook.

"What's wrong with you boys? Somebody hurt?" questioned Lott.

"Naw Suh, Mist' Wilson, ain't us," replied Andy. "It's Mast' Olliver! He's a fixin' to get himself kilt, sho' as hell!"

"Just wait a minute. What do ya mean 'bout Olliver going to get himself killed," probed Lott.

"Mist' Wilson, Skinner and his boys has took up at one of Mast' Olliver's old farms he ain't usin' no mo'. They's stayin' in an ole shack down there and they's been killin' his hawgs a runnin' in the swamp. Mast' Olliver is a goin' down there to run them off, and he's fixin to meet trouble. Ole Skinner and his boys has got guns, and they sho' as hell going to use them on him," explained Caleb.

Easing closer to the boys, John asked, "Where'd you hear such a thing, Caleb? How you know what you sayin' is the truth?"

"Mist' John, I got up real early this morning and was just going to take a walk down to Little Rock. When I got down to the sto', I saw Mast' Olliver leavin' the place with some shootin' powder, and he told Mister Walker he was a going to go kill him some niggars. He told Walker it weren't so bad that Skinner was a stayin' on the place, but by damn, he weren't going to allow them to kill his hawgs. That's sho' what he said."

Tim hobbled out to the group. "Who'd he say was goin' with him, Caleb?"

"Didn't say, but he sho' better not go by hisself. That Skinner is one mean niggar, and his boys is just as bad. They's devils in the flesh. Mast' Olliver is a fixin' to walk headlong into one hellava hornets' nest."

Tim and John's eyes met. "Tim, he ain't going to go by hisself. You can bet Frankie is there with him."

"You got that right, John. They're going to need help."

"Toby!" screamed John. "Harness up the wagon and you saddle up the mare and head for Decatur. Get the lieutenant and tell him to bring some soldiers with him. Don't waste no time!"

"Yes Suh, Mist' John," came the reply. "Good as done."

"Got to get my gun," mumbled John, hurrying back to his room.

"You ain't leavin' me behind," stated Tim, buttoning his shirt.

"Me neither," added Lott.

"Ain't neither one of you goin'," announced John as he entered his room. "You'll just slow me down."

"Down, hell!" exclaimed Tim. "I'm still as good a man as you is, and if'n I need be, I'll get down behind them thick wagon sides and do my shootin'."

"It's yore life," grumbled John.

"Hope there ain't no shootin'," commented Lott, reaching for his coat and rifle.

Sarah and Sister, hearing the excitement, rushed outside to find out what was going on. Learning what might happen, they clung to each other in the early morning coolness.

In a matter of minutes, Tim and John were seated in the wagon, but as Lott stepped up on the wagon wheel, pain shot through the left side of his body. Sinking to the ground, he motioned for Sarah. "You better help me. My back's out on me again," groaned Lott, struggling to get in a position to relieve the pain. "Damn, you boys have to go without me."

"John, we lost ya once, you better come back without a scratch on yore body," warned Sister, giving her brother a hug.

"Heahh!" shouted John, slapping the reins. The wagon rattled and shook as John and Tim sped south.

"Despite the hard feelin' between me and Frankie, no way," thought John, "am I goin' to let that boy get shot down in cold blood. Becca or no Becca, this ain't going to happen to him."

Tipping a hill, Tim exclaimed. "We goin' right by Frankie's house. Can't be a mile from here. Better stop and see if'n they is left yet."

But, Frank Olliver, Frankie, and Frank's foreman, Sam Claborn, were already mounted and moving steadily down the narrow ill-kept road toward the farm.

Years earlier, this section of land had been one of Frank's more profitable farms, but due to overplanting, it had become worthless. All that was left of value was a large herd of hogs that roamed the swamplands below the old fields.

"Frank, you reckon they's armed?" questioned Sam, coaxing his horse down a steep gully.

"Damned if'n I knows," he answered. "If'n they is, Skinner don't know nothin' 'bout shootin'. And he knows better than to draw down on me. He know's I'll shoot him in the blink of an eye."

"We don't need to get in no shootin' with them niggars, Frank. You know, the military is protectin' them bastards. We'll be the ones in trouble," continued Sam.

"I ain't worried 'bout no military. All I know is I got some trespassin' niggars on my property, and I'm going to get them off."

Frankie, already nervous, suggested, "Paw, we don't need to start no shootin' with them folks. We just need to let them know they is a trespassin'."

"Hell, Boy!" exclaimed Frank. "The only thing Skinner understands is force, and he's going to get a double dose of it from us, you hear."

Rounding a bend, the men sighted the old farm house, practically in shambles, off to the left. To the right was what was left of an old barn and on the other side of the house was another building with a huge woodpile. A stream of smoke curled from the chimney.

"Let me do the talkin'. I know how to handle Skinner," ordered Frank as he led the men into the yard.

Hearing the horsemen approaching, Skinner had peered out the window, and recognizing Frank, quickly woke his sons who were in the back bedroom.

"Skinner, you in there?" shouted Frank, dismounting and striding toward the front porch.

"I'm here, Olliver. What ya want with me?" replied Skinner from behind the closed door.

"I see you is livin' on my property and I heard tell you is a killin' my hogs. That true?"

Skinner eased the curtain back. "Ain't nobody been a livin' on this here place for a long time. As for killin' hawgs, we don't know nothin' 'bout that."

Frank cocked the hammers on his double barreled shotgun and rested it against his shoulder.

"Skinner, you is a lyin' fool! You is either going to get yore black ass off my place, or you and yore boys is going to be a bunch of dead niggars," scowled Frank.

"Frank, back off a little," advised Sam. "They may be armed and have us outnumbered."

"That's right, Paw. Don't push so hard," added Frankie.

Skinner knew Frank would use the shotgun. "Seth, you and Jack sneak out to the barn. Ben, you and Clemmy get behind the woodpile. That way, you be on each side of them. Now git on quick," instructed Skinner under his breath.

"What about you, Paw?" questioned Seth.

"I'm a going to go out and face him. If'n he lowers them barrels on me, you better shoot, cause he's going to try to kill me."

"You comin' out Skinner?" called Frank. "I'm waitin' for ya."

The door slowly opened and the former slave came out wrapped in a thick blanket, his arms hidden behind his back.

"Skinner, it's real simple. Just get yore bunch and get off my place and get off right now," ordered Frank.

Skinner walked across the porch and down the steps.

"Frank, we ain't leavin', not just now, and I ain't takin' nothin' off you. I ain't yore niggar no mo'."

Frank's face turned red in anger as he stood facing the man he had once owned and hated. Without thinking, he eased his fingers down on the double triggers, not realizing that he had just given a fatal signal to Skinner's boys.

"Sorry you feels like that, Skinner. I'm going to send ya on to hell today," threatened Frank, lowering the gun in an attempt to frighten him.

Without warning, Skinner threw off his blanket and drew his own shotgun from behind his back, firing both barrels directly at Frank. The double load struck Frank in the lower section of his body, taking his legs out from under him and knocking him backwards to the ground.

Almost simultaneously, Skinner's boys opened fire on Frankie and Sam. Frankie's horse went down, sending Frankie scrambling to avoid getting pinned beneath the animal. Taking cover behind the horse's body, he fumbled for his pistol, lost in the confusion.

Sam, luckier than Frankie but with shots whistling overhead, turned his horse and galloped toward a stand of trees several hundred yards away.

Frank lay sprawled on the ground with both legs shattered and bleeding, unable to pull himself to safety. Frankie, with a wound to his thigh and side, lay unarmed and huddled next to his fallen mount. Blood trickled down his pant's leg.

Skinner hurried back into the house and reloaded his shotgun. "This is some kind of good day. I'm going to get rid of both of them Ollivers," he mumbled. "Don't shoot Frank! 'Member, he's mine!" shouted Skinner to his boys.

"Paw, you alive?" muttered Frankie. "I'm comin' for ya."

Frank weakly called back. "Don't ya come out here. They's got us in a crossfire. You'll get yoreself killed." Twisting his body to where he could see Frankie, Frank murmured, "Frankie, if I don't live through this, you got to know sump'n."

"Paw, be quiet. You don't need to do no talkin'."

"Son, I didn't want Jake Wilson killed. Just wanted to get his money so he wouldn't pay off that Choctaw's debt. We needed that Indian's land. Didn't want him killed at all."

"Why you tellin' me this now?" questioned Frankie.

"If'n anything happens to me, I want you to know I might be a lot of things, but I ain't no killer," gasped Frank, drawing a labored breath.

Sam knew he needed to go for help but was afraid leaving his friends would mean a sure death for both of them. He prayed someone had heard the shots and would come to their aid.

Meanwhile, John pulled up to Frankie's house, leaped from the wagon, sprinted across the yard, and bounded up the steps screaming, "Frankie! Frankie Olliver!"

He pounded on the door, but there was no sound from inside.

Suddenly there were footsteps in the hall and the door slowly opened.

"John, what in tarnation is wrong for you to come out here so early?" questioned Becca, pulling a shawl around her bare shoulders.

"Becca, where's Frankie? Frankie, you in there?" John called out peering into the darkened house.

"John, what's wrong? Why do you want Frankie?" she asked, a sense of cold fear creeping over her.

John pushed her aside and stalked into the hall.

"Dammit, Becca, answer me. We ain't got time for games. Is he here, or ain't he?"

Becca was suddenly so weak with fear she could hardly speak. "John, he left about thirty minutes ago. Him, Mister Olliver, and Sam was going to go check on some hawgs, or sump'n like that."

"Damn!" replied John as he turned. "Tim, get that mule goin'!"

"John, what's happened? Is they in some kind of trouble?" questioned Becca, running after the wagon. "I'm comin' with you."

"No, you ain't goin' nowhere! Tim and me will take care of it. For God's sake, don't leave this house!" ordered John.

It took John and Tim only a short time to cover the four miles to the old farm. Coming up over a high rise in the road and descending a trail that led into a valley, John could hear faint gunshots in the distance.

"Tim, you hear them?"

246

"Damn sure do, John. They's already after each other. This remind you of anything?"

"Reminds me of the day we walked into hell up in Pennsylvanie."

Hearing another cluster of shots much closer, John ordered Tim to stop the wagon.

"I'll be right back," said John, jumping down. He darted through the woods at a dead speed and then returned in a short time.

"Tim, we got to hurry! Two men and one of the horses is down and they's shootin' at another man in a patch of woods. Looks like Sam."

"Get in! What's the plan?" questioned Tim.

"Well, there's some up in the barn loft to the right of the house, and one or two is behind a long stack of wood to the left of the place. The one on the ground is in a crossfire," explained John. "You take the wagon behind the barn so you can have the sideplanks for cover. Just keep them pinned down while I try to help ever who's on the ground. I'll get the one out in the woods to move around behind the woodpile and try to catch them from behind. That okay?"

"Sounds good to me. Be careful now, you hear."

John took his revolver and left the rifle in the wagon for Tim. By swinging wide to his right, John found a dry creekbed that gave him protection and brought him within thirty yards of where the gunman had taken refuge in the woods.

He soon spotted Sam Claborn crouched behind a large oak, reloading his rifle.

"Need some help?" whispered John.

Startled, Sam wheeled around and fired. In Sam's excitement, he had not even taken the time to remove the ramrod from his rifle barrel. John barely had time to duck as the ramrod and a bullet whisked past his head.

"Sam! It's me, John Wilson! This the way you treat folks tryin' to help you?"

Sam slumped back against the tree trunk in relief.

"John, damn glad to see ya. Sorry 'bout that shot. You might near scairt me to death. Frank and Frankie is down up front. Don't know how bad they's hit, but they's hit. You better keep yore head down. Them niggars can shoot a lot better than Frank claimed."

John sprang from his hiding place and dashed from tree to tree until he had reached a large hickory next to Sam. Bullets knocked bark off the trees as Skinner's boys released another round.

"Sam, listen to me. Tim is makin' his way over behind the barn to try to keep that bunch inside. I want you to follow that stream back there and work yore way down to where you can get behind them men at the woodpile. When you and Tim starts drawin' their fire, I'm going to see what I can do for Frankie and his paw."

Sam nodded his head. "Anything is better than what I been goin' through."

Sam dashed for the creek and with one mighty leap, tumbled down the bank and out of sight.

John crouched as bullets tore away at sides of the tree while he checked his pistol. Hearing shots in Tim's direction, John knew it would be only a matter of moments until Sam would make his assault on the ones behind the pile.

"There it goes," he thought. "Them's Sam's shots."

Without hesitating, John pushed himself from the protection of the tree and raced toward the house. Running in a zigzag fashion, he tried not to give the Negroes an easy shot. As John had hoped, Tim and Sam were now drawing the fire away from him. Not a bullet was fired in his direction as he made his move toward the fallen men. Approaching the downed horse and rider, John rushed up and lay as close as he could to his boyhood friend.

"Move over, Fellow. I got to get you out of here," insisted John. "Can't stay out in the open like this."

"John," muttered Frankie. "I'm hit bad. Got to get Paw out."

Just as Frankie spoke, one of the Negroes behind the woodpile darted out into the open. He brought his rifle up and fired a round at the two men. The bullet ripped a gash across the back of John's neck, sending a gush of blood down his shoulders. John instantly aimed his pistol and dropped the man in his tracks.

Suddenly, with a loud scream, Skinner threw open the door and rushed out toward where Frank lay helpless on the ground. Seeing Skinner running toward him, wild and crazy, Frank reached inside his pocket, pulled a derringer and fired both barrels at Skinner.

Skinner, without flinching, continued toward Frank.

"Frank Olliver, you beat me one too many times!" shouted Skinner, aiming his shotgun directly at Frank. "Me and you both'll be in hell today!"

The roar rattled the windows and the firing stopped abruptly. Swaying, Skinner tossed his shotgun toward Frank and slowly dropped to his knees, lowered his head and fell forward with two bullet holes in his chest.

"Throw them guns down! It's over," shouted John. "We don't need no more killin'. This fight was between two old men. Two old enemies. You all hear me?"

Skinner's boys threw their rifles down from the loft and made their way out of the barn to where their father lay. Another eased from behind the woodpile and went to help his brother sprawled on the grass in front of the woodstack.

"How bad is he?" asked John.

"If'n I hadn't shot him, he'd have got me. Tim, you and Sam all right?"

"Just fine, John. But yore wagon's kind of holey."

Leaning his brother up on some fallen pieces of wood, Ben, Skinner's youngest boy, exclaimed, "I thinks he'll make it. You just grazed his hide. Ole Clemmy is one tough niggar."

Frankie shakily got on his feet and stumbled over to his father.

"You don't need to see him, Frankie," warned John.

"He's my father, John, he's my paw."

Meanwhile, Becca had tried to saddle Lightning but had collapsed on the straw strewn barn floor.

"Been too sick lately. I'm just too weak to go lookin' for them men," she thought.

Lying on the soft hay, Becca tried to remember everything John had said. "He was lookin' for Frankie," she recalled. "Didn't mention Mister Olliver or Sam, so it must be Frankie that's in trouble. But, I didn't see no guns. Maybe Frankie got himself hurt."

"John'll take care of him. He always has. He'll bring him home. I know he will," stated Becca out loud as she pulled herself off the ground. "I wouldn't know where to go to find him, anyway."

Back at the old farm, Frankie had collapsed when he saw his father. John and Sam had placed him in the wagon.

"I'm dyin', ain't I John? Just like my Paw," said Frankie.

Tim placed a blanket under his head and covered him with another. "You ain't dyin', Frankie. Them two shots went clear through ya. Didn't even break no bones."

"I is dyin', too. I ain't even going to make it home. And me with a young un on the way."

"You ain't going to die. I seen Doc Caulder save a whole bunch of folks worse off than you is," added John. "Ben, help me get Mister Olliver's body up in the wagon. We got to get them all home."

"John," said Frankie, tugging on John's sleeve. "Before Paw died, he told me he didn't have nothin' to do with yore uncle's death. Only wanted to take that gamblin' money. He weren't no killer."

Just as they were placing Frank's body on the wagon floor, calvarymen led by Lieutenant Robinson galloped into sight. Riding up front was Toby.

Ordering his unit to halt, the lieutenant exclaimed, "Seems like I'm a sight late."

"Mist' John, you all right? You got blood all over yore back," observed Toby, getting down from his horse.

John closed the wagon tailgate. "I'm fine, but Frankie's shot up pretty bad. Got to get a doctor for him. Toby, ride up to Union and fetch Doctor McLauren. We's carryin' him on home."

"Hold up, men," ordered the lieutenant. "There's been a killing here. Somebody's responsible and somebody has to be charged."

John glanced over to where Seth, Skinner's oldest boy, stood.

"Lieutenant, this here fight was between Mister Olliver and Skinner. The rest of us kind of got caught up in it, and at the end, we all stopped it. As you can see, Olliver and Skinner is both dead. If'n you want to charge somebody, it'll have to be them. You can carry them to jail, if you want, or you can let us bury them."

"Is what John said right?" the officer asked.

Seth nodded his head. "That's right, Mister Soldier. This here fightin' was between them two, not us uns."

"Then you bury your dead. And hurry that man on home," stated Lieutenant Robinson. "And John, I want you to come down to Decatur first thing Monday morning to give me a full report, you understand?"

"Yes Sir, I'll be there," he replied. "Tim, get this wagon movin' while I try to stop the bleedin'."

As the they approached the house, Becca rushed out across the yard toward the wagon, but her heart sank when she recognized only John and Tim. She nervously scanned the road.

"Get out of the way Becca," called out Tim. "We comin' up to the house! Get back!"

He pulled the wagon to a stop at the front steps and John leaped to the ground. He hurried toward Becca so she could not see the men lying in the back.

"Becca, Frankie's going to be all right. He's been shot," said John, grabbing her by the shoulders.

"Shot!" stammered Becca. "Frankie's been shot? How'd it happen? Who done it? Let me see him," cried Becca, breaking free and running to the wagon.

"Don't look in there, Becca!" snapped John, trying to catch up to her.

But Becca had already seen the horrifying sight. Frankie was lying pale and motionless, covered with a bloodied quilt.

John placed his arm around Becca's waist to steady her in case she fainted.

"Becca, he's lost a lot of blood, but he's got clean shots. We got to get him inside. I done sent for a doctor."

Becca mumbled, "Who's under the quilt?"

Picking Frankie up in his arms, John replied, "It's Mister Olliver, Becca. He didn't make it."

Reaching the doorway, John turned to Tim. "Take him on home, Tim. You might want to stay there a while until neighbors can be notified."

"Becca, get some whiskey to clean his wounds and I need some clean cloth for bandages. You got a bed downstairs?"

"We got both," answered Becca breathlessly, rushing to the kitchen. "Put him on that cot in the study to yore right."

Becca soon returned with whiskey and bandages and John began cleaning and dressing the wounds.

"He's going to need water, Becca. We got to get it down him."

"He looks mighty pale," mumbled Becca, tears trickling down her cheeks. "We can't let him die, John. He can't die."

The hours passed slowly as John and Becca sat by the cot watching Frankie's ever move. Every so often he would moan, twist slightly and then fall back into unconsciousness.

Finally, his eyes opened. "I ain't going to die, am I?" he whispered.

John reached over and took his hand. "I done told ya you going to live. You think I'd lie to ya," reassured John. "We still got things to do and places to go, Frankie."

Frankie smiled weakly and gently squeezed his hand.

"I knowed you weren't going to let me down. You saved my life. If you hadn't come down there, they'd killed us all."

Becca reached over and wiped the moisture from his brow and gave him a gentle kiss. "You going to be just fine, Frankie. We ain't going to let nothin' happen to ya."

Six hours had passed before Doctor McLauren arrived and after examining the wounds, he closed his medical bag and extended his hand to John. "Son, don't know where ya learned doctorin', but you did a fine job with this boy. Couldn't have done better myself."

"Appreciate that, Doctor. I learned it from Doctor Caulder. I helped him doctor soldiers up North."

"Well, just keep him still and change them dressings often. He should be fine," concluded Doctor McLauren. "I'll drop by to check on him in a couple of days."

It was now late afternoon and shadows had crept across the room. Outside a cold November rain was falling and a brisk wind pushed the rocker out on the porch back and forth, just like someone was sitting there, waiting for some unknown event to happen.

Back in the stillness of the room, a sense of intense loneliness swept over Becca. "John, will you stay with us. I don't want to be alone. I need yore help with Frankie. He might start bleedin' again."

John got up and walked to the window and peered into the gathering darkness. "You got a mighty nice place here," he commented.

"Mister Olliver give it to us for a weddin' present."

"You always wanted a house like this. Farmin' like me and Papa does, a house like this would take a lifetime to build."

Becca thought to herself, "I always admired fine homes, but John, I would have lived with you in any kind of a house and loved every minute of it."

The newly lit lantern glowed on Becca's face. To John her beauty was both enchanting and disturbing. His mind wandered to another time, a time when things were at peace in his world, a time when bloodshed and killing were unknown, a time when a certain young man pursued a girl that would someday share his life, his joy, and his sorrow. A girl who was his best friend.

"John, you lookin' at me awfully strange."

John returned to the bedside. "My mind just goes off sometimes. It does that since I got that head injury."

"Will you stay the night?"

"Sure, I'll stay. Plannin' to anyhow. First thing I'm going to do is to get a fire started in here. The weathers changin'. Ole winter time is on the way."

Soon the fire popped and crackled as its warmth filled the room.

"Becca, you still want to hear what happened to me in the war? Going to be a long night. We got plenty of time."

Becca didn't respond at first. She just sat and stared into the fire. Finally she replied, "Only if you will listen to what has happened to me."

The hours slipped away as the two shared the years stolen from them. Sometimes they would laugh and at other times they wept. With the light of dawn, Frankie awoke, too weak to speak, so he listened as best he could to what John and Becca were saying. Their voices seemed like a dream echoing in an empty hall.

As the morning sunlight brightened the window, John stood up. "Becca, I need to be gettin' on home. You going to be just fine."

Becca smiled and nodded. "I hope so. Thank you for what you did for Frankie and thank you for talkin' to me. I think we both have a understandin' of what happened to us."

Suddenly, Becca noticed the blood stains on John's back. "John, you got hurt too. You got blood all over yore shirt," she continued, turning him around to get a better look.

"Just a scratch on the lower part of my neck. I ain't hurt."

"Let me see," she said. "Let's get that shirt off. There's a nasty gash across yore neck. We got to clean that up."

John stripped off his upper clothing and stood silently as Becca cleaned the wound. He didn't know what bothered him the most, the whiskey burning the open flesh or the sensuous touch of Becca's hands on his body.

"John, you got a terrible scar on yore back. I don't see how you lived through it," she whispered, softly running her fingers across the old wound.

John turned to her. "You brought me through it. I was determined I weren't going to die up there. I meant to come home to you. You mind holdin' me for just a minute?"

John wrapped his arms around her waist, and pulled her to him. Without thinking, he gently pushed the curls out of Becca's face and stared deeply into her eyes. They could restrain their feelings no longer. As their lips touched, it no longer mattered that Becca was another man's wife and that this kiss should never be. For that moment, deep within their hearts, they were totally alone; other people and time did not exist.

Becca pulled John closer and without thinking caressed him so violently it left red streaks across his shoulders and back as her long fingernails tore across the flesh. For years he had dreamed of the moment when she could be in his arms, feel the wet touch of her lips. He had longed for the time when she would be his wife, cuddled next to his bare body, with no feeling of shame or regret in what they did.

Still holding him close and savoring the softness of his warm body, she slowly started to untie the lace that held her blouse. Without warning, the clock on the mantle began to chime and like a bolt of lightning, reality shook them both.

They were no longer carefree youngsters. Time had torn their lives apart. It was time for dreams to end. They pushed away from each other, embarrassed.

"Becca, I shouldn't have. Please forgive me. It will never happen again," whispered John. In his heart, he wanted to tell her how much he loved her, but he knew this would only make things worse.

Becca smiled, reached up and ran her fingers through his hair, smoothing the tangles. Feeling his moist breath against her face, she knew that their lips would never touch again and her fingers would never explore the warmth of his body. Never again would she feel this closeness. Never.

"It weren't all yore fault. I wanted to be in yore arms. I wanted you to love me. We were both wrong," she whispered.

The rain had now stopped, the morning was extremely cold and a white coat of sleet covered the grass. John carefully made his way down the icy steps as Becca stood in the doorway.

"Want to ride Lightnin'? Going to be a long walk home. You best take him," she suggested.

"I can walk it. Lightnin's yores anyhows. Don't want to get attached to him. Might need a ride 'bout fifty years from now when I get old."

Crossing the place where the wagon had stopped the day before, John noticed a puddle of blood the rain hadn't washed away. In a flash, like a revelation, he remembered standing with his parents on their front porch one early morning years ago when a wagon pulled up to their house with blood dripping to the ground. He remembered his uncle gripped in pain and struggling for breath. He remembered Hatta huddled close to Jake's side and the yearning look in his uncle's eyes as he stared at his wife and fought for each precious second. John remembered what his father had said, "Someday, the scales will be balanced."

26

A LOST CROP

"Frankie, " called Becca from the back kitchen. "Got some fresh brewed coffee ready for ya. Want some?"

Only a mumble came from the study.

"The first cup, early in the morning, is always the best. I'm bringin' one."

"I don't want nothin' from you," grumbled Frankie. "You can drink it all yoreself."

"My you's grouchy this morning," replied Becca. She thought he should be feeling better by now. No infection had occurred and he was quickly recovering. But instead of being relieved, Frankie had become a troubled young man.

Becca walked up the hall. "Why you been so cross lately? You is one bad patient. I'll be glad when you get well. Maybe yore temperament will improve."

Frankie refused to look at his wife. "I said, leave me be." Becca turned quietly and left him to his thoughts.

While Frankie had lain wounded and helpless, Becca realized how much she really cared for him. Frankie had been a faithful, loving husband. He was always trying to please her and make her happy. She wondered why he was treating her with such indifference now.

Becca realized she could forget her youthful feelings for John and build a home for Frankie and their baby. She knew she could be the wife Frankie wanted. She had made up her mind.

Lately, everyone had noticed the change. She no longer slipped into periods of depression or went on long rides over the countryside. She was more the happy, boisterous young woman people had always known.

Meanwhile, sitting in front of the window staring out at a gray early dawn, Frankie pondered this change in Becca.

"Them dreams about Becca and John sittin' there talkin' weren't no dreams at all," thought Frankie. "They was talkin' and holdin' each other and kissin'. I think I recall Becca takin' her clothes off. I don't remember nothin' after that. Maybe they done sump'n else. What if they did?"

Without thinking, Frankie dropped the blanket from around his shoulders and wandered to the front porch. As he stood in the cold morning air, his tangled memories brought a frown to his face.

"I understand why Becca has changed, why she's so happy. She's still in love with John. Damn his sorry soul! I bet she was a meetin' up with him when she took them rides. I bet that baby ain't mine at all. Paw told me to watch that Wilson boy. Damn!"

"Frankie! What is you doin' out there in the cold? You ain't even got on no jacket. Here, take this quilt," urged Becca, running up to him. "You ain't going to get well actin' like this."

Without answering, Frankie took the quilt and went into the house. Becca tried to place her arm around his waist, but he pushed her away.

Later that night, Frankie determined to get John out of the way.

I

Chickens, cackling and flapping their wings, came from all directions as the corn was thrown out.

"Chick,chick, chick," called Sister. "Come get it, you hateful pesky devils. All you do is make racket every morning. And you leave messes in the yard I'm always steppin' in. I don't like yore eggs, either. But I do love chicken and dumplin's," she concluded, shaking out the front of her dress she had folded back to hold the feed.

"You hate them birds, huh," came a voice from behind.

Turning quickly, she recognized Thomas Walker.

"You scairt me, Mister Walker. I guess I was makin' too much racket myself to hear you ridin' up. What can I do for ya?"

"I'm sorry I scairt ya Sister. I came by to talk to John."

Sister pointed. "He's down on the lower field. Next to the creek. You can follow the trail down past the barn."

"Good seein' ya, young lady. Give yore Paw and Miss Sarah my regards," he said, tipping his hat.

Toby's two sons and John had been working for over a month to finish the cabin that would be Caleb and Sadie's new home. Andrew, not contemplating marriage, stayed with his parents.

"Need some more clay, Andy. Got to finish this chimney before dark. Yore brother is ready for a home of his own," said John, settling a large stone in place.

"Shore is. And I'm tired of livin' all cramped up in that little room. Hurry up, boy!" ordered Caleb.

Wasn't long before Andy came running up the trail with two large buckets of red clay.

"Hey, Mist' John. We gots company headed this way," exclaimed Andy, pointing to the upper edge of the clearing.

"Looks like Mister Walker."

"Woaah, here horse," commanded Walker, reining in Lightning. "Good to see ya, John. Looks like you is elbow deep in mud. Got a nice place goin' here. Is it for you?"

"Naw Sir, it's Caleb's. Would shake yore hand, but you see they's kind of a mess. Get on down, if'n you will."

"Thank you, Sir. I think I will take a break and get out of this saddle."

They had not spoken to each other since John had questioned him about the telegram.

"Mister Walker, I don't want to be disrespectful, but I've got work to do and I know this ain't no social call. What can I do for ya?"

Thomas pointed to the new barn near the edge of a freshly picked cotton field. "Heard tell you got some fine cotton. Just wanted to see for myself. Looks like you Wilsons done gone and built a big new barn too."

"We is kind of proud of our crop. Especially since it's done been picked and ready for the gin. Lot of hard work, you know," replied John. "We think it'll put us back on our feet."

Pushing the door open, Thomas stared at piles upon piles of fluffy white cotton. "Damn, boy. You Wilsons is got a good crop. This is everything I heard about and more."

For several minutes John and Walker discussed farming, cotton prices, and work. Just passing time. But when Caleb and Andy began arguing, John turned and used this as an excuse.

"Mister Walker, I'm proud you come by to see the cotton, but I need to get on back to work and I feel that you has got more on your mind than cotton. What exactly do you want?"

"John, I want to thank ya for savin' Frankie. You didn't have to go help him," emphasized Walker, extending his hand. "You could've got yoreself killed."

"Wait a minute, Mister Walker. I weren't by myself. Tim was with me. If'n it weren't for him and Sam, I couldn't have got up there. They helped save his life just as much as me," insisted John, reluctantly raising his hand.

"Say what you will, John, but it was you. It was you that was out in the open and might near took a bullet in the neck."

They made their way to the edge of the field where Caleb and Andy were laying stones.

"John, that's a mighty fine place for a niggar, ain't it? You sure this ain't yore place they's a buildin'?"

"Naw Sir, it's his. And come next fall, them eighty acres down there near the barn'll be his and Andy's too."

"You givin' them niggars a house and land?" exclaimed Walker, surprised. "You think that's smart? Folks round here won't take kindly to that. Got to keep them in their place, you know."

"Maybe not. All I know is them boys has helped us get this farm goin' again and we made a deal with Toby. They help us make two crops, and my Daddy and me is givin' them a place of their own," added John, walking up to Lightning. "Come here, boy. Give ole John a kiss," he continued, grabbing the reins and pulling the horse to where he could tickle his nose. "Going to be mine again, if'n I pay you back before Christmas, ain't he, Mister Walker?"

Walker stepped up in the stirrups and settled himself in the saddle. "That's our agreement, John. Pay me before Christmas. Still say you makin' a mistake with them niggars. But you is the one that has to take the consequences."

"Good afternoon, Mister Walker. Take care of my horse, you hear."

Meanwhile, Frankie continued contemplating how he could deal with John and not make the same mistake his father had made with John's uncle.

Late one night, thinking over what Mister Walker had recently told him about his visit to the Wilsons, Frankie formed a plan. If it worked, he would be rid of John and the entire Wilson family.

Frankie knew all the Wilsons had was that cotton crop he had heard about. If it were destroyed they would have to sell and move out.

He needed someone to help him. No problem. When people around Little Rock had heard about the Wilsons giving the Negroes land, some had voiced their anger publicly and even threatened to go down and burn them out.

"John Wilson, no more makin' a fool out of Frankie Olliver. It's time I dealt with you for the last time."

"Frankie," exclaimed Becca, waking up. "You havin' one of them bad dreams again, ain't ya?"

"Best dream I've had in years."

I

"Mist' John, here comes company," announced Andrew.

John, standing on the roof trying to place a stone that wouldn't fit, threw it to the ground in disgust.

"How can we finish this thing with folks worryin' the hell out of us. Might as well just quit," he complained.

"Mist' John, this uns Mist' Tim. You don't mind seein' him.?" said Caleb.

"Naw, don't mind it. Just want to finish yore house."

"Evenin' to ya, John. You in the mud pie bus'ness?" joked Tim, pulling his horse up. "A little mud becomes ya."

John scooped up a handful of red clay and hurled it toward Tim, intentionly missing him. "Next time I'll get ya, you ole jackass. What you doin' down here this late in the day?"

"Want you to go somewhere with me tomorrow night," replied Tim.

"Caleb, you and Andy finish it up. And Caleb, you and yore ole lady can move in anytimes you want. I'm goin' down to the barn and get one of the wagons loaded for the gin. Tim, come on down with me."

Tim gave John a hand with the cotton and before long had a wagon loaded.

"Tim, this here is the best cotton crop we has ever had. Don't it look good?"

Tim, lying down on a soft pile, exclaimed, "You got that right. You going to be in good shape now."

John flopped down beside Tim and asked, "What devilment has you got up yore sleeve that requires my presence?"

"How'd you like to go dog fightin'? Might even have some women lined up to go with us," he replied.

"Well, that depends on who they is. My papa always told me never go out with no ugly women. Too many good lookers out there. And mamma says you don't go out with no gal that you's ashamed to bring home, or marry. So, how would you rate these you talkin' 'bout?" teased John.

Tim smiled and then paused a moment before answering. "My woman is Sally Parker."

"Sally Parker!" exclaimed John. "Don't she let the men folks have their way with her?"

"You is exactly right, Mister John. Miss Sally and I is going to have us a fling come Saturday night. We might even decide to get ourselves hitched, that is, after we get ourselves good and drunk."

A frown came over John's face. "Tim, if you's with Sally, who's you got me fixed up with?"

Tim leaned up on one elbow and gave John a serious look. "You like fat, short women, don't ya? Well, Sally is got this friend that . . . ."

"Just stop it right there," interrupted John. "You can just take on two of them whores by yoreself. Mister John won't be there."

Tim began to laugh. "I'm just kiddin'. I got ya a date with Suzanne Olliver."

"Suzanne! You lyin', Tim. Just a lie," snapped John, jumping on him and pinning his arms down. Her mother sure wouldn't let her go to no dog fight."

"Well, I'll put it like this. Sally is spendin' the night with Suzanne, and Suzanne is stayin' over at Sally's. Outcome is they is stayin' the night with you and me."

Shocked, John released his hold and sat back in disbelief.

"Tim, I don't want to get those girls in trouble. Them Olliver's has enough problems like it is. I don't know about this here plan of yores."

"You don't want to go out with Suzanne? She sure wants to be with you. And I tell ya, she is sump'n to look at," continued Tim.

"That ain't it at all. I know what she looks like, but I just don't want to get mixed up with no Ollivers."

Everything was quiet for a few seconds, then John asked, "Where's this fight going to be?"

"Up at Union in the barn out behind Boler's Inn. Got some men comin' out of Jackson with some big money. Ole Tim is going to get some of that purse and then me and Sally is going to have the fling of our lives."

"Well, you can count me out. Last time any of my folks went dog fightin' in Union, one of us got killed. I ain't goin'."

As he thought about Tim's proposal, John's thoughts raced around in his head and he blurted out, "Tim, what do you see when you look at me?"

Puzzled, Tim stammered, "Well, I just see a man in front of me, I guess. What kind of a dumb question is that?"

"I'll tell ya what you see. You see the biggest fool God has ever created. That's what you see."

"What do ya mean? You ain't makin' no sense."

"It's like this. I got myself mixed up in a war I didn't know a damned thing about. Got one brother killed and another deserted and run off to God knows where. I almost starved to death. Froze my pore ass off more than once. Got the hell shot out of me. Finally get out of prison only to get throwed in jail on the way home. And when I get home, the girl I was plannin' to marry was married to a friend of mine. You see what I mean?"

"I see it clear, John. I guess I is one of them fools too. When I decided to join up, I figured a few soldiers would get killed, not many and nobody I knowed. And them men I seen lying out there on that ground in my dreams, they didn't have no faces. They weren't nobody real. But I was wrong. Them men, torn to pieces and screamin' for somebody to finish them off, were my friends, just like you. What I remember from them fields haunts me most near every night. That war weren't the party I dreamt of. Yeah, John, you is also lookin' at a fool. A one-legged fool."

"One more thing. When I joined up to fight, I weren't fightin' to keep no slaves. We never has believed in holdin' slaves. I was fightin' cause the State of Mis'sippi needed me," explained John. "Mister Lincoln, made this war to get them freed. The funny thing about it, was that most of the South would've gone along with him to free them, if'n he'd tried a little harder and given us a little more time. But Tim, you know what's sad? Mister Lincoln and his politicians got them pore Negroes freed, and they still ain't got no freedom. How many of them own a piece of land or a house? How many of them can read or write and go to school? I ask you how many? Not a damned one of them. And I tell you one more thing. As soon as the military gets out of the South, them Negroes is going to be just as bound to the white man's law as they was under the master's whip."

"John, I think you going to be proven right, but I'll tell you one thing. Toby and his family has got a house, and come next spring this here land we's sittin' on is going to be theirs. Seems like you and yore Paw has freed them more than once. Might be some more folks just like you out there."

I

"Frankie, didn't you enjoy havin' our families together for dinner? Even your mother seems in better spirits," Becca said as she straightened the furniture in the parlor.

"I guess it were all right," replied Frankie.

"Seemed like you and my daddy had a lot to talk about. "Frankie, has you noticed I'm gettin' a little bigger in the middle," continued Becca, turning so he could see. "We'll have a young un here 'fore you know it."

"I've noticed," replied Frankie, rising from his chair. "Think I'll take a walk. Need to get out for a spell."

"Mind if I go with you?"

"It's too cold. And I need some time to myself," he answered.

Frankie headed down toward the corral. As he crawled through the boarded fence, he called Lightning and began rubbing him down with a brush he kept on one of the fenceposts.

"Ole John ain't never going to get you back, you warhorse. You's mine till the day you die," muttered Frankie. "And Becca, I did enjoy yore paw's visit.

The more he talked about the Wilson's cotton, the more I'm ready to put my plan in motion."

Hearing that the Wilsons were about ready to move their cotton to the gin, Frankie knew he could wait no longer. He had overheard Suzanne talking to one of her close friends, Betty Hudson. Betty said Tim was carrying one of his dogs to the fight in Union and had invited John. But, what Frankie didn't know was that Suzanne was going along as well.

"Need about three men to do the job," thought Frankie. "And I ain't going to get none from 'round here. I know some folks over in Meridian who'll help me and will keep their mouths shut. Might cost me a bit but it'll be worth it. But there can't be no killin'."

▌

"John, you cleaning up mighty early, ain't ya?"questioned Sister, walking boldly into the kitchen where John was bathing.

"Get out of here!" complained John, sliding down into the soapy water. "Can't a man get a little privacy around here?"

Pulling up a chair just to annoy him, she kept up the harassment. "I know where you goin' tonight, Big Brother. You and Tim's goin' dog fightin' over in Union."

"Mamma, get her out of here before I kills her!" John shouted.

But Sister sat straight-backed, not making any effort to leave. "She can't hear you. She and Papa's gone for a walk. Holler all you wants."

"Sister, I don't bother you none when you's fixin' up. Just get up and leave me be."

"I will if'n you'll tell me what you up to. I bet you got some girls you going to be seein'," she continued, with a smirk on her face.

John shook his head and smiled, "You could be right, Little Sister. You know Sally Parker?"

"Sure, I does. Who don't?"

"Well, I'm going to be with her tonight," grinned John.

"Sally Parker! No you ain't either! I know what that girl does, and no brother of mine is going to be seen with her."

"She ain't as bad as folks say, and it certainly ain't no worse than courtin' a Yankee. Could be a lot of fun," explained John, with a serious face to disguise the fact that he was only teasing. He had actually become quite fond of her Lieutenant Robinson.

"You is a terrible person, John Wilson, and I'm going to go tell Mamma," replied Sister, rising from the chair. "Mamma!" she shouted, reaching for the door latch.

"Whooa, Sister! I'm just foolin' with ya. I ain't goin' with her. Tim is."

"Tim!" exclaimed Sister, returning to her seat. "Now I'm gettin' to the truth. And just who is you going with?"

"None of yore bus'ness. You know, Sister, when I come home last year, I thought you'd growed up a bit. But you ain't. You is still nothin' but a pest and a nag. Hell, I don't know how even a Yankee can stand bein' with you."

"Can't stand bein' with me, you say," she snapped. "Just for that remark, I'll stay right here till Mamma gets home."

"Sit if'n you want, but I'm gettin' out of this tub whether you's here or not. Like right now," announced John, easing out of the soapy water.

"Mamma! Papa! John just showed himself to me." screamed Sister, throwing the door open and running down the hall toward the front porch.

"Thought that'd get her out. She won't pester me no more while I'm washin'," chuckled John, wrapping himself with a towel. "I still can't believe I has changed my mind and am goin' with Tim, especially to Union," he thought. It's going to be as cold as all get out tonight. Suzanne, I hope you can keep this ole boy warm."

A few minutes after three that afternoon, Tim drove up in one of the finest carriages John had ever seen.

"Where'd you get that rig, Tim? Got a top and all. You steal it?"

"Nah, I didn't do no stealin'. I is gettin' pretty good at the cards. I won the use of this rig for the night. It'll have to go back in the morning," explained Tim.

Hearing the conversation, Sister strutted out to the front steps. "Tim, that sure is some kind of wagon. I mean buggy, or whatever it is. It's fit for a queen."

Tim, knowing how Sister liked to joke, but not be on the receiving end, took the initiative. "Sister, you is so right. It is fit for a queen. Somebody just like you, or maybe Sally Parker."

"Sally Parker!" she exclaimed, "You is as bad as John. You know sump'n else Tim? You is just as bad as that woman. You is a whoreman. You deserves each other."

I

"Frankie, who are those men up in the parlor and what do they want this time of the night?" questioned Becca.

"Just some friends of Paw's and mine from Meridian," he answered, reaching for his coat. "We goin' out for a spell. Be back before daybreak."

"Where you goin' this late? It's cold and you is still weak from the shootin."

Buttoning his coat, Frankie reached for his pistol lying on the mantel. "We goin' coon huntin'. That's where we goin'."

Confused, Becca sensed he was not telling the truth. "Frankie, you ain't been coon huntin' since you was a boy. And you don't shoot coons with no pistol."

"Dammit woman, just leave me be. We goin' huntin', and that's all you need to know," scowled Frankie. "Come on men. Times a wastin'. Get out of my way, Becca."

"He has just gotten through one scrap that almost took his life," Becca thought. "Is it happening all over again?"

The carriage moved gracefully through the streets of Union. In the middle of town they took a left turn onto Jackson Road which stretched westward toward Jackson, the state capital.

"Won't be long now, folks," exclaimed Tim, looking back at John and Suzanne cuddled under a large, thick quilt. "About a half mile to the inn. Just wait till you see them folks with all that big money. Mister Tim is a going to bring it on home tonight."

Sally, huddling close, giggled. "Tim, is you going to bring me home tonight?" she whispered. "You and me know how to have a good ole time. Right?"

"That's all you thinks about, Sally. We is fightin' and gamblin' first. Then we'll see."

"John, I don't care where we go tonight. I'm just enjoyin' bein' with you," whispered Suzanne, reaching over and kissing him on the cheek. "You remember that afternoon we went for a swim? We had some kind of good time, didn't we?"

"How can I forget. I can still see you comin' out of that water all wet and . . ." replied John, pulling her closer.

"There it is up on that hill—Boler's Inn. John, my dog's been pretty quiet back there in the back. That's a good sign, you know. When he's quiet, he's going to give us one helluva fight. Just look at all them horses and buggies up there 'round that place!"

Boler's Inn was a large two-story building that served as a stagecoach stop. It's wide open hall ran through the middle of the lower level and out back was a massive barn where the guests' horses, wagons, and buggies were kept. When dog and cock fights were held, or an occasional bare-fisted brawl, the barn was cleared for the event.

Boler's Inn had become a well-known historic site. It was used as General Sherman's headquarters when he led a raid on Meridian. And it was rumored that two members of the Murrell Mauraders, outlaws who robbed stages and trains throughout Mississippi and Alabama, spent the night there once. One of the outlaws buried a box containing loot, but was killed before informing his partner. The box was never found.

Meanwhile, another party was making their way down the dark road toward Little Rock. When other travelers on the road appeared, they would take to the woods to keep out of sight.

"How much farther, Mister Olliver? It's mighty cold out here tonight," stated one of the riders.

"Not far now. 'Bout two miles. We'll take to the swamp a piece up. Won't nobody see us there," answered Frankie, pointing up to his left.

"You say nobody's going to be there," questioned another rider.

"Naw, the house is almost a mile to the north. Just the barn and a house the Wilsons is a buildin' for some niggers. They ain't moved in yet. Nothin' to it."

"What if'n somebody shows up? Do we kill them?" asked one of the men.

"Naw, we don't kill nobody! There's going to be no killin' tonight," stated Frankie. "If'n it'll make ya feel better, I got sump'n to put over our heads where nobody can tell who we is," continued Frankie, handing the men cloth hoods.

"Here we go. This swamp'll lead us right up to the barn."

Earlier, Caleb and Andy had finished the chimney, and Caleb could wait no longer. Even though it would be a couple of days before they could use the fireplace, Caleb and Sadie had quickly moved their few belongings. The cold didn't bother them.

Lying in their bed in the still of the dark December night, Caleb nudged his wife, "Can you believes we's got a place of our own, Sadie. It's better than a lot of white folks, ain't it?"

"The Lawd's done come and blessed us, Cabe. I don't know of any other colored folks that's got their own place," replied Sadie, pulling the covers up. "Still can't believes the Wilsons going to give us this house and maybe some land, come next year."

A little later, Sadie was awakened by their hound barking outside. Listening intently, she thought she heard a horse whinny in the distance.

"Cabe, dog's a barkin'. Somebody's out there. I heard a horse," she whispered, shaking her husband. "You best get the lantern."

Throwing the cover back, he moved quickly to the window as a glow of light from outside filled the room.

"Sadie, sump'n ain't right out there. Sump'ns lit up. My God Woman! The barn's on fire! I sees some men down there," exclaimed Caleb, pulling on his pants. "Got to get down there and stop that fire!"

"Don't ya dare go to that barn, Caleb!" pleaded Sadie. "You go get Mist' John, or Mist' Lott. Don't go by yo'self. You might end up one dead nigger."

"Where'd that hound come from, Mister Olliver?" called out one of the men. "Where there's dogs, there's people. You sure them niggars ain't moved in yet?"

Frankie, astride Lightning, turned to the men. "Don't worry 'bout no dogs or niggars, just finish torchin' the place and let's get out of here."

I

"John, he's got him by the throat! He ain't going to let him go!" shouted Tim above the roar of the crowd. "We is fixin' to get ourselves rich."

Suzanne turned from the bloody fight and placed her hands over her face. "How can you watch sump'n like this? How can anyone watch one animal kill another and cheer about it? Take me outside, John."

John led her through the screaming mob and walked toward the inn. Taking a seat on one of the benches in the hallway, he placed his arm around his shivering companion.

"I'm tired of it too. I like Tim, always have, but I can't take no more fightin'. There's going to be a day when this ain't going to be allowed. And I don't think it's long off."

"John can we go inside? It's cold out here."

"Sure, they got a big fire goin' in there, and I'm gettin' a little hungry. Looks like it's going to be a long night."

The couple took stools next to the counter and ordered some hot tea. An older woman pushed the cups out to them and stared at John. "I ought to know you, boy. Where's you from?"

"I'm from Little Rock. I'm John Wilson. Lott Wilson's boy."

"Little Rock, you mean Coon Tail," she laughed. "Yes, I know yore Paw and Miss Sarah. Seen them many a time. Used to live down there before we lost our land. Damned ole Choctaw Land Company took it. Better still, stole it. I knowed yore Uncle Jake, too. He was somethin'. The most drankin', gamblin', dog fightin' and horse racin' man that ever hit this country. Weren't none like him. Hated to see him get killed. I was there that night when him and that Choctaw won a bundle of money. They was sump'n."

Suddenly, Tim, with Sally hanging on his arm, burst through the door swinging a large sack in the air. "Over four hund'rd dollars here, Big John. Big money. Big time. Drinks on me, folks. Get that liquor flowin' pretty lady!"

Tim had barely finished his first drink when a well dressed man stepped up to him. "Sir, I'm Vardeman Townsend from Jackson. We're goin' to have a little game upstairs, if you'd like to join us. That is, if you care for the cards."

Tim winked at John and then turned back to accept the invitation. "Sir, I'd be glad to join ya. I feel poker is indeed a gentleman's game. Shall we play?"

Suzanne leaned over to John. "What do we do now? I've got a feelin' this is going to be an all night affair."

John turned to their hostess. "Miss, you got an extra room tonight?"

She smiled. "With this crowd, you got to be jokin'. Ain't a bed that ain't took. This yore wife, Mister Wilson?"

The young couple blushed and Suzanne finally answered, "Not yet, but maybe one day soon."

"Then you two better behave yoreselves. 'Cause like I says, I know this here young man's folks," she chuckled.

Under his breath, John exclaimed. "What did you say that for, Suzanne? We ain't thinkin' about no marryin'."

"Why didn't you answer the woman, John? That was embarrassin', you askin' for a room. I just said the first thing I could think of."

"I would like to spend the night with you," Suzanne thought, admiring how handsome John looked as the light from the fire flickered across his face. "And I do plan to marry you one day, and not too long off, at that."

Miles away, Caleb, with a lantern in one hand and a large stick in the other, was running toward the flaming barn. The fire was streaking hundreds of feet into the sky and Caleb could clearly see four men on horseback watching the flames race through the building.

"That does it, men. Let's get out of here," ordered Frankie. "You is seein' John Wilson's future go up in smoke. No cotton! No farm!"

"What you doin?" shouted Caleb, rushing up to the burning building.

"What's that niggar doin' down here, Mister Olliver? You said that house weren't occupied," exclaimed one of the men in surprise.

Caleb not thinking of his own safety, ran past the flaming building toward the hooded horsemen. "You is a bunch of fools! I'm going to find out who you is," screamed Caleb. "You's going to pay for what ya done!"

"Let's get out of here!" shouted Frankie.

"That niggar's in our way. Want me to kill him?"

"No killin', I told ya!" exclaimed Frankie, spurring his horse.

Caleb was now running directly at the group as the horses galloped toward him. As they approached, one of the riders pulled his horse in front of Frankie, forcing Lightning to veer to his right and straight into Caleb. With a sickening thud, he was knocked to the ground and underneath the horse's hooves. Another horseman, unable to stop, also pounded into the fallen figure.

Frankie ordered the men to stop. "He don't seem to be breathin', Mister Olliver," announced the man. "I think you is lookin' at one dead niggar."

Frankie slumped over in his saddle. "I didn't mean to hit him," he stammered. "I couldn't get out of his way."

"Job's done, Mister Olliver. That barn's burnt. It's time to get out of here."

Crouched behind a cluster of cedar trees, about a hundred feet from where the men were talking, Sadie shook in fear. She was afraid she would be seen in the light of the roaring fire. "Dear Lawd, please let my Cabe be still livin'. And Lawd, please take them men away from here," prayed Sadie, dropping to the ground and hiding her face in the dried grass.

Back at the inn, tiring of the loud talk and tobacco smoke, John and Suzanne had lain down in the back of the carriage. They made a pallet out of one quilt and covered themselves with two other blankets to keep warm.

"Well, at least we is out in the fresh air," shivered John.

"You can put yore arms around me, if you likes. We'll make it just fine," Suzanne said.

"I can just see myself in bed with him, a fire burning in a fireplace and a thick feather mattress," dreamed Suzanne. "Just me and him for the rest of our lives."

"Hey folks! Stir out from under them quilts. It's might near daylight and this has been a profitable night for Tim Johnson," called Tim as he lifted his battered dog and eased him down next to Suzanne.

"Where's Sally?" asked Suzanne, rubbing her eyes.

"John, come upstairs and help me fetch her down. She's as drunk as a cooter bug. Been drinkin' shine liquor for over two hours," explained Tim.

"We'll be right back, Suzanne. Wait here," insisted John.

"Tim, how'd you come out tonight. You do any good?"

"Naw Sir. Not a bit. I was too busy gamblin' to fool with Sally," he replied.

John slapped him on the back, "I ain't talkin' about Sally. I'm talkin' about money. Did you make any money?"

"Sure I made money. Over six hund'rd dollars. Ought to help me and my paw pay a few bills and have a dab left over. And, how about you? Did Mister John Wilson do any good out there under them quilts?"

"Naw, I sure didn't. Didn't even try. Suzanne ain't that kind of gal."

The sun was just coming up as they pulled away from the inn. It had been a long and busy night. Sally and the dog lay in the back while Tim, John, and Suzanne sat up front.

"Tim, we best take our time gettin' home. Sally needs to be able to walk before we gets to her house," suggested Suzanne. "Her paw can be some kind of mean man when he gets roused up."

"And Tim, I think it's better for you to carry Suzanne on to her house. I don't feel right goin' over there," suggested John.

Suzanne placed her arm around John's waist and eased closer. "Mamma don't mind if'n you come callin'. She ain't got nothin' against you, John. She thinks the world of you. She won't mind none at all."

"I don't know, Suzanne. I need a little more time before I can be around yore folks."

"Time," thought John. "Is I ever going to get over Becca? In the dark last night when I was kissin' Suzanne, all I could see was Becca. When I held Suzanne close, it was Becca I felt beside me. Will I never feel free to hold another woman?"

"I'll take her on home, John," added Tim. "If'n we take it slow, we'll be there about nine."

Tim had little liquor that night, but his winnings had him as high as a Georgia pine. He felt like he owned the whole state of Mississippi. Having only one leg didn't bother him at all. He had a woman who seemed to love him and he had a bag of money tucked in his pocket.

Sally was drunk, but happy. She enjoyed going places with Tim. He was carefree and entertaining, totally unlike her father. Ever since Sally's mother died, her father had been almost unbearable. Nothing she did suited him. To him, her mother had always done things right.

Looking over at Suzanne in the morning light with the sun reflecting across her dark hair, John felt a sudden desire to touch her, to be with her. "Could I care for her more than I think?" John's mind floated back to a field in Pennsylvania. He remembered the angel that had stood over him with the sun sparkling through a mass of golden curls. He recalled the time he had spent with that young girl and her family, her gentle touch, and the evening when he gave Lucretia her first kiss. She had sent him scores of letters, but he had answered very few.

"She was just a child when I last saw her," he thought. "Probably about seventeen or so by now. I wonder what she's growed into. Guess I'll never know."

27

THE HEARING

THE SUN HAD BEEN UP FOR SEVERAL HOURS BY THE TIME THEY left Sally's house and the carriage now headed for the Wilson home.

"He didn't seem to be in too bad a mood, did he John?" asked Tim, hoping for a positive response. "Seemed almost pleasant."

"Weren't bad at all, considerin' you fed him a bunch of lies. If he knowed you kept his daughter out all night, there might've been a shotgun waitin' for ya," replied John.

"I don't know about that. One day I might just get hitched to that little ole gal of his. She ain't as bad as folks make out. And she does put up with my galavantin'. No sir, I don't think Mister Parker would shoot his future son-in-law."

"Tim, I think Sally's a sweet girl, and you can't believe everything you hear. If'n I had a father that treated me like he treats her, I'd run off with the first man who would take me.

"Well, there's the house. Our dog ought to be a comin' to greet us by now. He's a pesky ole rascal," remarked John, stretching up to get a better look.

Suzanne tugged John's sleeve, "Looks like Sister sittin' out on the steps."

Hearing the carriage, Sister started running toward them. As she approached, John could see the pain on her face. She almost collapsed as she grabbed the side of the carriage and tried to speak, her face a mask of tears.

John jumped down and placed his arms around his sister and pulled her to him.

"What's wrong? What's happened?" asked John, taking his handkerchief to dry her tears, but feeling a sick fear in his stomach. "You can tell me. Is it Mamma or Papa?"

"It's gone," cried Sister. "Gone."

"What do ya mean, gone?" questioned John, now alarmed.

Sister pointed. "It's burned up. Somebody burned it."

"You mean, our cotton?" probed John, his voice rising.

"Our cotton," shuddered Sister.

On the horizon John now noticed a slight haze of smoke rising in the direction of the barn.

"Suzanne, stay here with Sister. Tim, get this rig turned around and get down there as fast as it'll go," ordered John. "Push it!"

With the crack of the whip, the horses bolted into a gallop. The carriage was moving so fast Tim almost lost control.

"Slow it down, Tim! Won't do no good if we is killed."

Tim pulled back on the reins. "You the boss, John. You know yore sister makes things bigger than they is sometimes. They probably put the fire out and everthing is fine."

"Dear Lord, I hope what Tim's sayin' is the truth. We can't lose our cotton. That's all we got, Lord," prayed John.

Clearing the last rise in the road, Tim jerked the carriage to a stop. John stood up for a few seconds and then slumped back in his seat.

Tim sat motionless, too stunned to move.

After a few moments, Tim, dry mouthed, managed to speak. "John, it's all gone," he groaned. "There ain't a board left."

John remained silent, staring at the smoke rising from the ashes.

"It's all gone," he thought. "The only cash crop we got. All them long hot hours in that sun, and it's all gone." Recovering his wits, John mumbled, "Tim, pull on down. I see my folks."

Lott and Sarah were sitting on the ground, a safe distance from the smoldering remains of their barn. Lott had his arm around his wife's shoulders, her head resting against his chest.

They did not hear the carriage approaching.

John quickly got down and slowly walked over to his parents. He turned toward the fire, unable to face them.

"I ought to have been here. I might've stopped this thing."

"You couldn't have done a thing, John. Can't blame yoreself," replied Lott, looking up at his son.

John eased down next to his mother.

"Why didn't Cabe get you to help him fight it? You, Toby and Andy could've helped him."

Sarah lifted her head. "John, Cabe tried to fight it. He got killed down here last night."

"Killed! How did that happen?" whispered John in disbelief.

"From the looks of things, a bunch of riders come down here, and he tried to take them on by hisself. They run him over with their horses," his father explained.

"What about Cabe's wife? She see it?"

"She seen them. But I can't get nothin' out of her," continued Lott. "She's just sittin' in the cabin next to his body and won't say nary a word."

"We got to find out who done this and who murdered Cabe. There is got to be justice served. If the law won't do it, then I'll see to it myself."

"John, you remember, 'Justice is mine sayeth the Lord,'" his mother said. "Somehow, this here's got to be the Lord's work."

"The Lord's work! I guess you think He served justice when Uncle Jake was murdered. I don't see a thing He done, do you?" protested John. "I'm goin' up to Cabe's place. Let Tim carry you on home."

"John, there was three, maybe four of them. Can't tell for sure. But they really tore up the ground gettin' out," explained Tim, pointing to the loose dirt.

John walked up the steps to the cabin and tapped lightly on the door. It creaked open and Toby motioned him in.

"Toby, I'm sorry. Is Sadie talkin'?"

Toby shook his head. " I'm tried to get it out of her. She just won't."

John went back to the bedroom and over to where Sadie was sitting. Placing his arm around her, he looked over to Cabe and whispered, "Sadie, there's got to be justice. You got to tell me what you knows."

"Justice. You white folks talk about justice. There ain't ever been no justice for none of my people," she cried.

"Damned if'n that's so. You tell me who done this and I'll show you justice," promised John.

▌

"You going to sleep all day? It's done past dinner time," called out Becca, standing at the bottom of the stairs.

Waiting for a reply, she remembered the previous night's visitors. "He and them men didn't get back till sometime after one this morning. They sure didn't look like no hunters. They was a mean lookin' sort. I don't think they did no huntin'. Don't care what they says," thought Becca.

"Time to get up! Want to go see Mamma today, and I want you to go with me."

"I ain't ready to get up. Just shut that loud mouth of yours," grumbled Frankie.

Becca slowly climbed the stairs and quietly pushed the bedroom door open.

"You didn't do no huntin' last night. Them weren't hunters."

Her husband shuffled the covers and turned on his side away from her.

"You look out on the porch. You'll find a dead coon lyin' out there."

"I seen that stinkin' ole varmit. That thing's been dead at least two days," said Becca. "Stiffer than a beanpole."

Irritated, Frankie threw back the covers and shouted, "Let me tell you one damned thing and you best remember it well. We went coon huntin' last night and there sure as hell is a dead coon out on that porch. You remember that, woman!"

▌

After running all the way from Cabe's cabin, John stumbled up the porch steps, gasping for breath. Trying not to be heard, he tipped quietly down the hall.

But Lott heard his footsteps. "Kind of winded, ain't ya, Son?" he commented, easing the door open. "What you changin' yore boots for? Get anything out of Sadie?"

"Found out enough," snapped John. "Excuse me, Papa," he continued as he walked over to a chest next to his window. "Got to finish some longtime bus'ness."

"What kind of bus'ness you talkin' about, John?"

With his back to his father, John reached into the chest and slipped a revolver under his coat.

"The least you know about it, the better you'll be," advised John, closing the lid.

Lott caught his son by the arm and pulled his coat open. "What you going to do with that pistol?" he questioned, reaching for the weapon.

John grabbed his father's arm and pushed him backwards, knocking him into the bed.

Reaching out to his father, John exclaimed, "Didn't mean to push you. I'm sorry, but I know who fired our barn and I know who killed Cabe. Can't depend on no military law to help us. I heard tell there ain't much to them courts," concluded John as he walked out of his room.

Lott rushed after him. "Son, don't do no fool thing. Give the law a chance to help us. Let's go get Lieutenant Robinson. He'll know what to do. Let me go with you."

"You ain't goin' Papa. This is sump'n I got to do on my own."

"Sarah, you better get out here and help me with this boy of ours before he does sump'n that we'll all regret!"

John quickly saddled the family's mare. As he stepped up into the stirrups, his father caught up to him.

"John, for God's sake, don't do no killin'. If you do, it might be you who gets hung. No mountain of cotton is worth yore life. You has got to have faith in God."

"Papa, I ain't known no justice since I left Newton Station for the war. That God of yores has had me in a hell of one kind or another for too long. You keep yore faith. I'm fixin' to break hell wide open."

"Who you goin' after?" shouted Lott.

John turned back to his father, "That's not yore problem."

I

"Where is that wife of mine? When I need her, she ain't around," complained Frankie. With a blanket around his shoulders, he bounded down the stairs and into his study where Becca had a fire burning.

"Need some coffee," shouted Frankie, pulling a chair up to the fire.

"You been wantin' me up. Well, here I is."

In a few moments, Becca eased into the study. "Bringin' it right to you. Fresh and hot." Hearing someone approaching, she paused and glanced out one of the front windows. Astonished, she dropped the cup. "Frankie, it's John!"

The door slammed open and everything happened so quickly Frankie didn't

270

have a chance to get up. John rushed into the study and ripped out the revolver and pointed it directly at Frankie's forehead. With sweat rolling down his face, he pulled the hammer back.

"Frankie, I can't believe what you done to my family. Just a while back, I put my life on the line to save yores. And this is how you thanks me."

Becca rushed over and stepped between the two men, "John, what in tarnations you mean stormin' in our house and pointin' that pistol at Frankie? What has he done to yore family?"

John pushed her aside and kept his revolver leveled at Frankie. "Tell her. Tell her what you done last night. Tell her what kind of man you is."

Without changing his expression, Frankie muttered, "I didn't do nothin' to yore family. Don't know what you talkin' about."

"You's a damned liar, Frankie. Becca, last night that husband of yores and some other men burned our cotton, ever bit of it. And worst still, when Cabe tried to stop them, they killed him."

Becca walked over to where Frankie was sitting and looked down into his eyes. "Is that so, Frankie? Did you do them things?"

Frankie sat glaring at John. "We went coon huntin' last night. Remember."

"Frankie, you weren't huntin' last night. Them men weren't no hunters."

"Shut yore mouth, woman. We was huntin'," replied Frankie, rising from his seat. "Go ahead. Pull the trigger. You two been wantin' each other since you got back home. Go ahead and kill me. Then you'll be the murderer. Go ahead, Big John Wilson. Do it, if'n you got the nerve. Shoot me!"

Again, Becca stepped between the men. "There won't be no killin' in my house and especially between you two."

Frankie pushed her out of his way.

"John, you was braggin' about savin' my life. I remember that day. There I was lyin' on that bed all shot up. And what did you do? I seen you two kissin' there in front of the fire. And I seen Becca start to take her clothes off. I say that baby Becca is carryin' is probably yores, not mine."

"Frankie. This baby is ours. Yores and mine," exclaimed Becca. "It's ours."

Guilt began to creep over John and he lowered his pistol. "Frankie, it was only one kiss and that's all we done. Nothin' else."

John eased backwards toward the door. "I ain't going to shoot you, Frankie. You're right. I ain't going to murder nobody, especially you. You going to be tried for arson and murder, and when it's over, they's going to hang you. They going to string you up. How you like that?"

Frankie smiled. "You ain't got no proof, 'cause you ain't got no witnesses. That's how I like it, John. No witnesses."

"Sorry Frankie, but we has got a witness. An eye witness. And this time you ain't going to have yore Daddy around to buy yore way out."

"What does he mean yore Daddy buyin' yore way out?" questioned Becca.

"Tell her Frankie. Tell her why you didn't show up at the station when the rest of us left for Virginie. Tell her who took yore place."

John turned and abruptly left the house without another word. On the way home, John met Lieutenant Robinson and a small detail of soldiers. The lieutenant ordered, "Woaah horse! Hold it up men!"

Shifting back in his saddle, he turned his attention to John.

"You got trouble, John? You haven't shot anybody, have you?"

"Lieutenant, I sure come close to it," explained John, pulling his coat tighter to his body so as not to reveal the pistol hidden underneath.

"I almost shot Frankie Olliver for what he done to us."

"Mister Wilson told me what happened to you folks last night and he was afraid you might be headed for trouble. Might be going after the wrong person. Toby told me where you were headed."

"I weren't goin' after no wrong person. Frankie done it."

"You got proof, John? There has got to be proof in a matter like this."

"Is an eye witness proof enough, Lieutenant?"

"Damned well is, if you got one."

"Then I want to see just how good that military court you got down at Decatur is. I want to see how you Yankee's dish out justice."

Finally, on March 18, 1867, three months later, the Wilsons were summoned for a court hearing. They had been instructed to present their witness and Frankie Olliver, now formally charged with arson and murder, was ordered to be present to defend himself.

Even though it was only a hearing, the courtroom was filled with spectators because of the circumstances surrounding the case. Tobacco smoke floated in the air and there was a din of chatter as people crowded in to find seats.

At two o'clock in the afternoon, the back door of the courtroom opened and a tall uniformed officer entered followed by several other armed soldiers. Seating himself, he looked solemnly around the room, and then picked up his gavel and struck the top of his desk.

"This hearing is now officially open. Private, open some windows so we can have some fresh air in this place," ordered the officer as he pointed to the windows on the west side of the room. "And I want to tell you folks something right now. This is just a hearing and none of you was invited. So if you stay, you will not talk, and you sure as hell won't smoke."

The officer then took out his spectacles and for the next few moments fumbled through the papers lying on top of his desk.

"Fourth case today," he mumbled. "But this one does appear interesting."

Looking up at the people patiently waiting before him, he exclaimed, "I'm Captain Williamson, and I want to say again that this is only a hearing. Nothing else. I see here that a Frank Olliver Junior is being charged with arson and murder. That's some strong allegation. Stand up Mister Olliver. Let me see you."

Frankie slowly rose and replied, "Sir, I'm Frank Olliver."

Frankie, along with Becca, Suzanne, and Judith Olliver were sitting to the captain's left. The Wilson family sat across the open aisle on the other side of the room.

"Mister Olliver, come on down and have a seat up front here," beckoned the captain. "Lieutenant, swear him in and let's get this thing over with."

Frankie nervously made his way down the aisle and took his seat. After taking the oath, he twisted slightly in his seat waiting for the questions.

"Mister Olliver, that your family back there with you?" asked Captain Williamson.

Surprised, Frankie turned and glanced back. "Yes Sir, that's my mother, sister, and that's my wife, Rebecca. She's expectin' our first young un in about two months."

"Got a fine looking family there," continued the captain. "You fight for the Confed'racy?"

"No Sir, I didn't," replied Frankie.

"That's good," nodded the captain. "You know you are being charged with arson and murder, and either one of them is a hanging offense. How do you plead to these charges?"

"Not guilty, Sir. The night all that happened, I was coon huntin' a long way from the Wilson's. My wife can vouch for me. And the Wilsons has always been just like family to me. I wouldn't do nothin' to hurt them."

"I hope you wouldn't," responded Williamson. "Alright, Mister Lott Wilson, please come on down here with Mister Olliver."

Lott rose and addressed the captain. "Sir, if'n it's fine with you, I'd like to bring my son down with me."

"If he can be of help, he can come on down." replied Williamson.

After Lott and John had been sworn in, the questioning continued.

"These papers state you have proof that Frank Olliver here burned your barn containing cotton and then killed one of your fieldhands. Mister Wilson, that's some mighty strong charges. It also says you have an eye witness, that so?"

John stood. "Sir, I'd like to answer the questions, if'n I may."

"That all right with you, Mister Wilson?" asked the captain.

"That'll be fine with me, Captain."

"Your name is John Wilson, isn't it?"

"Yes Sir, it is," replied John.

"I guess you weren't no rebel either, were you?"

John paused for a moment. "Yes Sir, I fought for the South. That is till Gettysburg."

"You at Gettysburg, huh. We worked on you boys pretty good up there, didn't we."

"There was some mistakes made up there. Costly ones," added John. "If we'd had Jackson commandin' our left flank, could have been a different story. Would've won it the first day."

The captain nodded, "You well could be right, young man. We'll have to talk again sometime about that battle. Mister Wilson, I want to hear from your witness now."

Frankie watched John closely as he motioned toward the back of the courtroom. Fleeting memories of their boyhood days flashed through his mind, their days at school, hunting and fishing together, and the fun times he, Tim, and Robert had together before the war. But as Frankie's thoughts flashed to Becca, his past memories of John were pushed aside.

"Sadie, come on down here with me and Papa." She had never been in a courtroom before, and Sadie had only once before been in a place this crowded with white people. She had remembered, but tried to forget, that selling block in Meridian. Walking slowly down the aisle, she became terrified. Halfway down, she stopped and looked around at the strange faces peering up at her.

"Mist' John, I want to go home," she murmured. "I don't want to be in here."

John motioned to her. "It's going to be just fine, Sadie. Nobody's going to hurt you. Toby, will you come down and sit with her?"

Toby got up and helped his daughter-in-law to a seat in front of the captain and took the seat next to her.

After she had been sworn in, Captain Williamson continued. "It says here that you are Sadie Wilson, Caleb Wilson's wife, and that you saw what happened that night. You saw your husband killed. Is that right?"

Sweat stood in droplets on Sadie's face, and she shook so violently her shoes could be heard tapping on the floor.

"Woman, you have got to answer the questions. If you saw what happened, and if you want justice, then you have got to speak up," stated Williamson.

John got up and went over beside her. "Captain. I think I can get her to talk."

After the two spoke quietly for a few moments, John turned and addressed the bench.

"Sir, may I do the questioning?"

"If you can get her to talk, then proceed," replied Williamson.

"Sadie, on the night Caleb was killed, will you tell us what you seen," insisted John, quietly.

Softly Sadie replied, "I seen the fire a burnin', and my Cabe done run down there to see if'n he could stop it. I waited a spell, then I runned on down there too. When I got there, I seen some hants on horses with tawshes in their hands."

"Hants! What is a hant?" exclaimed the captain, puzzled.

"A hant is kind of a ghost to the colored folks," replied John. "Kind of like a spirit."

"A ghost! You mean we are talking about ghosts and spirits burning and killing things. That is got to be the most ridiculous story I have ever heard," said Captain Williamson amid the laughter in the courtroom.

"I don't think this hearing needs to go any further."

"Please Sir, let me explain," insisted John. "These men weren't ghosts. They had white hoods over their heads. They only looked like ghosts."

Sadie nodded at John's explanation.

"Well, Miss Sadie, if they were real people, and if they had hoods over their heads, how did you know Frank Olliver was one of them?"

Gathering courage, Sadie replied, "I thinks I heard one of them call another one Olliver. I thinks I heard the name Olliver."

274

"Thinks! You think you heard the name Olliver?" snapped the Captain.

"Mrs. Wilson, a young man's life is resting on what you say. Did you actually hear the name Olliver or did you only think you heard it called?" scolded the Captain.

Becoming more unsettled by the Captain's voice, she dropped her head and began crying.

"Take me home, Toby. I didn't wants to come here no hows. None of this is a going to bring my Cabe back. I don't likes this place."

"Take her on outside. I may call her back later," the Captain instructed.

Turning to the officer behind him, Williamson whispered. "I've heard so many cases, I don't think I can stand six more months of this. These people are driving me completely insane. Can you believe we are now hearing about hants, I mean ghosts. This hearing isn't going to last much longer."

Williamson then turned back to face the court. "Mister Olliver, I'd like for your wife to come down. I have some questions for her."

Becca stood and moved clumsily down the row and as she neared the aisle, tripped over a man's foot and almost fell. Captain Williamson motioned to Frankie. "Mister Olliver, I think your wife needs your assistance." He added, "My, are all your Southern women as pretty as this young belle? If so, I should have thought twice before fighting for the Union."

A light laughter passed through the courtroom. The Captain carefully studied the young woman sitting in front of him. She appeared to be about the same age as his daughter back in New York.

"Mrs. Olliver, I'll keep this as brief as possible since I know this has got to be uncomfortable for you. Just tell me where your husband was the night all this happened?"

"Captain Williamson, all I know is that about ten or eleven o'clock, three men come to the house to go coon huntin' with Frankie. And I'd say they were back at the house somewhere about one in the morning. Really, that's all I know about it, Sir."

"Did they bring any coons back from the hunt?" probed the Captain.

"They brought one stinkin' ole coon back and left him on the porch. Still there the next morning," replied Becca.

Laughter trickled through the silence in the court.

"One more question. How long does it take to ride from where you live to where the Wilson place is?"

Becca thought for a moment, "It takes a good hour of steady ridin' to get up there. Maybe less, if'n you ride hard."

"Thank you, young lady. You may return to your seat."

Becca glanced over at John, sitting with his father. In her heart, she felt Frankie was guilty, but what she had related was the truth as she knew it. Seeing him, she couldn't help but remember the happy times she had spent with the Wilsons. Her eyes began to water. "Those two were supposed to be my husband and father-in-law. I loved them to the depths of my heart," she thought.

Looking up into her face, John experienced the same burning love he had felt since boyhood. As their eyes met, John forgot she was pregnant with another man's child and that this hearing could cost her husband his life. All he saw was the girl he had loved since childhood.

Captain Williamson silenced John's thoughts as he brought the gavel down hard on his desk.

"All right. Get quiet in here! Let me tell you how I see this hearing. First, with the men wearing hoods to cover their faces, there was no way to identify the riders. Second, Sadie Wilson said she only thought she heard the name Olliver called. And if she did, just calling a person's name out doesn't mean that person is present. And since the hunters were gone about two hours, I don't see how they could have traveled the distance, burned a barn, and killed a coon.

"Mister Wilson, if I send this case on to a court and this young man is convicted, he could be hanged. You want that lady back there expecting a baby in two months to lose her husband? I sure don't. Not with the evidence presented here in this courtroom. If I sent this case up, they'd laugh me out of this state," Williamson explained. "This hearing is concluded, and I find Frank Olliver Junior not guilty because of lack of evidence," concluded Captain Williamson, striking his gavel a final time.

Frankie and his supporters yelled and hugged each other at this ruling.

But the majority of the spectators who knew the reputation of both families remained silent. Rumors filtering in from Meridian had confirmed that Frankie was involved and that some men were paid to burn the barn.

John looked over at his father, "This the justice you keep preachin' about?"

He then stood up and called out, "Sir, may I say sump'n?"

Captain Williamson, already on his way to the back door, stopped and turned back to the courtroom. "What do you want, Mister Wilson?"

"Sir, there might not have been enough evidence to bring that man over there to justice, but I do know what he done to my family. When he burned our cotton, he destroyed our only money crop. My Mamma and Papa is only got two five dollar gold pieces to their name. In other words, we have nothin' left. Sir, you can't start a spring crop on no ten dollars. My Papa, God bless his soul, keeps talkin' about justice. Captain Williamson, there weren't no justice here in this court today."

The captain flushed in anger. "Mister Wilson, are you making light of the way I handled this case?"

John pointed toward Frankie. "Sir, Frankie Olliver had sump'n to do with firin' our barn, and one of his bunch killed Caleb. I know it and he knows it. If'n you'd tried to listen to Sadie a little better, we might could've found out more about what happened. She knows more than she told."

As John finished speaking, almost all the people in the room stood and applauded. Seeing the support given the young man, the Captain replied, "Mister Wilson, I have the authority to have you bound and sent to jail, if you give me due cause. One more disrespectful word out of you and you'll spend thirty days behind bars."

"Sir!" John persisted.

"John, just be quiet," pleaded Becca. "You can't help nobody if'n you's in jail. Please just go on home for now."

John opened his mouth to speak again, but thought about what Becca had said. He nodded his head in agreement and stood quietly to regain his composure. Reaching to help his father up, John said softly, "Papa, let's do go on home. Becca's right about this." Meeting Toby and Sadie outside, the Wilsons walked slowly down the street to where their wagon was waiting. John turned to Sadie. "You think of anything else that might've helped us?"

"Mist' John, I'm scairt most to death of them Yankee soldiers in there. They was a mean lookin' bunch, but I does 'member that one of them hants was a ridin' yore horse. One of them was a ridin' Lightnin'."

"I wish you could've remembered that in there, Sadie. The only ones that ride that horse now is Mister Walker and Frankie," said Lott.

"Mist' Lott, did we win or lose in there today?" questioned Toby.

"We lost, Toby. I guess we lost it all," replied Lott.

John placed his arm around Toby. "Toby, I see it a different way from Papa. This is the first time a black woman has ever testified in a white man's court in Newton County. That's got to be some kind of a victory. And us tryin' to seek justice was the right thing to do. Naw Sir, Papa, today we made a step in the right direction. There's going to be a time when right will prevail around here," said John reaching, over and placing his other arm over his father's shoulder.

"Until then, I guess we'll just have to let Papa's Good Lord take care of all this injustice," smiled John.

"What did you think about it today, Sister," asked John.

"Well, I hate to admit it, but I was kind of proud of the way you spoke up to that judge, I mean captain. You did just fine for a country boy."

"There was a time when I wanted to be a real lawyer, but that seems long ago," commented John.

On the way home, John kept thinking back to the night when it all happened. "Why did he go to Union when something kept telling him to stay home? Was Tim and Suzanne in on the plan to get him away from the farm? Not Tim," John reasoned. "He would never do that to me. But what about Suzanne? If it hadn't been for her, he certainly wouldn't have gone. Yes, Suzanne must've been in on the whole scheme."

28

JUSTICE COMES IN MANY WAYS

"Papa, I'm goin' to brush down the mare," announced John, getting up from the breakfast table. "She's been lookin' pretty shabby lately."

Lott pushed his chair back from the table. "Hold up a minute. I'll go with ya. I need to work these ole legs a little."

As they reached the stables, John turned to his father. "Papa, for the last few days, I'm been doin' a lot of thinkin', and I'm not sure I can start farmin' all over again. When I think about all them long, hard hours out there under that sun and all the sweat and havin' sore feet and hands, I say, it ain't worth it. Even lost my horse, too."

Lott sat down on the straw and began packing his pipe.

"I understand how you feels, and I can't blame you none. But you ought to have been here when we first come to this country. Year after year yore Uncle Jake and me worked this place and it seemed like we would never produce any crops," explained Lott, lighting his pipe. "But we just kept on a workin'. We wouldn't quit till we made a go out of it. It were just Jake, Minsa, and me that took this land on. After about five years, we made a good farm out of it."

"You sure did, Papa. But I got two things I'd like to do."

"What's that, Son?"

"When I was in jail up in Kentucky, I heard sump'n that kind of excited me. When the jailor heard my name was Wilson, he told me about another man named Wilson who had been through there about three weeks before I got jailed. He said he was a large fellow with reddish hair, and the funny thing about him was that his skin was as dark as an Indian," explained John, working to untangle some briars in the mare's mane.

"Man said he looked like a halfbreed."

"So, what you tellin' me, John?"

"What I'm tellin' you is that this man he was describin' was takin' a string of thoroughbreds back to the territory. Papa, that man had to a been Homer. Couldn't been nobody else."

"Damned thing won't stay lit," complained Lott, relighting his pipe. "Sounds like it could have been him. So, what about it?"

"I'd like to go out to Oklahoma and look him up. I'd like to see him and Hatta. Just see how they is makin' out."

"It's a long way out there and some mighty rough country, I hear. But it's yore life, Son. You ain't no slave to this place," replied Lott, blowing smoke into the air.

"I know I ain't, Papa," acknowledged John. "But another thing. I want to see Thomas again. I want him to know I didn't get killed in that war. Where you think he is?"

"Don't know for sure. Only got one letter from him and that was back before you come home. Come from somewhere out in Texas. Maybe near the Mexican border."

Putting the brush down, John seated himself across from his father. "You write him back?"

"Yore mother did. Never heard another word from him," said Lott, pulling himself up from the ground. Deliberately changing the subject, he said, "Going to be a nice day today, John. Let's get the family and walk around the place. Too pretty a day to stay inside."

Sarah was excited about getting out of the house, but Sister stayed home since Lieutenant Robinson was coming to call. Toby and his wife were sitting on their porch and were asked along.

They wandered out past the fields and into the woods owned by Jake. For several hours they took their time casually exploring the forest. Tiring, they stopped at a small stream for a drink and some rest.

John lay down on the deep grass growing by the water and looking up into the sky, he remarked, "Papa, I still say we ought to sell some of this land. We could get enough for it to start another crop."

Lott ignored his son's suggestion and pointed through the woods to a small clearing. "Toby, what you see when you looks down yonder?"

Toby thought for a minute, then said, "Mist' Lott, down there where you's pointin' is where I first laid eyes on you and Mist' Jake. Mast' Olliver was a workin' me down there on the edge of Minsa's land. And through them woods ya'll comes a ridin' like bats outta hell," Toby chuckled. "And I thought shore Mist' Jake was a going to kill Mast' Olliver. And ya knows what? I thinks Mast' Olliver thought the same thing."

"Seems like yesterday, Toby," replied Lott.

Sarah placed a wild flower behind her husband's ear and ran her fingers through his thick white hair. "Yore hair tells me it's been a long time since you two met. Long time, Mister Snow Top Wilson."

Lott looked over at John. "What do you see down through there, Son?"

Confused about his Dad's question, John answered, not thinking, "I don't see nothin', I reckon. Just a lot of woods."

"Look closer, John. What do you see now?"

John's eyes brightened. "Papa, I see some of the prettiest woods that God has ever made. Woods that human hands ain't ever touched."

"That's right, Son. Them woods you's lookin' at is just like they was when them Choctaws lived here. We ain't touched a stick. They is just as pretty as that morning when yore Uncle Jake and me first laid eyes on them. If'n you ride around the countryside now, you'll see a lot of the woods has been cleared for farmin'. Every year more and more is bein' cut out. One day all this virgin timber will be gone and yore chill'un, maybe grandchill'un, won't be able to enjoy this beauty. See what I'm gettin' at, Son?"

"Yes Sir, I think I do, Papa. You is sayin' we can't sell none of this land," smiled John.

Lott looked over at Sarah, "Sometime I come down here and think of my brother. He loved these woods. You know, Sarah, when I walk through here and everything is still and peaceful, I just expect to see that big ole brute of a brother of mine walk out from behind one of them big oaks with that ridiculous smile across his face." Lott cleared his throat. "I miss him," he whispered hoarsely. "Just to see him one more time."

Lott turned to his son. "This land reminds me of him. Sellin' it would be like killin' part of that memory. When Jake and me first come here, we said we'd never leave it. And I don't plan to. When the Lord calls me home, I want you to place me over yonder on that hill right next to my brother."

For a few moments all was silent and then Sarah bent down and kissed her husband's forehead. "Don't even talk about that. You going to be here when that new century comes in. You and me has got a lot of things to do yet."

"Papa, talkin' about our farmin'. If'n we don't sell some of this land, how's we going to get money to start farmin' this spring?" asked John.

"The way I see it is we still got our land. We got our plows and mules. And I saved a good bit of the cotton seeds from last year. If'n you and Andy is willin' to try one more time, and if'n Toby and me can do what we can to help, then we can make a crop. We might have to scale down our farmin', but if'n you got the will to work and try it again, then Lord willin', we'll make another crop."

John reached over and clasped his father's hand, "Oklahoma and Texas is just going to have to wait. I ain't going to let no Olliver nor a burned up crop stop us. Let's head home."

"About time you people came out of those woods," called Lieutenant Robinson, as he lifted his hand to wave. "Sister and me were about to come looking for you."

"Lookin' for us. You Yankee boys weren't noted for yore ability to survive in the woods," joked Lott. "You'd get lost where we been a walkin'."

"Not with me with him, Papa," said Sister. "I knowed them woods as good as any of you, maybe better."

"Know them. You ought to be livin' in them," teased John. "We got some nice fat hogs down there in that swamp."

"Papa, you going to let him talk to me like that? Especially in front of James," scolded Sister.

Walking toward the back of the house, John replied, "Papa, you don't have to say it. Sister, I do offer you my sincere apology. Oink! Oink!"

"John, you ought to be ashamed of yore behavior. You is a growed man now, but you still acts like a child," said his mother.

Sweaty from the walk, and deciding to wash up, John headed to the well at the side of the house. He had no sooner removed his shirt when he heard his name called. Walking back to the porch, he saw a Negro man on a horse talking to his father.

"John, this here man brought you a message. Won't tell me what he wants," remarked Lott.

"Mist' John, I works for Mast' Olliver and he wants you to come over to his house. And he says you is to hurry."

John rushed over and angrily yelled, "Frankie Olliver wants me to come to his place. You is crazy as hell if'n you expect me to do a fool thing like that. In fact, I'm fixin' to pull you down from that horse right now. You tryin' to get me off to no tellin' where and kill me. That's what you's up to."

John suddenly reached up and grabbed the man by the arm and jerked him off his mount. No sooner had the man hit the ground than John was on top of him.

Seeing John drawing his fist back, he brought his hand up to protect his face and shouted, "Don't hit me, Mist' John! I ain't lying to ya! Miss Becca done had her baby, and she ain't doin' too good. She's been a askin' for ya. Doc is with her right now."

John slowly opened his clinched fist, "You say Becca is havin' problems?"

"Yessuh. Mist' John. She ain't doin' no good at all," he pleaded. "And I ain't doin' no lyin', neither."

Lott pulled John off the frightened messenger and then reached down and pulled the man up by the collar. "Let me tell you sump'n right now. If'n you is lyin' and somebody jumps my boy, you is going to be one dead man. You hear me?"

Shaken, the man replied. "Yessuh, Mist' Lott. I shore does understands ya. But, I ain't a lyin'. They says Miss Becca ain't gonna make it."

"Ain't going to make it! You mean she's dying," exclaimed John.

"That's what I heard him say, Mist' John. And that's the truth."

John turned and ran toward the stables. Lieutenant Robinson leaped down from the porch and quickly mounted his horse.

"I'm going with him, Lucretia. If this is a trick to kill him, then they are going to have trouble with both of us."

As the two men raced out of sight, the Negro man straightened his clothes. "I ain't never going to bring no message to you folks no mo'. That boy of yores scairt me. Ya'lls been rough on this Niggar."

Toby walked up and stared him in the eyes. "Let me tells ya sump'n, niggar. Ain't nothin' wrong with these Wilsons. If'n anything happens to them men, you ain't never seen rough like I gonna show ya."

Pulling up at the Ollivers, John and Lieutenant Robinson dismounted, tied their horses to the hitching post and quickly climbed the front steps. Just as John was about to knock, the door opened and Doctor McLauren motioned them in.

"John, she's been askin' for you. I'm glad you could come," he said.

Shaking the doctor's hand, John replied, "How's she doin' Doc?"

Doctor McLauren shook his head, "Don't look good, John. Baby came too soon. And I can't stop the bleedin'. I had a lot of trouble deliverin' the child."

"Is the baby all right?" asked James.

McLauren smiled wearily, "Baby's going to be just fine. It's the prettiest little gal I ever seen."

"May I see Becca now?" insisted John.

"She's upstairs to the left."

Suzanne was sitting outside the bedroom door, pale and tired. But seeing John, her eyes brightened.

"She's been askin' for ya all day," Suzanne whispered. "Just go on in."

John reached out and gently embraced Suzanne, then eased the door open.

Becca was motionless, her face colorless and pale. Frankie was sitting next to her with his head resting on the edge of the bed.

Frankie looked up and motioned for him to come on in. John quietly pulled a chair up and then gazed down at Becca. Never had he seen her so quiet. Only a slight movement of the blanket gave any indication of life. Memories from the war flooded John's mind, men's expressions as they lay patiently awaiting death.

John looked over at Frankie. "I came as fast as I could."

Frankie nodded.

Hearing his voice, Becca slowly opened her eyes. "Knew you'd come," she whispered, reaching out her hand.

"Becca, Doc McLauren said you ain't needin' to do no talkin'. You has got to rest," warned Frankie.

Becca extended her other hand toward her husband. "It's time to talk. I want you boys to listen to me," she said, struggling to move their hands together.

"Becca, you has got to be still," begged Frankie.

John interrupted. "Do what she tells us, Frankie. She needs to talk."

Becca squeezed their hands as hard as she could. Looking first at Frankie and then back to John, she mumbled, "You boys has got to stop yore fightin' and make peace. If you don't, hate will destroy both of you."

Exhausted, she paused for a moment and then continued, "There's a little girl that's going to need a lot of love. And I want you both to promise me you is going to give her that love."

Looking into Becca's eyes, Frankie replied. "Becca, we all's going to give that little girl a lot of love. Me, and John, you, all of us."

"Frankie," gasped Becca. "I do care for you." Slowly turning, she smiled slightly. "John Wilson, you going to make some woman a fine man." She then closed her eyes. "I'm going to rest a spell now," she whispered.

Later that night, the dream that had haunted Becca returned. Looking out her window, she could see John running up the path to her parents' house in Little Rock. He was dressed in his gray confederate uniform, thick black hair bouncing with each step and a smile across his face. At this point in the dream, he would suddenly stop and then vanish. But this time, instead of disappearing, he walked up to her window and motioned for her to come outside. Becca smiled and softly whispered, "You didn't leave me. Not this time."

I

Looking up from the marker, John turned to his mother. "I don't understand why God does the things he does to folks. It ain't right. Becca never harmed nobody. When does my hell on this earth end?"

Sarah placed her arms around her son and pulled him close. "Son, it ends when you take yore last breath here on this earth. Life ain't easy, but it can be good to you when you got someone who loves and cares for you." Pointing across the cemetery, she continued. "Look down yonder. Them small markers is where my babies, yore brother and sister, is a restin'. And somewhere up in Virginie, James Earl . . . . "

"Mama, I think I understand. This love we have for each other helps us get through them hard times. That's what the Lord gives us to keep us goin'."

Glancing over her shoulder, she added, "Yore Papa's been waitin' for us out there in the wagon for a long time. Let's get on home."

John took his mother by the hand, "You know sump'n. You ain't never give up on me. You ain't never let me down."

"Like I always told you, Son. You, Thomas, and Sister are my million dollars, the most precious gifts God has ever given me."

During the following days, John worked every minute, trying to forget his loss. He and Andy were in the field by daybreak and often John would work into the night.

Because of the rain-soaked earth, farming was almost at a standstill. John and Andy were afraid they still might not make it. Without a cotton crop, the Wilsons could lose their land.

A heavy thunderstorm late one afternoon forced the men out of the field. By the time John reached the house, he was drenched and tired. Following supper, he bade his family goodnight and retired.

Early the next morning, John was awakened by barking. As he lay in bed, he could hear the sound of horses. The barking ceased and he could hear voices.

"Must not be a stranger or that hound of ours would still be barkin'," thought John. He got up and eased to the window, but it was still too dark to see. John quietly took his revolver out of his chest and crept into the hall.

Lott, who had also heard the sounds, called quietly, "You hear sump'n out there, John?"

"Yes Sir. I'm checkin' on it."

As John reached the front porch he could just make out a mounted rider near the steps.

Bringing up his pistol, John called out, "You can hold it right there, ever who you is! I got a loaded pistol, and I'll use it, if'n I have to."

"Lay yore gun down, John. I ain't meanin' no harm to ya," came a familiar voice.

"Frankie! What in tarnation is you doin' here?"

Frankie pointed over to a horse tied to the hitching post.

"Brought yore horse home. Brought Lightnin' back."

John walked slowly down. "Frankie, I had a deal with Walker. I wasn't able to fulfill my end of it. This horse ain't mine."

"It's yores, John, saddle and all. And if'n you'll check them saddlebags, you'll find more than enough money to cover yore losses," explained Frankie. "And there's some money in there to help Cabe's woman. If'n it weren't for me, none of them things would have happened to you."

Surprised, John exclaimed, "Frankie, you know what you doin'? What you sayin' and doin' here could cost you yore life, if'n this went to a court."

Frankie dropped his head. "I don't care no more. If'n you want to tell, go ahead. Even if'n they hangs me, the law can't hurt me as much as I done been hurt. I lost my father. Then I lost my wife. And along the way, I lost my best friend. And I've lost my self respect too. John, that night we burned yore barn, we didn't want no killin'. Cabe just come out of nowhere wavin' a stick in one hand and a lantern in the other. We was on our way out when he come a runnin' right at us. He spooked the horse next to me and that spooked my horse. John, my horse run right over him. I couldn't stop him."

Lott called out, "John, you all right?"

"I'm all right, Papa. Everything's fine," he answered.

John turned back to Frankie, "You don't have to say them things."

"I do have to say them. When I watched them place Becca in her grave, I felt like I was the one who put her there. I was so jealous of her feelings for you I wasn't the husband I should've been. I was mean to her at times. Her problems began at that trial. She was so upset she collapsed and fell as we was leavin' the courtroom. She knowed I was lyin', yet she never turned against me."

"That ought to told you sump'n, Frankie. It ought to told you she loved you."

"I know that now, John. But it was me that killed her."

"When I got home from the war and heard you two was married, I hated you more than them Yankees we was figthin' up North. I was tryin' to figure some way to get Becca free from you. But you know, Frankie, I couldn't do it. Things weren't the same. I knowed Becca cared for me, but I could see she loved you and weren't about to leave ya. We both made things hard for her."

"You's right, John," agreed Frankie. "But do you think we can ever forgive each other, be friends again?"

John looked out at the early morning light glistening through the leafy tree tops.

"Frankie, I don't know. Our lives was torn apart just like the war tore this country apart. Things happened to us we couldn't do nothin' about. It's like jumpin' in a storm swollen river. You can fight the current all ya wants, but it's going to carry you along with it. We all got carried downstream and it dropped us off at different places. The South we knowed as boys ain't here no more. It's a new way of life. And I don't know if we can ever go back."

Frankie slowly extended his hand. "I hope we can start again, and I'm going to count on it."

John smiled, reached up and clasped Frankie's hand. "About this horse and money. I ain't going to turn you in. Let's just say that you paid an old debt."

The sun was just tipping the trees as Frankie rode off. John stood motionless in the freshness of the early morning. Off behind the house a whippoorwill could be heard and down in the creek bottom, a couple of owls screeched. In the distance a hound was giving hard chase to some critter.

Suddenly, words formed in his mind. It was a Bible verse, his father's favorite. "If My people, which are called by My name, shall humble themselves, and pray, and seek My face, and turn from their wicked ways; then will I hear from heaven, and will forgive their sin, and will heal their land.

John walked slowly to the edge of the yard and looked out over the fields and woodlands below. A sense of peace settled over him. His wars were over and the scales finally balanced. His hillcountry was now his future.